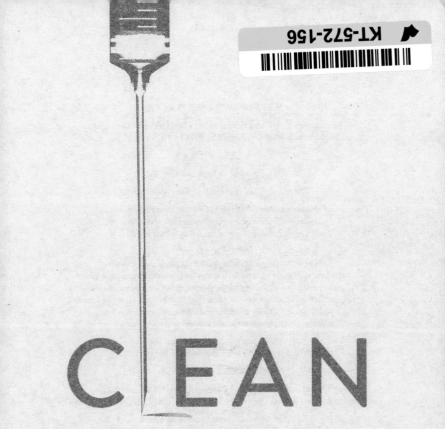

C|EAN

JUNO DAWSON

Quercus

QUERCUS CHILDREN'S BOOKS

First published in Great Britain in 2018 by Hodder and Stoughton
This paperback edition published in 2018 by Hodder and Stoughton

1 3 5 7 9 10 8 6 4 2

Text copyright © Juno Dawson, 2018

The moral rights of the author have been asserted.

A CIP catalogue record for this book
is available from the British Library.

ISBN 978 1 786 54036 2

Typeset in Adobe Caslon by Hewer Text UK Ltd, Edinburgh
Printed and bound in Great Britain by CPI Group (UK) Ltd, Croydon, CR0 4YY

The paper and board used in this book
are made from wood from responsible sources.

MIX
Paper from
responsible sources
FSC® C104740

Quercus Children's Books
An imprint of
Hachette Children's Group
Part of Hodder and Stoughton
Carmelite House
50 Victoria Embankment
London EC4Y 0DZ

An Hachette UK Company
www.hachette.co.uk

www.hachettechildrens.co.uk

Author Note

Clean is a work of fiction but it deals with many real, sensitive subjects including mental health, eating disorders, self-harm and addiction.

Links to advice and support can be located at the back of this book.

Juno x

*Dedicated to anyone who has ever
fallen over and then got back up*

STEP 1:
I ADMIT I HAVE A PROBLEM

Face-down on leather. New car smell. Pine Fresh.

I can't move.

I'm being kidnapped.

But I can't move.

My arms and legs feel like they've been deboned, dangling like jellied eels. Sick or dribble is crusted on my chin and cheek. With great effort, I peel my face off the seat.

My lips and tongue are chalky dry. I open my eyes, and blistering daylight burns them right out of the sockets. It hurts. I screw them shut but snatch a glimpse of Nikolai. From this angle, I only see the back of his head; his high fade haircut, and his hands on the steering wheel. I recognise his Rolex.

I don't understand what's happening.

Where am I?

Where *was* I?

Rewind the night. The last thing I remember, I was at the hotel. Yeah, that's it. We were in a penthouse. I got a key from reception. Me, Kurt and Baggy and that girl. The Fashion Week party . . . the bar . . . we left the bar to get high.

Oh yeah. The blue chaise longue. A needle.

Shit.

Is this what an overdose feels like?

I can't remember anything after I came up. I run a trembling hand over my body and I'm still in the gunmetal Miu Miu dress I was wearing last night. I'm covered in a scratchy plaid blanket. My feet are bare.

'Nik?' I croak. My throat feels like it has barbed wire stuffed down it.

'It's OK, Lexi. I'm getting you help.'

What now?

Oh fuck me hard, it's an intervention.

I start to argue, but my eyes catch fire again. I squeeze them tight and let darkness wrap around me like a sushi roll.

Can't sleep now.

I gotta wake up.

I claw my way out of the brainfudge and back into the car.

I'm coming down at speed, all backwards and bent. I'm cold and my skin has scales. Usually I can sleep it off, or I do a tiny bit more stuff to smooth the edges. A pill works too. Oxy or Vicodin or tramadol or diazepam. Whatever's to hand.

A man's voice. Not Nikolai's. 'She all right, bruv?'

'She took a sleeping pill,' Nik says. 'She'll be out of it for a while.'

Where are we? I try to roll over but can't. I can smell the sea: briny depths and salt air and seaweed. Seagulls shriek like bastard demons. Shut up, you flying dickheads. My head is pounding. Dehydrated. Mummified.

Where is he taking me? The seaside? How long have we been driving for? How is it even light outside? How long was I out for? Where's Kurt? The questions squawk louder than the seagulls. Perhaps this man can save me. I'll tell him I'm being kidnapped. I'll say I've been raped.

'Help ...' I mutter. My lips are scabby and my tongue is suede and I don't really muster more than a mumble. 'Help ...' I try again.

'She's my sister,' Nikolai says loudly, drowning me out. 'Hungover. Do you need our passports? Sure, here you go.'

The BMW rolls off and jolts as we go over a bump. 'Nik ... Nik ... where are we going?'

He casts a quick look back over his shoulder. 'You're gonna be fine. Just get some rest.'

5

I remember laying back on the chaise. I remember Kurt sliding the needle in my arm. I never do it myself, obviously – that's sketchy. I remember looking out of the window and seeing all the lights, all the tiny little lights of London. Amber and gold and glitter. Boats on the Thames, headlights, the Shard on the horizon. Everything went blurry, everything was fireflies.

Fireflies.

I dream of fireflies.

Tyres crunch over gravel. Sleep hasn't helped. I still feel like I've been scraped inside out with fish hooks. My teeth are spongy; porous.

The car door opens and Nikolai steps out. I hear footsteps approach. Lots of feet.

Wherever we are, we're here.

Where's Kurt?

It takes a lot of effort, but I drag myself upright by clinging to the door handle and the rim of the back window. It's still blindingly bright. Oh, I see Nik remembered his own Ray-Bans but didn't think to bring any for me. I need my phone. I scan the backseat for my purse, but I remember my phone was attached to the speakers in the penthouse anyway. It must still be there. Shit.

I squint. Nik shakes hands with a super-tall man with a beard. He's a bit 'Hagrid's more attractive brother'. Blazer, open collar, no tie. He's accompanied by two women in sharp, futuristic nurses' whites.

Shit just got really real. Oh god. He's threatened it before – *Lex, you need help* – but I totally thought he was kidding. Now he's actually doing it. I'm at a hospital.

I'm at *rehab*.

Not. A. Chance.

Dress around my hips, I scramble between the driver and passenger seats and flop down into the driver's seat, reaching for the ignition. He's taken the key. Damn. I'll have to run for it. I tug on the door handle but my balance is shot. A breeze catches the car door as I open it, flinging it wide, and I tumble onto the asphalt. I put my hands down to break the fall and feel gravel dig into my palms like studs.

'Lexi, wait! Be careful,' says Nikolai.

Bodies and dark shadows circle me. Hands reach for me, fingers come at my face. I wave my arms like a messy windmill, trying to swat them away.

'Let's get her inside, shall we?' says Dr McBeardy.

'No!' I cry. My volume button is broken. I scream my throat out of my neck and it echoes around the garden.

I peep through the jungle of legs and see we're on a long driveway leading to a gorgeous country mansion. Downton fucking Abbey. It's weathered, grey and mottled; partially covered in ivy. The main entrance is flanked with handsome columns. The grounds must be acres and acres – all I can see for miles is trimmed green lawn, surrounded by lush forest.

I'm hauled to standing, but the gravel hurts my bare feet. 'Ow!' I howl like I'm dying, even though it's not that bad. The nurses sort-of-lift, sort-of-drag me in the direction of the house. 'Nik! Please!'

I turn and face him, my eyes as big and innocent as I can make them. Little Sister Lexi. Sweet Little Lexi. Protect her, she's a girl, a bone china baby.

'Sorry, Lexi . . . you need help.' He doesn't look me in the eye.

'Let's all talk in my office,' McBeardy says soothingly. I am far from soothed. I can't go to rehab – mainly because in about four hours I'm going to *really* need a bump. I start to kick and flail, then when that doesn't work I go floppy like a toddler in a supermarket aisle. The nurses, who must pound protein shakes

8

or something, hoist me up using some amazing technique they learned in Nurse Army Camp.

'Put me down, you cunts!' I scream. 'Let me go!'

They ignore me so I just start screaming CUNTS over and over again because it's the worst word I know.

I sit in McBeardy's office, knees pulled to my chest, in a sleek, tan leather chair. There is definitely vomit down the front of my dress. It reeks. He hands me a bottle of Evian and I take a sip. It helps the mouth-rot.

Tell you what'd be nicer than mineral water: heroin.

Nikolai sits sheepishly next to me. 'Are you OK?' he asks quietly.

'Fuck off.'

'You did the right thing, Mr Volkov,' says McBeardy, taking his seat on the opposite side of a burly chestnut desk. The furniture is trying very hard to be masculine and I wonder if he's compensating for a tiny little penis. 'Nice to meet you, Lexi.'

'Fuck. Off.'

The doctor has the smug audacity to *smile* and fold his hands around a mug of black coffee. 'I'm sure you have a lot of questions, Miss Volkov.'

'Just one: will you please fuck off and let me go?'

'Technically speaking, that's two questions, and no, I'm afraid I can't. At least not just yet. This isn't a prison and you haven't been sectioned. You are free to leave, but I hope you'll stay.' I'm about to protest but he goes on. 'Let me bring you up to speed. My name is Isaac Goldstein and I am lead doctor at the Clarity Centre.'

'This is rehab, right?'

'It's a residential treatment facility.'

'So, rehab.'

'If you like.'

'Lexi,' Nik butts in, 'it's the very best, OK. The best of the best.'

'Oh yeah?' I say, turning back to Goldstein. 'Who's the most famous person who's ever been here?'

'Our reputation is built on our discretion, Miss Volkov.'

So discreet I've never heard of it. Nik could have at least taken me to The Priory. 'A Kardashian? Khloé? Kylie?'

Dr Goldstein ignores me. 'Don't get me wrong – we're not a hotel, but we do have world class facilities: luxury rooms and villas, heated indoor and outdoor pools, gym, spa treatments and chefs from Michelin-starred restaurants. You'll be very well looked after during your recovery.'

Nice try. *Recovery* is the key word. 'But it's still rehab. Like, can you even get a vodka tonic?'

'Obviously not.'

'Jesus Christ. Can I smoke in here? Do you have a cigarette?'

'Yes, smoking is allowed. Although I don't have a cigarette.'

Nik reaches into his inside pocket and pulls out a packet of Marlboro Lights and a lighter. I snatch them off him and spark up. Oh man, that's better. I almost suck it down to the filter in one great greedy gulp, until I realise Nikolai is staring at me with a cocktail of horror, pity and stank disgust. It's the kind of look you might give a filthy homeless person eating out of a bin. 'What?'

'I thought you were dead, Lexi.' His eyes glaze over like Krispy Kremes.

'Boo hoo! We all learned and grew as people. Can we go home now?'

'No.' He dabs his eye with a Kleenex. 'I'm not taking you back.'

I roll my eyes. 'Fine. I'll call Kurt and he'll come and get me.'

'The Clarity Centre is on a private island off the south coast,' Goldstein says. That explains the sea smell. 'We're a very successful treatment facility, Miss Volkov, and we don't let just anyone board the ferry – every vehicle that crosses must have clearance. We can of course choose to restrict access – for obvious reasons, we have to be very careful who we let on the island.'

'You have *got* to be kidding? How is this not a prison?'

'I already said, you're welcome to leave any time you like.'

'How? If I swim?' I turn to Nik. 'This is insane. Nik, I can't stay here.' I push back my chair and start towards the door. 'Come on.'

'It was Kurt who called me,' Nik says, and I stop. 'They thought you'd overdosed. When I got to the penthouse, you were blue, Lexi. Your lips were fucking blue.' He reaches into his pocket again and takes out my phone. He brought it! Only then he slides it over the desk to Goldstein.

'Hey!'

'We can look after that for now,' Goldstein says, dropping it into his drawer.

'You can't do that! I know my rights!'

'Standard practice.'

I throw myself down at the side of Nik's chair. If we leave now, we can be back in London before the cravings get really bad. 'Look. Nikolai. I'm totally a recreational user . . . it's not a biggy.'

'Can you hear yourself? I thought things were getting out of hand when it was pills and coke. But *heroin*? Lexi, people don't use heroin recreationally!'

12

'They totally do! That's why I couldn't handle it . . . I hardly ever use. It was just a bit of fun, I swear. I'm not an addict! Do I look like a junkie to you?'

My brother's eyes gape. Another tear falls. He's silent for a moment. 'Yes,' he says finally. 'You absolutely look like a junkie.'

I've lost him. There's nothing I can say. I'm on my own. I march to the door and yank on the handle. It's locked. 'Let me out! Let me out right now, you fat fucker.'

'Sit down please, Miss Volkov.'

'Give it a rest, Lexi. You're staying and that's that.'

'You can't make me!'

Nik stands, hands on hips. 'Well you're not coming with me and they won't let your sketchy friends on the ferry, so I guess you'll just have to ask Dad to come get you. And then you can explain why I brought you here.'

That stops me. Daddy would kill me. Or worse, cancel my credit cards. 'You wouldn't.'

'I bloody would. This is where it stops. I'm not covering for you any more. I took pictures last night, Lexi. You either stay here or I show him his little princess covered in puke, track marks on her arm.'

I scream and scream and scream. Blood-red vision. I pull a bookcase over. I swipe a load of shit off the doctor's desk. I try to throw an armchair out of the window but it's too heavy to shift so I just look stupid.

Two stacked guys in the same starched white uniforms enter the office, hanging back to the sides of the room, waiting for their instructions from Goldstein. In the midst of the chaos I'm making, he remains infuriatingly calm. 'Mr Volkov, as Lexi is under eighteen and you're her next of kin and an adult, you can authorise us to sedate Lexi if need be.'

'Don't you dare!' I scream. 'You can't do that!'

'Do whatever you need to do,' Nikolai says without hesitation.

The boynurses move in on me and I shrink into the mess I've made like a cornered animal. One of them flicks the tip of a needle. As twisted as it sounds, the sight of the hypodermic briefly calms me until I remember it isn't a hit. That said, if I've learned one thing, it's that a drug's a drug. It's probably a downer, so it'll def take the edge off, but it means I'll have to stay in this hellhole. Dilemma. They stalk closer. My time is running out. I have to decide. And I decide I want to stay conscious. 'God, whatever. You don't have to sedate me. Look! I'm calm. I'm Zen. I'll pick up the books. Jesus.'

The boynurse stops. I'll cooperate for now. I need time to cook up a plan. I can't have Daddy cut me off. I'll play nice and get off Rehab Island when they realise this is all a catastrophic clusterfuck and acknowledge I'm not Amy Bloody Winehouse.

I make an attempt to lift the bookcase, but it's actually pretty heavy. 'That's OK, Miss Volkov. I'll get someone to tidy the office,' says Goldstein. 'For now, you need to say goodbye to your brother and we'll get you settled into your suite.'

'I have to go?' Nikolai says. 'Already?'

'I think it's for the best.'

Nikolai uses the bathroom before we walk back to his car. I'm wrapped in a blanket and have been given some box-fresh white Vans for my bare feet. Goldstein and one of the boynurses lurk behind us.

'I've got to go and collect Tabitha from Heathrow later, but I'll get someone from the hotel to send some clothes and stuff,' he tells me. I try to remember where his girlfriend's been this time. Milan? She interns at *Tatler*. 'I'll make sure they're discreet.'

I wrap my arms around my body and it legit feels like I'm holding my skeleton in formation. I'm coming apart at the seams, but can't show him that. Junkies would call it 'clucking' but I'm no junkie, so I don't call it anything. 'Nik, this is crazy,' I tell him, making my voice Sunny Delight. 'As if I need to be here. Look, I swear if you take me home I'll never ever do Brown or Oxy or Vicodin ever again. I *promise*. And I'll see my therapist twice a week like a good girl.'

I see his resolve waver, just for a second, and then he shakes his head. 'No, Lexi. You need to get away from your shitty friends. Look . . . I really think this place is the nuts, yeah. Just give it a go. Please?'

'Nik . . . I can't stay here!'

'It's only a few months, Lexi.'

'MONTHS?'

'It's a seventy-day programme.'

'You might as well kill me now.'

He pulls me into a hug but I push him off me. Bastard Judas. 'You'll be fine, Lexi. I'm gonna tell Dad you're with Mum. He's hardly going to call her to check, is he?' He climbs into the BMW. 'Just get better. I'll be back to visit you.'

I cling to the door. 'Please . . .' I'm crying now, and not even pretending.

'Let go of the door, Lex. This is for the best.' He slams the door out of my hands and starts the engine.

'I can't believe you're doing this to me!' I shriek, pounding the car window with my fist as he pulls away.

Dr Goldstein is already at my side with the boynurse. 'Come along, Miss Volkov. Let's show you to your suite.'

I look up at the mansion. The windows look down at me like eyes. Judgmental, condescending eyes.

They got me.

They fucking got me good this time.

At least the room is nice. I'm on the ground floor – which I'd normally complain about – but I remind myself this isn't a hotel, however much it looks like one. As I'm whisked towards my suite, I get the gist of the Clarity Centre: plush carpets in palliative jade; ecru walls; walnut trim; soft up-lighting; creamy orchids in goldfish bowls. Classy 101.

Goldstein entrusted me to the hunky boynurse. After some seriously disorienting corridors – you think I'd be used to them – he stops outside Room 11 and opens it. With no luggage, I shuffle in behind him like Orphan Annie. 'This is your room,' he says simply. 'Let us know if there's anything you need. There's a call button next to the bed.'

'Bit of Vicodin?' He's himbo-hot – steroid shoulders and thick neck, reddish hair. I perform a smile for him.

He manages a polite, if fake, laugh. Like he's never heard that one. The colour scheme is the same as the halls – ocean greens and pale greys. All very feng shui, I'm sure. There's even a decorative bowl filled with pebbles on a side table near the door. Basic bitches. If I see a fucking Buddha statue I swear I'll club someone to death with it. King-size bed with suede headboard; a cubist desk and sofa; patio doors on to some sort of terrace . . . an outdoor pool, covered. Beyond that I see endless, shifting silver water. Sea view, lucky me. 'Dr Goldstein will be back with your meds in a second.'

'What's your name?'

'I'm Marcus, Miss Volkov.'

'Hello, Marcus.' I smile sweetly again, cocking my head to one side like some sort of jailbait porn fantasy. It'll pay to have the nurses on-side. 'May I look on the terrace?' I want to plan possible escape routes.

He shakes his head. 'Not yet; not while you're detoxing.' He turns to leave. 'I'm on duty all day. Call if you need anything.' He's professionally disinterested. He leaves.

What do I do now?

This is absurd. Back home, I had a mani-pedi booked for two this afternoon.

There's a Clarity Centre Welcome Pack leaning against glass bottles of mineral water – one still, one sparkling – on the desk. Great. I ignore it.

I go to the en-suite. Marble sink, jungle shower over man-sized tub. Again, could be much worse. I flick the light on and flinch from my reflection in the mirror. It's no wonder Nikolai freaked out – I look like something off *The Walking Dead*. Either this is *very* unflattering light or my skin has a definite green tinge; waxy and corpsy. Shit. I wonder if it was a bad batch. My eyes are bloodshot and racoon-ish – smeared with last night's eyeliner and mascara. My hair is a greasy blonde bird's nest.

There must be a god because a wrapped toothbrush is waiting in a glass with some toothpaste. I reach for it and try to take the cellophane off but my hands are shaking like mad. It's kicking in. Fuck.

It starts like flu, that fever in your bones. But it's about to get so much worse than the flu.

I manage to brush my teeth and decide a shower might help me feel more human. With any luck, I'll come down nice and easy, like a feather on a breeze. The shower beats down on my head and I have it as hot as possible, hoping to scald the ache out from under my skin.

It doesn't work. As soon as I turn off the jet, I start to shiver. A deep-freeze from inside my marrow. I'm rattling.

I dry off before finding some clean Calvin Klein pyjamas in the wardrobe. I don't have a brush – I think about calling Marcus to bring me one but decide against it – so I towel off my hair as best as I can and comb it with my fingers.

I'm having a cigarette (Nik left me the whole pack) cross-legged on the bed when there's a knock at the door. 'Miss Volkov, it's Dr Goldstein.'

I let him in.

'Is it Volkov or Volkova?'

'Just Volkov.' My name actually *is* Alexandria Volkova, but we never use it. The gendered names thing only confuses English people, and it benefits Mummy and I to have the same name as Daddy.

'How are you feeling?'

'Like shit.' I cross to the sofa and sit down, my limbs on backwards. The shower hasn't helped; I'm itching all over. Ants tunnel just under my skin. Worse, I'm starting to feel nauseous, a sour milk taste on my tongue.

Goldstein pulls out the desk chair. I see he's carrying a pharmacy bag and it's all I can do not to tear it out of his hands. 'A couple of questions first. When did you last use, Lexi?'

Use makes me sound like a *user*. I roll my eyes. 'God, is that what we're doing?'

'The most important thing, before we can do any *real* work, is to detox your system. While there are drugs in your body, that's all you'll be able to think about.'

I try to laugh it off, all the while thinking only about drugs. 'Dr Goldstein! This is all a huge mistake,' I say, jaw clenching up like I've boshed about twelve pills. 'I'm *not* a heroin addict. I only ever use a bit of brown to mellow at the end of the night if I've done MDMA or coke.'

He doesn't miss a beat. 'Do you think that's normal behaviour for a seventeen-year-old?'

I shrug. 'Yes. Like, if you're on a big night, yeah.'

'Lexi, it really isn't. Listen. At the Clarity Centre, we operate on a specially adapted *Ten* Steps programme . . .'

Big surprise there.

'And the first step is admitting you have a problem.'

'But I don't have a problem! It's not like I'm a homeless junkie selling blow jobs for crack or some shit, is it?' My spine hurts and I shift on the sofa, trying to get comfortable.

'When did you last use?' he repeats.

I sigh. Play the game and I'll get out sooner. 'Last night. About one in the morning . . .'

Fashion Week isn't about the shows – although some still are worth showing up for, and it's always amusing to see the bloggers try to outdo each other in the crazy fancy dress stakes (oooh you're wearing a Wendy house, how innovative, how Fashion Week). No, it's about the parties.

Burdock & Rasputin had their party at the Shoreditch hotel. Y'know, my dad owns V Hotels? Yeah.

I wore Mui Mui and some Jimmy Choo boots with a vintage faux fur. I thought it'd be tacky to wear Burdock & Rasputin to their own party. It was pretty cool. Miguel, our mixologist, created a cocktail to go with the line. It tasted of mouthwash, but in a good way. It was heaving, obviously. Actual A-List too, no reality TV, no girl-group members: Chloe Sevigny, Rihanna, Lupita, Karlie and Gigi. Love Gigi, she's a doll.

I don't know why I was surprised, but I forgot Nevada was doing her internship at B&R so *of course* she was there. Awkward. We sort of collided in the smoking area; no way to avoid each other. 'Babe!' I said. It was either that or pretend to be my previously undisclosed identical twin.

'Lex! I wondered if you'd be here.' Well, duh – it's my hotel. Nevada is originally from Hong Kong and was always destined to work in fashion. She wore a gold turban on her geometric bob and an outsize men's blazer over a sequinned bra and acid-wash Mom jeans. She smokes Djarum Blacks. Insufferable, right? Being your own project must be exhausting.

'I totally forgot you were doing B&R! How was the show?' The bass wasn't as oppressive outside; I didn't have to shout to be heard.

'Sick! How are you? You look . . . good.' I noted a moment of shady hesitation.

'Yeah, I'm sweet, babes.' I wanted the exchange to be over.

'I better get back inside. I'm supposed to be running the official Insta.' She paused and stroked my arm. 'You should come back to school, Lexi. It isn't the same without you.'

'Well, duh!' I smiled.

'You know, no one blames you—'

'I know.' I cut her off.

'So you'll come back?'

I couldn't tell her I wouldn't be welcomed back to St Agnes with open arms. As far as my friends knew, I dropped out. 'I don't know. Maybe. I like being free.'

'So what are you going to do? Work?'

What is with the interrogation? 'I'm not sure yet. I'll take some time out and think about it.'

Nevada scurried off to hashtag or whatever and I hung out for a while. Fashion Week parties always wind down about ten because everyone killed themselves the night before getting the show ready. The after-party moved on to a tequila bar underneath a Mexican restaurant. I went with some of the models, TT Burdock himself and some hipster asshole who called himself Sylvester The Camera. We did some coke in the Uber. We did more coke and tequila shots at the bar. It was trashy cool – red light bulbs and Day of the Dead skulls. It smelled of chicken fajitas and salt-rimmed margaritas.

Everyone wanted to go home – the bug-eyed models had fittings early the next day – I guess that day – but I was just waking up. I swear I was always meant to be nocturnal. Being awake during the light feels like my head is full of bleach. It's unnatural and perverse. I crawl out of my coffin at ten p.m. like a vampire.

I had sworn that I wouldn't call Kurt again unless he called me first. I don't know why I'm always the one who has to make the first move. But when TT and Sylvester said they'd had enough, there was no way I was going home for cocoa so my resolve flew out the window. I called him.

'Hey, it's me,' even that sounded needy.

'Babes! Where the fuck are you?'

'I'm in Hoxton. El Bandito.'

'Oh, the tequila place? Cool.'

'Where are you?'

'Camden.'

'What you up to? Can I hang?'

'I'm with Baggy.' So called because he's never without a baggy of something. 'Just waiting for Steve.' The Dealer. My skin crawled. I hate Steve; he's a creep.

'Oh cool. Let's party. I'm not tired.'

'Sure. Come over. You got any cash? We owe Steve like two-hundred squid.'

'What the fuck? As if.'

'Nothing comes for free, babes.'

'Whatever. I'm getting an Uber.'

Mustafa arrived in his Prius and took me to some cocktail bar near Camden Lock playing Guns N' Roses and Metallica non-ironically. It was mostly full of unbuttoned City Boys on Tinder dates, and groups of girlfriends taking advantage of two-for-one mojitos. Kurt and Baggy were already there in a vinyl booth with some suicide doll, all ruby-red collagen lips, Betty Page bangs and liquid liner. 'Hey,' I said, sidling in next to Kurt and hating myself a little bit.

'That was quick.' He kissed me on the lips and draped a tattooed arm over my shoulder. I nestled against him. 'Lexi, this is Kitty Amour.'

'Hey.' She was stoned off her tits already, slumped against Baggy. She held out a limp hand with red talon nails and I shook it. One set of false lashes were coming unglued so she looked like she had a lazy eye.

'What are we drinking?' I asked.

'Hemingway daiquiris,' Baggy explained. He's a funny one. He's not conventionally attractive – in fact he's distinctly toad-like – but always has some girl on the go. It could be, of course, that his dad owns a football club. Kitty Amour (her real name, I'm sure) is the latest in a long line.

'Cool,' I said. 'I'll get the next round.'

Steve The Dealer arrived as I got back with the drinks. I gave Kurt the cash we owed him and the two guys went to the gents in staggered trips: Steve first, then Kurt. Steve swished past our table with a wink before leaving the bar for good. Kurt came back to the table a minute later. 'OK. Let's finish up and get out of here, yeah?'

He was twitchy – I guessed he must really need a bump. I was still a little high from the coke at the club so wasn't feeling it so bad. Also, I'd had a cheeky diazepam while I was getting ready at the hotel.

For now, Kurt was staying on a family friend's sofa – some lawyer and his fiancé – so we took another Uber back to the hotel on the river in Vauxhall. That's where me and Nikolai live most of the time, because it's the biggest. We have a whole floor to ourselves when Daddy is away. Which he usually is.

While Kurt, Baggy and Kitty (that limpet wasn't going anywhere) waited in the lobby next to the fountain, I went to the office and booked us into one of the penthouse suites. There's usually one empty, and we keep one reserved at all times for the Prince of Oman or something, so that's nearly always free. I took a key card and we headed on up in the glass elevator.

Our hotel is world class. Like, not the sort of place you'll ever find on lastminute.com. The penthouse suite overlooks the Thames for miles. You can see the Shard and the London Eye in one direction, Battersea Power Station in the other. I opened the balcony doors and the curtains billowed. It wasn't too cold. I hooked up my phone to the Bluetooth speakers – something to chill to.

I've been to New York, LA, Dubai, Hong Kong, Moscow, Paris and Tokyo, but there's something about London. It's got dirt under its nails, British teeth and a permanent resting bitch face. The people, the clubs, the fashion, the traffic, the weather. London gives zero fucks, has zero chill, and I love it.

As soon as we were in the room, Kurt rolled up a plaid sleeve and slipped his belt around his bicep. I was drunk, dancing to the music. I think it was The Weeknd, I'm not sure. It was that thing when you're drunk and you think you're ten times sexier than you really are. I kicked my boots off, swaying to the beat, teasing the hem of my dress up. 'Lex, you're killing me, girl!' Baggy mimed stuffing a fist in his mouth. 'Hot as hell, man!'

Kurt was focused only on finding a vein, so I continued to put on my show for Baggy. I tossed my hair over my head and beckoned Kitty over with a single finger. She knew where I was coming from and we danced close, grinding our hips together. My lips found hers and we kissed. Girls' lips are so subtly different: plumper, softer.

I'm not a lesbian, or even bi, it's just sometimes fun to fool around with hot girls and guys think it's the best thing ever. When I pulled away from Kitty, Baggy was fumbling with his crotch like he might be about to have both kinds of stroke.

There was a warming, familiar vinegary smell as Kurt cooked the heroin on a spoon. It's cute. He has a favourite spoon. It goes everywhere with him. I call it Spoony. He dipped the syringe in the bubbling brown liquid and drew the plunger out with his teeth.

'Hey,' I said. 'Me first.' He started to protest until I reminded him who theoretically paid for it. I took myself over to the chaise longue and reclined, arching my back. 'Do I look like Cleopatra?'

'I'm not sure Cleopatra was a white girl with blonde hair,' he replied, irritably.

He crawled over and tugged on my arm. He slapped my forearm a few times, trying to pop the veins. I don't really like slamming – I'd rather smoke it or do a pill – but this way you get the high ten times faster. You can feel it swimming through your veins like glitter. The light flows to your fingers and toes. It's toasty and warm. It's liquid gold.

'Hey,' I said. 'Tell me you love me.'

He looked right into my eyes. He has gorgeous grey-blue eyes and deadly serious black eyebrows. 'You're a pain in my ass,' he said. 'But I fucking love you.'

I gave him a proper kiss. He tasted of daiquiris. There was a sharp scratch as the needle slid in my vein. 'Not too much,' I told him, already feeling it swim up my arm.

I don't do brown so often that I don't feel the high any more. As it washed through my body, I felt tingly all over. I sparkled like champagne. I looked out of the big windows and saw the lights of London twinkling. Strawberry crème on the inside, just for a minute. All the lights, they looked like fireflies and they pulsed like a heartbeat around me.

It was like sinking into a hot bubble bath.

It was an embrace.

It was . . .

Dr Goldstein jots something down on his clipboard. 'And that was when you passed out?'

Passed out is so undignified, but . . . 'I guess so. But like I said . . . it's probably Kurt's fault. I told him not to give me too much.' I feel really sick now. Like I might be sick. I need to get near a toilet.

'And, to clarify, in the last twenty-four hours you've taken diazepam, cocaine and heroin?'

I shrug. I'm shivering now, grinding my teeth, and it's only going to get worse. 'Well . . . yeah. Look, when you put it like that . . .'

He writes something else and then clicks his ballpoint shut. 'OK, Lexi. Here's what we're going to do. I'm prescribing you Suboxone to help you come off the opiates you've been taking. It's a mixture of two drugs – one to replace the opiates, and one to help with the side effects of withdrawal.'

Thank god for that. I thought for a horrible moment they were going to make me go cold turkey. And I'm glad it's not methadone because that's for homeless skagheads. 'OK. How long do I have to take that for?'

'The Detox Stage usually lasts about a fortnight. We'll reduce the dosage of Suboxone daily to wean you off. I won't lie to you, Lexi – it's not going to be pleasant. When was the last time you went a day without taking an opiate . . . heroin, Oxycontin, Vicodin or tramadol?'

I honestly don't know. I don't really think about it any more. Not since . . . well. I shrug again.

'As they say . . . no pain, no gain. Believe me when I say, it's going to hurt, but it'll be worth it.'

I hold out a sweaty palm for the pills and scowl. 'Hon, I've had a hangover before.'

I'm dying.

I am dying.

I can't take it.

Get me the hell out of here.

Just let me die.

I writhe on the bed. I'm so hot. I'm melting. I'm wet. I peel the pyjamas off my skin. I try to pull the skin off too because I AM TOO HOT.

I'm going to burst like a sausage. My skin's going to split open and my bloated organs will slither out like eels.

It hurts all over. It hurts on the inside. It hurts on the outside. My bones are calcified, gnarled and stiff, twisting my body into ugly shapes. I'm a gargoyle, knotted in salty bedsheets.

My kidneys have their own throbbing heartbeat.

There's glass in my tubes, in my piss.

I tumble off the bed and puke on the carpet. It comes in gushes and gushes until there's nothing left and I'm dribbling Berocca-colour bile, dry heaving, retching. I'm turning myself inside out, boomerang-shaped. I can't breathe. I don't even notice the nurses enter my room and scrape me off the floor. They try to wipe my face, but I lash out with my elephant legs. They feel obese and swollen. 'Get off me!' Their touch hurts. I'm a cactus girl, everything prickles. I try to curl up into a foetal ball. 'I need more pills . . .'

'It's not time yet,' a black nurse says kindly, her face zooming in and out of focus. 'In the morning, my lovely. We've just got to get you through the night. I can give you some ibuprofen for the pain.'

'Fuck that!' I start crying. 'Please . . . please . . .'

'Here, love. Sip some water.' She brings a glass to my cracked lips and I take a little, only for my stomach to slap it right back up.

I think it's morning. Grey light bleeds in around the curtains. I'm frozen, cocooned in the duvet. I don't remember if I slept at all. All I remember is hurting. It hurts so much. It feels like my bones are trying to hatch from under my flesh and make a run for it. My body doesn't feel like mine, bent into a pretzel by giant hands.

Boynurse Marcus comes in with a breakfast tray and my medication. 'Morning. You should try to eat something if you can, and there's a pot of tea too. It will make you feel better, I promise.' There's toast, pastries and granola, but the thought alone of food reminds me of vomiting.

I drag myself off the bed, shuffling to the desk like a ninety-year-old woman, arthritic and hunched. I greedily snatch the tablet and gulp it down with some orange juice. I see that I have Marcus alone. 'Can you get me another one? Dr Goldstein obviously hasn't prescribed enough . . . I feel awful.'

He nods sympathetically. 'The first couple of days are the worst.'

'So can I have another?'

'No. Not until this lunchtime at the earliest.' He checks his chart. 'Yeah, you get another at one, Miss Volkov.'

I sidle closer to him, but he pulls back. 'Marcus, please, call me Lexi. I won't tell anyone. It'll be our little secret!' I try to look cute, but I don't know if I can pull it off in crumpled pyjamas and with vomit breath.

'I'm sorry. I can't change prescriptions; I'm not a doctor.'

'But you can get in the pharmacy, right?' I figure he lives on the island. How much action can he get? I move closer. 'Come on, Marky Mark … you scratch my back and I'll scratch yours …' I stroke his bulging bicep.

He rolls his eyes and backs towards the door. 'Get some rest. I'll be back with lunch.'

'Whatever, you faggot.' I throw the glass of orange juice at the closing door. It's actually plastic so doesn't even smash. Pulp dribbles down the wood.

'If you want Kurt's face in one piece, you'll suck my dick.'

'Fuck off, Steve.'

'I'm not fucking about, Lexi. He owes me a lot of money.'

I shook my head. Steve's high-rise council flat, overlooking Chelsea Bridge from the poor side of the river, stank of skunk. It was last Christmas. A sad, wonky angel sat atop a threadbare tinsel tree. Steve's mole eyes were squinty, pink-rimmed. 'I just paid you everything he owed.'

Steve grinned like a Great White at his massive goon bro. 'So let's call this interest.'

'Then get Kurt to suck your dick.' I held my Alexa in front of my body like a shield.

'That shit would make me gay. I want you to do it.'

'Steve, I'm not sucking your dick, so forget it.'

'Well then, Kurt can forget having teeth.' He gave his goon a nod. The hulk moved towards the door.

'Wait,' I said.

The Suboxone kicks in and I drift off again. My body shakes and spasms. My arms and legs jerk around like I'm a puppet on invisible strings. I don't understand how I can feel so awful. I don't get it.

I snooze until I feel something warm on my thighs.

With wide-awake horror, I realise I've shit myself.

I have literally shit the bed.

With diarrhoea.

It stinks the room out in seconds.

I try to stand but slump down next to the bed.

Not sure what else I can do, I reach up and press the call button. It takes everything I have. I'm face-down on the carpet when Marcus comes in with a young woman I've not seen yet. She helps me into the shower – I can hardly plant one foot in front of the other I'm so drowsy – and strips off my soiled pyjamas. The water feels like it's shedding my skin off, but she holds me up under the jet.

It's so humiliating.

I'm naked and covered in shit.

I cry. I fold in on myself, crouching in the tub and rocking like mad people on bad teen soaps do.

She envelops me in one of the plush white towels and steers me back into the suite. There are fresh sheets and a clean set of pyjamas waiting on the bed.

I can't sleep, I'm in too much pain. The ache is at the core of every bone. If I could dig them out I would. I've never had the bends, but I bet this is what it feels like, like I'm going to fucking snap.

I've had it.

There is a way, a really easy way, I could stop the pain.

I'm getting out.

I drag my carcass off the bed and go to the terrace doors. They're locked but I tug and tug on the handle, trying to force them open. I start screaming, banging on the glass. Maybe someone will come and let me out. If I have to make a run for it and hide away on the ferry, I will.

They can't leave me like this. It's torture. It's a human rights violation. I need more fucking pills.

I look around the room. The desk chair is too heavy for me to lift. My arms feel like stringy prosciutto, but I look for something else I could throw.

The bowl of decorative pebbles. Yes.

I grab a rock and hurl it at the sliding doors. It pings off without even making a scratch. I try again, pelting stone after stone at the window. How sodding thick is the glass? By the time the nurses come running in, I've crumpled to the floor, my energy sapped. As they try to restrain me, I start to lash out with the now empty bowl. 'Let me out!' I scream. 'I'm going home! You can't keep me here!'

'Come on, Lexi, back to bed, please . . .'

'Fuck off!' I roll across the rug, ducking out of the nurse's arms. I crawl into the corner and hide behind the thick drapes.

'What's going on?' From my hiding place, I hear Dr Goldstein's voice.

I crawl out. 'Please . . . I need more pills. Just a diazepam or something! It really hurts!' I sob.

'I did warn you it would,' he says, crouching to be on my level.

'I can't do it!' Snot dribbles down my chin. 'I can't do pain! I have a really low pain threshold!'

He clutches both of my arms. 'Lexi, you *can* do this. Please don't give up.'

'I won't . . . I just need something to take the edge off . . . please. There are things . . . moving under my skin.' I hold out my arms to show him where my skin is squirming and bubbling.

'I'm sorry, Lexi, I'm not prepared to give you any further opiates. We have to wean you off or you'll never get any better.'

I throw myself back into the corner and start chewing on my wrist. If I hurt myself they *have* to let me out. This is such a good idea, I don't know why I didn't think of it sooner. I'll get the lumps out myself.

'Lexi, what are you doing?'

I start scratching at myself with chipped silver fingernails, leaving red marks all up my arms. 'Get me out of here or I'm going to kill myself. I swear I'll do it. Who's gonna come to your shitty clinic then?'

'Lexi, are you going to calm down?'

'Stop saying my name you patronising cunt!'

He stands wearily and turns to Marcus. 'I'll have to sedate her. Then please take her to the Safe Room.'

I don't like the sound of that one little bit. Marcus and a newly arrived boynurse surround me. Between them they drag me up and pin my arms at my sides. I kick out with my legs but they just flail. Goldstein comes at me with another syringe. 'No! No! Get off me!' He efficiently slides the needle into the top of my arm. I gob right in his face. It trickles down his glasses and I feel something like glee. 'Fat Jewish twat.'

For the first time, I see him flinch. Good. He retracts the needle and the boynurses hustle me out of the room. I go floppy again, my neck can't hold my head up, and they sweep me down the corridors, my toenails dragging across the carpet.

They put me in a different room with grey slate tile floors, high rectangular windows and a less lavish (double) bed, albeit one nailed to the floor. If this is their version of a padded cell, they need to try harder. It's not much different to a budget hotel room. There's even a boxy en-suite in the corner. Hardly a punishment.

I already feel woozy from whatever Goldstein gave me. They flop me onto the bed and I'm too tired to argue. I still ache all over, but I can't fight any more. 'Get the fuck off me,' I say, mostly to make a point, but my speech is slurred like I've had a stroke or something. My slug tongue lolls around in my mouth.

I let myself drown into sleep. Oh, it's lovely. It's the same as brown, it's a hug.

A hug . . . from a big bear.

A big brown bear.

A big cuddly brown bear.

A big brown

Bear.

When I wake up, I'm FREEZING cold again. I pull the duvet around my body and nest all the way under the covers into the dark.

It hits me. I'm trapped here. I'm in a luxury cage. No one is coming to help me. I'm a prisoner. Maybe it's time to call Daddy, but what would he say? Dr Goldstein will tell him the truth . . . they've probably tested my piss or something. They'll show him a junkie. Maybe for the first time *ever*, I don't think I can flutter my lashes out of this one. What if Daddy sent me to live with Mummy in Cayman? I don't think I could stand it.

They'll tell him I'm a heroin addict.

My bones jangle like a windchime.

I shudder.

Maybe I am a heroin addict.

When did that happen?

Fuck my life.

I put a pillow over my head. With any luck, I'll just die.

Night comes again and it's worse. I dream Nikolai is eating Mummy and trying to shove bits of her flesh in my mouth. There are tiny, gerbil-sized naked human babies all over the floor of my room at the hotel and I keep treading on them. I dream that I wake up and feel better.

I dream of Kurt. I dream of lazy Sunday mornings with room service. Eggs and soldiers, stacks of pancakes with bacon and maple syrup.

I dream of Antonella; Antonella passing me notes in Latin. I dream about her laughing. The notes spell out what I did, all in elegant calligraphy.

I dream of going to the bathroom, but wake up desperate for a pee and too cold to move.

I press the call button. This time, an older man with a shaved head enters. He has tattooed arms and a beard. 'You all right, love?' He has a thick Scouse accent.

'Please help me . . . I think I'm dying.'

He chuckles but I'm too sick to be cross. 'Aw, you're not, pet, I swear to god. I seen this a million times. It'll be better in the morning.'

'Please . . . please call Nikolai and tell him I'm dying.'

'Tell you what, I'll leave a note for the morning nurse and how about you call him when it isn't two in the morning?'

'He'll be up,' I say, and a tear finds its way out. I want Nikolai. If I'm going to die, I want him to be here.

He offers me a tablet. 'Here, love, take this for the fever.'

I do as I'm told. My hair is matted to my face in greasy knots. 'Can you help me to the bathroom?'

'That I can.' He almost lifts me off the bed and carries me to the little shower room. Using the walls and sink I can manage. After I've been, I'm too tired to move so I just fall asleep on the loo.

I wake in the morning and the pain is less. I feel solid. I feel . . . fluey, I guess, but at least I'm not human ramen and my kidneys aren't on fire. I'm back in bed, but I don't remember getting here. I wonder, honestly, if I dreamed the Scouse nurse. I figure someone must have scraped me off the toilet and put me back in bed.

When the black lady nurse comes in with my breakfast, I realise to my surprise that I actually quite fancy a cup of tea. Yeah, I'm *theoretically* Russian, but I was born in London and there's *nothing* like a cup of English Breakfast tea.

'Morning, Lexi!' she says brightly. 'How are you feeling?'

'Awful.' I drag myself upright.

'You're looking a bit brighter. You've got some colour in your cheeks.'

I'm about to tell her to fuck off, but hold my tongue. My being here is not this woman's fault. Her name badge says JOYCE.

'I feel like I'm full of cold.'

Joyce nods. 'Totally normal. It'll pass. You're well on your way, love. Keep going.' She hands me my medication and some water.

'Is there tea?' I ask.

'There is. Do you want any cereal? Toast? You should try eat something.'

'No. No thanks.' The thought of food still turns my stomach.

'Fair enough.'

I sip my drink, and it's *everything*, but the Suboxone soon makes me drowsy again. I put the cup on the built-in bedside shelf (no one is destroying that any time soon) and lay back down.

I drift in and out of sleep for what feels like hours. Still running hot and cold but not to such extremes, thank god. I have strange dreams again. I can't decide if they're memories or not.

I dream about being at my grandmother's little flat in Highgate. Lace table cloths, tea sweetened with black cherries. Daddy brought her over from St Petersburg. She died when I was five, but I remember our visits. My dress was plaid with a frilly white collar. My hair, naturally blonde back then, was in little curly bunches.

She had an open fire, which I was always entranced by. I sat with my baby dolls on the hearth listening to her stories. Baba Yaga, Vasilisa the Beautiful, Alenushka and Ivanushka. She spoke very little English, and I spoke hardly any Russian, but I understood enough to know I should be terrified of Baba Yaga.

She used to braid my hair while I sat on her lap.

I wonder what *Babushka* would think of me now. Lexi isn't made of sugar and spice and all things nice any more. There's a certain grim fascination in watching little girls ripen and spoil, isn't there. Everything inside is gangrene and cigarette butts.

Oh, I've been bad.

I wasn't always.

I don't think.

I wake properly when there's a knock at the door. 'Lexi? Are you awake?' It's Dr Goldstein. He enters and I sit up. 'How are you feeling?'

'Like shit.'

'You look better than you did the last time I saw you.'

I shrug, although it feels like a storm blew over in the night. I feel calm now. Sick, but calm. 'I'm sorry,' I say.

He looks a little taken aback. 'For what?'

Now I'm shocked. 'For calling you a . . . you know. That's like the worst thing I've ever said.' It actually isn't by some margin, but he doesn't need to know that.

'One would hope so,' he laughs a little, ruefully.

'Like, my mum's side of the family is Jewish, or at least Jew-ish . . . so I can't believe I . . . I shouldn't have said that.'

He sits down on the chair by the bed. 'Lexi, you and I haven't really met yet. All I've met thus far is the addiction that lives inside your body. But I'm confident the real Lexi is still in there somewhere. There's plenty of time for us to get acquainted. Until then, I won't hold anything against you.'

Therapyspeak. I'm fluent.

Regardless, maybe he's not so bad. We want different things, but I'm not convinced he's evil. I don't think he wants to hurt me. I say nothing.

'Now,' he says, his eyes on mine, 'do we have to keep you here or can we trust you around decorative pebbles again?'

Back in my suite (from which they have actually removed the decorative pebbles) I put the TV on and half doze, half watch re-runs of *Friends* on Comedy Central and *Big Bang Theory* on E4. This scheduling tells me it *must* be a weekend. God, how long have I been here? The days and nights are a blurry blob. I wish I were at home. Usually Nik and I slob out and watch this shit in our pyjamas and order room service.

The Suite Life of Nik and Lexi.

Utterly drained, I only move when I need the bathroom and even that is a massive undertaking. I'm saggier than a used condom. I stare up at the ceiling. For the first time I wonder what exactly I've done to my body. If I feel so wretched now, it probably wasn't good. Was I running on drugs? It never really seemed that bad when I was high.

My appetite starts to return and the sensation is alien. I can't remember the last time I was properly ravenous. I usually just pick at nuts or have a yoghurt or something. I've survived on canapés for about a year. As evening drags in (E4 is now showing bloody *Transformers 2*), the gay Scouse nurse returns.

'All right, sweetheart? You're looking better.'

I see his name is Gary. 'Thanks.' I'm glad I didn't hallucinate him; he was nice.

'Can I get you anything?'

'I am a bit hungry.'

'Good! That's a good sign. Heroin totally kills your appetite. It means you're nearly clean.'

I don't feel anything close to 'clean'.

'What do you fancy, hon?' He picks up the remote control and presses a button so an interactive screen pops up. He clicks through to today's menu. I'm dimly impressed.

'I don't know, just something light. I might still shit it all out.'

Gary smiles. 'A distinct possibility, but at least you'll be shitting out really nice food, eh?'

'I'll just have minestrone soup, please.'

'Sorted.'

'Don't suppose I get a little glass of Moët for good behaviour?'

He laughs. 'What good behaviour is that?'

'I didn't try to smash anything today.'

'There's no alcohol on the whole island, babes. But we do a nice banoffee pie?'

'I'll pass. But thank you.'

'All part of the service.'

He returns with my soup about fifteen minutes later and puts it on a bed tray for me. The smell turns my stomach and I think for a second I'm going to vomit, but I wonder if it's actually my tummy rumbling. There's a hunk of crusty fresh bread alongside the soup and it smells wonderful, like the hipster artisan bakeries in East London. That reminds me of Kurt, of brunch, of flat whites, of eggs benedict.

'I'll just sit here,' Gary perches on the armchair. 'I've got to make sure you don't choke or spoon yourself to death.' He gives me a wink. 'But I'm not gonna stare at you while you eat, promise. What are we watching?'

'*Transformers 2*. It's bloody awful.'

The soup, however, is delicious. It feels warm all the way down.

More days roll by. I feel defeated, deflated. I can only submit to feeling like crap. Weirdly, the more I eat, the better I feel, and the food coming from the kitchen is always yum: scrambled eggs and avocado; quinoa salad; chicken and kale; apple and spinach smoothies.

OK, I admit it: I can feel the goodness going in and the crap coming out. I guess I can go back to London and tell everyone I've been on a nice juice detox.

Can I go now?

Or is the plan to bore the drugs out of me?

Daytime TV is the *worst* and if I have to watch any more antique-hunt, property-auction shows I'm going to go legit insane. I spend hours navigating Netflix but finding nothing I can focus on for more than twenty minutes. I'm not so sleepy any more and I'm starting to get restless.

I think on Day 7 (although who can tell really?) Dr Goldstein comes to my room wheeling a Louis Vuitton suitcase.

'Oh my god! Is that my clothes?' If I never see another pair of Calvin Klein pyjamas it'll be too soon.

'It is. Your brother sent them a couple of days ago. We've searched the bag, I'm afraid – it's our policy.'

I don't care. I'm too happy to have my things. 'What about my phone? When do I get that back?'

Goldstein pauses. 'We would prefer to hold on to it until you're further along with your recovery. It's standard practice for all our patients. Connections to your life in London won't help you focus, Lexi, believe me.'

No. No way. 'I . . . I just want to let my boyfriend know I'm OK.'

47

'Kurt? I'm sure Nikolai has kept him informed. At this stage, I would strongly advise you to trust me. We usually allow use of phones from about three weeks into treatment – this is for all our patients; it's nothing personal. Digital detox is just as important as drug detox.'

A month without Facebook? Sounds quite nice actually. Eating my eggs this morning felt weird: because I didn't Instagram it before I ate it. 'Whatever, but I need to speak to Kurt. Just Kurt? Please?'

He hesitates. 'We can certainly talk about it. Now ... Miss Volkov, would you care to get dressed and accompany me on a walk around the grounds?'

I blink. 'For real? I can leave my room?'

'I think it's about time, yes.'

I don't need to be asked twice.

He waits outside while I review my outfit options. Predictably, Nikolai has packed a bizarre mish-mash of clothes – clearly the first things his hand landed on in my wardrobe. Why would I need a D&G cocktail dress in rehab? They don't even serve cocktails. Regardless, I find some skinny jeans and a vintage Britney Spears tour tank that'll do. Bless Nik for packing my pewter Manolos, but I think I'll stick with the Vans the hospital gave me.

I'll shower later, so I just shove my post-apocalyptic hair into a knot on my head. I'm so desperate to get outside, I couldn't give a rat's ass what I look like.

I let Dr Goldstein back in once I'm dressed and we go to the terrace doors. He pulls back the curtains and I'm almost blinded.

'Wow, that's bright.' I rummage in my suitcase and see Nik has tucked some Ray-Bans in the lid section. It's colder that I thought it would be so I grab a cashmere pashmina too.

I turn back to the sun and take a tentative step out of the suite. I feel like Bambi learning to walk, unsteady on my legs. I've become so used to the funky smell of my suite, the fresh air is like *insanely*, Nordic-glacier-made-of-mineral-water fresh. 'Oh god, that's better.' Hazy clouds muffle the sun, but it's still a glorious, crisp morning.

'Welcome back to the world.'

'How long was I in there?'

'Eight days.'

Shit. 'Eight days? Wow.'

He smiles, and his eyes crinkle at the corners. Beards make men hard to age. I guess about forty, forty-five? 'Still a long way to go, but you're almost off opiates. Your dose is next to nothing now. You'll be clean by this time next week.'

I say nothing, because there's nothing to say, but also because I'm still slurping in the fresh air. Clarity must be at the top of a hill because the garden looks down on to the sea and I can still get just a hint of salt and seaweed. The view is spectacular, although I feel about a trillion miles away from home.

'Quite something, isn't it?' Dr Goldstein says dreamily. 'I never get bored of that view.' I mutter an agreement and we stroll around the pool. 'The pool is heated, and there's an indoor one in the gym also. There's even a jacuzzi.'

'Great.' Doesn't he know I've grown up in hotels my whole life? Shit like that quickly loses its appeal. Trinkets for idiots. Jacuzzis are a bubbling soup of other people's bodily fluids, frankly.

49

It's pretty here though. Rabbits scurry over the lawn, little white bums flashing as they hop. The grounds are set in a lush pine forest that tumbles all the way down the hillside. God, it really is Alcatraz. Alcatraz with a spa. 'Does anyone else live on the island? Like normal people?'

'We avoid terms like "normal", Miss Volkov, but no. It's a private island. There are small properties, all owned by Lord and Lady Denhulme, that the staff live in.'

'They can't stay here all the time . . .'

'No. We rotate the staff in shifts. I go to the mainland most weekends, but I quite like living out here. It's very tranquil.'

I look at his hand and see he's not wearing a wedding ring. We walk around the side of the mansion where there's some modern raised decking. I hear voices and freeze. I don't know why but I didn't really think anyone else would be here.

'It's OK,' Goldstein says. 'You don't have to meet the others yet if you aren't ready.'

I don't intend on staying past a week or so, so what's the point in getting chummy with the inmates? 'I look like shit,' I say – and that's partly true – but also I don't know if I have the strength yet. They're junkies. Or worse: Recovery Junkies. There's always one at a house party or whatever. They always make grand song-and-dance numbers about how long they've been abstinent for. They're *so* pious about it. I'm always like *take your Perrier and shove it up your—*

'That's OK. You'll meet them in Group soon enough.'

Something to look forward to.

We follow a path that leads away from the house and down to a beautiful pond with mermaid fountains and lily pads. I chance a look over my shoulder and see some fellow hostages have emerged onto the decking, straining to get a look at me. I wrap the pashmina tighter around me. I don't kid myself I'm famous, but people sort of *know* me because of Daddy. I'm sometimes in *Hello* or *The Evening Standard* and I get papped if I'm out with Cara or Karlie. This is embarrassing.

I sneak a look back and see five bodies – I *think* two boys and three girls – looking down at me. I can't make out their faces, only shapes. One of the girls is very overweight and black, and another has bright ginger hair, but that's as much as I can make out from this distance.

I do note one similarity though. 'Why are we all so young?'

'Didn't I say? This facility was set up especially for young adults. There's no lower age limit but we cut off at twenty-four.'

'Why?'

'That's the way Lady Denhulme wanted it.'

I guess this lord and lady are the owners. How philanthropic.

Goldstein continues. 'I've always preferred to work with young people.'

Paedo. 'Why?'

'Because rarely have you gone past the point of no return.' We're now at the front of the mansion, where Nikolai dropped me off. 'As I said when you first arrived, we run an abstinence-based programme based loosely on the Twelve Steps often used in recovery programmes, just with two fewer steps. Tell me, Lexi, are you religious?'

'A lot of my shoes are Christian.'

He looks confused. 'Ah. Well, a traditional Twelve Steps programme refers to a "Higher Power". At the Clarity Centre,

51

we just encourage you to think of the bigger picture. Addicts tend to see their addiction as the centre of the universe. Here we think there's a lot more to life than your next hit. For some people that's God; for others it's family, or friends, or even belief in love or nature.'

That's what the Scientologists said too. 'OK. Whatever.'

He smiles at me. 'Come on. Let's go up to my office and take a look at your schedule.'

'Schedule?'

'Therapy, group therapy, activities ... the hours can go by pretty slowly out here if you don't have something to do.'

I follow him up the stone stairs towards the front door. 'So, like basket weaving?'

He chuckles. 'Arts and crafts are certainly an option.'

'Oh goodie.'

'How can one so young be so cynical?'

'Let's save it for therapy, yeah? I don't want to give you any spoilers.' My face contorts into something like a smile for the first time in eight days.

His office looks precisely as it did before my temper tantrum. I sit in the same seat while he runs me through how my days will be from now on. Apparently I'll have individual therapy *every* morning, even if it's just to check in with him or his colleague, Dr Ahmed, who I'll meet tomorrow. There will follow group therapy until lunchtime and then our afternoons are free for 'activities'. I wonder if 'masturbate in the bath' counts. The evenings will be 'structured', which sends a shiver down my spine, but Dr Goldstein assures me it's only a mixture of film screenings, games nights and speakers coming to the island to 'share their recovery stories'.

'Our clients often find evenings are the hardest,' he explains. 'That's when many would traditionally use, so we keep you busy.'

'OK.' It sounds like hell on earth. Two months of a regime even stricter than St Agnes, and look how well that turned out.

'Bother. My printer is on the blink,' Goldstein says. 'Just wait here a moment while I get your schedule from the office.'

He darts out and the door clicks shut behind him. I wonder if my phone is still in here somewhere. There aren't any windows to the corridor so I have no idea how long it'll take him to return. I drum my fingers on my knees.

Worth a quick look.

I hop out of my chair and go around to his side of the desk. His desk has four drawers on either side. They're not locked either. Amateur. The first is full of stationery, the one below that paperwork. I go over to the left and the top drawer contains assorted knick-knacks but also a plastic pharmacy bottle.

Huh.

Score.

My heart flutters up into my throat. Sudden dry-mouth. Oooh, naughty, NAUGHTY thoughts. Inquisitive little fingers, minds of their very own, scurry to the bottle and give it a shake. It rattles.

The label reads DIAZEPAM 10MG. A pretty strong dosage too. The prescription is in Goldstein's name.

I look to the door. The coast is clear. I fumble with the child-proof cap and get it off. There are like five pills. I doubt he'd miss one. I mean, it's one poxy diazepam – what harm can it do? It'll just take the edge off. I still feel like I've been sucked out with a Dyson through my ass and one little pill isn't going to fix that, but it might get me through the day.

It's just Valium. It isn't even an opiate.

With a final glance at the door, I pop a pill and swallow it back. I thrust the bottle back in the drawer and return to my seat about three seconds before the door opens.

That's when the minty taste hits me.

Goldstein stands in the door, disappointment – no, resignation – all over his beardy face.

What fresh hell is this?

'That was a Tic Tac,' he says. 'I was watching you via a video link.' He points to a tiny, subtle lens hidden high on a bookshelf next to a wise owl ornament.

Busted as fuck. 'You set me up.'

'No one asked you to rifle through my desk, Lexi.' He returns to his seat, calm as a summer cloud. 'Why did you do that?'

'I don't know! I was looking for my phone!'

'And why did you take the pill?'

I push myself out of the chair and stomp to the window. I'm so embarrassed, I can't even look at him. 'Because it was there.'

'And that's something you do? Just take prescribed medicines you find lying around in drawers?'

I don't know. I don't know why I did it.

Why I wanted it.

But I really, *really* wanted it.

I slump down next to the radiator under the window, head in hands. He's got me. He's totally caught me red-handed and I am such a twat for falling for something so blatantly obvious. Junkie honey trap.

'Lexi, why did you take that pill?'

I look up at him through my hands and knotty hair. 'Because I guess I have a problem,' I say. 'Happy now?'

STEP 2:
THE CHOICE TO RECOVER
IS MINE TO MAKE

I smoke a cigarette on one of the sunloungers outside my suite. It's a pretty dusk, the colour of pink grapefruit juice. Apparently my little breakthrough in Goldstein's office earned me an unlocked patio door. I see now that my room is part of a modern annex grafted on to the side of the mansion.

I sigh.

It's all so improbable. How can I be 'an addict'? I'm seventeen years old. I always sort of aspired to a coke problem as I turned thirty, but never this. This is mortifying. When Nik sat me down about six months ago, after . . . well, when he sat me down to lecture me about my behaviour, I thought it was *cute* in an unnecessarily concerned big brother way. I didn't realise he *saw* me. He really saw me. Why didn't I see it too?

The crazy part is, I can almost hear a separate little voice, almost identical to my own but *not quite* telling me I *need* to score and that Goldstein is a quack.

Don't get me wrong, I still feel like twice-baked crap, but I don't *need* to score. I just really *want* to. What's up with that? I know my body is getting better, I can feel normality is just around the corner, but it's pretty clear I was topping up with drugs just to achieve an even keel. I guess that's what makes an addict an addict.

If this is how rancid I feel without the pills and stuff, I suppose I have a *dependency* and that might as well be an addiction. Is there even a difference? I cringe like there's nails on a blackboard. I shouldn't have let it, let *anything*, get the better of me.

I stub out one cigarette and light another immediately.

What about Kurt? Does that make him an addict too? I've never thought of him that way – we just got high sometimes. It was supposed to be fun. It *was* fun. It's not fucking fun now.

I know, like I KNOW, that Kurt won't stop using even if I do. And where does that leave me? The shrill-bitch, nagging, sober girlfriend is where. A part of me wonders where the problem is . . . I don't think anything we were doing affected anyone but us. Maybe it's only a 'drug problem' if you can't afford them? And I can. It's not like I have or need a job. Maybe we can carry on the way we were?

It's only when we're high that I truly *have* Kurt. That's when he's most mine. It's what pins us down together.

But a voice that sounds a lot like me refuses to be a bitch to the chemicals in my body. I had no clue how much I was using really. I was that metaphorical frog in the pan of boiling water: it got hot so gradually I didn't realise I was cooking.

I almost light a third cigarette, but then spare a thought for my lungs.

I'm weirdly nervous about my first therapy session. I don't know why; I've been seeing therapists since I was fourteen. Daddy was worried about us when Mummy finally left. It had been a long time coming though. I wonder if it's more the prospect of *group* therapy that's bothering me. The prospect of performing some contrite flagellation before total strangers doesn't exactly fill me with glee.

I'm feeling a little better, although I have horrific toothache. I've been clenching my jaw all through the night. I'm still having messed-up dreams and night-sweats.

It feels like the first day at school after the holidays and I now have sufficient energy to give a shit what I look like. Being a total boy, Nikolai didn't think to pack any make-up – or even any moisturiser – so when Joyce comes with my breakfast I ask her if there's any way I can get my hands on some. Sure enough, when I get out of the shower a little goodie bag from Kiehl's is waiting on my bed. It's pretty basic supplies, but it's better than nothing.

I select the skinny jeans again, this time pairing them with a retro Miami Dolphins sweater I love. It's about twenty sizes too big and slopes off my left shoulder. I braid my hair into a messy plait and note my roots are coming through at pace. My natural hair colour is muddy-puddle-brown and I've been dying it since I was about eleven. I sometimes forget I'm not an actual blonde. I wonder if the five-star treatment stretches to root touch-ups?

After room-service breakfast, I head to Goldstein's office for my individual session.

'Tea? Coffee?' he offers, fussing around with his notes as he shows me in. He's rearranged the corner of the office: three armchairs circle a coffee table on a shaggy rug, removing the desk-shaped barrier between us.

'Coffee, please,' I say, hoping it'll kick-start my brain. I take one of the seats and wonder if it's a psychometric test . . . like, what does taking the *left* seat really say about my personality? In this case, it means 'from this position, Lexi can stare out of the window because she thinks therapy is for bed-wetters'.

Goldstein sorts the coffee as we're joined by a super-stylish Asian woman with her hijab tucked into what appears to be a Burberry trenchcoat. 'I am so sorry I'm late. Ferry didn't leave on time.'

'Not a problem,' Goldstein says. 'Lexi Volkov, meet Dr Samia Ahmed, our other lead therapist. Coffee, Samia?'

'I'll take mine black, thanks, Isaac. Nice to meet you, Lexi. How are you settling in?'

Is she for real? 'Oh, it's like that time I was at Disneyland Paris.'

'But with less heroin, I assume?'

I can't mask a smirk. 'Marginally.'

'Do you mind me sitting in?' she asks. 'Dr Goldstein is your primary contact so I completely understand if you'd rather work with him alone. I promise I won't take it personally.'

She has a homely Yorkshire Pudding accent and I quite like her already. Not sure why. I don't really see what difference it makes whether she's here or not. 'I don't mind,' I say.

'Good. I like to get to know all our residents.' Interesting choice of words. 'And this way Isaac and I can work together to decide how best to support you.'

'Whatever.'

Coffee made, Goldstein takes his seat. They both look to me expectantly. It's Go Time.

I take a deep breath. 'So what do you want to know?'

'Let's start with the facts. I always think facts are easier than feelings. Why don't you tell us about the first time you used opiates?' Goldstein asks.

I smile again. 'Well, I think I had some codeine after I had my tonsils out . . .'

'Recreationally?'

This is going to hurt, isn't it? Fuck it. It's not like I didn't know this was coming. 'Well, I suppose if we're going to talk about that, then I need to start with Kurt . . .'

You hear people talk about love all the time. It's just flopping out of people's mouths every minute of the day: *I love you, I love this burger, I love my mum, I love my new Balenciaga.* Love, love, love, all the goddamn time, right?

I *thought* I knew what love was. When I was younger, I had a gorgeous Haflinger pony called Pepper and I *loved* him, I really did; it felt like my heart got bigger the day I got him. But this was something else. I wasn't ready for it.

We met at a St Agnes party. St Agnes is a fancy girls' school in Kensington. Think of a slightly more competitive version of *The Hunger Games* with fewer winners and you've probably got it. High Achievers wall-to-wall. I think it was Florentine Harvey-Lenk's Sweet Sixteen. She'd hired a bar on Clapham High Street and invited about two hundred of her closest friends and family. By day, Clapham is the domain of leafy Boden mummies and their labradoodles, but by night it becomes a cautionary tale of rugby-playing estate agents fingering barely legal girls in neon-lit cocktail-bar doorways. Each bar is punctuated by a different grizzly fried chicken shop.

Luckily for everyone, Florentine's event was private. Importantly, there were boys there. I was never a boarder, so boys were never especially exotic, but for a lot of girls, a willy in the room was like being dropped in a vat of catnip.

Kurt wasn't invited, but he was there. He knew the bar owner. He knows all the right people: the door whores, the DJs, the bouncers, the bartenders. He never pays, he glides through the red rope like a ghost.

I was bored shitless and ready to leave. I think I was wearing a midnight blue slip dress and a sheepskin coat. I'd lost

Antonella, Nevada and Genevieve: Genie was on Jägerbombs which *never* ends well and I'm so not the hold-back-hair type. I weaved my way through the crowd – mostly St Agnes girls trying to twerk on boys from St Barnabas. Prosecco-fuelled Drake fans. What price dignity?

And then I saw him, slouched over the end of the bar like silk. Quiff collapsing over black eyes, sleeves rolled almost to the shoulder, skin crawling with mermaids, anchors and krakens. Oh god, you know what? *He* was my first opium. He was blue smoke curling across the bar, contorting into the shape of a summoning finger. I just knew. I knew as soon as I saw him.

He looked a little older than us – but not by much. Not Sex Offenders Register material. Suddenly, I wasn't going anywhere. Other girls – basic bitches – were staring at him and whispering oh-so-subtly behind their hands like debutards, so I just walked on over, lion-tamer chill. The only reason to fear boys is if you think you're unworthy somehow. 'What are we having?' I asked.

He looked me up and down, but I was cute AF and knew it. 'I'm on dirty martinis. Can I get you a cherryade or something?'

'Adorable.' I turned to his bartender chum. 'I'll have the same – vodka, not gin, two olives.' He was about to ask for ID so I just handed over my platinum card. *Volkov* is all the ID I've ever needed. He scurried off to mix my drink.

I knew I'd have to play it cool. Kurt is a COOL GUY so I'd have to be a COOL GIRL. No strings, no label tags, no thumbscrews – at least none that he's aware of.

He glimpsed the name on the card. '*The* Alexandria Volkov? My lucky night.' He oozed sarcasm.

'Lexi. And don't believe everything you read in the diary pages.'

'I don't read them full-stop. My little sister wants to *be* you.'

'Who doesn't?'

'You?'

I barked out a laugh. His Playful Banter game was strong. I'm not loveblind; I know part of the appeal was that I didn't impress him, or if I did, he hid it well. Like, why should people be impressed? I didn't ask to be born an 'heiress'. I didn't work for it; I work *with* it.

'Well, you've got me there.' The bartender slid my drink over on the ubiquitous black napkin. 'Cheers . . .?'

'Kurt.' He clinked my glass with his own. 'Kurt Blakeney.'

I established he'd just graduated from St Martin's College with a First in Fine Art and Sculpture. His family are somehow related to the royals, through marriage. Dad is a stockbroker, Mum works at Sotheby's. Grayson Perry handpicked and bought one of his final-year sculptures. Sipping martinis, we talked about South London as the new East London; how sick we were of 'gourmet' junk food; Uber versus black cabs; the art scene; closeted gay actors and models we both knew and how reductive that was.

Of course, it was what we *didn't* say that was more telling. Underneath the words there was something much more seductive, more suggestive, happening with our eyes and lips.

By the end of the conversation I was hooked. I wanted him like I'd never wanted anyone or anything before, including my alligator Birkin. Full disclosure: I was saving my virginity for Prince Harry, but this was virgin territory. As fate would have it, Daddy was in London and was blowing up my phone asking when I'd be home – he's weirdly protective for an absent father.

Daddy sent one of the hotel drivers to bring me home. Shameful. Kurt, oddly old-fashioned, offered to walk me to the car. Clapham High Street was in full swing: lads looking to start fights, girls carrying their Primark nude pumps to the bus stop. I wouldn't normally do what I did next, but Kurt wasn't normal.

'Can I give you my number?' I asked, breaking my personal rule about making anything resembling a first move.

'Sure,' he said, non-committal.

I can tell when I'm being humoured. 'I'm not what you think I am. I'm not a schoolgirl.'

A thick brow flickered in disbelief. 'How old are you?'

'In socialite years? About twenty-eight.'

He laughed. 'You can hold your booze, I'll give you that.'

'I'm Russian. My blood is forty per cent distilled.'

He laughed again and handed me his phone. I typed my number in and gave it back. 'Well maybe I'll see you around then,' he said with a vague smile.

I wasn't going to beg. 'Maybe you will.' I swung my legs into the limo and didn't look back.

You can only imagine my surprise and delight when I woke up to a message from him. It had come through at four a.m. and said: *We should check out that pop-up Mexican in the church.*

I'd heard the legend of *La Casa de Jesus*, a temporary street-food venture in Peckham. It was meant to be amazing, but if you ran to Peckham for every 'amazing' pop-up restaurant in a car park, tattoo shop or Portaloo you'd need more than seven days in a week.

Call me names, but I'm not a game-player. I replied as soon I was done hitting the snooze button. *Sure. When?*

Kurt is nocturnal so I got the reply at about one. *Tonight? 9?*

And I guess that was where it really began. Is that when I first used? No! That night I wore Balmain and we ate the best quesadillas I'd ever tasted. I would have married one if I could.

'Don't you go mental living in a hotel?' he asked me as he sipped his margarita.

'I haven't ever not lived in one, so I wouldn't know the difference. I mean, it's pretty clean, but like, who doesn't have a cleaner?'

'We don't have one every day, princess.'

'Uh, don't call me that! I know some princesses and they're either part-pony or bulimic coke fiends.'

He grinned. He has a little chip on his front tooth. I always liked it. Veneers are creepy. 'And that's not you?'

I sensed I was being tested. 'I could never be bulimic. I like my food too much, as you can clearly see, and enjoy digesting it.' I gestured at my third quesadilla. 'And coke is only OK if everyone's doing it, otherwise you're just the most annoying cunt in the room.'

Using the C word has to be well-timed. I love that there's still a word in the English language that has any power to shock whatsoever. I'm like, it's just another word for my bits, you guys, chill out! You know what I think it is? I think guys don't want girls to have that word, even though it's ours.

Anyway. His grin broadened to Cheshire Cat proportions and I knew I'd passed. Oh come on, St Martin's art student with trader father? They probably sprinkle gak on their cornflakes every morning. 'Such a wise head on such young shoulders.'

'I don't know what I'm doing,' I told him with a shake of my head. 'Like, ever. I make it up as I go along. But Daddy always says life's too short to not try everything new. I'm only here for, what, sixty good years, and I want to do it all. On my deathbed, I don't wanna be like, *shit I forgot to try absinthe* or whatever.'

'I hear that,' Kurt said. 'With that in mind, there's some things I wanna do with you.'

I looked up at him coyly over my mojito. 'I'm sure there are.'

'Wait two minutes and then follow me to the bathroom . . .'

It so wasn't me, but when I'm with Kurt I'm not me. There's something red hot between us – a mist, a crazy mist – and when he said 'follow me' I did because I *couldn't not*.

I counted to one hundred and twenty, put down my napkin and wove through the tables towards the toilets. With every step my heart climbed my ribcage to my throat.

He was waiting for me.

We locked ourselves in the toilet and did a line of coke before we kissed. It was urgent and hungry – animal hands pulling, tearing at each other – but I wasn't going to go all the way in a lavatory and told him so. 'I just wanna taste you,' he said with half-closed eyes. His hands slid into my pants and moved them to one side.

Well, I think you get the picture. It felt . . . singular, like nothing else on earth. I can still remember my heart pounding in my skull and the earthquake that followed. Was it Judy Blume who said an orgasm is like a sneeze in your between-me-down-there? She's wrong – it's like the moment just *before* the sneeze.

Well, OK, yeah, I guess we did use on the first date, but only a cheeky line. The first time I did heroin I didn't even realise it was heroin.

Sometimes Kurt was like trying to capture smoke in your hands. Sure, he'd always reply when I messaged him, but it was always me that made the first move or, if it wasn't, I'd get messages like 'we're on Primrose Hill – come join us', when I was away skiing or at school or something. He was impossible. It was sexy as hell.

It's important to go to charity functions or award ceremonies, especially if V Hotels are a key sponsor. It was the Brit Awards last year. V Hotels were one of the sponsors and had a table. If I recall rightly, Antonella was skiing in St Moritz, so Nevada and I went along because everyone knows limitless free champagne and Brit School try-hards are always a hilarious combo. Either that or some has-been pees themselves or tries to start a fight.

I was sent a whole bunch of dresses but chose McQueen in the end. Ivory ruffles, as light as air and embellished with embroidered butterflies and pearls. Misha XN, the stylist at the Shoreditch hotel, did my hair – taking about three hours to make it look like I'd been dragged through a hedge backwards. It was plaited and twisted up into a knot, with a haberdashery of jewels, charms, pearls and brooches woven into the curls.

Nevada, who was signed by Models 1 when she was basically an egg – she's got that Asian/Western mix that's bang on-trend

– wore Marchesa and we huddled for warmth on the red carpet, posing for pictures. Let me tell you, avoiding accidentally being papped next to a reality TV judge or, worse, a YouTuber, is no small feat.

Daddy wasn't even vaguely interested in attending, so our table was made up of Nikolai, his girlfriend, Tabitha, and some other hotel people.

It was fine – a girl band girl's boob fell out accidentally-on-purpose, and a number of popstars came out in support of famine in East Africa, five minutes after purging a three-course meal in the toilets.

While an unlikely – but wholly predictable – pairing performed a duet, I checked my phone. There was a message from Kurt. *Babes, were you just on TV?*

I replied: *At Brit Awards. It's absurd.*

We're in Chelsea, he messaged, *come over later.*

And so we did. The after-parties get messy and undignified so Nevada and I took a car to the house party. It was actually at Ferdie Brompton-Whyte's place – you know, the beer heir. Picture a smart townhouse like something from a Richard Curtis film – all window boxes and gleaming mosaic floors. The party was pretty chill, maybe about twenty people. Kurt stuck out like a sore thumb among the collar-up Ralph Lauren and Hackett crowd. Chelsea people always have the wholesome look of a Golden Retriever that's just bounded in from running in a cornfield. Kurt was hunched in a corner, smoking out of an open window. When he saw me, he looked genuinely pleased and I felt a little jolt of static electricity.

'Nice dress,' he said. 'You look naked.'

'Who says that isn't the idea?'

He pulled me in for a hardcore kiss I wasn't quite expecting. He tasted of Lucky Strikes and Jack Daniel's.

Nevada returned with two flutes of champers. 'Kurt, this is my friend Nevada Charles.'

'Nice to meet you,' Nev said. Kurt just nodded.

We all hung out for a while in the lounge, but it was pretty clear I had competition. Flossy Blenheim is the younger and slightly-less-perfect sister of Xenia Blenheim ... you'll have seen her in the Dior campaign? Anyway, it was clear Kurt had been invited because she was into his action. She was on him like she'd never even heard of personal space. Oh, she's OK, just clueless – but I was prepared to fight her for him.

I lost Kurt for a while and I was worried he'd sidled off with Flossy until I found her crying drunkenly on Nightingale Lowe in the wet room. Kurt was in the kitchen with Ferdie and Troy Chang. 'This shit is the purest,' Kurt was saying, rolling a spliff. 'Guaranteed mellow high.'

'What's this?' I asked.

'It's not for you,' Kurt said definitely, simultaneously throwing down the gauntlet.

'Oh, grow up. Puff?'

'Something like that.'

Troy sparked it up and inhaled deeply. His eyes rolled back in his head. 'Oh shit, that's good.' He passed it to Ferdie.

'Sharing is caring,' I said.

'It's not pot,' Kurt said with finality.

'Do I look like I'm troubled by that detail?'

Nevada appeared beside me. 'Then what is it?'

Ferdie and Troy chuckled like naughty school boys, their faces already glazed. 'It's *bliss* is what it is,' said Kurt.

'Lexi, don't,' Nevada warned. 'What if it's heroin?'

A bit like the word 'cunt', I didn't understand why one drug should be treated any differently to the others. Kurt smirked. I wasn't backing down. 'What if it isn't?' I took the joint from him and took a drag.

It was like sinking into a hot bubble bath. First I felt the warmth, like my insides were sticky toffee pudding. I won't lie – just one toke knocked my head off. I was so dizzy the room carouseled around me, everyone else bobbing up and down like fairground horses, wild eyes rolling. I clung to Kurt as we came up, knowing we were experiencing the same rush. I felt closer to him than ever. It's like we melted into one person.

That was when I lost my virginity to him. We went to a spare bedroom, bodies entwined on a pile of coats, and he was right, you know: it was bliss.

'Anything else?' I ask. 'I can go into more detail if you'd like.'

'I think that'll suffice,' Ahmed says.

'How often did you use after that?' Goldstein asks, offering me a chocolate digestive, which I refuse.

I shrug. 'I dunno. Sometimes. At first it was wicked every time. It's like any drug, though – the very highest highs wear off pretty quickly. Why can't they do that? Make a drug that feels as amazing as the first time every time?'

'So . . . occasionally?'

'Mostly at the end of the night. We'd usually go back to Kurt's – Daddy doesn't like boys coming back to the hotel – smoke a little before bed.'

'Just smoking?'

I squirm. 'Sometimes we'd take a pill. Like, Baggy would sometimes get hold of Oxy.'

'And when did you start injecting?'

Embarrassed, I pull my sleeves down over my wrists. 'Not until later. When smoking it didn't really get me high any more.' Slamming is much more efficient. Direct into the bloodstream.

Now, that is pretty shameful actually. Worst part is, I *knew* that was proper junkie behaviour and I did it anyway. But I don't know if I'm really selling the high. That's the thing with drugs. All my life people have told me that 'drugs are evil' and 'drugs are bad' but I knew they *had* to be lying because if there was literally nothing good about drugs no one would ever do them. Why can't we just be honest and say 'drugs are boss until you almost snuff it, your brother abducts you and you start shitting the bed'?

Or until you look like a living corpse?

Or until you're sweating pellets?

Or until you basically offer to blow a nurse for a hit?

Or until your best friend . . .

Shut up, head, just shut the fuck up. I know.

Suddenly I don't feel too good. 'Can I get a cigarette?' All of the ones Nikolai left me with are gone.

'Of course,' says Goldstein, closing his notebook with a definitive pop. 'We're about out of time anyway. Have a break. You can get more cigarettes from the main reception and we'll both see you for Group at eleven. Before that, do you want some time with your phone?'

It's so predictable, isn't it? I rolled over and begged like a good doggy so now I get Scooby Snax. 'Erm, yes. Thank you.'

He fetches it from the main admin office along with a charger. It'll have been dead for days. He and Ahmed stand up to leave. They're trusting me alone with a smartphone?

'Am I being listened to?' I say, fumbling with the plug socket.

'No,' Goldstein says. He turns back to me as he exits. 'I'll be back in ten minutes. But be mindful of the people in your life who can get to you, even when there's a sea between you.'

Thanks, Oprah. I'll take that into consideration. He leaves and closes the door behind him. The phone comes alive and lights up. I hold my breath as the phone takes what feels like *weeks* to wake up. The first texts and messages come through. Mummy and Daddy (both generic 'hope you're OK' texts which lead me to believe Nik *hasn't* ratted me out. Yet). Nikolai (an

apology – and asking me to check in with him as soon as I can).
Baggy (clearly dying to know where I am).

No Kurt.

No voicemails.

Are you fucking kidding me?

I dial into my voicemail to check but there's nothing. Not even a PPI claim robot.

I don't get it. I've been here over a week. You'd think I'd have more messages. Like, I was supposed to see people. I had lunches and a manicure booked in. Last week was the Asperger's Ball. It was *at the hotel*. Why hasn't anyone asked me if I'm sick or something?

But more than any of that, why hasn't Kurt asked if I'm alive? I resist the urge to go full Naomi and hurl the phone across the room, as that wouldn't do me much good in the long-run. Instead I dial Nikolai. He answers at once. 'Hey, Lex?'

'It's me.'

'Are you OK?'

'Have you spoken to Kurt?'

'What?'

'I'm not messing around, Nik, just tell me. Have you spoken to Kurt?'

A pause. 'Yes. I told him if he tried to contact you, I'd rip his nuts off.'

I feel like *my* nuts have been ripped off. 'Jesus, Nik.' I'm winded. 'I can't believe you did that. You have no right—'

'I don't care, Lex. The guy's scum. You wouldn't be in this state if it weren't for him.'

'That's not true,' I squawk down the phone, although it's probably (OK definitely) true. 'Nik. I *need* to speak to him. You have no idea what it's been like here. It's awful! I shit. The. Fucking. Bed.'

He laughs and I can't help but laugh too, although I'm crying and my nose is running. 'Good. I think that's what's supposed to happen.'

I sniff.

'Are you off the drugs yet?' he asks.

'Almost. I feel like shit.'

There's another silence. 'I just want my sister back.'

I don't really know what to say to that. 'Has Daddy said anything?'

'He's taken Anja to Mauritius for her birthday. He thinks you're with Mum.' His gold-digging child-bride must have turned twelve or whatever she is.

'OK. That's OK.' I chew my nail. If I can get through this without Daddy finding out, that's definitely a bonus. 'Are you OK?' I add as an afterthought.

'Me? I'm fine. I was worried for you, Lexi. I was scared to death. What if you'd . . .? I don't think I can manage Mum and Dad by myself.'

It's hard to imagine I died because I did not die. Unless this is purgatory. Actually, that's disturbingly accurate. Is this where you come when you OD? Eternal rehab? Chilling.

For the first time, I try to picture how I must have looked that night – unconscious and pale in the penthouse. I never meant to scare him, or anyone, like that. Ms Grafton's barn owl schoolmarm tones echo through my head: *When will you acknowledge, Miss Volkov, that your actions have consequences?*

I always knew they had consequences. I just thought I was the only one they affected. And I'm fair game.

'I'm sorry,' I say in a very little voice. 'I didn't mean to scare you.'

He pauses. I guess it's been a long time since I apologised to anyone, for anything. 'Well, you did. You scared the shit out of me.'

We say bye and I check the other messages. Mummy asks how I am and is then sniffy when I haven't replied. I do so now and tell her my phone was stolen by Muslim immigrants outside Clapham Junction. This plays gloriously into about nine of her prejudices. Daddy has sent a selfie of him and Anja – wearing a standard issue dial-a-bride gold bikini – on some white sand beach. I hope she gets swallowed by a shark even more vicious than she is.

Baggy wants to know if I'm OK. He's a sweet boy. I tell him I'm fine but give no details as to my whereabouts. I don't trust him to not blab. Even sweet boys have their price, and I have no desire to be a *Mail on Sunday* exclusive.

I take a deep breath and call Kurt. It rings and rings before it goes to a voicemail I'm way too familiar with. 'It's Kurt. Leave a message.'

'Hello. It's me,' I say. 'Shit, I sound like that Adele song. Does that get a laugh? Look, I know what Nikolai said to you and that was bang out of order. I guess, when he saw me . . . he freaked out. But I'm fine now. I'm at a clinic. It's probably not a bad thing to have a detox or whatever and I'll see you soon.' Do I say it or not? Fuck it. 'I love you. Call me, OK? They let me check my phone every day.' I hang up. God, I hope he's OK. It sounds mental, but he's not as tough as he looks and London can be a soul-sucking vampire leech.

He needs someone.

He needs me.

I inhale two cigarettes back-to-back on the communal decked terrace. It's fucking freezing, but I'm trying to put off meeting the other fuck-ups for as long as possible ahead of Group. I suppose it's better to get it over and done with; rip off the plaster. As I light my third cigarette, I'm joined by a very posh boy. I can tell he's posh before he even opens his mouth. He's got that inexplicable floppy posh-boy Boris haircut and his collar is turned up. They always look a little like confused hedgehogs coming out of hibernation.

'Hello,' he says. 'I'm Guy.'

Plum firmly in mouth. 'Double barrel surname?'

He scrunches his pedigree face. 'That obvious? Samson-Reed.'

I shake his hand. He looks about my age, but it's harder to tell with boys. 'Sorry. That was rude. I'm . . .'

'Alexandria Volkov. I thought I recognised you earlier when you were with Goldstein.'

Great. 'Great,' I say. 'So much for going under the radar. But call me Lexi. Have we met?'

'No.' He lights his own cigarette. 'I think you might know my sister. She graduated from St Aggy's two years ago. Clarissa? Clarissa Samson-Reed?'

It doesn't ring a bell. I shrug.

'You are a St Agnes girl though, right?'

'I was. Not any more.'

'Were you there last year when that girl died?'

'No,' I say.

There's an awkward silence as we both smoke. I wonder if the first rule of rehab is no one talks about rehab. I suspect he's dying to ask 'what I'm in for' but I wouldn't want to give away any hints before Group. 'What are you smoking?' he asks.

Ah, two smokers will always have something to talk about. 'Marlboro Lights.'

'Cool. I like Camel.'

'Hardcore.'

'I know. Terrible habit. But they say if you stop before you're thirty, your body miraculously heals itself or something.'

'Who says that?'

'Smokers, one would imagine.'

I nod and stub my cigarette out.

'Don't be nervous about Group. It's not that bad, I promise.'

I think I am a little bit nervous. Even talking to Guy feels weird, like I'm learning to interact again; like some sad terrier that's been kept in a shed too long. At this stage I might bite. I don't trust him. I don't trust any of them, including – especially – the doctors. 'Cool,' I say.

'Come on, I'll show you the way.' He stubs out his cigarette and leads the way. Only then, as we arrive at the door, does he turn back to the ashtray attached to the railing. He checks something, then walks past me to the door again, then goes back *again* to check the ashtray. 'Sorry,' he says, and this time he walks through the door and I follow him inside.

Oh yeah, just for a second I forgot everyone here is broken.

Group is held in a different room in the old part of the house, possibly a dining room, library or billiard room at some point. This house is a life-size Cluedo board. There's a handsome fireplace, in which a low flame crackles, and two big windows looking out over the lawn. Vaguely arranged around the fireplace and coffee table are three sleek grey sofas and two armchairs.

Guy and I are the first inmates to arrive, although Goldstein hovers at the fireplace. I want to sit alone, so select an armchair and tuck my feet under my butt.

'Relax,' Goldstein tells me. 'You're not going to be forced to talk if you don't want to – I'll ask you to introduce yourself. That's all.'

I nod. I can manage that. I can't deny I'm curious to see who I'm locked up with.

The others arrive in a noisy clump, spilling through the door like a human clot. There's four of them. Three girls and a guy. I see him first: surfie hair, wet sand colour, stubble, Malibu tan. *Vice* magazine masturbation material . . . just utterly East London gorgeous. He looks my way and gives a polite nod. He has Ryan Gosling eyes that I expect cause knickers to spontaneously drop with one glance. He's wearing a grey T-shirt and his left arm is covered in tattoos. That reminds me of Kurt and I get an ache under my ribs. I return his nod.

Behind him is the massive black girl. Christ, she's big. God, I'm such a judgey bitch. I avert my eyes so she doesn't catch me staring, although not until after I clock her expensive weave and diamond-flecked Rolex.

82

The second girl comes through the door backwards – shouting something to a nurse down the corridor – and I sit up straighter in my chair. I do a double take, sucking breath in through my teeth.

Antonella.

Just for a second, I swear it's her: same dead straight raven-black hair, same waifish build. But then she turns around and I see, although they're similar, this girl isn't quite as gorgeous. This girl is tall, painfully thin and gangly – collarbones, cheekbones, wrists and knuckles. Her friend – they're linked arm-in-arm – is a booby red head.

They settle in their seats. I wait quietly, avoiding eye-contact.

'Let's get started then, shall we?' Goldstein asks.

'Where's Samia?' asks the tall skinny one. As she tucks her hair behind her ears, I see a ladder of shiny silver scars on her wrist. A cutter, but a cutter a long time ago, I'm guessing.

'We're expecting a new arrival,' he explains. 'Dr Ahmed is going to greet him.'

'Ooh a new boy!' says the red head with a clap. 'I hope he's cute.'

Simpering moron. We're all so young. It could so easily be a seminar group at school, but it isn't. I really, *really* don't need an hour of group hugs and Kumbaya.

Excruciating.

I wish I were high.

I want to get obliterated, to blast my head out of reality and reality out of my head.

The desire, the thirst, shocks me a little. I sit up straighter.

Goldstein sits next to the big girl on one of the sofas. 'So it's our first Group with Lexi.' He says in a cotton-wool voice, like introducing a timid new puppy to infants. 'Before we get started, Lexi, why don't you tell us a bit about yourself?'

It takes everything I have to not simply scream and throw myself through the window pane. It's really hard to Be Nice when you're just fundamentally not. 'Hi, I'm Lexi. I was basically abducted and brought here in a coma.'

The skinny girl smiles slyly. The hot guy looks at me with *pity* in those puppy eyes. Oh well, you can fuck right off, mate. I doubt you're here for addiction to prayer. 'Apparently I'm a heroin addict,' I say, more bitterly than even I'd intended. 'So there you go. You can stop trying to figure it out.'

The skinny girl's smile broadens. 'Wow. Rock and roll.'

Huh. Interesting. I think she might be trans. It's in the voice. Strong jawline.

'Kendall,' warns Goldstein. (Make-believe name. Definitely trans.) 'It's not your turn to speak.'

'It's OK,' I say. 'I'm done.'

'Very well. In that case, as it's your final Group, Melissa, why don't you start us off?'

The red head nods. 'By the way, before I start, can everyone keep looking for my silver locket? I can't find it anywhere. I don't wanna leave without it. It didn't cost much, but it was my grandmother's . . .'

Goldstein nods. 'We'll do a search this afternoon, I promise. So! It's your last day at Clarity. How are you feeling?'

'I dunno. Good, I guess. Nervous. I'd be happier if we found my locket!'

'Why nervous?'

84

'It feels like I've been here for ever.' Too bloody right, hon. 'I'm just worried the world has changed while I've been away. Like, I won't know how to function any more.'

Goldstein leans forward and nods. 'Perfectly understandable and something I'd say nearly all of our patients go through. There is something very safe about institutions. What did you observe on your home visit?'

Melissa shrugs. 'Mum and Dad didn't really let me out of their sight, so it was hard to tell, you know what I mean? And I knew I was coming back.'

'Did you face temptation?'

I bristle at the quasi-religious flavour of that word. You don't face *temptation*, you face *life*. Life is full of nice things that are bad for us. Temptation is just a fancy word for wanting them. It's the same as 'demons'. The first time someone says I have 'demons' I'm out of here. I don't need an exorcist. I need a drink.

'I wouldn't have drunk at home anyway. I definitely didn't *want* to go out and get drunk.'

'Good. That's good.'

'Like, I know I'm going to want to drink. Probably in a few weeks when the novelty's worn off and I'm not expecting it.'

'And what will you do when that happens?'

'I can't avoid alcohol for ever. It's out there, right? I'll have to explain I'm sober now. If they're truly my friends, they'll understand.' It all feels so scripted. I think that's what therapy is. It doesn't change your behaviour, but it gives you a vocabulary to discuss how screwed up you are: therapese.

'Honesty. It's so important.' Goldstein nods. 'To be honest with yourself and with other people.'

'This is for ever. I have to exist in a world with booze everywhere. I hope I don't relapse . . .'

'But if you do?'

'I know I can stop. I know I'm better now. I know I'm stronger than drink.'

Goldstein makes us clap like performing seals. I half expect him to reveal a bucket filled with slimy whitebait to reward us.

He opens the floor for comments. 'How do you respond to that Ruby?'

'I mean, how is that supposed to work for me?' asks the big girl in an American accent. Again, I feel like a thundering bitch for even noticing her size. Like, I couldn't give two shits if someone is overweight to be honest – god, I wish I had more tits and ass – but this girl can't be healthy. Watching her move, it's like her body's holding her back somehow. I'm not *disgusted*. I'm sort of sad for her. Is that the PC way to feel? Who the fuck knows. 'What am I meant to do? Avoid food for the rest of my life?'

'Kendall?' Goldstein asks. 'Anything to add?'

'What she said. Food is everywhere. It's all anyone ever talks about. Ever. People are obsessed with it, planning out their lives around where their next meal's coming from. It's hideous.'

'Brady?' Goldstein says, gesturing at the surfer guy. 'Any comments?'

He smiles affably. 'Not today, Doc.' He's American too. It's odd, I'm sure I recognise him, but I can't quite figure out from where.

He says nothing else, doesn't give any clues as to what his Issue is. He looks too healthy to be a junkie: teeth too white, tan too golden. I'll find out soon, I'm sure – like, why would he get a free pass in Group?

'Very well. I still think what Melissa said is relevant.' Goldstein makes a steeple with his fingers, elbows resting on his knees. 'It's not about pretending our triggers don't exist – it's about accepting our relationship with them and making adjustments to protect ourselves.'

I wonder how Kurt and I will manage. He's my trigger.

Maybe we can compromise. We can still do some stuff, like puff or MDMA, but no brown. No pills. I can't go through that withdrawal again, that's for sure.

'That's the thing with food,' Ruby says. 'Like I don't even need a drug dealer or ID. There's a Krispy Kreme on the corner of 3rd and Lexington. There's a Dunkin' Donuts a block over. McDonalds is twenty-four hours.'

'Food is easy to get hold of,' Goldstein says, 'but believe me – an addict will find a way, whatever their poison is. We have to be very clear: addiction is a loaded gun, make no mistake, but it's harmless until a hand picks it up. Drink, drugs, food, sex . . . these things are not necessarily harmful in themselves. They are inherently neither good nor bad. In a world where most people sensibly follow their prescriptions, avoid illegal drugs, or maintain a healthy relationship with food and drink, we must deduce that *we* are the problem. They existed long before we did and they'll exist long after we're gone. What we have to deal with here is ourselves and the compulsions we have.'

Compulsion. Another word for want.

All *I* want is to get away from these freaks.

I'm nothing like these people, these pitiful things.

If I am, then I hope someone puts me out of my misery like squishing a bug underfoot. It'd be kinder.

After a circle-jerk goodbye for Melissa, we head to lunch. It's my first lunch in the 'restaurant' and it's not as high-school-canteen as I'd feared. It's sleek and modern, with two circular white tables, each seating eight. Everyone sits together and I can't very well sit by myself. Guy explains there's restaurant staff. I guess this is where our money's going. I admit I've probably eaten in worse restaurants.

Today's options are seafood linguine, cheese and tomato tartlette, or soup. 'What's good?' I ask.

'It's all rather tasty,' Guy tells me, sitting on my right. He seems distracted, checking something back in the corridor. I look but there's nothing there. He settles, aligning his cutlery before sitting on his hands.

'It is if you're not on a goddamn food plan,' Ruby says, lowering herself on to her seat. 'I'll be right over here with my rabbit food.'

I look to Kendall on my left, who seems equally uncomfortable. It seems extra cruel to treat an overeater alongside an anorexic. They must find each other so bewildering.

Brady sits between Ruby and Melissa.

A starched woman with a heavy accent takes our orders. I order the tartlette. Kendall orders soup and Scouse Gary, hovering on the next table, reminds her she needs bread too to fulfil her calorie requirements.

This is how it is: like a Dali painting at a distance, we all *seem* pretty normal until you look closely. Kendall is now sulking about a bread roll, Ruby pouts at a chicken salad, Guy is still counting something under his breath. There's only Brady I haven't sussed out yet.

'So is Kendall your real name?' I ask, trying to snap her out of her mood.

'It is now,' she mutters.

'After the model?'

'Well, it wasn't after the mint cake,' she says with a smile. If she weren't so scarily thin, she'd be quite stunning in a high-fashion way.

'You're trans, yeah?' I don't know. Is that a question you're not meant to ask? There was a trans guy at St Agnes and we literally protested on the front lawns to allow him to stay at the school. He remains the first and only boy to have ever attended.

'Yeah, it's not a big secret or anything. I've been Kendall for, like, four years now, and I knew I was a girl *long* before that.'

I tell her about Jake, the guy from our school, and she seems impressed.

'Where are you from?' I ask.

'Surrey,' she says, 'but I have my treatments in London. I'm going to move there as soon as I can. I wanna be a model.'

She seems almost too frail for London. It'll snap her.

'London is pretty cool,' I say. 'I guess I take it for granted.'

'I'm sorry, this is so basic, but I can't believe I'm actually having lunch with Lexi Volkov. I totally upvoted you on socialite.com.'

I can't help but smile. She's so provincial. 'You didn't!'

'I did!'

'Thanks, I guess! Cringe!'

'I know. Look, I'm the only trans person in my village . . . I had to create my own fun, and it's not like I'm gonna bake a cake, is it?'

The food arrives and it's not bad, although I'm now craving a glass of cabernet like mad. Eating food without a proper drink seems alien. I might not mention that in my session.

I watch Brady pick at his linguine, trying to place his face. I'm sure I've seen him *somewhere*, but don't know if it's from the scene or the TV. 'Do I know you?' I eventually ask.

Ruby bursts out laughing. 'Busted!'

'Let's see if she can work it out!' Kendall giggles. 'It took me three whole days.'

'What?' I say. 'Are you famous? Sorry, I'm pretty shit with stuff like that. Are you a popstar or something?'

'I'm not famous.' He's softly spoken. With the hair and stubble and dreamy demeanour, he could be a cult leader. 'My family are.'

I squint and then the penny drops. 'Brady . . . you're not from *Brady's Bunch*?'

The rest of the table applauds my accuracy.

'Guilty as charged,' he says with a little curl of the lips.

'You're *Junior*?' Junior was a chubby little thing with acne and jam-jar glasses. That's why I recognise him! There was this Buzzfeed piece about child stars who grew up to be hot, Neville Longbottom style. 'Wow, good job, puberty.'

He laughs. 'Thanks. Only Pop calls me Junior.'

'No fucking way.'

Brady's Bunch was a craptacular reality show about Brady Ardito (Sr) who used to be in an eighties hair metal band called The Glasshearts. From what I remember, he was a slurring former alcoholic and his long-suffering former-soap-actress wife, well, suffered. Everyone knows what happened to Venus Ardito – the big sister. She was the breakout star and has like seven albums and a movie under her belt. At the moment she's in some HBO thing I'm watching on Netflix.

Brady was a kid at the time; he was 'the nerdy one'. I wonder how old that makes him now. It was on when I was about eight, so I guess he must be nineteen or twenty now.

'How's your family?' I ask.

He plucks a mussel out of its shell and pops it in his mouth. 'They fully support my choices,' he says eventually.

'You're here willingly?'

'I am.' He fixes me in his stare and I feel it acutely in my vagina. He should definitely look into that cult thing. I'd join.

'What are you going to do this afternoon?' Kendall asks.

'What is there to do?' I ask, keeping it vague. I like Kendall, but I don't want her latching on to me now that Melissa is leaving. Never been a fan of clingfilm friendships. And the fact she looks so much like Antonella ... well, it's ... weird.

'Girl, you're in rehab now!' Ruby says, waving a bit of rocket towards me. 'What you think you're gonna do? You weave a motherfucking basket.'

My eyes widen. 'You're kidding, right?'

'Aye, she is,' Gary butts in.

'I'm telling you! One time in Arts and Crafts, Janet had us weaving baskets and I was like, hell no.'

'Ruby, babes, wind your neck in,' Gary says patiently. 'Lexi, we'll talk after lunch about your options.'

'No, go on. Tell me now,' I say.

'There's a personal trainer,' Guy says. 'Brady and I have been training.'

'He's insanely hot,' Kendall adds. 'His butt is like the peach emoji.'

'Or, as Ruby said, there's Arts and Crafts, or we can arrange a tutor for you if you need to continue studies.'

Oh, sweet Jesus. Again, where do I sign up for oblivion? I don't even want to go back to my room. It feels too much like a cage. I'm irrationally worried they'll lock me in again.

'Or there's the swimming pool or stables,' Melissa adds absentmindedly.

I rest my fork. 'Stables? I'll do that,' I say instantly, getting major Pepper flashbacks. There – that's something I can live with. I love horses, and I can get out of this bloody building for a bit.

There's a sudden commotion beyond the dining room window. Someone screaming. Kendall is the first out of her seat, closely followed by Melissa and Guy. 'New guy?' Ruby asks.

Bored more than curious, I join the others at the window. On the driveway is a cavalcade of official-looking Bentleys, all gleaming. An accompanying entourage of bodyguards in Ray-Bans stand next to their cars as a super-glam looking Middle Eastern family gather around a weeping woman in a hijab. Oil money. Like oil, it's always glossy, always slick. The boynurses drag a brown boy in an expensive suit towards the front doors. He's the one kicking and screaming.

He looks pathetic, like a well-dressed toddler having a

tantrum in Tom Ford. Only this toddler is jaundiced and clammy, clearly in withdrawal from something.

'Shit, was I like that?' I mutter under my breath.

'You were *worse*,' Ruby says.

Brady volunteers to take me to the stables and I don't mind one bit. Not only is he easy on the eye, he's also the most chill of my fellow inmates, and that suits me. It seems we're to be trusted. I guess it's not like there's any *temptation* on the whole island. Nikolai only sent my mauve Marc Jacobs biker jacket, but Kendall lends me a scarf and a beanie hat. It's not quite spring yet.

We walk away from the house down a forest trail. The woodchip is damp and squishy underfoot. It's a long time since I walked through a forest. The light goes shamrock green and glittery. It's pretty and it smells – in a good way; all leafy, garlicky and earthy. I breathe in, hold it in my lungs and purge. I wonder if I should smoke less; I feel cloggy.

We used to have weekends away to the New Forest. Mummy and Daddy and Nik and I. Feels like a million years ago – and some other me. There was once a cute little girl, but she was a shell, a shell *I* was latent in; a larva waiting to hatch inside her body and seize control.

'So. What are you in for?' I ask as we stroll downhill. Wow, that sounded more blunt than I thought it might. I try style it out. 'What? Is it like *Fight Club*? Aren't I meant to ask?'

He laughs a little. 'I don't mind. I needed to get away.' He's in no hurry, kicking through leaves with his hands in pockets. 'I think it's safe to say my family have addictive personalities.'

'What was your weapon of choice?'

'What wasn't?' he says with a sigh. He says no more.

I'm not sure what else to say. 'What does your dad think? Wasn't he in rehab for most of the eighties?'

'I love my parents,' he says after a pause, not actually answering the question. He snaps a twig off an overhanging branch idly. 'They always did what they thought was best for us.'

'This is pretty embarrassing . . . but I saw your sister at the O2 when I was, like, thirteen.'

He laughs. I hope he doesn't think I'm a massive loser. 'Who didn't? She any good?'

'At the time it was basically a religious experience.'

He laughs louder. 'I'll tell her that. She'll get a kick out of it.'

'Wow, that's surreal. You know Venus Ardito. Well, duh, of course you do.'

Why am I babbling? I never babble. 'What's she like . . . in real life?'

He shrugs. 'She's my big sister. She's a pain in the ass!' He doesn't mean it, I can tell. 'She works too hard. Way too hard. Like I said, addictive personalities. She's hooked on fame. I don't know who's worse off – her or me.'

About three years ago, Venus dropped the Ardito part professionally, joining the Cher, Madonna, Britney gang of women who require no surname. I wonder why, but don't ask.

The path cuts down behind a neat, single row of stables and we enter through a back gate. I see a training ring and a mud-splattered four-by-four parked outside. 'Who lives here?' I ask, pointing at the cottages next to the stables.

'Some of the nurses I think. And Elaine. She looks after the horses.'

'Can you imagine living here? On the island? You'd go mad.'

'Or maybe, just maybe, you'd go sane,' Brady says with a Hollywood-white smile.

As we walk around the paddocks, a forty-something woman in jodhpurs with killer cheekbones and strawberry blonde hair brings a foal around on a guide rope. 'Hello there, Brady,' she says. 'Who's this?'

'This is Lexi,' he says. 'She's new.'

'Nice to meet you, Lexi.' She holds out a hand and I shake it. 'I'm Elaine.'

'Hey,' I say. 'She's very beautiful.' I stroke the foal's flank. She's going to be big someday, but right now she's all Twiglet legs.

'This is Clover,' Elaine says. 'Isn't she precious? Are you here for a ride?'

'Lexi is; I just delivered her.'

'You aren't gonna come?' I ask, slightly disappointed.

'I promised Rob – the trainer – I'd train. I've got a triathlon thing going on with Guy.'

'OK,' I'm suddenly nervous. 'I haven't ridden in a few years . . . I don't know if I should . . .'

'I'll make sure you're all right before we let you off, don't worry,' Elaine tells me. 'That's what I'm here for. Come on, I'll introduce you to Patty. She's a doll. And let's get you some gloves and boots . . .'

'I'll see you tonight at dinner,' Brady says. 'It's Melissa's big farewell meal.'

'Sure.' I doubt I'll go. I don't know Melissa from Eve. It's weird.

I follow Elaine and collect some boots, gloves and a helmet. Bits of jigsaw come back to me as if it's second nature. It's like my body knows what to do even if my head doesn't.

97

Elaine shows me to a stable and I stop dead in my tracks. Patty looks so much like my old Pepper. Same conker brown colouring, same dots on her flank. It's uncanny.

In the end we sold Pepper. I didn't pay him enough attention so Daddy said he had to go to a family who'd take better care of him. That thought feels like leeches in my stomach. It wasn't like he wasn't looked after – the stable girls doted on him – it was just that I grew out of ponies. It's not my fault.

It is your fault.

I screw my eyes shut and squeeze the thought from my head.

As soon as I'm in the saddle, I feel at home. As we trot around the ring, it sort of hurts my lady-garden, but that's all part of the fun. Patty is docile and clearly used to carting junkies around the estate grounds. 'There you go,' Elaine shouts from the side of the training ring. 'You're a natural, darling. Do you want to take her out for a hack?'

I'm still terrified I'll break my neck, but Patty, frankly, seems a little stoned. 'Why not?'

'That's the spirit.' Elaine opens the gate to let us through. Patty clomps onward, needing only minimal encouragement. I soon realise she must know a route around the island. We stroll off down a well-trodden bridle path, Patty seemingly on autopilot.

I feel a bit nauseous and wonder if it's more withdrawal fun.

We've only be riding about ten minutes when I slide out of the saddle to puke in a bush. God, when will it stop? I climb back on Patty – an enormous effort – and try to focus on deep breaths. I listen to the birds singing and try to take in the forest. A babbling stream runs through it, and I follow it as closely as

I can so I don't get lost. We pass a crumbling ruin of a little . . . brick house thing. Three walls, a fireplace and a bit of a corrugated steel roof remain and I wonder what it used to be. When we were little, Nik used to call huts like these 'witch houses' to freak me out. It worked. I think about Nik and miss him. I wonder what he's doing right now.

Only then I'm pretty sure I see a red squirrel and it snaps me out of the funk. Well, isn't this wholesome PG-rated fun. I realise I have *time*. I'm not going anywhere fast, so I might as well *relax*. I feel my shoulders unclench with an almost-audible snap.

Patty snorts and I give her a rub to reassure her. I wonder if she's up for a trot and I prompt her to speed up. The wind on my face snaps me out of the nausea. We ride past a little row of twee cottages that I guess house more staff and on to a hillside track that overlooks the beach.

I'm not even gonna lie – it's stunning. This side of the island is uninterrupted beach, curving like a C between two rocky crops. Gulls swoop and soar, and gentle waves fizz onto the sand. Out here, exposed, it's even gustier, and I feel like I'm truly being detoxed – rinsed out. I'm two kale smoothies, an avocado and a bit of yoga away from being very 'lifestyle blog' right now.

The sun starts to sink. Red sky at night, shepherd's delight. I don't know how long we've been walking but I don't want to kill poor Patty. I take what I sense will be the quickest route back through the forest.

As we plod back through the stables, I see Elaine struggling with a fearsome colt. He's absolutely the most handsome horse

I've ever seen – hide the colour of rippling silver – an almost platinum shade. It's pretty clear he doesn't want to be saddled up. He sidesteps awkwardly, tossing his head back and forth.

'Hi, darling, could you just hang back for a minute?' Elaine calls to me.

'Are you OK?' I dismount Patty, keeping a hold on her reins. 'Do you need a hand?'

'Oh, I'm fine.' Elaine doesn't look fine, she looks red-faced and irritated. 'It's just Storm being, frankly, a man.'

Once I've untacked Patty and made sure she's had a good drink, I find Elaine still struggling with Storm. He's now pacing the training ring uncertainly, clearly stressed. Elaine has backed off, hands up in surrender. 'What's his problem?' I ask, climbing on to the bottom rung of the fence that runs around the ring.

'He's an arsehole,' Elaine says, joining me at the fence.

'Fair.'

'I adopted him from a friend of mine on the mainland. She bought him for her daughter, but it's pretty clear he's not child-friendly. I said I'd see what I could do, but I think some horses just aren't made to be rode.'

'Did they break him in?'

'No. He's almost three now. I think he might be a lost cause.'

'Don't let the doctors hear you say that.'

She laughs. 'Quite! I'd settle for him letting me take his saddle off. Shall we gang up on him?'

In the end – with a couple of carrots – we entice him to the fence. I distract him with food while Elaine promptly whips his tack off. He takes the bait but there's some real *fury* in those black eyes of his. 'That'll do for today,' she says. 'Thank you so much, Lexi. Hadn't you better be getting back for supper?'

I remember Melissa's leaving dinner. I think I'd be in their way. I shake my head. 'Nah, I'm saddle sore. I want a bath and some room service.'

Elaine smiles. 'Well, that sounds rather lovely. Now, run along. It'll soon be dark and I don't want you getting lost in the forest.'

She's the first person in a long time who's treated me like a little girl. Weirdly, I don't mind.

I can't sleep.

My bones feel hollow and my blood synthetically blue like that stuff they pour on sanitary towels in adverts.

I feel hosed down, bleached and disinfected. Sterilised.

Pure and clean. White tiles and enamel.

Like a hospital. Like *the* hospital: corridors and machines, tubes and bleeps.

No, don't go there. Don't think about that. Don't think about her.

I roll over. I flip the pillow so it's cooler.

Why can't I sleep?

I stare at the ceiling, indigo grey. If I look too long, I can see faces in the shadows.

I don't want the telly on. Can't focus on a book; the letters crawl like ants at a picnic.

It feels like there's static under my skin; electricity. My feet and fingers twitch with it.

I'm awake and I can't stand it.

I wonder if they'd give me a sleeping pill if I asked.

No. Of course they won't. Not even a Nytol Herbal.

I feel stretched, taut like an elastic band, ready to ping across the room.

I dig my nails into the bedsheet and claw at it.

I want to slow it down.

I want the edges filed off.

I want something.

I need something.

I start to cry and bury my face in the pillow in case a nurse is listening at my door.

'So, tell me about your family,' Dr Goldstein says. Today Dr Ahmed hasn't joined us.

'Isn't that a little predictable?' I ask, cradling a coffee mug the size of my head. I must have got some sleep, but it was so reedy, so shallow I don't feel the benefit of it at all. Little birds twitter just outside the window and I wish they'd shut up. What have they got to be so cheerful about? Beaky little twats. Christ, I'm in a foul mood. Yes, even more so than normal.

'Is it?'

'Come on . . . "Blame the parents"? Really?'

'Should I?'

I laugh. 'Probably. They're not perfect; not even close. I figured that one out when I was about twelve. OK, my dad. My dad is stubborn, he lies, he treats women like shit. My mum is a drama queen, she's selfish, she's insecure . . . shall I go on?'

'Those are very mature observations.'

'Hon, you're not my first therapist.'

He smiles. 'Well, why don't you tell me how you arrived at these conclusions?'

Because I'd rather die.

If we pull this thread, the whole sad jumper's gonna unravel.

When I was about ten, Daddy made me and Nikolai have a Russian tutor. Like he felt it was important for us to connect with our heritage or something. The tutor was kinda cute in a dorky way – he was finishing his Masters at UCL I think.

'Something Russian,' I said, and he told me I'd done very well. So impressed was he that he said I should go and tell Daddy.

We had our lessons on the terrace restaurant of the Vauxhall hotel and I knew Daddy would be in his office on the ninth floor – the executive suites. So off I went, skipping into the lift and down the corridors. As I got nearer, I heard voices coming from within and just assumed he was in a meeting or something. I knocked and opened the door, just a crack.

I caught him with one of the waitresses – I can't even remember her name. Do I need to tell you what they were doing on the desk? No? OK.

He chased after me. 'Lexi,' he told me. 'What did you see?'

'Nothing,' I lied.

'I was just helping Vanessa –' that was her name, *Vanessa* – 'with a problem. A grown-up problem. She was very sad, so Daddy gave her a hug. That's all.'

'OK,' I said, chewing on the end of a plait. I was *ten,* we'd had sex education at school and also, I'm not an imbecile. I knew *precisely* what they were doing.

'Now, Lexi, it's very important you don't tell your Mummy what you saw. It would make her sad. She would not understand. We don't want to make Mummy sad, do we?'

'No,' I agreed at once.

However, what poor Daddy didn't know was the briefing I'd had from my mother a year or two earlier. She sat on the toilet seat sipping a cocktail while I was in a bubble bath, again in our suite at the hotel. 'Alexandria, *malysh*,' she said. Mother's accent is much stronger than Daddy's because she grew up in Siberia while he's lived in London almost his whole life. 'I want you to do for me little job. Can you do that for Mummy?' She took a sip of her vodka martini. Her acrylic nails, although expensive, looked so cheap.

'Yes!' I said, still so eager to please the adults in my life. At that point, I thought they were worth pleasing.

'Good.' Mum was runner-up Miss USSR 1989, but now she's had two facelifts; monthly Botox; a nose job; one boob job to make them bigger; another to make them perkier; and dermal fillers every few months in her lips and cheeks. She's got that 'surgery look', like she's wearing a puffy papier-mâché head. Her hair is always platinum blonde, and you will never, ever see even a millimetre of dark root poking through. 'Listen, I want you straight away to tell me if you see Daddy talking ever to other ladies. Do you understand?'

I was confused. 'Which other ladies?'

'Pretty ones. Pretty and young ones. You just tell Mummy.'

And so I did. It became a bath time ritual. I'd feed the information back to Mum and wait for her eyes to light up. I was programmed like Pavlov's dogs. Tell Mummy a secret, get the reward. The next day we'd go to Hamleys or Harrods and she'd buy me a new toy or a dress.

One night, just before the divorce circus came to town, they were screaming at each other in Russian. I crouched underneath the grand piano, absorbing as much as I could like a sponge. Kids that age are like radars – they hear *everything*. I could only pick out the English bits of it, but Mummy was yelling one word over and over: *proof*, now she had *proof*. She was going to take everything, the hotel, the money, the cars, the jet. Us. We were about fifth down the list. From where I was, I saw their legs pacing back and forth, vodka sloshing over the rim of Mummy's glass as she waved it in Daddy's face.

When I heard something smash – probably one of them hurling their drink at the wall – I slipped out from my hiding place. Quiet as a mouse, I tiptoed down the corridor and knocked lightly on Nikolai's door.

'Come in,' he said.

I opened the door a few inches and slipped through the gap. 'They woke me up,' I said.

Nikolai, who'd have been about fourteen, shuffled to one side of his bed. 'For god's sake, Lexi, you're such a baby.' He made a show of seeming annoyed, but he was happy I'd come in, I could tell. I ran over to his bed and wriggled in.

'I hate it when they're like this.'

'Grow up. *All* parents argue.'

'That's not true,' I said. 'Charlotte's mum and dad hold hands and kiss each other in public.'

'Exactly – in public. Who knows what they do when they're not in public.'

We lay side by side, not saying anything else. Mummy screamed about sluts and whores and bitches. 'Do you think they'll get divorced?' I finally said.

'No,' Nik said quickly. 'Maybe. Maybe it would be better if they did . . .'

'It wouldn't!' I cried out louder than I'd intended to. Sure, we'd had nannies and tutors our whole life, but everything

106

always felt shaky until it was just the four of us. That was when I felt normal. That was when I could sleep soundly.

'Lexi, get real. They hate each other.'

'No they don't!'

'They do. You can only *truly* hate someone you used to love.' I remember thinking about that for a long time and not getting it. I get it now. 'What's the point of them being together if all they're going to do is fight all the time?'

I wanted to tell him that I couldn't relax unless we were all together; that I didn't like not knowing where we all were; knowing we were all safe; but I said nothing.

'Whatever happens,' Nik went on, 'we'd still see both of them. We'll be fine.' I don't know which of us he was trying to convince.

My little head was whirring like an engine. Where would Mummy go? She wouldn't be able to stay in the hotel – and despite her threats there was no way she was getting her hands on them. Would we go with her? Would one of them take me, and one take Nikolai? The thought alone made me feel nauseous.

'They're stupid,' Nik said suddenly. 'It's all about money. He doesn't want her to get his money and she wants as much as she can get. That's what all of this is about, you know. It's not about us, it's about money.'

He looked so angry. I didn't want to know that information. I was happier not knowing, but I guess their fighting was like toxic waste, seeping through the carpets and dribbling down the walls. It got to us both. Radiation sickness.

'You won't leave me, will you, Nik?'

He turned to me. 'No. No way. We'll be fine. Don't tell *anyone* I said this, but you and me are gonna have to stick together. Whatever happens.'

That made me feel better. 'Whatever happens.'

We shook hands. 'Now go to sleep,' he told me. 'They'll still be here in the morning.'

But he was wrong. In the morning, Daddy was already sleeping in a different penthouse.

OK, I know I'm tired and emotional because the memory of that night makes my eyes sting. 'Would you like a tissue?' Goldstein asks.

'No, I'm cool.'

'You don't have to be brave in our sessions, Lexi. There's no one else here.'

'You're here.'

'I don't count.'

I shrug. 'That's it, really. Big long ugly divorce. This was before pre-nups, but they'd both had detectives following each other for years. They were both unfaithful but, in the end, she got a decent settlement: eighty million and the New York apartment.'

Inevitable question: 'And how did that make you feel?'

Thinking about the night in Nikolai's room has left me feeling exposed, like a kitten clinging to a branch too high in a tree. 'Well, we saw it coming, didn't we?'

'That doesn't make it any less painful.'

'God, whose parents *aren't* divorced?'

'Again, that doesn't make it any less painful to *you.*'

I smile. 'I really don't think it's that simple, do you? "Her parents split up so she became a drug addict." Like, really?'

He holds his hands apart, surrendering. 'You're quite right, of course. It's never that simple. But I'd like you to tell me more about that "shaky" feeling, that feeling of not being able to relax when you were apart from your family. Did that ever go away?'

I think about it. I rifle through the mess in my head and

wonder if it's still there under unopened credit card bills, memories, blackouts, and scraps of paper with numbers on. 'No. Probably not. I think I probably got used to it. Maybe that's when you become a grown-up – when you stop feeling safe.'

After the session, I'm allowed to check my phone again. This time there's a text from Kurt.

Call me whenever, babe. Phone will be on.

I'm not going to get another chance until tomorrow so I dial him up immediately.

It rings.

And rings.

And rings.

It rings again.

And then he answers. 'Babe.'

'Jesus fucking Christ, Kurt,' I say, suddenly filled with sulphuric rage. 'Where the fucking hell have you been?' I'm crying and I don't know why. Today is too much.

'I'm sorry,' he says. 'I'm sorry. When you called yesterday my phone was on silent and I was passed out. I'm sorry.'

That calms me down a bit. 'Where are you?' I regret asking such a needy bitch question. But if he is with some other skank, I'll kill him.

'I'm still at Jack and Helena's place. They're in Dubai so I'm looking after it for them.'

'Are you alone?' Neeeeeeeedy bitch.

'Yes, I'm alone. Fuck, Lex, it's good to hear from you. I was worried sick. You OK?'

'What do you think?'

'He, like, proper kidnapped you.'

I laugh a snotty laugh and wipe my nose on my sleeve. 'Kurt, I'm in *rehab*.'

He chuckles. '*No, no, no.* How is it?'

'It's so not The One.'

'Do they strap you to the bed?'

I roll my eyes. 'It's not an asylum. It's like being at a hotel. A hotel with no booze.'

'You can't even drink? Jesus.'

'Babe, it's rehab. I am surrounded by sketchy addicts. Seriously, they're all batshit crazy.'

'When are you getting out?'

'I don't know. How long have I been gone? It's meant to be a seventy-day programme, so like, another two months.'

'What? Really?'

'I know!' I'm not sure how to phrase the next question. So I just ask. 'Are you still getting high?'

A pause. 'Not last night.' Well that answers that question. Shit, I can't get into it now. 'Just do as they say and get back here, yeah?' he says, and for him, saying that's a big deal. It's enough.

'I am doing. And I'm . . . I'm clean now. It might not be a bad thing.' He's silent and I carry on all in a rush. 'Like, I was a hot mess. I legit thought I was going to die, it wasn't funny.' Still silence. 'We'll talk about it when I get back.'

'Tell you what . . .' he says slowly.

'What?'

'I miss you like mad, babe.'

That's all I really needed to hear. I close my eyes but not before another tear squeaks out.

We're in Group.

Come on, ladies, let's get in Therapy Formation. Ahmed's in charge today, but Goldstein looks on – Brady, Kendall, Ruby, Guy and then me, hovering like the angel of death, dressed head to toe in black Saint Laurent.

Ruby is telling us about her father. Her father, it turns out, is Dr Russell Kidd. He's the senator for New York State but he's often talked about as 'The Next Obama'. I knew he had daughters from the news, but I've never seen him with Ruby.

'So is your mum . . . Diandra Jordan?' I ask. I know next to nothing about sport but *everyone* knows Diandra Jordan. When we were kids, she won every sprinting gold medal at every Olympics. She's who you'd pretend to be on Sports Day.

'Nah,' Ruby says, 'she's my *step*mom. Daddy and my mom got married when they were real young, straight outta college.'

I had no idea he had a whole other family before the one I've seen on TV.

'Thanks to Daddy, we have nurses and stuff, but I had to help with Mom,' Ruby explains. 'She's pretty sick sometimes. Sickle-cell anaemia. When my friends were out getting tanked at parties and stuff, I stayed home with her. I'm a straight-A student, man, I got no time for pills and shit, but there's always food, right? Like, you can eat as much food as you want and no one cares. I could still study, I could look after Mom, I could see Daddy and Diandra and the kids. Everyone eats, it's cool.'

'Speak for yourself,' Kendall mutters under her breath next to me on the sofa.

'When do you think it became a problem?' Dr Ahmed asks.

Ruby shrugs. 'I dunno. Like, I was always kinda juicy so I don't think anyone noticed, maybe not even me. I think it probably started like when I *noticed* I was bigger than some of the other girls. Maybe when I was about eleven. I started to eat more at night when Mom was asleep. I'd sneak downstairs and sit next to the fridge. But I wouldn't take too much; I didn't need the staff telling Mom I was stealing food.' She takes a breath. 'That's something that drives me crazy, man. People thinking I eat all day and all night. As if! When you look like I do, you do everything you can to *not* eat in front of people. Otherwise they call you a fat pig and ignorant shit like that.'

'To your face?' Brady asks.

'That and worse,' she says with a dismissive flick of her French tip nails. 'Mostly people just stare. There's this look, this disgusted look. I ain't paranoid, either, it goes something like this . . .' She pulls what I'd describe as a stank face. 'So I ate at night, by myself, when no one could see.'

'What do you think prompted your family to intervene?' Dr Ahmed asks.

'That's an easy one. I looked too fat in photos. Daddy was embarrassed.'

'I'm sure there's more to it than that,' Dr Ahmed says.

She purses her lips. 'I'm sure there wasn't. Can't have the eminent ex-cardiologist, senator Dr Russell Kidd, looking like a deadbeat dad, can we? What would voters think?'

'You don't think they were worried about you?'

'Daddy worries about appearances. "Eyes on the prize, Ruby

114

my girl." That's what he's always saying. He worries about polls and voter turnout. Work . . . there's another addiction we never talk about.'

Kendall laughs. 'What? He's addicted to workahol?'

'Kendall,' Ahmed warns, 'it's not your turn. Ruby, I'm sensing a lot of shame today.'

She says nothing for a moment. 'Look at me,' she says finally. 'Just look at me.'

There's an ugly silence for about a second too long before Ahmed moves us on. 'Lexi, what are your thoughts on what Ruby's told us?'

I look around expecting there to be another Lexi behind me. 'What?'

'You've been very quiet. Part of the process is in talking and reacting to each other.'

I shrug. 'I don't think it's any of my business.'

'Ruby will have opinions about your recovery.'

'It's none of her business.'

'OK, let me rephrase.' Ahmed flexes her fingers. 'What could you learn from Ruby's experience?'

'I don't know,' I say. 'I've never really had an issue with food.' I shrivel like a freshly salted slug, awkward next to Kendall.

'Is it about food, though?' Ahmed swoops in, so clearly proud of the truth bomb she's about to detonate. 'Is it about alcohol, or drugs . . . or is it about the compulsion? Ruby? How often do you think about food?'

Ruby shakes her head like it's obvious. 'All the goddamn time. It never stops.'

Ahmed turns to me. 'Does that resonate, Lexi?'

I think about last night in bed. About how much I wanted something, *anything*.

'No. Not particularly,' I lie.

In the afternoon, I go back to the stables. It's that or fucking macramé.

I help Elaine to muck out the stalls. My back soon aches and I'm relieved when Elaine carries out a tray with two teas. It's the right shade too; I like it strong.

'So, what brings you to our island?' she says as we sit on a pair of grubby white garden chairs, the sort that topple over in bad home movies.

'Are you allowed to ask me that?'

'I'm allowed to say whatever I like the last time I checked.' She smiles. 'You don't have to tell me if you don't want, but it's all off-the-record and it gets quite boring down here. The horses have so little to say.'

The morning has been gruelling enough; I can't rehash it all again. 'I don't want to talk about it,' I say.

'Very well. Let's imagine you weren't here. What *else* is interesting about Lexi?'

Huh? I have 82,000 followers at the last check, does that count?

'What do you mean?'

'What do you do in your spare time? What sort of things do you like?'

'I . . .' I stop. I have nothing to add. Apart from shopping, drinking, partying and seeing Kurt, I don't really *do* anything. 'Not a lot really,' I reply, and wonder if that's normal.

'I'm sure that's not true,' Elaine says. 'You certainly are a dab-hand with the horses.'

After we finish our tea, Elaine sweeps out Storm's stable. While she's doing that, I observe him snorting and pacing around a pasture. I lean over the fence, holding out a carrot. With a haughty expression, he saunters over and sniffs at it before turning away, unimpressed. 'You,' I tell him, 'are an asshole.'

'Harsh,' says a voice behind me.

It's Brady. He's sweaty, a grey T-shirt plastered to his chest and torso. His hair is tied back into a messy ponytail. He leans forward, hands on thighs, trying to catch his breath.

'Well, he is.' He holds up a finger, struggling to breathe. 'Here.' I hand him a bottle of water I brought down.

'Thanks.'

'Working out again?'

'Goldstein thinks it's good for me. Body and mind working on a common goal, or something like that. I think he just means it keeps my hands busy. Anyway, I was out of shape.'

He certainly doesn't look out of shape now. He wears running shorts over a pair of those sporty Nike man-leggings. His thighs and calves are strong, muscular.

I can smell him. Deodorant and salty sweat. It's so male. It's not a bad thing.

God, I shouldn't even be looking. I literally just spoke with my boyfriend.

It must be pheromones. I take a step back. 'You going for a ride?' he asks.

'On Storm? Are you kidding? I'd die.'

He grins. 'Nah, he's just playing hard to get.' I'm not sure what to say to that. 'See you at dinner, yeah? I'll shower, I promise.'

And off he goes, jogging down the forest trail. I watch him go. Bum, as Kendall would say, like the peach emoji.

That night I do join the others for dinner. Not *just* because Brady invited me, but because I'll chew my own hands off if I have to spend another night alone in that room with the Kardashians on E!.

Tonight it's swordfish drizzled in lemon with asparagus. It's fresh and light. Kendall cries because she thinks the vegan option is too fattening. We all politely pretend it's not happening. Kendall remains at the table with a full plate and Gary standing over her shoulder long after we've retired to the room we usually have Group in.

Tonight we have a movie. 'Each movie is especially selected to avoid "triggers",' Brady tells me with a sly grin. Legs curled under him on the sofa, he's wearing baggy grey sweatpants, a vest and a baseball cap. Through the arm holes in his top I can see his left nipple on a muscular, tattooed pec. His time with the trainer is definitely paying off.

Shit, I really have to stop perving over Brady. I need to get back to Kurt or take a cold shower. 'No drinking, no drugs, no sex, no nothing,' he says. 'It's pretty much PG-13 fun for us.'

I'll say.

Tonight is one of the *Star Wars* ones. I've seen it before. Who hasn't.

Kendall eventually joins us, her eyes pink-rimmed. She looks a little lost without Melissa. She's a bit full on, but I don't hate her. I wonder if . . . she looks so much like *her* . . . is it getting to me? *Snap the fuck out of it.*

She sits cross-legged on the floor at the back of the room and starts to re-apply her make-up under the light of the lamp. I take my Diet Coke and join her, whispering so we don't disturb the others watching the film. 'Your make-up always looks awesome,' I tell her.

'Thanks, babe, but CoverGirl don't cover boy.'

'You don't look like a boy.'

'In my head I always do. I always will do.'

'Well, you don't.' I wonder if that's where it started – starving herself. Trying to make herself tiny, feminine.

She blushes a little, eyes down. 'Thanks. But look at my chin. Seriously. I want a chin reduction and maybe cheek fillers.'

I shake my head. 'No way, don't. My mum had her cheeks done and she looks like a fucking alien. Real Housewife of Silicone Valley.'

She giggles. 'You barely need make-up. Jealous.'

'I do for events and stuff.'

'Do you contour?'

I wince. 'I can't do it! I end up looking like I'm auditioning for *The Lion King* or something.'

She laughs and Guy shushes her from the sofa. 'Let me show you.' She takes out a contour kit and powders my nose, cheeks, forehead and chin. She shows me in the mirror. I look like I'm wearing a *lot* of make-up, but I do look more angular I suppose. Dare I say, healthier? She's taken the green tinge out of my skin. And I don't look like Mufasa, so that's a start. 'Oh cool,' I say, tilting my head left and right to check out my cheekbones.

'You are welcome.' Kendall grins. 'Brady! I did Lexi's make-up! What do you think?'

He swivels around, looking over the back of the sofa. Shit, that's embarrassing. All I can do is pout like a thirsty Instagram whore. 'Beautiful,' he says with a gentle smile. I roll my eyes because praise is intolerable.

I wake up in the middle of the night. The clock on my nightstand reads 2.34 a.m. God, it's only about an hour since I finally nodded off. I roll over to go back to sleep when I hear footsteps – light, scurrying footsteps.

In my head, I irrationally go to 'puppet demons'. Childhood fear. Puppets are terrifying.

I sit up in bed and push the hair off my face.

The footsteps get louder and I see a shadow sweep along the gap under my suite door. What the fuck? Is someone escaping?

It's *probably* not puppet demons.

If they're going, I'm going with them, whoever it is. I jump out of bed and head to the door. I open it a crack and poke my head through just in time to see Kendall, running barefoot down the corridor.

What is she doing? Am I dreaming this? She vanishes around the corner. I look the other way and wait for whichever nurse is chasing her. After a minute, I realise no one's coming, my sleep-fogged head clearing. Kendall isn't running *away* – she's just running. Jogging.

She's exercising in secret.

That's sad.

I guess I have a choice. I can wait for her to complete her circuit and try to convince her to go back to bed, or just leave her to it. But I don't want to embarrass her. I'm not going to grass her up to Goldstein either – that's not cool. Snitches get stitches and are also bitches. I don't know what to do, so I just close the door as silently as I can and go back to bed.

Before I finally nod off, Kendall does four more laps past my door.

STEP 3:
I WILL LEARN TO TRUST IN MYSELF AND OTHERS

Dr Goldstein thinks my life has lacked routine since I left St Agnes. Now I have routine:

I have breakfast. Some form of eggs – poached, smashed or gooey; soft-boiled ones with soldiers. Sometimes muesli, berries and yoghurt.

I go to therapy. We talk more about the divorce and the custody battle: Daddy's campaign to prove Mummy was a pill-popping psycho who could barely care for herself, let alone two adolescents. Mummy tried to convince the judge Daddy used to hit her and was a risk to us. I don't *think* that's true. I hope it's not true. I certainly never saw proof of that and I honestly don't think Mummy could have – or actually would have – hidden it.

Goldstein waits for me to finish and reclines in his seat. 'Lexi, at what age do you think childhood ends?'

I frown. 'I don't know. Sixteen? Maybe younger.'

'At what age do you think *your* childhood ended?'

I roll my eyes and smile. 'Touché.'

'It just strikes me that your parents' behaviour perhaps forced you and your brother to grow up before your time.'

I flinch. I don't like him attacking my parents. They're a shit shower, but they're *my* shit shower.

After therapy, I talk to Kurt. Calmer now, I tell him about Kendall's night-time runs and Ruby's midnight feasts. Most days, I think he's hanging, out-of-it. He's either been up all night or has just woken up, I can't tell. He denies he's high, I guess for my benefit, but I'm not sure I buy it.

Group is more interesting because I'm not the new girl any more. Today, the Saudi prince joins us for the first time. He looks waxy-skinned and dead-eyed now, but he should be handsome in sixty days' time. His chest and arms are huge, steroid huge, neck thicker than my thigh. Unimpressed doesn't even begin to cover his expression. It's like looking in a mirror.

Goldstein and Ahmed both sit in. 'Today we have a new guest,' Goldstein says. 'Would you like to introduce yourself and explain why you're here?'

'I'm Saif Omar,' he sighs. 'My parents think I have a problem with drugs. I don't, but whatever.'

He wears smart slacks, a Ralph Lauren shirt and a Rolex. Twinkle, twinkle, massive diamond in his left earlobe. His hair is razor parted, slicked back into a greasy quiff. He's dripping rich. He's like me. He's never had to worry about money for a single second of his life. It's a game all rich people play – imagining what it would be like to be poor. Because we never have been; we've never had to adapt or survive.

Daddy came from nothing, he tells us often enough: at thirteen, a recent immigrant, he started as a kitchen boy at a hotel in the West End. The chef took pity on him and let him eat any food that was left over at the end of the night. He always vowed that Nik and I would never have to know what hunger was like.

I think I've known hunger, just not the type he worried about.

'If your parents are suffering as a result of your drug use, wouldn't you say it was a problem?' Goldstein asks.

Saif sits back down. 'I guess so. I think it's a lot of fuss and a gargantuan waste of money, but I don't suppose there's a lot I can do about it.' His accent is all over the place: A little American, a little Arab, a little British. I'm guessing he's been educated in the UK, if nothing else.

'The first step, as ever, is in admitting you have a problem, Saif,' Ahmed says.

'It's bullshit, though,' he says. 'You know what this is about – they found some needles in my gym bag. But it was just growth hormones! Everyone uses steroids . . .' Ha! I'm right! 'And everyone does a bit of coke every now and then. It's not a big deal. I'm sorry, it's really not.'

I agree, but that attitude isn't going to get him out of here any faster. Amateur. It's like quicksand; if you struggle, you make it worse.

'You're wrong.' It's Brady. It's not like him to interrupt. I stop fiddling with my split ends and pay attention. 'If you surround yourself with addicts, you can convince yourself that anything's normal.'

'Brady,' Goldstein says, cutting him off. Damn. I wondered if, for a second, we might get some insight into Brady's Big Issue. Interesting. Must be an addiction thing, I guess. 'It's not your turn to speak. But he has a point, Saif. Think of your addiction as a living, breathing organism, one that will do anything to survive. One of its survival tactics is to seek out other addicts because there's safety in numbers. Each addict will reassure the others that the way they're living is the norm.'

I think about my friends at St Agnes and how I hardly see them any more. I see Kurt, I see Baggy. I see dealers and users. Is that it? Again – too easy an explanation.

'If that's true,' Saif says angrily, 'how the fuck will it help being stuck on Addict Island?'

Check, Dr Goldstein.

'Because here, with all our different afflictions, and everyone in different stages of recovery, you'll be able to see your addiction for what it really is. A disease. A sickness.'

Checkmate, Saif Omar.

In the afternoon it starts to rain, tip-tapping against the windows of the old house. Wind howls through the walls. The weather was bad enough for the ferry to be cancelled, and the personal trainer and tutors couldn't make the crossing.

I haunt the house, bored off my tits. Saif pummels the treadmill in the gym, sweat pouring off his face. Kendall, in head-to-toe athleisurewear, maintains a steadier pace alongside him. Still running, still burning those calories.

Moving past the lounge, I hear Ruby and Guy listening to the radio, talking about what bands they like and don't. I don't even realise Brady is in the therapy room until he moves. He's laid on the sofa, reading a dog-eared copy of *Catcher in the Rye*. Figures. He's the Clarity Centre's very own Holden Caulfield. Like, why is he even here? He says next-to-nothing in Group, and it's not fair. He knows more about me than I do about him. Is there a big mystery, or is he just a tourist?

'Hey,' he says.

'Cliché,' I tell him, nodding at the book.

'I always pretend it's my favourite.'

'And what *is* your favourite?'

'Easy. *The Hunger Games*.'

God, that takes me back. Me, Antonella and Nevada racing each other to see who'd finish the trilogy first. *Of course* Antonella won. She always did. 'Good shout. Team Peeta or Team Gale?'

'Team Katniss.'

I laugh. 'Correct answer. Ten points to . . .?'

'Please. Ravenclaw.'

I sit at the other end of the sofa. 'Interesting. Had you down as a Gryffindor. *Clearly* I'm Slytherin.' It was Harry Potter that first got me into writing stories when I was about eight. I used to make little books on hotel letterhead paper and staple them together. Man, it's been a long time since I wrote anything.

He puts the book to one side. 'You wanna do something?'

Is he flirting? The trouble is, the way his mouth curls at the edges makes *everything* seem like flirting. He has Resting Flirt Face. 'Such as?' I ask.

Five minutes later and we're cross-legged on the rug, either side of the coffee table, Snakes & Ladders between us. 'Fuck,' he says, sliding his blue tiddlywink all the way down a fierce-looking python. He looks up at me and smiles. 'Well, isn't this just one big fat recovery metaphor? Six steps forward, thirteen steps back.'

'And to think,' I say, 'we were born into houses with so many ladders.'

He laughs, properly laughs, and I smile because it's nice to make people laugh. I shake the dice.

Another day, another downpour.

Yet I'm standing outside Storm's stable.

I already know what Goldstein would say: that my cavalier attitude towards my physical wellbeing is indicative of crippling low self-esteem. Or something. I do not value myself, so I play Russian Roulette with a million different guns.

So, prime example: I'm here. And I'm going in.

I don't know why, but I want to.

The weather, appropriately, is stormy: right now it's stopped raining, but the wind persists. Everyone was cooped up inside the house and I couldn't take it any more. The walls were closing in. I had to get out. I borrowed a hideous cagoule from Elaine's house and went for a quick hack through the woods on Patty, although she wasn't feeling the weather one bit, even under the shelter of the trees.

Now my thighs hurt, my leggings are soaked, and I'm sweating inside the raincoat. And for whatever reason, my feet have led me here.

I can hear him snorting, kicking against the door. The whole structure shakes.

I must be insane.

This horse is gonna kill me.

Just in case, I put my helmet back on.

I just can't leave it alone.

Everything I do feels like it's driven by a grinning demon at my core. He's jet black with white teeth and eyes. *What can I make the mad bitch do today?* I'm his brainless puppet.

I unlatch the stable door and peep into the gloom. Storm whinnies, tossing his silver mane from side to side. Sweat shines on his flanks. He paces the stable, cursing the walls on all sides. His eyes are wild, rolling back into his skull.

'What's up?' I say.

Storm retreats into the darkest cobwebby corner, claws at the hay with a frustrated hoof.

'I'm coming in, OK?'

He doesn't charge at me, he doesn't do anything, so I unlatch the bottom half of the door. 'It's just me. Elaine isn't here, so you don't have to act like a dick. I won't tell anyone if you won't.'

He rears up, kicking his hooves. I don't move any further in. I freeze.

'OK, I get it. You're the boss. God, chill out.' He paces, almost performing a box-step.

I take another couple of inches towards him. 'See? I'm not so bad, am I? If you want to get out of here, you need to chill out. I'll let you in the pen.'

His head dips slightly. He snorts down his nostrils.

'But I need to put a bridle on and clip a rope on it, or we can't go. Does that sound fair? What do you think?'

He takes a step towards me and I very slowly reach out and stroke his head. He pulls away, but not viciously. He just doesn't want to be stroked. Fair.

I back to the wall and take the bridle off the hook. I show it to him. 'You ready?' He seems to know what to do. He bows his head and lets me slide the bridle over it. 'There. Painless, right?'

I attach a guide rope and he basically drags me out of the stable towards the pen, like it was all his idea in the first place. I'm not going to let him dominate me though. I'm no pushover.

I tug on the rope, letting him know I'm still there. He doesn't like it. I tug again, not giving up. Oh, I can be stubborn too, motherfucker.

I try to dig my heels in, but they just slide through wet mud. He's too strong for me. If I'm not careful, he'll drag me face-first along the track. I let him go and he runs into the pen, rope trailing behind him. 'Storm!' I cry after him. 'Stop!'

I give up and watch him careening in circles. I'll have to trap him in the pen and wait for Elaine to get back to help me. I hope she's not too mad I let him out. Still, I got tack on him. It's a first step. Maybe he's not such a lost cause after all.

There's more drama at dinner time. Kendall isn't gaining weight – and I know why – so they've upped her calorie intake. It doesn't go down well and she's kept back after we all leave to finish what's on her plate. The others gather in the gym for yoga and meditation.

Thanks, no thanks.

'Can I go make sure Kendall's OK?' I ask boynurse Marcus. She's still being force-fed in the dining room as far as I know.

'I guess. But then you both need to come down here. It's not optional.'

Mandatory meditation? That's relaxing. 'OK, I'll get her.'

I head back to the dining room, but she's gone. I follow voices and wander through to one of the activity rooms in the new block that looks pretty much like an art studio: there's screen-printing stuff and easels. Kendall is drawing at one of the workstations, making menacing black shapes with a piece of black charcoal. Round and round her arm swoops. Her fingers are coalminer filthy and she's chuntering angrily to herself.

I don't think she's aware of me. I clear my throat. 'You OK?'

In shock, she drops her charcoal. 'Fuck! You scared me!' She takes a breath. 'No, to answer your question. I feel disgusting. I hate it. I hate feeling food in my body. I'm bloated and fat.' She spits the last word out.

I went to a girls' school. I know it's futile to tell someone with an eating disorder anything other than what they want to hear, so I say nothing but enter the studio to join her.

'I'm so over how everyone wanks themselves off over food,' she goes on. 'It's a national obsession. I am a hundred per cent bored of talking about it.'

I smile. 'Like those basic bitches who take pictures of avocados every five minutes. I'm like, what is wrong with you? It's an avocado.'

She laughs. She stops circling. 'Oh my god, avocado is the very most basic. That or sourdough pizza.'

'I think there's like a periodic table of basic. Kale is high up on there too. Or any form of juicing.'

She laughs, throwing her hair back. 'We should totally make a periodic table of basic. What else would be on it?'

I pull up a stool next to her. 'Erm, I dunno. Like, Man Buns?'

'Brady sometimes does a Man Bun.'

'Basic.'

'Ooh,' Kendall claps, 'those colour runs with the powder paint.'

'*So* basic. While you're at it, those super masc obstacle courses where you pay to crawl through mud and shit.'

She holds up a finger. 'People whose favourite smell is earth after the rain.'

'So. Fucking. Basic. And extra points for basic bitches who think they're clever for knowing it's called "petrichor".'

'Is that what it's called? Who knew. Basic. The Kardashians?'

'Sorry, hon, but that's a given.' I hold up a triumphant finger. 'Got it – adult colouring books.'

'Yes. Megabasic.'

I pause. 'Hold up. Maybe saying "basic" is basic.'

'Shit.' Kendall considers her swirly artwork. She chooses her next words carefully. 'Look, *I know* I'm really sick. I know obsessing over the sugar content of a grape isn't right. I know that this thing might kill me. I might really die. But some days, I would rather die than eat. It's a contest. If I eat, I lose; if I die, I'm dead. Is that the most insane thing you've ever heard?'

I don't really want a Care Bear heart-to-heart. Do I bring up her night jogging? I don't want her to feel cornered or attacked. I can't *cure* Kendall any more than I could cure cancer like I was human chemo. I guess I just have to 'be a pal'.

'Fuck it. Maybe we're all sick. If we're sick, it's not our fault,' I say sarcastically.

Kendall's eyes widen and she looks confused. 'Lexi, it *isn't* our fault.'

There's a sudden crash – glass breaking – followed by the sound of shouting and screaming. Kendall looks at me and we both spring off our stools. We hurry to the corridor. The commotion seems to be coming from the entrance hall end. 'Is it someone new?' Kendall asks.

'Only one way to find out.'

We're about halfway down the hall when Marcus barges past us, almost flooring me in the process. 'Get to the gym NOW,' he barks. Clearly ignoring that instruction, we follow him at a safe distance.

As we enter the main hall, three nurses swarm over someone I can't see. The smashing noise was one of the huge jade green vases, which now lays in Easter-egg fragments all over the tiles. I see arms and legs squirming in the mass.

'You like that?' A girl screams, her voice hoarse. 'You like feeling my tits, yeah? You like having a good feel of my body? Keep doing it! I'm gonna cum!'

I hide a snigger behind my hand. Wish I'd thought of that one. First me, then Saif, now her . . . doesn't anyone *walk* into this place?

'Stand up, Sasha!' Scouse Gary yells.

'Have you ever touched a minge, Gazza?' the voice says. 'Does the thought of a wet pussy make you feel sick?'

Marcus gets involved and the others break to let him in. Between the four of them, they haul a surprisingly slight mixed-race girl to her feet. She's naked, except for some boy's boxer shorts and Doc Martens on her feet. Her hair flies around her face in long braids. 'Get the fuck off me! I can't breathe! Which one of you fascist fuckers gonna get sued first if I can't breathe? It's my asthma! I need an inhaler.'

'Sasha, honey, you don't have asthma,' says Joyce.

'You willing to take that risk? My Grandma got that asbestos in her attic, innit? Put me down!' Sasha flails her arms and legs around. She wriggles free and throws herself across the main reception desk like some sort of mad commando. I lurk in the doorway with Kendall. Brady, Guy and Ruby approach, coming to see what's going on.

'What's happening?' Guy asks.

'Some new girl,' I say.

Kendall, looking ghostly pale, shakes her head. 'It's not a new girl,' she says. 'It's *Sasha*.'

Ruby throws her hands up. 'Aw, hell no!'

'Ruby . . .' Brady tries to calm her.

'Who is she?' I ask, but I'm drowned out by Ruby.

'There's no goddamn way I'm staying here if that psycho's back.'

Sasha hides behind the reception desk, playing cat and mouse with the nurses. 'I can hear you, Ruby,' she calls. 'You lost some weight, sweet tits? I think I can see some neck peeking through.'

'Fuck you, Sasha, fuck you all the way.'

Dr Ahmed, in jeans and a blouse, and without her hijab, sweeps in through the front door, carrying her doctor's bag. 'Sorry it took me so long,' she mutters to the nurses. 'Hello, Sasha,' she says. 'It's lovely to see you again.'

'No, it bloody isn't,' Kendall calls.

Dr Ahmed glances over at us. 'All of you get to your rooms,' she calls. 'This is lockdown.'

What the hell is lockdown? Suddenly, I'm not at a fancy clinic – I'm in prison.

'Go, now!'

The nurses move in on Sasha and she starts throwing things. She swings the phone around by its cable like a lasso.

'Stay away! Stay away? This ain't gonna go down like last time. I ain't gonna play. Sasha don't play.' Suddenly she throws the phone at Scouse Gary and grabs a hole punch. She hurls it towards Ruby. As Ruby ducks out of the way, Kendall crashes into me and I feel the hole punch make contact with my head. 'Ow!' My hand flies to my forehead.

'Hold her still,' Ahmed says, filling a syringe. Marcus and Joyce restrain Sasha, and Ahmed delivers the injection to her arm.

'You should have let me die last time,' Sasha says, the whites of her eyes blazing from her sweaty face. 'You gonna regret saving me. Sleep tonight knowing that. I'm a pox on your house.

I am plague and pestilence.' She relaxes into Marcus's big arms, going floppy like a rag doll.

Kendall grasps my arms. 'Lexi? Are you OK?'

'Yeah, I'm fine.' I pull back my hand and see there's blood on my fingers. Maybe I'm not fine.

'You're bleeding,' Brady says.

'See? You see what she's done?' Ruby continues to rant. 'We are not safe with her here!'

Ahmed comes over, eyes blazing. 'You know I'm pretty sure I said "lockdown" and yet here you all are. Sasha will be in isolation until further notice. We'll talk about it tomorrow. Lexi, let me look.' She examines my head. 'It shouldn't need a stitch. Gary? Will you get Lexi cleaned up? Thank you.' She regards the rest of the group calmly. 'Don't you all have some meditation to do?'

I watch Joyce and Marcus drag the skinny topless girl towards the Safe Room. I look at everyone else's faces. They're all tight-lipped, grey and grave.

They all looked scared.

After Gary has wiped away the blood and cleaned the wound and stuck a plaster on my head, I go out onto the terrace for a cigarette. I feel a bit woozy. It's probably just adrenaline comedown. I've had worse comedowns; I'll live.

The rain has blown over and it's a clear, chilly night. The sky is cloudless, filled with more stars than I've ever seen. It's like God's spewed them across the cosmos. Are there really that many suns? I remember Nikolai once telling me that some stars are already dead, the light reaching our eyes long after they stopped burning. I wonder – if I pick one, and stare at it long enough, will it go out?

'Here.' I didn't even hear Brady slide the doors open. He places his hoodie over my shoulders. 'It's cold.'

'Do you smoke?'

'I'm trying to quit.' He takes one anyway and I offer him a light. 'I think I need one tonight though.'

'Who is she?'

He takes a long drag on the cigarette before answering. 'Someone we thought we'd seen the last of.'

'That bad?'

He smiles. 'No one's *that* bad.' He smiles more. 'But she's bad.'

I smile back. 'Great. Just when I start to think this place might not actually be Hades.'

'I think you should decide for yourself,' he says. 'But it's been a lot *quieter* without Sasha, look at it that way.'

'What's her story?'

'Lord and Lady Denhulme do some outreach work with a charity. Sometimes they accept a patient . . .'

'Who isn't filthy rich?' I finish my cigarette and stub it out. 'How philanthropic of them.'

'Philanthropic . . . good word score.'

'I read a book once.'

'I can tell.'

'Have you ever met this Lord and Lady?'

'No. No one has.'

'Ooh, spooky.'

'Sasha was already here when I arrived. She's . . . a lot.'

'Aren't we all?'

'I'll say.' He finishes his cigarette and reaches over me to dump it in the ashtray. He's close, almost up against me. 'How's the head?'

I grin up at him. 'Never had any complaints.'

I move an inch closer and he does the same. We're almost hip to hip. I can see his nipples erect through his baseball jersey. 'Aren't you cold?'

'No,' he says.

It falls silent.

Our eyes meet, then lock. Sometimes words are so unnecessary.

This is where the kiss goes. He lowers his head towards me. I know I shouldn't – hello, Kurt – but Brady is *right here* and he looks so good. I just want . . . I need the contact. I want him to hold me as much as I want him to kiss me.

We're so close.

But then he pulls back. 'Sorry,' he says.

For a second, I'm disappointed, but then I snap out of it. It's fine. He probably just saved me some inner turmoil. I have a boyfriend. 'Hey, no biggy.'

'Sorry! God, awkward. What was that?'

I bite my lip and shrug.

'I'm so lame! Shall we go find the others?'

'OK. Sure.'

'Hang on to the hoodie.' We head towards the patio doors.

My head is sore. I feel dizzier. That was unexpectedly intense. I really wanted him to kiss me.

I feel guilty.

But I *still* want him to kiss me.

'Would you say you were happy?' Goldstein asks. It is very sunny and I'd rather be outside instead of looking at blue sky over his shoulder through the window.

'I'm in *rehab*,' I say.

He smiles. 'When was the last time you were happy?'

I frown. 'I don't know. What sort of question is that?'

'It's not really a difficult question, Lexi. When were you last blissfully happy?'

My nails look like shit. I wonder if I can get a shellac. 'Is anyone "blissfully happy" past the age of about ten?'

'Yes. Plenty of people. All the time, in fact.'

I pause. What does he want me to say? 'I was low-key happy with Kendall last night until I got pelted with office equipment.' I don't mention I was happier with Brady. 'I'm happy when I'm with Kurt.'

'Happy? Or high?'

I laugh. 'That's a cheap shot.'

He smiles back. I try to look past the grizzly beard and wonder if Isaac Goldstein was in the Synagogue Hotties Calendar back in the day.

'I apologise,' he says. 'Were you ever sober with Kurt?'

'Yes,' I say, but it's a reflex. I don't know. I *must* have been.

'Can we talk about school?' he asks, changing the subject. 'You attended St Agnes in Kensington, is that right?'

I shoot back inside my shell. I wasn't ready for him to tap that nerve. 'Yes.' Where is this going?

'How was school? In many ways, I'd imagine that was one of the more consistent elements in your life?'

'I guess so. It was fine.'

143

'Friends?'

'I had friends.'

He smiles. 'Care to expand on them?'

We're not going there. Not now, not ever. He can't know what happened. My name was never in the papers. Or can he? 'They weren't into drugs or anything,' I say. 'They have nothing to do with anything.'

He nods, in an intensely irritating therapist way, and jots something in his notes.

After the session I try to ring Kurt. It rings, but then goes to his voicemail. I try three times but he doesn't answer. 'Pick up, you asshole,' I mutter.

I don't know why, but I feel weirdly guilty about what *didn't even happen* with Brady. And I'm bugged that it's bugging me.

And now my head starts telling tales, little film trailers showing me what's happened to him: he's with another girl, he's overdosed. He's in trouble.

'Babe, you do not mess with these people,' he once told me, pacing the hotel suite. I was naked on the bed, tangled up in bed linen. He was in a pair of saggy boxers, desperately trying to get hold of Baggy. 'Why the fuck isn't he answering?'

'Calm down.' I was still a little high, but he was seriously killing my buzz. 'Come back to bed . . . it's Sunday.' Sunday morning with hazy, honeyed light bleeding through the drapes. I wanted to snuggle, drink tea, get eggs. 'Should we make brunch reservations?'

Kurt turned on me. He pinned my arms to my side. 'Are you listening to me? These men will fucking kill me, Lexi. If I do not pay them, they will *kill* me.'

My head was foggy. He was serious. He was hurting me. 'Kurt, let go. Jesus Christ, if you just need money, I can get you money.'

'It's a lot of money, Lexi.'

'How much?'

'Like a grand; fifteen hundred maybe.'

I shrugged him off. 'I'll tell Daddy I bought a new dress. If he asks.'

He let go of me. 'Can you get it today?'

'Yes. God. Just chill out. Now, do we want to meet Antonella and Troy for brunch or not?'

He kissed me hard on the lips. 'Oh babe, you have no idea. You've saved my life. I love you.'

'Kurt, it's Lexi. I hope you're alive. Answer your phone for fuck's sake. I'll try again at the same time tomorrow.'

Group is lively today.

'None of us are safe while that psycho's here!' Ruby is still ranting. 'Look at Lexi's head, for god's sake!'

'I'd rather you didn't.'

Both Goldstein and Ahmed are present today. 'Ruby,' Ahmed says, 'you need to calm down. Sasha stopped taking her medication and that's why she's back. You know she'll be more stable in a couple of days. Until then, she's in the Isolation Suite, so you're all perfectly safe.'

'There isn't a drug on earth strong enough to cure that lunatic!' Ruby won't drop it. I wonder what went down last time.

'The drugs don't cure you,' Guy adds softly. 'They just make you quieter.'

Ahmed looks at him sympathetically. 'Guy, that's not true. The goal of medication is to offer a clear head so you can get some perspective on your problems. They're not necessarily for ever.'

'I've been on medication since I was eleven,' Guy says. 'Ritalin, sertraline, citalopram, escitalopram ... I don't remember what it's like to not be medicated to the eyeballs.'

Well, that shuts Ruby up. At least for now.

'The goal of recovery is *not* to surround yourself with like-minded people,' Goldstein weighs in. 'As we discussed in the last session, only enablers agree with your every action. Personally, I think it's important we bring different voices to the table.'

'Sasha certainly does that,' Kendall says archly.

I'm like, *What? Poor people voices?* That's really patronising. We're all supposed to learn how awful and privileged we are from the crazy street urchin? I'm already well aware of how utterly sickening my existence is, thanks, I don't need any help from Sasha. If I wasn't me, I'd loathe me. I only tolerate myself at best.

'This is all feeling a little charged,' Goldstein says, stating the abundantly obvious. 'Look at the weather outside. It feels like the first day of spring, and here we are cooped up in therapy. Go. Go play.'

We all look at each other. Is he serious? 'What?' Saif says. 'Are you for real?'

'Play is proven to improve mental wellbeing. Go on, the lot of you. Go and play outside.'

I sit on the back steps, the mossy stone freezing my butt. It's not nearly as warm as it looks. Ruby and Kendall sit alongside me as Saif and Brady half-heartedly pass a basketball between them. Guy is smoking a cigarette.

'This blows,' Ruby says.

'I'm too old for *playtime*,' I say.

'Do you think we should start a game of tag or something?' Guy asks.

Kendall points at her heeled boots. 'Do I look like I want to play tag?'

'What she said,' I add.

'What do you even do at recess in England?' Brady asks. 'Drink tea? Eat scones?'

'I wish,' Kendall says. 'I mostly got called "a girl" for not joining in with the football. Then I became a girl and they all started calling me "a boy" instead.'

'We mostly bitched about people behind their backs,' I add. 'All girls' school. Although you could watch the St Barnabas boys across the green.'

'I was more entrepreneurial,' Saif says, aiming the basketball at the hoop and missing. 'Damn. My junior high school was in Dubai. I made a killing selling beers and joints from my locker. Worst Muslim Ever.'

'What did you do, Ruby?' Guy asks.

'Like, jump-rope or making up dance routines to Beyoncé and stuff.'

'We did that too!' I say. 'Or practised cartwheels and handstands on the green.'

Kendall jumps off the step. 'We used to do that! I can still do a handstand up against a wall. Lexi, catch my legs!'

I follow her onto the grass lawn. 'You better not kick me in the face. I'm already wounded.'

She kicks her boots off and takes a step back. She pivots forward on to her hands and her legs rear up at my head. 'Holy shit, careful,' I yelp.

'Have you got me?' she wobbles.

I clutch her skinny ankles. 'I've got you!' She holds the pose for about a second before she folds in on herself like a concertina. She looks up at me in a heap and I have to laugh at her.

'That hurt!' she says, laughing too.

'I used to be able to do a cartwheel,' Guy says.

'Go on then!' Kendall picks herself up.

Guy performs a very poor cartwheel, his feet barely leaving the ground. 'That didn't work,' he says and tries again.

'Dude, that is awful,' Brady says. 'I used to pull some gnarly flips into the pool. I can do backflips.'

'As if!' I call.

'I can! How much you wanna bet?'

'I highly doubt gambling is allowed on Sinner Island, Ardito.'

'Good point,' he laughs. 'Stand back . . . I need a run up.' He takes a run over the lawn and springs into a forward flip. He lands funny and topples over.

'Oooh! Bad dismount!' Ruby calls.

'Come on then, Ruby!' Brady brushes himself down. 'Your go!'

'Ha ha!'

'I'm serious!' He's trying to include her to be kind, I guess. 'Do a handstand! I'll hold your legs.' He offers her a hand.

'Brady Ardito, if you come one step closer . . .'

'You'll what?' He goes to drag her off the step and she squirts her mineral water bottle in his face. It's one of the ones with the sip cap thing so it fires a perfect jet of water.

'Oh! Oh, is that how it is?' He grabs his own bottle and hits her right back with a stream between the eyes. She leaps off the step and chases after him shaking her bottle over his head. 'Kendall, back me up!'

Kendall grabs a water bottle, but Saif is already on her case. He fires an arch of water and it lands on her hair. 'Oh, you total dick! My hair will go curly!'

'*My hair will go curly!*' He mimics her tone and she chases after him. I grab a bottle of water off the picnic table and go after Saif too. Before long, we're engaged in the ultimate boys-versus-girls water fight. I'm soon soaked all the way to my pants and freezing cold, but I don't care. Brady empties a bottle right over my head. 'You arse! You're gonna die for that!' I jump on his back and wrap my legs around his waist. I tip my bottle down the front of his T-shirt.

'Holy shit, that's cold!'

'Good!' I scream as he tries to tip me forward over his head. 'Brady! Stop!'

From the patio doors, I see Goldstein watching us with a cup of tea. He smiles to himself and heads back inside.

After I've changed out of my wet clothes, my curiosity gets the better of me. On the way down to lunch, I see the coast is clear to the Safe Room. Interesting.

Sasha has been well and truly hyped.

I creep down to the Safe Room. No one is guarding her door and it all seems quiet.

Almost *too* quiet.

Things so rarely live up to the hype.

I tiptoe all the way to the door and press my ear to the wood. Nothing. Maybe she's not the Velociraptor the others made her out to be.

I'm about to walk away when I hear a faint voice. 'Gary? That you? Can I get a fag?' I wince and freeze. I wonder if she can see my shadow in the crack in the door. 'I can see you. Look, I'm not kicking off. I just want a fag, yeah?'

I figure I can help a bitch out. 'I'm not a nurse,' I say.

In the door there's a little hatch. This being a classy place, it's not like a police-cell letterbox. It's more like the quaint little door the cuckoo pops out of in a Swiss clock. Keeping a safe distance, I unbolt the hatch and open it.

Sasha is sat in 'classic squalid asylum hunch' next to the bed, arms wrapped around her legs. She might as well be rocking.

'I'm Lexi. You hit me with a hole punch.' I point to the plaster on my head.

Sasha gapes up at me with massively dilated pupils. Her mouth is slack, lips moist. Braids dangle over her face. 'Sorry 'bout that, Blondie. Hope you don't die.'

'I'm fine,' I say. 'Look, if you want a cigarette, I'll give you one. Just don't tell the staff, OK?'

153

She lumbers forward, feeling her way along the walls. Wow, she must be on the really good pills. I wonder what she's taking and if I can get some to help me sleep. 'I ain't no grass. I got more secrets in the crypt than the Catholic Church, babes.'

I'm wearing Brady's hoodie. It's not like a statement; it was just hanging on my chair, so I stuck it on. There's a packet of Marlboro Lights in the pocket. I slip my hand through the hatch and hope she's not gonna go Hannibal Lector on me. 'You got a light?' she asks.

I'm not sure about giving her access to a naked flame, but it's too late now. 'Sure.' I hand over the lighter and see her forearm is a criss-cross lattice of shiny scars, some razor thin, some like fat leeches on her skin. Burn marks too. There's not a centimetre of unmarked flesh. Wow, she doesn't mess about.

She sparks up and takes a deep drag. 'Oh man, feel them toxins. You know there's 4000 chemicals in a fag, forty-three of which are carcinogenic. That's a gorgeous word, innit? Wrap you tongue around that . . . car-cin-o-gen-ic.'

She's a very different beast on her meds. Her speech is slurred, her eyes glassy. I don't think she could attack me if she tried. 'Good to know. How are you feeling?' I ask.

'I feel,' she says, 'mighty real.' She shuffles to the bed and sits down. She's wearing the standard issue Calvin Klein tracksuit.

I wonder if I'm going to get any sense out of her.

'I been mostly thinking,' she goes on, 'about where they'll put me when they run out of cages. How do you solve a problem like Sasha?'

'Where have you come from?'

'London. Hackney.'

'I'm Battersea.'

'Lady cyclist.'

I frown. 'What?'

'When lady cyclists were banned from Hyde Park, they proudly took to their bikes and rode around Battersea Park. In 1890 it was quite the scandal. Glorious fucking women gallivanting on bicycles.'

I smile. 'Good for them.'

'What you in here for? Did you . . . cycle in Hyde Park?'

Despite everything, I flinch. 'I'm an addict. Apparently.'

Sasha smiles a Joker-like grin. There's a little gap in her front teeth. 'Tell me about the Bad Boy what gave you the bad shit.'

Oh, fuck her. 'There is no bad boy.'

'Do not lie, Blondie. Lying is a sign the devil's got your tongue, and if he's got your tongue he'll be after your ass next. Some South London gangster, yeah? Some rude boy? Princess thought she'd get back at Daddy by sucking some meaty black cock.'

'Oh, Jesus Christ,' I say, over it. 'You don't have the first fucking clue.'

'You drive him around town in your Merc? You give him money? He'll "pay you back", yeah?'

I can't not think about Kurt. It's not like I didn't have my eyes wide open. Money: he needed it, I had it to burn. Playmate and payroll. 'Whatever. I'm going now.'

'Wait!' She gets off the bed and comes right to the hatch. I take a step back. I'm not having her bite my nose off or whatever. 'Come closer, Blondie, I wanna tell you something.'

'I'm fine here, thanks.'

'Don't be a pussy, come here.'

'No.'

'It's a secret.'

'I thought you were good with secrets.'

'You know why they won't give me cigarettes? It ain't the cancer, darlin'.' She takes her cigarette and stubs it out on her forehead, in the exact position of my plaster. The skin sizzles and blisters at once.

'For fuck's sake,' I say. 'You're batshit.'

Sasha smiles. Her unblinking eyes glare through the peephole. 'Yeah? What was the first fucking clue?'

The encounter with Sasha weirded me out. I can't tell anyone she hurt herself without landing myself in trouble and I wonder if she'll grass me up. I get now why the others are so on edge. How do you ever relax around someone so unpredictable? I wonder . . . I wonder if that's what I was like to Nik?

After lunch, I'm all set to walk down to the stables when Kendall and Ruby chase me down on the back lawn. 'Wait up!' Kendall says.

'God, you walk fast,' Ruby moans.

'We told them we wanted to come to the stables with you,' Kendall explains.

I give her heeled boots a once-over. 'You want to come to the stables?'

'Obviously not. But come with us. There's something I want to show you.'

'Is this allowed?' I ask. 'I don't actually care what the answer is, but I'd like all the information.'

'It's not *allowed*, but we're not really doing anything wrong,' Ruby says.

I gesture down the path. 'Lead the way.'

We wander towards the stables, but this time, we carry on past the cottages and on to a path signposted 'Beach Path'. Winding, haphazard steps fashioned with planks, sleepers and the occasional slab of stone zig-zag all the way down the hill towards a shale and dirty sand beach. This is cool in a *Three Fuck-Ups Go On An Adventure* way. I've seen the beach while I've been out riding Patty, but never actually walked down.

It's clouded over since this morning and the wind is snappish, whipping in from the sea like lashes. It smells, and almost tastes, of salty seaweed beachiness. It's sour but organic somehow, like being in Whole Foods or something. The sky is artificially huge, like a painting in the Tate, doomy acrylic-paint grey clouds roll and swirl out to infinity. God fingers – that's what Nik used to call shards of light – pierce the murk and stab into the sea. The perspective makes my eyes go funny.

Kendall can't walk so ends up taking her boots and socks off, and carrying them across the sand, screaming as she steps on seaweed or shells. 'Girl, what are you doing? I told you not to wear those fool things,' Ruby says.

'Like, all my shoes have heels!' Kendall laughs. 'Do I bloody look like the outdoors type? Nature is gross!'

'God, I thought I was bad!' I laugh at her prancing across the sand. 'What is it you want to show me?'

'Just this, just the beach,' Kendall says. 'We're not supposed to come down this far without supervision. I guess the sea is a pretty big suicide risk and all.'

I hadn't even thought of that.

'Watch out for crabs!' Ruby says as we climb over rock pools.

'Always excellent advice . . .' I add.

'Gross!' Kendall squeals.

We walk along the beach until we come to a big sea-wall thing. We have to go up the slope to cross it, and on the other side is what I suppose passes as a marina. There's a network of wooden piers and then one, larger, concrete slope for the ferry. Further inland there's a little office and a barrier check for cars, but I can't see anyone about. 'Where is everyone?'

'I think there's a guy who comes down twice a day when the ferry comes in,' Ruby says.

A couple of ancient row boats, paint peeled away to almost nothing, clink against their moorings like ice cubes in a glass of Coke. 'Look at that,' I say, nodding towards the boats. 'Let's get the hell off this island. Quick, while no one's looking.'

'Girl, I'd sink that shit,' Ruby says and I can't help but laugh. She's laughing too so I guess it's OK.

We sit on the end of one of the jetties, swinging our legs. Kendall nudges me. 'So, guess what happened last night.'

'Besides that psycho bitch coming back?' huffs Ruby.

'I met Sasha this morning,' I say.

'She's out of Isolation?' Ruby's hackles shoot up at once.

'No,' I reassure her. 'She's a charmer. Anyway. What happened last night?'

Kendall smirks.

'What?' I ask.

'Last night, I totally got it on with Saif.'

Both Ruby and I erupt. 'What?'

'He was checking me out all night, asking me loads of questions and stuff. After lights out I knocked on his door and we fooled around a little. He made me promise not to tell anyone . . . but who are we kidding, I have a big mouth.'

'Was it good?' I ask. I'm actually not surprised. I thought I'd picked up on a little bit of something-something earlier when we had the water fight.

She shrugs. 'It was OK. He's one of *those*.'

'Those what?' Ruby asks.

'Those "straight" guys who just love trans girls. There's a reason so many of us are escorts or whatever – it's because there's like a thriving demand. But none of them want to get to know us, not really. It's like you're a kinky toy to them. It's bullshit. It was fun, I guess. Someone to do to pass the time, but it won't come to anything.'

'Why not? It might,' I say.

'Nah. He doesn't really see me as a girl. That's all I want.'

I don't really know what else I can say to that. Ruby fills the silence. 'You get yours, honey. That boy has arms for days!'

Kendall shrugs. 'Shame his dick doesn't match, really.'

And then we're laughing again.

'Well, where did you last have it?' Kendall asks. We're all in the dining room. Saif has lost his Rolex.

'I don't fucking know,' he snaps. Kendall's face falls. 'Sorry. I took if off when we had the water fight I think. I don't know.'

'It'll turn up,' Brady says. 'It's so bling, you can see it from space, bro.'

'Very funny, asshole. It was a present from my dad. If I don't find it, I'm dead meat.' Oooh, Daddy Issues, I think to myself. Something to look forward to in Group.

We're just finishing dinner (tiger prawns with glass noodles rounded off with truly excellent rhubarb crumble) when Goldstein comes into the dining room. He's got his coat over his arm and his briefcase. 'I'm off, but just to let you know that we have some family visits tomorrow.'

Everyone shuts up.

'Kendall, Saif, Lexi – you all have someone coming.'

'Nikolai?' I ask. I can feel tears bubbling up, but I swallow them back.

'Yes,' Goldstein says, and I nod, not trusting myself to speak.

'Any word from my dad?' Guy asks, his cheeks red.

'Not this time, I'm afraid, Guy. We'll have another slot next week.'

Guy just nods, he looks crushed. Poor Guy.

After dinner we have a night off – no organised fun for us. Well, at the Clarity Centre a night off is 'Games Night'. Cards are allowed as long as no one makes wagers (betting *is* forbidden), and Saif and Brady are locked in a frantic table-tennis death-match. Kendall is sulking because Saif snapped at her and Ruby is quietly plotting his death with her in a corner of the games room. Sasha is still in Isolation.

Guy is reading *100 Years of Solitude* un-ironically by himself on the sofa. I get the impression he's got the hump Saif has stolen his playmate. I've seen this before . . . it's how Baggy gets whenever there's another guy between him and Kurt. The beta male gets shunted out. I decide to take pity on him. 'They didn't have a copy of *Prozac Nation*?'

He looks up and smiles. 'It fell apart from overuse.'

'You OK?'

He closes the book and crossed his legs underneath himself. 'I'm more than a little fatigued, to be honest. I want to go home now.'

'How long have you been here?'

'Almost two months. Feels like an awful lot longer.'

'Sucks. You live with your dad?'

'Yes, Mummy died when I was ten.'

'Oh, I'm sorry.'

'It was a long time ago.'

'Still sucks.'

'Have you ever grown up on an army base?'

'No.'

'It *really* sucks,' he says. I smile. 'When Mummy died, Daddy decided I'd be best off away at school. Eton, no less.'

'Oh Jesus. How was that? Eton mess?'

Guy's one of those cuddly but entirely sexless guys girls adore. Of course, they are usually the first to go all 'Men's Rights' when girls friendzone them. I'm not destined for Great White greatness. I didn't quite fit in. They thought I was spectacularly bonkers from day one. I'm meant to be ruling the world, right? I'm The Elite, and look at me! They treated me like a defective Swiss watch. "The boy who touches things three times." That went down about as well as you'd imagine.'

'So . . . it's like, OCD?'

'It *is* OCD.'

'Shit. Sorry.'

'No, it's OK. I've had it so long I don't really remember how it started. Doctors have told me it's a bit like an addiction. I'm sure when it started I was doing weird stuff for a reason, but in the end you do them just to take the edge off the panic. If you don't you feel like you're going to die. I *know* I won't, but that's not what it feels like.'

I know I probably shouldn't ask, but I ask anyway. 'So why are you in rehab?'

He grins. 'Lexi! This isn't rehab, remember . . . it's a "treatment facility"! Daddy didn't know what else to do. I dropped out of university after three months because it got so bad. I could hardly leave my room and I was getting into fights and stuff.'

'Fights? You?'

He blushes. 'Yeah. I know. I don't look the type. I'm different after a pint or six. The irony is my OCD gets better when I'm drunk, but . . . well, that's clearly not the way forward.'

It's never easy, is it? It's never one thing, I think. I look around the room and none of us are easy, none of us are . . . *clean*. All our weird shit internally overlaps like tectonic plates, and we just wait for them to grind together, brace for the earthquake.

'I'm told I was becoming a problem drinker,' he admits. 'Who am I kidding? I was a mess. I kept waking up covered in sick in the park just outside my college. It wasn't pretty.'

'Isn't that what university is for?' I say with a grin.

'That,' Guy says with certainty, 'is enabler behaviour.'

He's probably right.

'I just want to have a normal life,' he says. He lets his guard all the way down, and he was already pretty bloody vulnerable. 'I don't want to feel like this for the rest of my life. I can't.'

I reach for a little white lie. 'You won't.' I take his hand and give it a squeeze. I see Brady briefly look our way. I wonder what he thinks of us holding hands. God, why is that even in my head? That isn't a thing. Being caged is getting to me. 'You're sick,' I say, 'and you'll get better. We all will.'

Would you look at that. I'm learning the lines.

STEP 4:
I AM STRONGER THAN
I THINK I AM

In the night I dreamed I'd be speaking to Nik through a Perspex screen via a telephone, but I'm told there's not a set 'Family Room' as such. The receptionist calls the phone in my room just as I'm putting some mascara on. 'Good morning, Miss Volkov. Your brother is waiting for you in reception.'

I stick on the Vans and string my Tiffany necklace around my throat. I look on the coffee table for my McQueen skull ring. It's like my every-day go-to ring. I rarely take it off. Where the fuck is it? I wonder if I took it off in the lounge last night – sometimes if I get too hot my fingers swell a bit and I take it off. It was my sweet-sixteen present from Nik. I should be wearing it when he's here. I pull all the bedding up, looking among the sheets and clothes I've discarded.

The phone rings again and reluctantly I head to reception without the ring. With every step I get a new butterfly in my stomach. I don't know why I'm so nervous. It's only been a few weeks.

I push through the door and see him sitting in one of the armchairs. He's reading a copy of *GQ* that's been left on the coffee table. 'Nik?'

He looks up at me, his eyes widening. He stands, letting the magazine flop into the chair. We mirror each other. I don't know what to do.

Then he holds his arms wide and I throw myself into them. He hugs me tight. It's weird, but it feels like he is the first solid thing I've held in a very long time. If he's real then maybe I'm still real too. He smells of home. No one aroma: a mix of his deodorant, fabric softener, the hotel dry-cleaners, Marlboro Lights . . . *home*.

He kisses the top of my head. 'Lexi, you look a million times better. Seriously. Thank god.'

I look up at him and wipe a tear off his face. 'Well, don't boo about it, you massive pussy.' I grin and he hugs me harder.

'Oh, I've missed you, you cunt.'

I laugh a huge, proper laugh, so hard it shakes my lungs loose. I cough. I smoke too much.

There's a polite throat-clearing behind us. It's Dr Goldstein. 'Good morning, Mr Volkov. How was the trip down?'

'Yeah, fine. How's my sister been? A nightmare?'

'Nik!'

'Not at all, Mr Volkov. Lexi is a delight. We'll chat before you leave, but right now, why don't you enjoy coffee in the lounge?'

The sun is shining so we get the coffees to go and walk through the grounds. 'It's pretty nice out here,' Nik says. 'Maybe I'll bring Tabby for a weekend break next time.'

'Very funny,' I say. 'It's not a spa, believe me. I was attacked with a hole punch.'

'What?'

'It was an accident.' I take a sip of too-foamy-to-actually-be-a-latte coffee. 'It's not so bad.'

'And you're off the drugs?'

I scowl at him. '*The drugs?* What are you, eight? Yes, I am fully detoxed. As of yesterday I am pill free. I guess they know what they're doing.'

'How do you feel?'

'*Now* I feel fine. *Then* I honestly thought I was gonna die.'

'Well, whose fault is that?'

I almost smash my coffee into his face, before biting my tongue. 'We do not *blame* out here, Nikolai. That's not our way.'

'Sorry.' He actually looks pretty sheepish. 'But that's the whole point of coming, right? To get it all out of your system. Now you're good.' He grins. 'You can come home soon and all this will be behind you.'

I shake my head. Can he really think it's that simple? That I'm a passive victim of evil substances? A couple of cute little birds are splashing about in the fountain on the lawn. They distract me while I struggle to make a sentence. 'Nik, it doesn't work like that. It . . . it's not just about getting clean.'

He looks confused. 'What is it about, then?'

'I dunno. I guess it's about me.' I cringe at my choice of words. Good one, me. 'Like, *why* I was getting so blasted all the time in the first place. It's complicated.'

Nik shrugs. 'No, it isn't. Just don't do drugs any more. You obviously can't hack it.'

I stop walking and sit on one of the stone steps. 'Nik, you've come all this way, can we not fight?'

'I'm not!'

'Can we talk about something else, please?'

'Sure.' He sits beside me. 'Like what?'

'Have you seen Kurt?'

He laughs. 'OK, and *I'm* the one starting fights?'

'Nik . . .'

'No, I haven't. But like I said, I did threaten to kill him if he set foot south of the river.'

I tilt my head. I don't know if the coy-little-girl shit ever really flew with Nik, but it's worth a go. 'Will you check up on him for me?'

'Aw, Lex!'

'Oh, come on! Please? I know you hate him, but I can't get better if I'm worrying about him.' Nik looks sceptical. 'I'm supposed to be focusing on myself, but all I can think about is if he's in a ditch in Shoreditch. Could you just find him and reassure me a little?'

He looks like he's biting his tongue pretty hard. 'OK,' he says finally, through a clenched jaw. 'If it helps.'

'It'll help.' I throw my arms around him. 'You don't have to spy on him, just let me know he's OK. That . . . he's looking after himself.' Truth be told, without my money, I don't know how he's doing. His parents cut him off not long after we started dating. Can't think why.

'Lexi,' Nik's eyes excavate mine, 'he's a junkie. Of course he's not looking after himself.'

He's got me there. 'Just keep an eye on him.'

Saif and his sister come around the corner, strolling together. She is stunning, feline face framed by one of those tall hijabs in peacock blue. It's all pinned together by a fabulous gold brooch. Saif and I exchange a nod, sharing in a moment of how absurd all of this is.

We fall silent until Saif and his sister have passed. 'So. How are Mum and Dad? Fill me in.'

When I get to the dining room that night, I see Sasha is there. They must have her meds sorted: she's neither lobotomy chill or freebasing. Still, Dr Ahmed is also joining us for dinner, which she doesn't normally. She sits alongside Sasha and tonight there are no tea lights on the tables, making it decidedly less 'bistro' and much more 'school dinners'.

'Thank you for not making a fuss,' Ahmed says, not aiming the comment at Ruby directly. 'Sasha is ready to join us again.'

Sasha hardly looks up. She's wearing a tent of a cable-knit fisherman jumper. It slopes off her left shoulder. Her clavicle is covered in little circular burn marks. She scowls up at us as we take our seats. 'I am sorry for my histrionic demonstration when I got here. I have a number of deep-seated issues. I know that may come as a surprise, but it's all true.'

'Thank you,' Ahmed says. 'Anything else you want to say?'

'Ruby, I'm sorry I was a twat. I was a proper cunt.'

Ruby throws her hands up. 'See? She's doing that because she knows I hate that word.'

'Sasha . . .'

'That is indeed one of my myriad issues. I just see a window and clamber on through it. In or out.'

'Sasha . . . don't even start.'

'I'm sorry,' she says. 'Ruby, I am sorry.'

Everyone looks to Ruby to return her serve. 'Whatever.' Rally over.

Dr Ahmed shakes her head. 'Ruby, you know that's not how it works. I know this isn't therapy, but there'll come a time for all of you when you seek forgiveness for the things you've done, and you're not going to want to hear "whatever".'

Ruby rolls her eyes. 'Apology accepted. Just don't get in my way.'

Collectively – or maybe it's just me – we all turn to Sasha to see if she'll make the obvious size joke. She refrains. For now. That's good because I'm kinda hungry – it's weird how much my appetite is back – and I can't be arsed with another kick off. I share a relieved glance with both Brady and Kendall and I sense they'd thought the same.

Sasha chews on a piece of crusty bread. 'So, you're Lexi Volkov, yeah?'

'I am.'

'I know about you.'

I sip on my mushroom soup. It's lukewarm. 'So do a lot of people.'

Sasha performs a theatrical wink. 'Nah, Blondie. I *know* about you. I suppose every tower needs a Rapunzel but butter always melts eventually. Retribution comes a-calling.'

'Sasha,' Dr Ahmed warns her, 'can we just have a peaceful meal, please?'

I stare into my bowl. She doesn't know *anything*. She's talking shit. How could *she*, she of all people, know about what happened?

I try to shake it off, but now I feel nauseous. I abandon the soup.

So this is life with Sasha. We're holding our breath, stepping around broken glass, eggshells, other clichés.

After dinner we have a guest speaker – a former patient who's now six years sober. Good for him. Six years without a drink. Jesus. Where will I be in six years? I'll be twenty-three. I try, but I can't see past the island perimeter.

He finishes up at about eight so we have an impromptu board game night. This shit must be kicking in because the idea doesn't make me want to jab knives into my eyes or down Cillit Bang. They have Cluedo, Monopoly, Mousetrap, Game of Life . . . all the classics. I dimly remember playing games like this at prep school or with Nik. You can't play Cluedo with two – it's too easy to work out who the killer is.

I scan back through memory photos, trying to remember if I ever played with Mummy or Daddy. I don't think we ever did.

Oh, poor little Lexi. Take some pills to ease the pain.

I snap out of it. I refuse to attend the pity-party.

Wisely, we've been split into two groups. I'm playing Cluedo with Sasha, Saif and Kendall. I'm glad. I want to keep a close eye on Sasha. I want her where I can see her. 'I think,' I say to Kendall, 'that it was Mrs Peacock in the conservatory with the lead pipe.'

Sasha and Saif hide their eyes, and Kendall shows me Mrs Peacock's haughty face. I quickly cross her off my list. So it's definitely Reverend Green. He's probably a kiddie fiddler too, the beady-eyed freak.

While Saif rolls the dice, I see Sasha dig the tiny little dagger playing piece into her forearm. Boynurse Marcus is playing Game of Life with Brady, Guy and Ruby. 'Hey,' I whisper. I don't want to grass her up. 'Don't do that.'

She looks at me through hooded eyes. 'Bored of board games, innit. I'm trying to stay awake. Not hurting anyone but Sasha.

She's fair game, says so in four out of five toilet doors in Hackney.' She presses it deeper into her flesh and a bead of blood forms a little jewel on her skin.

'Sasha . . . come on. You don't wanna go back in that room. I was in that room. It's shit.'

'Spoiler alert. It's all shit, Blondie.'

I laugh and then she laughs. 'I think shit exists on a spectrum,' I tell her. 'This is less shit.'

'You got me there.' She throws the now bloody dagger onto the Cluedo board.

'Oh, gross!' Kendall says.

'I'll clean it up,' I offer. 'You should get a plaster or something too.'

We take a break while I wipe the board and Sasha goes to find a first aid kit. She got away with it this time, I think.

'C'mon then!' Saif says, clapping his hands as I join them again. 'I think I know whodunit.'

'Really?' Kendall says. 'I have like no idea!'

'I just gotta get one of you in a room and I'm so gonna nail it. This murderer is going down. Going downtown.'

Something familiar in his voice – a breathless, manic quality – makes me stop and look at him. Pearls of sweat dot his upper lip and his eyes are as wide as saucers. I don't need to be a sleuth to deduce that Saif is high. It's the first time I've seen him not-sulking. It's an open-and-shut case. I doubt he's even aware his knee is bobbing up and down like a hummingbird at a flower. I check his nostrils for powder, but there's nothing incriminating.

He's coked up. So blatantly coked up.

How the hell did he get coke?

His sister.

His sister brought him drugs.

Clever little bitch. Both of them.

I wonder if she smuggled them inside her hijab. That's actually pretty ingenious.

'Saif!' I say. I'm about a second away from asking him what he's got when the words stall on my tongue.

'What?' he says, blinking like a psycho with hayfever. He's coming up.

'I . . . nothing. I mean, it's Kendall's turn anyway.'

'Yeah, and then I'm gonna win. Then we should do Monopoly. Aw man, I am so down for Monopoly. Can I be the top hat? Fancy-ass motherfucking playa in a top hat. Yas!'

I say nothing. As with Sasha, I don't know if anyone else – least of all Marcus – has noticed, and I don't wanna grass him up. I'm not a grass, period, but second of all, a wicked little part of me wants some.

It's all kicking off in my head.

Good Lexi (in white, angel wings): you're clean now, you don't do drugs. That would be bad.

Bad Lexi (in red latex corset and devil horns): fuck it, a tiny bit of coke isn't gonna do any harm, is it? It'll make Monopoly way more fun.

Good Lexi: you've come this far.

Bad Lexi: yes, and you can therefore do it again. And coke isn't heroin, anyway.

Good Lexi: what were the last three weeks for if you can't resist coke the first time you see some? Are you that weak?

Bad Lexi: probably.

Good Lexi: and you literally just promised Nikolai this morning.

Bad Lexi: how would he ever know? It's not his X-Men power to know when I've done blow.

Good Lexi: and what about the others? What if there's a demented gold rush for Saif's gak and everyone falls off the wagon? What if *Brady* falls off the wagon?

I look over and see Brady laughing at something Guy is saying. I know, just *know* that Brady – with all his polite, concise answers in Group – would think less of me if he knew I'd done coke.

Fuck me hard. Am I that co-dependent? Kurt likes me more when I'm high so I do drugs, Brady likes me less so I don't. It's a good job I'm in therapy, right? As Bad Me grumpily gives up the fight, Good Me feels a little glow of smug satisfaction. I can't be that addicted, can I?

After we've had hot chocolate and marshmallows – which I can't even pretend to hate – we head off to bed. Brady, Guy, Sasha and Kendall are all upstairs, while Ruby, Saif and I are on the ground floor in the 'villas'. I think we have the more expensive rooms.

This means I have a chance to get Saif by himself once we've bid Ruby goodnight. By this point, I'm actually quite tired and have no desire to be wide awake and chatting utter nonsense. I was always quite practical with my coke or speed – I knew exactly how much I'd need to stay awake for the duration I wanted. 'Hey,' I say.

'What's up?' He's coming down now, twitchy and rubbing his nose a lot.

'How did you get it in?' I ask. This feels illicit. I want to fold myself into his secret, show him how cool I am for not ratting him out. Then, if my resolve breaks, I know he'll trust me.

'Get what in? I don't know what you're talking about.' Balls. I forgot he'd be in the paranoid stage. Only in this case, he's absolutely right to be. He leans against his villa door, trying – and failing – to look casual.

'Come on, Saif . . . you can't play a player.'

His face changes, like a sudden storm rolling in. His thick brows meet in the middle. 'Look, I don't know what the fuck you're talking about, but keep your mouth shut, yeah? Or I'll shut it for you, bitch.' He spits the words in my face.

Wow. I actually have to stop myself from reacting. I don't back up, holding my ground. Cokeheads are truly the worst. A snarl on his lips, he turns and barges into his room. I take my time to blink. 'OK,' I call after him. 'Whatever. Rude much?'

Screw him. I guess it's his money, his rehab, his waste of time. I ruffle my hair and slope off down the corridor, hoping he doesn't think I was shaken.

The next day starts with the arrival of a jumbo-size, ultra-heavy-flow period. It looks like the last scene in a slasher movie down there. With everything going on, it didn't even occur to me that I've unwittingly come off the pill. This is my first period in about a year. No wonder I nearly had a little boo-hoo when Saif shouted at me.

Awkward. God, now I'm the girl who shat the bed and then bled all over it. If I'm not careful, they'll have me in adult diapers. I strip the bed and make a little ball of sheets by the door. I'll explain to Joyce or one of the other women nurses. I already clocked some tampons in the little cupboard under the sink, thank Christ.

Breakfast – egg white omelette and hot water and lemon – is followed by therapy. I'm pretty much over it now. The novelty has worn off and I think Goldstein, curse him, is actually good. He's chipping away at me and I don't like it. I slump in and find Goldstein already waiting. 'Good morning, Lexi. How are you today?'

'I'm on my period. It's distressing. You wouldn't get it.'

'No, no I wouldn't and I won't pretend to. We'll go easy on you.'

'Thanks.'

'We've talked a lot about your family. Can we talk about your schooling?'

I bristle and I'm pretty sure he notices. Oh, who am I kidding, of course he notices. He notices everything.

'Sure, what do you want to know?'

'Well, it's something you don't seem comfortable talking about. Why is that?'

'It's nothing to do with comfort. It's just boring. I went to school. Now I don't.'

He looks at me over the rim of his glasses and I wonder if he was ever young. He seems like the sort of person who was born with a beard. Geography-teacher chic.

'You were an exceptional student.'

I shrug. 'Was I?'

'Don't be modest. I asked St Agnes for your reports.'

I swallow. 'Yeah? I bet that made for a riveting read.'

'It was enlightening. You won an award for your writing?'

'I was like twelve.'

'Still. You beat thousands of other writers. You got to meet royalty. You must be very talented.'

I remember that day well. The prize-giving was held at Kensington Palace. Princess Kate shook my hand and everything. I curtseyed, cute as a cupcake. It was a lovely, sun-washed July day and, at the time, I was very proud. Admitting that now feels like I'm letting him win. 'You can meet royalty at any bar in Chelsea any night of the week.'

'You do realise you're deflecting praise?'

'I'm British.'

'If I were a therapist, I'd argue that on some level you don't feel you're worthy of praise.'

'For writing some dumb story and winning a prize?'

'It's not just that, Lexi. You were a straight-A student until you turned sixteen. Then what? You just dropped out of school. Why?'

Tears sting my eyes. Antonella's face fills my head – her silky black hair, her smile, her dimples. In all the darkness, there's a glimmer – a single match lighting at the bottom of a mineshaft. And then it blows out.

'I was just over it. You know?'

After the session, I'm allowed my allotted phone time. I have a text message from Nikolai: *I saw Kurt. He's fine. You can stop worrying. N x*

I call him at once. He answers right away. 'Hey. You OK?'

'Nikolai.' I punch out each syllable. 'You can't just say "I saw Kurt". Where was he? How did he look?'

'He looked like a hipster douchebag. So, pretty normal.'

'Ha ha. Where did you see him?'

'Tabby was invited to some gallery opening in a shipping container in Shoreditch. I figured he'd be there.'

That sounds fairly accurate. 'And he was?'

'Yeah, he was there. With that inbred pug Flossy Blenheim.'

My grip tightens on my phone, almost crushing it in my palm. 'What? He was with Flossy, or he was *with* her?'

'I don't know. They were there together.'

I can feel myself about to Hulk out. I swallow hard. 'Was he high?'

'It was an opening. *Everyone* was on coke.'

'Were you?'

'Jesus, Lex. Yes, I did a line.'

'Great. So you're allowed drugs, Kurt's allowed drugs, everyone's allowed drugs but me. That's just peachy.'

'Grow up, Lexi. I didn't nearly OD on junk, did I?'

'This is bullshit!' I snap and hang up on him. I know I should wait before I call Kurt, I'm going to sound like a cracked-out fishwife but I can't wait twenty-four hours to calm down.

I dial his number and wait. He answers after about five rings. 'Hey, babe. How you doin'?' He sounds crusty, like he's in bed, just waking up. It's ten in the morning and it feels like I've been up for an eternity, which makes me even more furious.

'Are you alone?' I bark. Zero chill.

'What?'

'Do you want me to break it down? Are you in bed with Flossy Blenheim having recently put your penis inside her vagina?' I hate this. I hate that he's turned me into Archetypal Psycho Girlfriend. Where's Cool Girl now?

'Have you lost your fucking mind?'

'Kurt, I know you were with her last night.'

'Yes, in that we were both at the P!nk Wa!fer launch.'

'Nikolai said you were together.'

'Nikolai hates my guts. Jesus, are you spying on me now, Lex?'

I tug on my hair. It's somehow both dry and greasy at the same time.

'Lex, are you there?'

'Kurt. I don't know what's going on. I feel like I'm wearing a blindfold and I can't pull it off.'

'I was just at a party with friends. I got shitfaced on warm chardonnay and fell asleep on the night bus.'

I want to believe him, but it all fits, doesn't it. Flossy: stupid, rich, dying to rebel, to get her mummy and daddy's attention.

And who does that remind you of?

Is that all I am to him? A cashpoint vagina? He puts his card in and I dispense twenties. I feel sick. I don't want to *want* to control him. I don't want to *care*. How did I end up like this? Is this love? It feels nasty and puce.

'I'm sorry.' Why am I apologising?

'Lexi, you gotta trust me, babes.'

'I do.' I don't.

'You know what Flossy and that lot are like. They're always good for a laugh.' He means they're always good for drugs. He's see-through.

After we say goodbye, I sit for a while on Goldstein's office floor. I feel about as bad as when I first arrived. I vividly picture inhaling a joint and the cloudiness that would follow, the haze, how smudged my edges would be. I want to feel pastel again. *Millennial pink.* I feel too well defined.

Saif. Saif has coke. But coke isn't what I want. The last thing I want is to be more alert. I want to zone all the way out.

Flossy Blenheim? Jesus, even I'd hit Xenia Blenheim, but Flossy looks part-moose. She's got the posh-girl teeth. I can't not see them together. I know every inch of Kurt's body. The tattoos, the way they ripple over his skin. His scar where a dealer stabbed him to the left of his armpit.

I picture his lithe hips sinking between Flossy's legs and I blaze with anger, like my skin's burning off, just leaving rage and sinew.

Well, he's not the only desirable one. I look at the clock and see we still have thirty minutes until Group.

And that's plenty of time.

I check no one's about and breeze upstairs. I'm powered by anger. Anger and hormones. I'm on the blob, so I won't fuck him, but there's plenty of other things we can do.

If Kurt can be bad, so can I. I'm every bit as bad as he is. Two wrongs don't make a right – they make us even.

I steamroller down the hallway, creating a tailwind as I go. I stop outside his door. Do I really want to do this? Yes, yes I do. The other night on the terrace, I felt something and I've never been wrong before. He wants it too.

I knock on the door.

I don't look great, but my teeth are clean.

He opens the door. 'Hey, Lex. You OK? Am I late for Group?' Brady's wearing Abercrombie and Fitch sweats and a wife-beater. 'I can't find my Lakers cap anywhere. Have you seen it?'

'No. Can I come in?'

'Sure. It's a bit trashed. Lemme just do a sweep for dirty underwear.' Well, if he cares enough about that, he obviously cares what I think. 'I think we're good, come in.'

I slink into his room. I follow him closely. The room smells boyish, musky.

'What's up?' he says.

I stay close. I'm right under his nose. 'I just needed to know,' I say. 'The other night?'

He looks sheepish. I move closer, so our hips are almost touching. He still does nothing. I reach up and cup his cheek with my hand. He swallows, but doesn't move. Christ, he's making this harder than it needs to be. I instigate. I press my lips to his and for a moment he freezes like a statue and then he comes to life. He grabs my head and sucks me into a vortex of a kiss. It's powerful, stronger than I thought it would be.

Just when I start to purr, he stops.

'Lexi, I can't.' He pulls away.

I blink. 'What? Why not?'

'I . . . I just can't.'

Well, this is awkward. 'Oh. OK. I thought I . . . I felt something the other night and . . . you know what? I'm sorry . . .'

He at least has the good grace to look mortified. He gives me a squeeze on the arm and very gently plants a kiss on my forehead. 'Lexi, it's not you . . .'

I frown. 'You're gay? Cos that's cool . . .'

'No! I'm not gay. I'm a sex addict.'

I was not expecting that. 'What? Are you kidding?'

He drops down on the edge of his bed. 'No. I wish I were. I did tell you there wasn't a drug I hadn't got into.'

I sit next to him, close. 'Brady, I'm not sure sex is a drug. You can't get addicted to sexahol.' I can see the outline of his semi through his joggers. 'And if you're a sex addict, I'm more than happy to help you out with that.' I put a hand on his thigh, but he stands brushing it off.

'Lexi, stop. I'm not kidding. I'm in recovery. Abstinence is abstinence. You can get addicted to anything that reinforces a pattern of behaviour.'

I let it sink in. 'So . . . *no* sex?'

'Not right now, no.'

'Wow. Can you have a wank?'

He laughs and, damn him, it's sexy as hell. 'Nope. Could you just have a "little bit" of heroin and stay clean?' I don't tell him how much I would *love* a little bit of heroin. 'It's all-or-nothing with me. I've done "all" and it didn't end well.' He pauses. 'It didn't end well at all.'

What does *that* mean? He's obviously not going to share further. Awkward silence fills the room like a gas. 'This is *really* embarrassing,' I say, getting up off the bed.

'No. It's not, if we don't let it be.'

'Can we just pretend this never happened?' I start to back out of the room. 'I guess I was imagining things.' I collide with the door, erasing the last shred of dignity I had.

Brady follows me and takes my hand, gently pulling me back. 'Lexi, wait. We're cool and you're not imagining things. I wanted to kiss you on the terrace. I want to kiss you now. I've wanted to kiss you since the second I saw you.' My heart swells. I thought I was coming up here because I was pissed at Kurt, but . . . I like what he's saying. 'But I can't. I really can't.'

I'm not ready for how disappointed I feel. It's like a slap. I don't know what to think. 'It's fine,' I say. 'And don't worry – I won't say anything. About anything.'

'It's cool. The others – except Saif – know about my sex addiction from Group before you arrived.'

Huh. I'm irrationally *furious* at Kendall and Ruby for saying nothing, but it's not like I've mentioned my feelings for Brady, so . . . wait, I have *feelings* for Brady? I'm actually shocked at the notion strolling into my head so casually.

'Give me a sec to get changed and we can walk to Group together.'

I wait in the corridor and I'm shaky. The adrenaline, no longer needed, rattles my bones. Nothing is making sense. I feel almost *relieved* he rejected me. Not because I don't want him, but because I *really* do.

And that's problematic.

'It's never one thing,' Brady says in Group. I wonder if he feels the need to explain himself after what just happened. 'You know, I'd go sober for a while ... say that I won't do it again, but then – just when you let your guard down – you hit the Fuck-It Button. You tell yourself, "oh, it's so-and-so's birthday and it's just this one last time".'

Rain pelts against the windows.

'You have it all to look forward to: the ritual. You kind of plan it out ... you'll have some drinks, some party, some dope, some girl. You're high so you tell yourself it was this magical special night and you've fallen in love. It's all the same chemicals in your head. You go for more drinks; you do another line. Because I was always drunk or high when I met a girl, I couldn't ever tell the difference between love and drugs, if there even is one. It's all euphoria, right? Totally co-dependent for a few intense weeks and then we'd break up – screaming rows, throwing shit, slapping, biting, spitting. I'd get out and get sober. Tell myself never again, ready for it to start all over.'

Sasha is curled into a knot of arms and legs in an armchair. 'It ain't the drugs. It's you.'

'Exactly.'

They're right. I know they're right, but it's an exhausting thought. It means admitting I haven't even started. There's no dope in my body any more, but what if that's not – never was – the issue?

Sasha smiles cruelly. 'How stylishly broken we all are.'

Dr Ahmed steps in. 'Sasha. It's not your turn. Brady?' she says. 'You done?'

'Sure.'

'It's lovely, isn't it?' Sasha continues. 'That we have such time and privilege to sit around having a cry-wank about our issues. Just using tears as lube.'

'Sasha, that's enough!'

'Gross!' Kendall adds.

I stifle a giggle behind my hand. C'mon, the lube thing was funny.

'But it's true. Most people don't have the time to get fucked up all day because they gotta go to work and make ends. Or if they do, they end up covered in piss and shit in a doorway, sleeping under cardboard boxes.'

Dr Ahmed opens her mouth to speak, but Goldstein holds up a hand. 'Sasha. *If* you can stay calm, I think this is a valid discussion.'

Now she's being taken seriously, she shrinks a little. 'I'm just sayin'. It's bullshit that we can all sit in a mansion talking about our adorable flaws because we got money.'

'You don't got money,' Ruby chips in.

'That was uncalled for,' says Guy next to her.

Sasha laughs and tugs up her sleeves to reveal her collage of scars. 'Well, aren't I the lucky one?'

Brady speaks again. 'I hear what you're saying, Sasha. Inequality sucks. But to be real, I don't think depression or anxiety or bipolar or OCD or whatever else we've got going on . . . I don't think those things give two shits about how much money we have.'

Goldstein grins. 'And there we hit the nail on the head.'

I don't think it's that simple. It never is. OK, maybe I am fucked up. Maybe what I was doing back in London was fucked up. I don't think sticking on a label, calling it a sickness, *diagnosing* me, is going to help.

It's not going to fix me.

It's not going to fix what I did.

It won't bring Antonella back.

STEP 5:
I ACCEPT I AM NOT
A BAD PERSON

I remember the day I first met Antonella. It was Second Form at St Agnes. On the first day back after the summer vacation, we had a year-group assembly. That August, we'd been on our final holiday as a family to Antigua. I know now it was a last-ditch attempt to hold the marriage together. It didn't work.

I was excited to be back at school. After four weeks of palm trees, glorious sunshine and white sands I was dying to see Nevada and Genie. We excitedly caught up on boyband gossip. Luka from *Stand As 1* was seeing some skanky backing dancer and we plotted her violent death. We *were* twelve.

St Agnes is a little Hogwarts, tucked away in the heart of Kensington – not far from the Natural History Museum and the V&A. It's the same sort of red-brick building on a much smaller scale, hidden from prying eyes by a high wall topped with spikes. A private garden called The Green and a busy road separate St Agnes ladies from the gentlemen of St Barnabas.

Assembly was held in the chapel, and it smelled of church – a lingering scent of myrrh and crusty Bibles wafting through the pews and stone columns.

'Ladies . . .' said Ms Grafton. Over the summer she'd had a haircut, but the bob didn't suit her – too much like a Lego woman. 'Today we welcome a new girl to St Agnes. I just know you'll all do your very best to make her feel welcome. It's never easy starting somewhere new, is it? Come on up, Antonella.'

The new girl was *gorgeous*. Not in a generic, pretty Insta-Girl way, more like a renaissance painting in the Louvre or an Italian screen siren. Her black hair was dead straight and parted in the middle – in stark defiance of the rest of us, who were still very much into big, tonged waves. Her eyebrows were seemingly un-tweezed – unthinkable – but she looked straight out of *Vogue*. She was much hipper than us, and I knew at once I wanted to be her friend.

Despite Grafton's words about how hard it is starting a new school, she didn't look like she had a single fuck to give. She joined Grafton on the stage, her uniform new and immaculate. 'Hello,' she smiled and gave a coy wave, her hand twitching at her hip. She was coolly confident without being a dick. 'I'm Antonella Hemmings. I just moved here from Zurich. My dad is an ambassador.'

That explained the cool – she must have been to some awesome places, collecting all the best bits from each culture as she went.

'Alexandria?' Grafton addressed me. 'As you're Head of Year, you'll be in charge of showing her around.'

'Of course,' I said, still so keen to please, so eager for empty praise. Antonella came and sat between Nevada and I. 'Hi, I'm Lexi. Welcome to St Agnes.'

'Thanks,' she said. 'God, sorry you're lumbered with me. I swear I won't follow you around like a lost sheep.'

I grinned back. 'You say that now . . . this place is a labyrinth.'

'I'll get the hang of it. I like your earrings. Are they Tiffany?'

And just like that, we were best friends.

The rain has eased off. In fact, from the terrace, I can see black clouds carrying it out to sea like a sky armada. And yes, it smells of Basic.

Kendall and I have a cigarette while Saif, Guy and Brady throw a rugby ball around on the wet grass. At the other end of the lawn, Sasha sits by herself in an old swing tied to a sturdy oak. I think she's probably doing it to psych me out, but I swear she's staring at me. She isn't even swinging, just watching.

With a war cry, Saif tackles Brady and they both slide through the mud. 'Dude, I look like I shit myself!' Brady shouts. Saif can hardly breathe for laughing. Mud really does cake his arse. It's still a lovely bum. I crease up again inside, remembering the shame-a-thon in his room. I stub out my cigarette.

'You like him, don't you?' Kendall says. 'Brady.'

I give her a withering look. High school gossip is not my fave. 'Really?'

'Lexi, what else are we going to talk about? How many days clean are we?'

'Valid. What do you want me to say? That he's gorgeous? He is. That he's lovely? He's that too. Oh, but wait . . . what's that? *He's* a recovering sex addict and *I* have a boyfriend.'

Her eyes widen. 'You have a BF? You never said, you shady bitch.'

'I do. God, give me another fag if we're gonna have a big bloody chat. Yes, I have a boyfriend. His name is Kurt. I'm sure if you could read Goldstein's notes he'd tell you it's not massively healthy. I don't know.' I take a deep drag. Then another.

'Don't know what?'

'This. Being here. It's like my life got snapped off into a right angle. It was all heading one way. I thought I knew *everything*. Now I'm not so sure. Of anything. It's not like I planned on being here.'

'I hear that. Where do you think you were headed? The doctor told me I was going to die if I didn't eat. At one point I was just over six stone. I didn't care.'

'Do you care now?'

She finishes her cigarette. 'I'm happier than I was. I don't want to die. I just don't wanna eat. And don't change the subject. This is about you.'

I scratch my ratty hair. It needs a wash. 'I don't think I'd have died. It really wasn't as dramatic as it looked and I'm not a moron. This is going to sound insipid, but I didn't really see a future. Just Kurt. He was it.'

'OK, that's a little depressing.'

She's right. It is. 'I didn't realise how high I was. I was ten feet off the floor. Like a ghost . . . disconnected from everything, walking through walls.' I wave my cigarette around, brushing off the unease. 'Hey, will you do me a favour? Don't tell Brady I have a boyfriend. I know nothing can happen . . . but I don't know what's going on with either of them right now.'

Kendall's eyes blaze with scandal. 'I *knew* you liked him!'

When people say you're 'out of it' they mean it. I was. I'd checked out of life in London and now everything feels … well: I *feel*. Heroin is an anaesthetic, after all. I was pleasingly numb. Now, it's all tangible and I feel both the goods and the bads again. This Kurt and Brady stuff is somehow like a migraine and indigestion at the same time. Great.

It bothers me all the way into therapy the next morning. I pace around Goldstein's office like I have haemorrhoids and can't sit down.

'Like, it can't be that easy,' I tell him. 'I was miserable so I did a ton of heroin to numb the pain? As if. You can't walk down Oxford Street without seeing at least two hundred utterly miserable people and they aren't shooting up.'

Goldstein takes off his glasses and wipes the lenses with his tie. 'Addiction is never so simple. Are you going to sit?'

'No. I need the cardio. I mean, Sasha was right. What have I got to be miserable about? My life is …'

'Perfect in every way?'

I stop pacing. 'No.' I gesture with my arms, reminding him where we both are.

'Then what? Sickness – and I would stake my entire career on addiction being a sickness – doesn't care where you come from, Lexi. So your family is rich? So what? Do you think that makes you immune?'

I cross my arms, shielding myself from his words. 'I don't feel sick.'

'The first thing an addiction tells you is that you're not addicted. It sounds like your own voice, but it isn't. It's the addiction and it's how it takes control. You've been telling yourself there isn't a problem for how long now? Two years? Longer?'

I shrug.

'What's striking, Lexi, is how few emotions you seem able to identify or even recall. You can't tell me the last time you were happy . . . sad . . . excited. I think you used drugs so you didn't have to *feel* things.'

'That's not true. Love is an emotion. I loved . . . *love* . . . Kurt.'

'You allowed yourself one outlet, but that relationship is harmful. By persisting with it you harmed yourself and furthered your addiction.'

'Love hurts.' I think of Mummy and Daddy, and the ways they knew how to wound and scar each other better than anyone else ever could.

'No. I don't believe that. Love worth having shouldn't hurt, not ever.'

'Are you married?' I ask, feeling bold.

'Not any more. My own addiction problems saw to that.'

'What?' Now I do come and sit down on the sofa. This shit just got a lot more interesting.

'Oh yes. Much of my twenties and thirties were a spin cycle of drinking and sobriety. My wife did all she could until I comprehensively broke her down. She stayed with me for fifteen years, a good ten years more than most would have. When she left me, she says now, she did so because she couldn't bear the thought of witnessing my inevitable death.'

'Oh,' I say. 'Did you have kids?'

'Yes. A little girl. Well, she's not so little any more. I see her sporadically. I . . . we felt . . . it was better for me to be away when she was young. I was still drinking. She has a stepfather she loves very much.'

That's gotta sting. 'Is that why you're out here in the middle of nowhere? In case you relapse?'

'No. Not really. I was a doctor before. I realised in time, with the experiences I'd had, I was more use here than I was in dermatology.'

I laugh politely, humouring him. Now he says it, it makes sense. He always seemed to be on my level, never above me, talking down. We're all junkies on this island.

'As much as I admire how you steered the conversation away from yourself, let's get back to you, shall we?'

I grin. 'If we must.'

'Let's talk about anger. Anger isn't an emotion,' he says. 'It's a reaction to stimuli. When we first met, Lexi, all I got was anger. How about now?'

'I'm not angry now.' I take a couple of seconds to realise that this is true and it feels quite nice. 'Now I don't know how to feel. I feel . . . nothing. And everything. Like I'm back at the beginning, or something.' Restore factory settings. Without London, without Kurt, without context, I'm nothing. I feel like one of those naked, bedraggled Barbie dolls you find in 50p boxes outside charity shops.

'What makes you happy . . . other than drugs or Kurt?'

Well, there go the top two options. Brady, as close as he was yesterday, fills my head. I push the image aside and hope Goldstein isn't psychic. I don't trust my feelings for Brady any more than I trust my feelings for heroin. I'm bored and I'm lonely. It figures I'd fixate on the hottest guy in close proximity. 'I like being with the horses.' That is not a lie.

'Good!' Goldstein actually claps, just once. 'There's actually a wealth of research to suggest simply being in nature is good for one's state of mind. I encourage it.'

I nod.

'Lexi,' he says. 'Beyond anger, you seem to have a strong sense of guilt. To welcome it, almost. And I don't see the point in you feeling guilty for your upbringing. You still deserve to be well, you still deserve to be happy.'

I look into his eyes. There it is. It slithers in my gut like a serpent in tar. I am. I am guilty. I don't deserve good things.

Because, and I think I've always known this, I'm no good.

I spend the afternoon at the stables as has become my new regime. Feeble spring sunshine is giving it like thirty per cent, but still trying to break through. I busy myself, helping Elaine with Patty and an injured mare called Tia before turning my attention to Storm. 'Do you want to see my bruise?' Elaine says. She rolls up her trouser leg to reveal an almost perfect hoof print. It's a painful purple and yellow.

'Oh god. Did Storm do that?'

'Yes. And he wasn't even trying. Oh Lexi, what am I going to do with him?'

He seems calm enough now, greedily eating out of a nosebag at the side of the paddock.

'I've been trying.'

She doesn't seem to hear me, her forehead creased. 'I know an organisation that frees horses to be wild in the New Forest. Maybe that'd be the kindest thing to do. Just let him go.'

I look Storm in the eye and wonder if he can, on some horse level, understand. I place a hand on his flank. I can feel his heartbeat. 'Don't give up on him.' The words catch in my throat, for some reason. Maybe it's because I'm still on my period. 'Let me try.'

'Are you OK?' Elaine asks.

I swallow whatever it is back. 'Yes. I just think . . . the other day it felt like I was getting somewhere with him.'

Elaine rests her head against Storm's and he permits the closeness. 'It's so funny, isn't it? How animals make us more human.'

Storm's eyes are black, lashes enviably long. I look deep into them. Silently, I make him a promise. I won't give up on him if he won't give up on me.

I wait for Elaine to head off to Patty's stall before I give Storm a firm talking to.

'You heard her, right? Is that what you want? To be sent away, to be wild? It's cool if you do, I guess. Maybe I'm transferring or whatever, but I'm not ready to give up just yet, OK? So here's what we're going to do. I'm going to mount you. I know. Shocker. Please don't throw me.'

God, it's like *Buckaroo*. I vault over the paddock fence and *very* gingerly start to tack him up. He takes the saddle and headstall with no fuss, but he won't tolerate a bit in his mouth. He snorts, paces back and forth. I step well back, having no desire to get a bruise to match Elaine's. He'll take a carrot, but stubbornly refuses the bit again.

I must be mental, but I can mount him without a bit. I can attach the reins to his headstall. It's practically suicide if he kicks off. I won't be able to stop him, like getting in a car with no brakes.

I steer him into the training pen. If I come off, at least I'm guaranteed a soft-ish landing.

'Are you listening, Storm? I'm going to get on now. We don't have to go anywhere or do anything. We just have to *be*. Does that sound like a plan? You ready?'

When he doesn't kick off, I place a foot in the stirrup. I count to three and boost myself up, swinging my left leg over Storm. I land in the saddle.

Storm doesn't like it. Not one bit. He reverses and threatens to rear, his head tossing back and forth.

I cling to the reins. Maybe I should just get off.

No. I'm not scared of him. He might look big and scary, but he's just a horse. 'Oi!' I say. 'Stop being a little cunt! I'm just

204

sitting on you, you twat. I'm trying to help you!' I rub his crest. 'It's just me. It's just me.'

He calms down. He stops and tries to style his little tantrum out, looking moodily into the middle distance like Edward Cullen or something.

'See? That's not so hard, is it? Here we are. You and me.' Tears suddenly sting my eyes and I don't know why.

I play it down to Storm, but maybe it's harder than it sounds. Perhaps the hardest thing of all is just *being*.

I remember Mummy's 'spiritual phase' of three years ago. She hired some charlatan called Guru Rachel as her life coach. Rachel – a sinewy, blonde, yogic husk – kept repeating this 'all life is suffering' mantra, which I always thought was pretty bleak. I wonder if this is what she meant: just being alive is dying a minute at a time, and we have to make peace with that.

I don't ride him, I don't try to make him do *anything*. Birds, like a hundred birds, chatter as they dip and dive overhead. I strain to hear the sea over their racket. We just exist together, still. For now, that feels like progress.

Everyone loved Antonella Hemmings.

Not because she was cool, although she was, but because she was delightful and kind.

'You girls did all this?' I remember Grafton's slack jaw. The hall, and St Agnes has a *huge* hall, was almost stacked to the ceiling with boxes. Most of them contained tinned goods, but some also held nappies, sanitary products, shampoo, soap, scarves and gloves. All were destined for refugee camps in Calais. Grafton smoothed back her dyed auburn beehive. 'I can hardly believe my eyes. Lexi, Antonella, Nevada . . . this is just wonderful.'

'It was all Antonella's idea,' Nevada offered giddily. It's odd, on reflection, that we never called her Toni, Ant or Nels. Everyone else had a nickname, but never Antonella. I sometimes called her 'Hems' and she hated it. Every syllable is meant to be savoured like a delicious Italian aperitif.

Antonella, as ever, shook it off. Not false modesty: modesty. 'I was just the first to *suggest* it. Total team effort.'

'Well, I must say, I'm very impressed, not to mention touched, at your selflessness, girls. And the fact you've organised everything with only minimal help from your teachers is even more impressive. Good on you, ladies. Good. On. You.'

I lizard-basked in her praise, wholly undeserving of it. Sure, I got Daddy to send a truck load of food from the hotel, but it was all Antonella. Like everyone else, I'd seen the sad, ashen faces of those kids living in shithole campsites – while politicians and journalists discussed their fate over negronis at Soho House – and thought, *wow, that's bad, poor people.* If it hadn't been for Antonella throwing herself into organising the food drive, my mental and moral exertion would have ended right there.

Antonella made things happen. She made you believe it could work. 'We should do something,' she said quite unexpectedly as we were having a picnic in Regent's Park. She was leafing through that day's *Metro* as I braided Genie's hair.

'Tonight?' I said. 'I thought we were going to the cinema with those St Barney's boys?'

She rolled her eyes at me and held up the front page. A crying child, looking for his mum, clutching the ubiquitous limp, dirty teddy bear. 'No, silly. We should do something *to help*. These people have risked life and limb, fleeing war and despots and fascists and rapists, and we're making them live in what is essentially a shanty town by a railway because bigots don't want a few extra children in their dreary towns. It's bullshit. We should help.'

'Help how?' Nevada said, popping a grape in her mouth.

'Well,' she replied, 'we could either do a crowd-funding thing for a charity, or we could do a massive food drive at school? Just think, if every girl brought like five tins of soup, we'd have . . .'

'Two thousand tins of soup,' I said.

'And that's a lot of soup.'

'Do refugees even like soup?' Genie asked, because she isn't very bright, bless her.

'It's not just soup,' Antonella explained, not a hint of mockery in her voice. I'd have told Genie she was being thick, but not

207

Antonella. 'They need warm clothing, toys, books . . . anything really.'

'OK,' I said. 'What do we do with all the stuff once it's at the school?'

'OMG!' Nevada said. 'You know that TV presenter? Dawn thingy? She's been sending trucks over from London. I bet if we tweet her, we could arrange a truck to collect the stuff.'

'And the teachers would totally go for it because it's good citizenship . . . and more importantly, it makes the school look awesome.'

And thus a plan was hatched.

Just because she did nice stuff, she wasn't Sister Antonella of the Sacred Tedium, make no mistake. She was a riot. She called it 'minxing'. 'Lex? Are we minxing tonight?'

Even at fourteen we could easily pass for eighteen. Daddy preferred us to hang out in one of the hotels where someone could keep an eye on us, but determined teenage girls will always find a way to test the electric fences. It's like chaos theory. Probably.

One night I got absolutely spannered on Jägerbombs at Shadow Lounge. Antonella's big brother is gay and was hanging out there with some mates. I wasn't used to drinking in the way that Antonella was. Sure, I'm Russian, and vodka is The Way, but Antonella had been gently sipping red wine and grappa on vineyard terraces at twilight her whole life. Like any good friend, she held back my hair as I nostril-puked, legs poking out of the toilet cubicle. Even once my stomach felt hollowed out, I was still in no fit state to go home.

'Daddy will kill me. I told him we were seeing *Mamma Mia*.'

'Come on,' Antonella said, her Jägerbombs apparently not touching the sides. 'Follow me.'

We left the club and she propped me up all the way down a thrumming Old Compton Street, dodging bears, drag queens and kamikaze rickshaw drivers. It was almost midnight, but somehow she knew where to go. We turned on to Frith Street, avoiding a manic G-A-Y promoter thrusting wristbands in our faces. 'How have you never been to Bar Italia?' she said, catching me as I tumbled off a heel. Christ, we wore some skanky jailbait stuff when we were kids. 'It's open until five a.m. every night.'

We darted over the road, a black cab honking at us. Bar Italia was long and thin, with a coffee bar on the right and a narrow row of stools all the way down the left wall. It was crowded, but not too crowded. We wove through snogging couples and loud Italians to get to the very back. Antonella put me on a stool and returned a couple of seconds later carrying a second for her to sit on. 'Ciao!' she called to the cute guy behind the counter. 'Due espressi doppie mio amico!' The waiter called something back with a broad, and very minxy, grin. 'Sei piuttosto carino troppo!' she replied.

'What are you saying?' I slurred. I was starting to get floor-spin, sobering up.

'He says the espressos are free because we're cute. I told him he was cute too.'

He brought the espressos over and I took a gulp. 'Holy crap, that's strong!' I gasped. It was so hot I think it stripped the top layer of my tongue clean off.

'You're supposed to sip it, Lex! God, you're so not Italian!'

We laughed. Antonella and I sat, people-watched, and sipped bitter espresso until I was so sober my legs quivered with caffeine and I was ready to go home.

Since arriving at Clarity, I've been slumming it: ignoring make-up and grooming completely. For whatever reason – or because I know Brady will be at Group – I put on a little kohl, mascara and Chanel lip stain. I rarely see Brady at breakfast – he works out in the morning so he eats early, or 'juices'. When did we allow *that* to become a verb?

I have a one-on-one with Goldstein first, of course. He toothpicks more into my time at school.

'Have you thought about resuming your education?'

'Not really.'

'But what about your future?'

'My father owns twelve international hotels. The future is New York, or Singapore, or Beijing, or Cape Town . . . shall I go on?'

'But what will you do?'

I waft a hand lacily. I'm in that sort of mood. 'Shop.'

He smiles. If I squint, he looks like Aslan. 'I don't believe you mean that, and neither do you.'

'I wouldn't be the first heiress to travel, eat, shop, drink and party. There's a different charity benefit seven nights a week if you're feeling humanitarian.'

'What happens when fun stops being fun?'

I say nothing. He's got me there.

'You're worth *more* than your inheritance, Lexi. Can't you see that?'

I can feel tears burn, but I divert it into a bitter laugh. 'Well, that's lovely. Can I put it on a cushion?'

Sadness dims his gaze. 'You can do whatever you like with it.'

Before Group, I have a fag and think about Siddhartha. The prince who would eventually become the Buddha. Guru Rachel told me all about him. He grew up in a palace with bling and privilege. So sheltered was he that he didn't even know about illness or ageing, until he escaped beyond the gates. Once he saw suffering, he rejected his royal name and dedicated his life to poverty, spirituality and the quest for Nirvana.

Is that what Goldstein wants? For me to cast off the Volkov name? The money? Get a nice job in PR, do Hot Yoga and get Deliveroo on a Friday night with some nice Netflix David until I die? That . . . that is utterly terrifying to me.

It's like a multiple choice: Why did Lexi end up in rehab off her tits on heroin?

a) Her shit parents neglected her.

b) She was sad. Boo hoo.

c) She was bored and already had everything else except an addiction.

d) She hated herself because of a, b and c.

Or, of course . . .

e) All of the above.

It's all of the above, and then some. I'm so fucking sick of thinking about 'Lexi'. I'm starting to break away from myself and become a concept. #ProjectLexi. I'm bored of me. I have cabin fever in my own skull.

'Lexi!' It's Ruby, calling from inside. 'Hurry up! We're starting!'

'Coming!' I stub out what's left of my cigarette and slouch through the patio doors. This is the first time I'll see Brady today and I suddenly wish I had a mint. I should be able to get some from somewhere, right?

'Oh, there you are,' Dr Ahmed says, hovering in the doorway. 'Is Saif out there with you?'

Despite being all alone on the terrace I look over my shoulder like a twat. 'No. Just me.'

'For crying out loud. Will you go give him a knock?'

I sigh, but I nod. I drift down the long corridor to the entrance hall, across reception, brushing my fingers among the leaves of the potted palms. I'm dawdling, avoiding as much dreary therapy-time as I can. They can wait. In fact . . .

I remember I have gum in my bag and dart into my room, giving Saif a knock as I pass. 'Saif! It's time for Group!' I shout, popping gum in my mouth and shutting my door.

I go back to Saif's room and knock again. 'Saif! Are you taking a dump, or what?'

That reminds me that you shouldn't eat too much sugar-free gum because it contains xylitol and that's a laxative.

'Saif? Are you in there?'

It's silent beyond the door. I can hear the light bulbs in the hall buzzing.

It's weird, isn't it, that thing where you just *know* something's wrong. Sixth sense. I think back to breakfast. People coming and going . . . but no Saif.

'Saif?'

We aren't allowed keys to our rooms, obviously. I put my hand on the door handle. If he's having a wank or something . . . well I don't think he's my biggest fan anyway. 'Saif? I'm coming in, yeah?'

I press down on the handle.

His room is identical to mine, but smells like boy. Trainers and deodorant and testosterone musk. I take two steps into the suite.

My heart clambers up my throat.

And then it falls all the way down.

Because you're never wrong when you want to be.

He's on the bed in his boxers, duvet bunched around him like tissue paper.

His grey fingers are still wrapped around the needle in his thigh.

At first I freeze. I just stand there.

He's definitely dead. He's staring at the ceiling with cloudy fish eyes. His lips are blue.

Is that what I looked like in the hotel suite?

I knew he'd smuggled shit in and didn't tell anyone.

Some emergency protocol kicks in. *You must get help now.* I collide with the door to his suite before backing into the corridor.

But then something overrides my emergency protocol. A voice that sounds a lot more like me. *Get his stash first, moron.*

Before I know it I'm beside his body, scanning. Sure enough there's a silk pocket the exact same shade as his 'sister's' hijab. I pick it up and rummage through with my fingers. Blow, gear and some little bottles of what I assume must be growth hormone or steroids or some shit. Saif had no intention of getting clean.

Maybe I could just take the coke?

Yeah, I'll take the coke and leave the junk. Easy.

A new voice interrupts. This one also sounds like me. *What the fucking fuck are you doing, you fucking ghoul?*

'Lex? Saif? What are you doing?' It's Kendall. She must have been sent for both of us.

She sounds close. Without thinking, I stuff Saif's entire stash in the front of my knickers. I don't know what I'm doing. I do it anyway.

'Lex?'

'Don't come in!' I cry. I turn and crash into her as she arrives at the threshold to his room. 'Get an ambulance!'

'What?'

'I think he . . .'

She pushes her way around me. She reacts like a normal human would. She cries out, covering her mouth with both hands. She tumbles into me.

'Help!' I cry to no one in particular. 'Saif needs help!' I know he's well beyond help. 'Help us!'

The receptionist appears at the end of the corridor. 'What's wrong?'

'He overdosed! Saif! He overdosed!'

The poor receptionist's face changes shade, from St Tropez to living dead in a split second as she sees I'm not kidding. She launches herself at the phone and activates the nurse bell. I take Kendall's hand and drag her out of the room, down the hall, away from the body.

Goldstein and Ahmed appear in reception along with Scouse Gary. 'Saif's dead!' Kendall screams. 'He's dead.'

The doctors and Gary push past me and Kendall towards Saif. I feel dizzy. I feel the ground vibrate as they charge.

'What?' says Guy. The others are filing into the hall now, their faces pale. 'Are you serious?'

'He's dead!' Kendall repeats. 'There's a needle sticking out of his leg!' Kendall crumbles entirely, flopping into Guy's arms, inconsolable.

I look to Ruby and she shakes her head. 'Kendall, let's get you some water or something. C'mon.' Ruby steers Kendall and Guy towards the dining room.

I sort of black out for a second. Suddenly Brady is holding me up by the arms. 'Lexi? Are you OK?'

I shake my head. The pieces are falling into place. If they catch me with drugs, they'll think I'm using again – or, even worse, that I gave them to Saif. I don't know what to do. Brady seems so solid. I don't have much choice. I pretend to hug him. I whisper into his ear. 'Brady, I took drugs off his bed. I don't know why.'

He hugs me tighter. 'Give them to me.'

'Brady, I can't . . .'

'I haven't been in his room. They might search you, they won't search me. Where are they?'

'In my pants. I know. I don't know what I was thinking. It's fucked up.' I look up into his eyes.

'Hand them over. I'll flush it.'

By now, the entourage is halfway down the corridor, Ruby demanding to know what's going on. Kendall is now in floods of tears in Guy's arms. Checking no one's watching, I thrust my hand into my underwear and retrieve the sachet. In one fluid movement, Brady stuffs it into his own crotch. 'It's OK,' he says. 'It's OK. You found him?'

I nod.

'And he's definitely . . .?'

'Yeah.'

'Oh, man. Fuck. Fuck this shit.'

This time I hug him for real. I feel his hand on the back of my head, stroking my hair. I'm glad I don't have the drugs.

Now it hits: Saif is dead.

How? He was just here last night. Like there was no . . . warning. No sign. No breadcrumbs or clues. No final words.

I suppose, in real life, there never is.

And I know this shouldn't be about me, but I can't help it. I'm glad it wasn't me. It could have been. It almost was.

A movement in the corner of my eye catches my attention. Her white eyes blaze through the darkness at the end of the corridor; Sasha melts back into the Group room.

Shit. I don't know what she saw.

Shit.

While Ahmed waits with the body – with *Saif* – Goldstein takes control and I am grateful. It feels like nothing bad can happen with him around. Father figure/Daddy issues.

For the first time since I got here, he raises his voice. 'Into Group NOW!'

We're kettled in the room, Ruby and Guy's questions ignored. Kendall is hysterical. Hardly aware I'm doing it, I shove my fingers in my ears, blocking it all out.

Goldstein returns to Saif's room and leaves us under the watchful eye of Gary, who quickly agrees it's probably for the best if the smokers are allowed to smoke for the sake of everyone's sanity. On the terrace, I smoke with Guy and Kendall, her fingers shaking. Brady goes to use the loo and, I guess, flush Saif's stash.

The din dies down, replaced by a bulging silence. I'm not sure which I like less. I'm waiting for an ambulance to come caterwauling up the drive, but I realise it's not gonna happen. We're on an island. There's no A&E. Goldstein and Ahmed are it. Are either of them even medical doctors? Goldstein was a *skin* doctor, what's he gonna do . . . take a look at his eczema? I look to the patchy white sky and squint for a helicopter – I suppose that's what'd happen if . . . well, if there was anything they could do to save him.

'Do you think he did it on purpose?' Sasha asks suddenly. She's reclining on a sunlounger wearing sunglasses, her hands a pillow behind her head.

'Jesus,' Ruby says.

'Plenty of people OD on purpose,' says Sasha matter-of-factly. 'He sucked Kendall off, right?' How does she even know that? She seems to know *everything*. 'Maybe he couldn't deal with the gay Muslim shame of it.'

'I swear to god,' I say through my teeth, 'Sasha, either shut up or I will knock you the fuck out.'

'And I ain't gonna lift a finger to stop her,' Ruby adds.

Sasha laughs. 'I'm actually quite tempted to see the pair of you try, but I'm sorry Kendall, that was some shade. My tongue got loose from my brain and set out to cause mad mischief. She's a cunt, that tongue of mine.' She holds her hands up in surrender. 'Kendall. I'm sorry. Here . . . bite me. I deserve it.' She holds out a chopping board arm.

'I'm not going to bite you. That was an awful thing to say.'

'That's why I said it. You know me by now.' She reclines once more. 'Tell you what though, Blondie, we got a saying on the estate where I come from: It's "you wouldn't trust a junkie with your granny's handbag".'

'What's that suppose to . . .'

Brady.

How long have we been out here? Ten minutes? Fifteen? More?

Time aplenty to flush that stash.

Like two baggies and a wrap . . . and the little vials. Shouldn't take long.

It's like Guy read my mind. 'Where's Brady? He's been ages.'

Sasha smiles like a psycho.

No! No, he wouldn't. Brady is so . . . together.

But then again, *I'm* pretty together when I'm sober and I just took a load of gear off a corpse, so . . .

Bollocks.

I throw my cigarette out on to the lawn and turn back to the house. 'Where are you going, pet?' Gary asks. 'You need to stay together, doctor's orders.'

Oh, for crying out loud. 'I just need the loo. I'll be two minutes.'

Gary steps aside and I hurry along the bottom corridor until I reach the entrance hall and then I dash upstairs, straight to Brady's room. I hammer on the door. 'Brady? Brady, are you in there?' I knock again. Oh Jesus, what if it was a bad batch? He wouldn't, would he? I can't do this twice in one day, but I'll have to. I push down on the handle and this time, I *pray* I'm wrong. 'Brady?'

The room is trashed, but empty. Brady and the stash aren't here. So where is he? I run to his bedroom window and look out over the front lawn. I don't see him. Think, think. He wouldn't do a whole bunch of drugs in the middle of a rehab centre, so . . . I look towards the forest. It's not a big island, but it's a crumpled one with infinite nooks and crannies.

Which Step is accepting responsibility? I gave Brady – a recovering addict – a load of coke and heroin. This is so, *so* my fault.

Antonella.

No. That was different.

How?

Shit. I have to find him.

I hear something. A helicopter – in the distance but getting louder. This is it. Everyone is bound to be looking the other way.

I'll be faster on horseback. I slip out of the building without being seen and pelt through the woods. I tumble out of the overgrown pathway that leads to the stables and mess up my footing. I sort of flop to the gravel track, my left knee taking all the impact. Pain shoots all the way up my leg and through my spine. My tights rip and I see I've skinned it – mud mixing with red blood. Shit. I hope it's not as bad as it looks.

Now I limp towards the stables. 'Elaine?' I call, but there's no reply. Probably for the best. I go toward Patty's stable but see the doors are open and on the hook. Well that explains where Elaine is.

Of course, there's always Storm. He'd be way faster than Patty.

Yes, but he'd also probably kill you.

Well, that's true of so many things in my life. Never been an issue before. *Wow, maybe I do have a death-wish.* I'll save it for the next session. I go to Storm's stable and unlatch the doors. 'Hi, boy, how are you today? We're gonna try something, OK?'

He seems pretty pleased to see me. I give him some love, stroking his flanks to butter him up. 'We're gonna try a little hack. You up for it?'

He tosses his head a bit and I lose patience. I haven't got time for his shit today. 'Enough! We're going for a ride, just deal with it, you giant manbaby. Remember Brady? He needs us, so you can't dick about. Got it?'

In record speed, I tack him up, taking absolutely zero per cent of his shit. This time he, albeit reluctantly, takes a bit in his gob. By the time I'm finished, he almost looks sheepish. 'You ready?' I mount him. 'Come on, Storm, you got this. We got this. You're a fuck up, I'm a fuck up – we cancel out each other's crazy. Let's go.'

He needs only a gentle heel tap of encouragement and we're out the gates. It's like he's seen freedom and he's going for it. He lurches straight into a canter and I tug on the reins to remind him who's in charge. If we go too fast, we might miss Brady.

My brain is whirring. If I was going to do a whole bunch of drugs on a remote island, where would I go? Maybe the beach? It's as good a place as any to start, I figure. I steer Storm on to the beach path. It's soft – mossy and woodchip – underfoot, and he doesn't protest too much, following the path in an unsteady trot. 'You are doing *so* well,' I tell him.

Once we arrive at the seafront, I let Storm do what he really wants to do, and *run*. There's a long sandy ribbon in front of him and this is the nearest he's had to freedom in weeks, I'm betting. I kick off and we charge over the silt, salt air whipping through my hair. It's only now I realise I've forgotten a helmet. Still, I let him run, like a plane accelerating down a runway, his hooves mash up the damp sand.

All the while I cast my eyes across the beach and up into the hills for any sign of Brady. We gallop and gallop until we run out of beach – the cliffs stop it from running the whole perimeter of the island. All I can think to do now is head up into the forest and take the trails.

I'm turning Storm around when I see a silver sliver curling into the whitewashed sky. Smoke. It rises up out of the trees. 'Smoke signal,' I tell Storm, and wonder if Brady is either careless or *wants* to be found.

Wait . . . the Witch House. That funny little ruin in the middle of the forest has a fireplace. And it's *such* a good junkie hangout. That *has* to be it. 'Come on.'

We take it more cautiously back into the woods. There's no bridle path as such any more. Storm's strong legs pick through brambles, thorns and nettles. I wish we could gallop, but the terrain isn't right. The longer it takes . . . the worse he'll be.

Unless – and I hope this is true – I'm totally wrong, and he's with everyone else back at the house wondering where I've gone.

Wait.

Now I *smell* smoke and see the grey Witch House peeping through the trees.

I dismount and lead Storm the rest of the way. A path has been trodden to the little house. 'Brady?' I now say, keeping my voice calm and soothing. 'Is that you?'

I secure Storm to a gnarled stump thing and I take a breath, and then I go in.

He's not dead.

But he's not *good*.

He's . . . slimy. He's crying and he's snotty, squished in the corner of the dank bunker. The fire crackles politely in what was once a chimney, like any good boy scout's fire would. The stash is set out before him, orderly, the heroin, coke and steroids all in neat piles.

'Brady, what are you doing?' I keep my tone steady. I want to throw my arms around him and hold him tight. But I don't.

'What is wrong with me?' he sobs, dribbling a little. He's a mess.

'Did you take anything?' I ask.

'I did some coke.'

I kneel before him, keeping a distance. I wouldn't want to be crowded. 'Well . . . that's OK.'

His head falls back and he cries.

'It is!' I say. 'Goldstein is always saying it's not a test . . . we don't fail. It's a blip or whatever. Snakes *and* ladders, remember? Brady, it's my fault. I shouldn't have let you take this shit.'

'It isn't. It's not you. This one's all me. I thought I could do it. Just flush that shit down the toilet. But I couldn't. I was already telling myself I could do a little bump of coke. To prove I wasn't a junkie. How am I here again? Again? What is wrong with me?'

I sigh. 'Brady, this is because you're high or coming down or whatever.'

'No, it isn't! It's because I'm weak. I am *so weak*. I couldn't even be *near* drugs. What the fuck am I going to do? How am I meant to live in this world, Lexi? Where am I going to go?'

Well, he's got me there.

'Look at this. I snorted a dead guy's blow. I didn't even think about Saif. I just thought about me. It's always been me. I'm fucking rotten inside. There's dog shit where my heart should be.'

I shake my head. Very carefully, I reach for his hand. 'Brady . . . come on.' I do what I think Kendall, or Antonella, would do in this situation. Kind lies. 'You aren't – we're not – bad people.'

He laughs and more snot shoots out of his nostril. Sexy. 'You think?'

'You're *not* a bad person.'

'Lexi, yes I am. I'm worse. I'm worse than you know.'

'I doubt that so very highly, but it's not a contest.'

His blue eyes go arctic-clear for a second, drilling down into me. 'I killed someone, Lexi.'

The words ring in my ears and I swear my heart just stops for a second before rebooting.

'Are you serious?' Brady always made me feel so comfortable, so safe. Less so right now. I wrap my arms around myself.

'Why do you think I'm here? I hit rock bottom.'

I crawl closer and sit alongside him, my back against the wall. 'What happened?' I take his hand. 'Brady, it can't be any worse than what I've done.' I stop myself. 'I . . . I mean look at us *all*. We're all such damaged goods.'

'Lexi, I killed a woman.'

Oh.

OK.

I let go of his hand. Should I be getting the fuck away from him? No one knows where we are. I wonder how fast I could mount Storm if I needed to. 'Brady, you're freaking me out. Tell me what happened.'

He takes a deep breath and wipes his nose on a sleeve of his Yankees hoodie. 'Only Goldstein knows this, OK. None of the others. They can't know . . .'

'OK . . .'

He says nothing for a very long time. My heart, ironically, is going faster than if I'd done coke. Finally, he says something, staring at his fingers as he pulls a leaf apart. 'We were at a Vanity Fair party. I can't remember what it was for. Who am I kidding, I can't remember *it*. I was drinking. Champagne and vodka, and I think I had a hipflask of whiskey. It was in some house in the Hollywood Hills. I think it was Natalie Portman or Scarlet Johansson's place, or it used to be or something. Some Disney Channel girl blew me in the pool house and we did speedballs.'

Thanks for *that* image. I don't like how him and some Miley getting it on makes me feel. It's like hot knitting needles between my ribs and out my back.

'You know what it's like. You feel invincible. Untouchable. It was only a short drive back to our place.'

I can see where this is headed. 'Oh god. What happened?'

'I left with Venus and a couple of friends. The label had sent her a Range Rover, her new pride and joy. Anyway. We were cruising down Mulholland Drive, the stereo was really loud . . . Venus was playing us her new album. I was so out of it. I sort of passed out and the next thing I knew Venus was screaming at me. I was puking . . . puking everywhere, all over the car. Venus freaked out . . . she didn't want vomit all over the interior. She was so busy yelling at me, she wasn't watching the road. She didn't see the other car coming . . .'

'Oh god . . .'

'The driver had to swerve to avoid us and went off the road.' His head flops down and he smothers his face with his hands, sobbing harder.

I exhale. 'Brady, it was an *accident*. You weren't even driving. It's not a crime to throw up.'

He rests his head against the mossy wall, utterly dejected. 'No? It was Venus driving, sure, but it's my fault she wasn't paying attention. It's my fault.' He gives a hard little laugh. 'What happened next was really decent. When the cops came, they breathalysed Venus. She was sober, but more's the point: she was Venus Fucking Ardito. The cops were just thrilled to get a selfie with her.'

'For real?'

'For real. Their kids were her biggest fans. Officially, the other driver caused the crash. TMZ reported Venus had a near miss, and it made the papers, but she was never charged with anything.'

'Oh my god.'

'Her name was Dyanna Rodriguez. She was a make-up artist in the movies. She . . . she was a newlywed. I killed her. I should be dead. She should still be here. It's not fair.'

I pinch the bridge of my nose because I'm about to lose my chill.

I want to tell him. I want to tell him that I'm just as bad. That I'm worse.

But that's not what Brady needs to hear right now. I need to get him back into the house and make sure Goldstein doesn't see him like this. 'Nothing is fair,' I say. I sigh for a long time. 'We are living, breathing proof that nothing is fair. We need to get over it or it's going to kill us.'

'I don't think I can go on,' he says in a tiny voice. He means it.

Oh no. I shake my head. 'What? Then she died and you die too? What's the point? You're *here*, Brady. What are you going to do about it? We can get better. We can *be* better. God, take some of your reality TV money and do something *good* with it. Help somehow . . . support a drink driving campaign, I don't know.'

He looks up at me. 'Thank you.' We sort of crumple into an awkward hug, all angles and elbows. 'I don't know if I'm as strong as you,' he says.

'If that's true,' I say, 'we're all screwed.'

Our foreheads are resting together one second and the next we're kissing. This kiss is all fire and frenzy, all tongues and teeth. It's like we're both being pulled into a whirlpool, our edges blurring. Feeling the fire on the side of my face, he rolls on top of me. Just having him on top of me is divine. Our hands go crazy, grabbing and gripping at each other's bodies. I roll my hips open and feel his weight between my legs. That switch flips inside and I want him inside me, nothing else will do.

At the back of the carnival in my head, I identify a nagging little voice. And it's saying, *stop*. I know this isn't right. Is this Brady or coke? He's a sex addict. I'm pushing him further off the wagon.

Fuck. My. Life.

'Brady, stop.' I push his hand off my breast.

He looks so lost, so vulnerable. Brady's hurt is all in his eyes, there for everyone to see. I want to take the pain away. But I can't. Not like this.

'Sorry,' he says.

'Don't be,' I say as he rolls off.

He lays next to me and I nestle in the nook of his arm, resting my head on his chest. He's so warm. He smells so good. We catch our breath. The sex haze evaporates and we're left as two – relatively – sane people once more. 'I want you so bad,' he says, the words whispered through my hair. 'I want you so much it hurts, but I don't know if that's my heart speaking or my addictions.'

'I know,' I say, and I think I do know. I know what it's like to not trust yourself. To trust yourself least of all.

He strokes my hair. 'I think . . . I think I want to love you, Lexi. But I can't just *love* you, not without it destroying me. Or worse, you. I'm toxic. I can't hurt anybody else. I don't wanna hurt anyone else. The people closest to me suffer the most.'

Why is it that, sooner or later, everyone disappoints you? Everyone slips off their pedestal eventually. I sit up and look at him, faintly disgusted. 'Gotta say, I think the family of the woman who *died* suffered the most, Brady. Snap out of it – it's not all about you and your bullshit.'

He blinks like I've slapped him really hard around the head. I went too far. 'You're right. That was a dumb thing to say.'

'It happened,' I say, and I'm not sure if I'm talking to him or myself at this point. 'So, what next? Where do we go now? I'm sorry for snapping, but it's true.'

He says nothing for a second. 'It's OK,' he says. 'It needed saying. I was being a selfish prick. I think sometimes I get lost in my own corridors, y'know? But I don't know. I don't know where we go from here.'

'Neither do I.' I bury my face into his T-shirt and close my eyes.

We lay by the fire until we, and it, are all burned out.

I think about him, and Kurt, and Antonella.

I almost tell him, but hold my tongue. I can't say the words because then it would be real and I'll have to deal with it.

I'm a killer too.

STEP 6:
I WILL STRIVE TO BE
A BETTER PERSON

'We should head back,' I say when the fire is embers and the sky is dark like a bruise. 'We're gonna be in so much trouble. They must be looking for us.'

'Can't we just stay like this for ever?' This sad ruin is an apt home for two sad ruins.

I prop myself up onto an elbow. He looks and sounds like the real Brady again, but he's different now. I realise I was a little in awe of him before. We're more equal now.

I snuggle against him. Something inside me glows like the ashes. 'That would be nice, wouldn't it?'

Only then I remember long, lazy Sundays in bed with Kurt and almost spasm with guilt. I think I preferred it when I was numb inside.

'But before we do, we gotta deal with this shit.' He sits up and gestures to the array of narcotics we kicked over as we made out.

'Burn it,' I say. 'We have to.' I'm sure the doctors or police or whatever will wonder where Saif's stash has gone, but nothing is more dangerous, right now, than having this shit in close proximity.

And we do. We rebuild the fire and throw the whole lot on. It smokes like hell and we get away before we choke ourselves to death, or get really, really high.

Storm is where I left him, and seems quite content. I untie him and lead him on foot so Brady can walk alongside us. 'I'll have to take him back before we face the others.'

'Sure.'

'What do we tell them?'

'The truth?'

'No,' I say – my natural instinct to lie is strong. 'I mean, what good will it do?'

'Clear souls?'

I grimace. 'I think I'm a little far gone for a clear soul, Brady.'

He offers a kind half-smile. 'OK. We could just say I freaked out about Saif. I don't mind.'

I wonder if Goldstein will be impressed if I just admit to taking the drugs. The fact that I didn't touch any of them counts for something, surely.

We walk through the forest in amiable quiet. Our hands swing so close together that it seems unnatural for me to not take his hand. He squeezes it for a moment, but then pulls his away. 'I can't,' he says. He puts his arm around my shoulder in a bro move. 'You know, I so wish I could fall in love like normal people can, but I can't. If I could just date and watch movies and hold hands on the beach, I would. Like, I don't fall in love, I go *nuts*. I wish I could make people understand what it's like.' He doesn't sound maudlin, just defeated.

'So try,' I say.

'I once told Goldstein it feels like the forest fires in Cali. When I love, it starts like a little bonfire but within days it's all-consuming and out of control. It's an inferno and it levels everything in its path.' He shrugs. 'It's an addiction like any other, and it's as harmful as any of the other shit I was doing.'

I don't want to tell him about Kurt. I don't want to tell *anyone* about Kurt, because every time I do it comes out sounding sordid and seedy, and it wasn't. I don't think. But yes, absolutely, I was hooked on Kurt. 'I think . . . yeah, I know what you mean.' That'll do for now.

He lets out a big sigh. 'I hope one day I can do all that stuff – popcorn and ice-cream and stuff – without losing my shit.'

'You will,' I say, and I really mean it. I want him to get better more than I want myself to get better. I want to rescue him.

I give Storm a pat. I managed to tame him, I want to tame Brady, but who's gonna tame me?

When will you acknowledge, Miss Volkov, that your actions have consequences?

I remember Grafton's disappointment. On that occasion, we'd just got back from a trip to Paris. We were meant to be sketching in the Louvre, but I'd convinced Nevada and Genie to escape the Renaissance and come with me into Montmartre to find absinthe. Antonella stayed in the museum because she seemed legit into the wallpaper or something. Anyway, a few hours later Genie got so shitfaced she had to have her stomach pumped *en Français*. It was pretty funny *on reflection*.

When we got back to London, I was dragged before Grafton because Sir Randolph, Genie's dad, tried to pin the whole episode on me. Yeah, babes, I basically held a funnel in the silly bitch's mouth. Grafton's office is teak-panelled and musty. It smelled of shelves and shelves of old, leather-bound volumes of dead-white-guy poetry I can't imagine she ever reads.

'Alexandria, what's going on?' The headmistress changed her tone, taking off her glasses and her crow's feet deepening. 'I've known you since you were eleven and this isn't the girl I used to know.'

I uncrossed and crossed my legs. I said nothing.

'I know little girls become young women, but this . . . attitude lately . . . just doesn't seem like you. I know for a fact Antonella shares my concerns too.'

That was a cheap shot. Interesting though. I wondered, at the time, if Antonella didn't like Kurt. We'd been dating a few weeks at that stage and she seemed, at best, lukewarm towards him. I figured she was jealous because I'd got a cool, older boyfriend and she hadn't. I looked through spiky black lashes at Grafton. 'I think Antonella's good enough for the both of us.'

'Is that it? You think you're the bad twin?'

I hid a smirk behind my hand. Competing with Antonella was as futile as racing Usain Bolt. You'd only ever come second at best. 'No,' I said.

'Well then what is it, Alexandria? You had such phenomenal promise.'

God, what did she want from me? *Please Ms Grafton! I need help! I've sinned terribly and seek redemption!* 'I dunno,' I said. 'None of this really matters, does it?'

Grafton pursed her lips and reclined in her leather chair with a creak. 'I hope,' she said, 'that when you come to realise it *does*, it's not too late.'

Goldstein mirrors her expression now. Brady and I stand before his desk, metaphorical caps in hand. 'Do you have any idea how concerned we were? We were seconds away from calling the coastguard.'

'Sorry,' I say, and then Brady jumps in.

'I took Saif's stash,' Brady says, ignoring the minor detail that he was nowhere near Saif's room at any point. 'Lexi came after me to stop me using. She was too late. I did some coke. I'm back to zero days clean.' He toes the carpet like a little boy. 'We threw the drugs on the fire. They're all gone, I swear.'

Goldstein's icy glare defrosts a little. 'Well,' he says, 'at least that explains where his drugs went. I shall have to tell the police, Brady. You know that, right? Those drugs were evidence.'

He nods.

Goldstein rubs his beard like a wizard. 'Relapses, as you know, aren't the end of the world. It's understandable – with sudden access to drugs – and the impact of Saif's death, that you'd make questionable choices.'

'I feel like shit,' he says. 'And I'm sorry I was an asshole.'

Wait wait wait.

'I can't let Brady take all the blame,' I say with an almighty sigh. 'I took the stuff from Saif's room when I found him. I have no idea why. Brady took it off me so I wouldn't get in trouble.'

'Did you also use?'

'No. Honestly, no.'

'She could have, but she didn't,' Brady adds.

Who knew? Honesty feels pretty good. They should put that on the packaging.

Goldstein sighs an even bigger sigh. 'Well, it's been a bad enough day without me having to deal with you two. Go to dinner. But,' his eyes fix both of us, 'before you do, do I really need to spell out how ill-advised it is to form romantic relationships while in recovery? I'm not sure I've ever seen co-dependency build a solid foundation. Focusing on someone else's needs is a hugely efficient way to ignore your own.'

'I know,' Brady says immediately. 'That's not what this is.'

Wow. That stings like a wasp.

After a very sombre dinner, we're gathered in the drawing room where we have a very special edition of Group. Kendall cuddles up against Brady on the sofa and I don't mind – there's nothing between them; he comforts her like a brother. I'm with Ruby on the other one. Sasha plays with her braids in front of the fire. Our group feels a lot smaller. Now, with all the drama spent, we're left with an empty armchair.

Goldstein enters with a tray of hot chocolates that we *all* probably wish were something a lot stronger.

'Thank you,' Guy says, taking a mug. 'Are you allowed to tell us what's going on?'

'Thank you for your patience.' Goldstein hugs a cup of mint tea in his paws. 'And yes, you have a right to know what's going on. Saif's body has been flown back to the mainland and Dr Ahmed is meeting with his parents tomorrow. They're flying over from Dubai as we speak. The police have left for the day but they'll be back tomorrow – they might want to speak to some of you about how the drugs got on the island.'

With time tick-tocking at a vaguely normal pace, it kicks in properly. Saif is dead. Dead dead. Never coming back, never-gonna-walk-in-again dead. He was a bit of a cock, sure, but he's *dead*. He was only a year older than me and that's *it*. No wife, no kids, no car, no job. Ever.

Antonella.

I feel sick. I swallow hard and take a slow breath through my nostrils. Dinner was hoisin duck and rice noodles. I feel it all churn in my stomach.

'Did he do it on purpose?' Kendall asks, eyes pink-rimmed. I focus on her and the urge to vom passes slightly.

'No. We don't think so.' Exhausted, Goldstein sits next to Sasha on the rug. It reminds me, really, that he's just another one of us. Another fuck-up. 'The problem is that Saif didn't think he had a problem.'

'Isn't that a cheap shot?' Ruby says. 'He's not here to defend himself, Doc.'

'But *you* are,' Goldstein says and I glimpse a spark of anger. 'So listen up all of you. If dead addicts could speak, do you know what they'd say? They'd say "I didn't think it'd happen to me". Sound familiar?'

It's not like any of us need to put our hands up; it reads all over our faces. Dying is for losers, for homeless skagheads in doorways and tunnels. *If only that were true.*

'It's called "Unrealistic Optimism",' Goldstein goes on. 'The addiction reassures us *we're* in control, that we can stop any time we like, that it'll *never* be us. Until it is.'

It's quite embarrassing. I really thought that Kurt and I were somehow different.

Kindling crackles and snaps in the hearth. The flames glimmer in Sasha's eyes. She seems a million miles away. It's interesting that she didn't grass on me or Brady. Why not? I'll bet she was saving it – something to use against me when the time was right.

Goldstein goes on. 'Saif came here under duress. I don't think he had any intention of stopping. He was very young and thought he was immortal. He was only eighteen. It's a terrible waste. And that's addiction all over.'

There's another stifling silence until the door to the drawing room opens and Elaine enters, more smartly dressed than I've ever seen her, wearing a grey boat-neck dress and court shoes.

'Ah, Lady Denhulme, thank you for joining us.'

Shut. The. Front. Door.

I look to Brady and he frowns too. Elaine is Lady Denhulme? No way! She crosses the room and gives Goldstein a tender hug and kiss on each cheek. 'Not at all, Isaac. I came as soon as I could.' She turns to us. 'Good evening. Some of you I've met at the stables . . . some of you I've yet to meet and I apologise for that. I try to meet every young person who comes to Clarity.' She looks at each of us in turn. 'Sasha, it's good to have you back again.'

'Is it though?' she says. She doesn't look up, still twirling a braid around her finger.

Elaine continues as though she hasn't heard. 'If we haven't met, I'm Elaine Denhulme and this was my residence once upon a time. I founded the Clarity Centre just over ten years ago when my youngest son, Sebastian, died of an overdose.' She doesn't pause for dramatic effect; she just ploughs into the next sentence. 'It's unspeakably sad that a young person passed away here today. The sole aim of this centre was to prevent addiction and mental illness from claiming young lives. This will have been a terrible shock to you all, but while the investigation is ongoing I truly hope you can support and help each other through this. It's comforting, at least I think, that we aren't ever alone on the island. We have each other, if nothing else. It's easier said than done, but try to not let this affect your own recovery. We will grieve for Saif, but we are very much still here.' She pauses to compose herself. 'All I ever wanted was to give you the future that Sebastian didn't get.'

Her eyes glisten, but she doesn't cry. She blinks the tears back and smiles tersely. 'Thank you all. I'll let you get back to your evening.'

I look around at the others as she finishes speaking. A circle of scared faces, apart from Sasha, whose head is still clearly somewhere else.

The worst part?

It's still there: the voice in my head.

And it's saying:

'Yeah, but it wouldn't ever be you.'

Jesus knows we need something to lighten the mood, so before bed we watch *Zoolander 2* in the lounge. Kendall gets the hump because she says it's transphobic. Goldstein stays with us too. I can't deny I feel safer with him around tonight.

I'm restless though. I don't want another cigarette, but I can't sit still. 'I'm going to make some more hot chocolate. Does anyone want anything?'

Guy wants some tea but I say I don't need any help. Next to the dining room there's a 'kitchen'. It's not the main kitchens where our dinners are made, more like a tea, coffee and snack area with a fridge. They keep it full of fruit and chocolate and stuff for when the kitchen staff aren't in.

I turn the kettle on and go to the fridge for milk.

'They was strangling me,' a voice in the dark says.

I yelp and drop the jug. It shatters and milk sprays over the tiles to where Sasha is squatting in the corner, illuminated by the fridge light. Around her feet are her braids, coiled like dead snakes. She cuts away at them with a pair of craft scissors.

'Jesus, Sasha, what the hell are you doing?'

I didn't even realise she wasn't in the lounge. She must have slipped out while we were watching the movie.

'Cutting away the oppression, Blondie. You should think about this. I'm taking away the value the patriarchy assigned to beauty and femininity.'

The scissors are blunt (in case of occasions like this, presumably) so she's sawing, hacking away at her hair. What's left on her head is a fuzzy, uneven mess. I step around the milk. 'Sasha, stop! Your hair!'

'You Photoshopped idiot – this ain't even my hair. It's some polyester shit I got in Brixton. Proud black woman conforming to ideals as white as this milk. Semi-skimmed, pasteurised beauty. But beauty is in the eye of the beholder, and the beholder has a dick, Blondie. We cater ourselves on silver platters for them, to be desired and accepted. Pretty little canapés.'

I could argue that I just like to look the way I wanna look, but, judging from the mania in her eyes, it's totally pointless. She's not gonna listen. I crouch next to her. 'Sasha. You need to give me the scissors. If they catch you with them, they'll put you in the isolation room again, you know they will.'

'Maybe it's for the best. Maybe I'm safer in there.' She leans closer and whispers in my ear. 'He touched me, you know?'

What? 'Who did?'

'Marcus. He felt my tits while I was sedated. Thought I didn't know. But I felt his cold hands on my breast, fingering my nipple like this. Do you know what I think? I think all men are capable of fetid wickedness when they think no one's watching. Even your boy Brady. Especially him.'

I choose to ignore that last part. 'Jesus. Sasha, if that's true then you have to tell someone. I'll come with you, we . . .'

'Oh, she's as fucking vacant as she looks, is this one! Who you think they're gonna believe? Him? Or me?' Another braid tears off. 'So I remove beauty. I reject and rescind and renounce beauty. I am a blank slate: tabula rasa.'

I hear footsteps. 'Who's in there?' It's Joyce. 'Sasha?' She pokes her head into the kitchen. 'Oh, Lexi dear, have you seen Sasha? She went to the bathroom a while ago and . . .' She finally sees the hair swimming in milk and enters properly.

247

What else can I say? 'It's . . . Sasha.'

The manic glare dims and I swear Sasha smirks at me. Like I did what she was expecting me to do or something. Almost like she was playing with me. If she was, I think I just lost. 'Oh my days! Sasha! Get up now! What have you done?'

'I am a danger to myself and others. I was just about to cut Lexi's throat. It's a good thing you came along.'

'Put the scissors down. Look at your hair! Now, are you coming with me or do I need to call for help?'

Sasha walks through the milk. 'Oh, I'll come.' She lets the scissors fall. 'I'll come.'

Joyce leads Sasha away by the elbow. As she goes, she casts a look back over her shoulder and smiles at me again.

I'm deep, deep in a warm, porridgey sleep when I wake up. At first I don't even know why I'm awake until there's another delicate rat-a-tat-tat on the door of my suite. It's still pitch black outside the French windows and my body clock tells me dawn is still miles away.

I wonder if I'm hallucinating. I unfurl from my duvet and pad to my door. 'Hello?'

'Lexi, it's me.' Me is Kendall.

'What is it?' I ask through the door.

'Come with us.' I open the door and see everyone – except Sasha – lurking in the corridor. 'We're going on an adventure,' she whispers.

'Are you insane?' I look directly at Brady. 'Like we're not in enough trouble already.' When has that *ever* stopped me before? 'Whatever. I'll get dressed.'

'No need,' Kendall says. 'Just put something on your feet and meet us in the lounge.' She hands me a woollen blanket. I quickly grab the Vans and shove them on with my pyjamas. I meet them back in the lounge and Guy presses a finger to his lips, indicating that we follow him.

The mansion is seemingly deserted but there will be a nurse on duty somewhere, ready to spring out and bust us. We walk the halls in silence, on tiptoes. I realise Guy is leading us out of the front exit. 'What if there's an alarm?' Ruby asks.

'There isn't,' Kendall says, and I realise she'd know from her midnight exercise sessions.

'There's CCTV,' I whisper, and wonder if Kendall has learned a route without cameras. I bet she has.

'Why would they check?' Guy suggests, hustling us out on to the grand stone porch.

The night is crisp and cool; my breath hangs in the air. The stars are almost tacky, like a drag queen's been at the sky with Swarovskis and a glue gun.

'Wait,' I say more loudly now that we're out in the open. 'Do you think we should get Sasha?'

'God, why?' Ruby says.

'It feels shady to leave her out.'

'She's in Isolation,' Guy says. 'It's right next to the nurse's room. I don't think we can bust her out.'

I nod and we set out across the lawn. It's wet underfoot. 'Where are we going?'

'Wait and see,' Guy says. He's wearing some hugely dorky pug slippers, which is kinda cute. 'This is gonna blow your mind.'

I've never been to this part of the garden. Sweeping stone stairs lead down to an ornamental garden and rockery. It's like a viewing platform looking out over the sea, over the treetops. There's two wrought iron benches to sit on.

'Is this it?' Kendall asks.

'Just wait,' Guy says. 'I get insomnia. On top of everything else. Sometimes I come out here and wait for sunrise. The sun comes up in the east. Right over there. I thought it'd be a nice thing to do, you know, for Saif.'

We don't say anything. Yeah, it's pure fromage, but Guy's heart – as ever – is in the right place.

'This is a cool thing, man,' Brady says, putting an arm around Guy. 'When's sunrise?'

'I don't know. Usually about six.'

'Cool. We got a little time.'

I sit next to Brady and Guy. Ruby and Kendall take the other bench, Kendall resting her head on Ruby's shoulder. Aside from Guy, who seems wide awake, we all look bleary.

'Sasha told me something earlier,' I say when the silence is too much.

'What?' Kendall asks.

'I don't know if I should say.'

'Girl, you can't say "I got a secret" and then not tell us the goddamn secret!' Ruby says.

I sigh. 'She told me that Marcus felt her up while she was sedated.'

'Shit,' Brady breathes.

'No way!' Ruby snorts. 'As if!'

'When did she say that?' asks Kendall.

'Tonight, before they put her in Isolation. Do you think I should tell someone?'

'No! Because she's a crapsack. A sack, full of crap,' Ruby says, needlessly defining that term.

'Brady? What do you think?'

He shrugs and considers his answer for a while. 'Do what you think is right, but here's the thing with Sasha – she contradicts herself all the time. I've known her the longest and she tells outright lies.'

'Like, she told me she was the illegitimate daughter of a Tory politician and that's how she got into Clarity,' Guy says.

'But then she told me she never knew her dad and that her mum was a prostitute,' adds Kendall.

'Sometimes she says she grew up in foster homes, other times she talks about her mum and brothers and sisters. She once said she was an orphan,' Brady continues. 'I think she does it on purpose. I think she doesn't want us to know what's real and what's fake.'

'If that's true, I dread to think what's real,' I say.

'You know what I think?' Ruby says. 'I think she probably lives in a totally normal house with totally normal parents and she's making shit up to explain why she's so screwed up. Like, if she comes from a crack whore it all makes more sense.'

Sasha makes no sense. Which makes me want to make sense of her.

Brady leans in to me. 'If it's worrying you, tell Goldstein. He knows Sasha better than any of us.'

I nod. *If* she's making it up, *she's* part of the reason why Genie wouldn't go to the police that time Giles Gilhooley forced himself on her at that rugby fundraiser, and I'm angry. *If* she's making it up, I might get a perfectly good nurse sacked for no reason.

If she's not making it up . . .

It might be my imagination but I think the sky is turning indigo.

'Should we say something about Saif?' Kendall says.

'We hardly knew him,' Ruby says, and I'm getting a little tired of her sourness.

'Kendall knew him pretty well,' I say with a smirk.

'Too soon!' Kendall says with a tiny side-smile. 'He was good in bed. There. That's my contribution.'

'He was mixed up,' Brady says. 'He had an ego, he was a little arrogant, but I think he was a good guy underneath. Just immature. Even more so than the rest of us.'

That's fair. 'I wish I knew him better,' I add. It feels like a dumb thing to say and I wish I hadn't said it. It just keeps occurring to me that I knew nothing about him. I don't know what food he liked; what his favourite movie was; who his friends were. And I never will. Y'know, because he's dead.

'I thought the dude was a bit of a douche, actually,' Guy says.

'Guy! Way harsh!' Ruby chides.

'Let me finish. I should have known better. He had a problem and I didn't want to help him because it felt like he was stealing my friend, which is nuts. I'm sorry I didn't try.'

I reach over Brady and give Guy's knee a squeeze. 'It wasn't your job to save him.'

Guy shrugs. 'I don't know. I think you guys are helping to save me.'

Again, cheesy, but he's probably right. Between us we have more issues than *Glamour*, but we're like a circle of mirrors facing inwards; we can't hide from each other or ourselves.

We fall silent.

'It's time,' Kendall says.

It happens more quickly than I thought it would. The sky turns electric blue and the clouds are black for a second, but as the sky becomes lavender, the clouds are baby blue. It reminds me of the MAC eyeshadow counter for a second, before everything becomes the softest, palest pastels.

And then the sky is on fire. Amber gold leaks from the horizon like a fried egg yolk stabbed with a fork. We're dazzled for a second and then the sun hatches from the ocean, dribbling over the waves.

I'm crying and I don't know why.

All my bullshit and bitterness and cynicism is burned off for a second and I just roll with the emotion. It very much feels like a rush, like I'm coming up, and I can't control it. I'm too weak to resist, too weak to pretend this isn't majestic and powerful and beautiful. Everything I've ever said or done feels stupid and irrelevant. *I* am stupid and irrelevant.

I'll be myself again once the sun is up, but right now I have no more fight left in me.

Ski trip. Val d'Isère. 'Lexi . . . Lexi . . . wake up! We're going to watch the sunrise.'

'Fuck off, Antonella . . .'

'It's beautiful, come on.'

'Go away . . . I mean it.'

I cry.

I feel Brady take my hand and I let my heavy head rest on his shoulder.

STEP 7:
I WILL EMBRACE CHANGE –
IN MYSELF, OTHERS AND
MY ENVIRONMENT

The next few days are subdued. It's clear Goldstein and Ahmed are going through the motions with slightly deflated tyres. In One-To-One, I tell Goldstein that Saif's death wasn't his fault: 'Wasn't that like Step 2? We can only get better if we want to. Saif was pretty happy. It . . . it was just an accident.'

Goldstein smiles a half-hearted smile. He looks tired, bed-creased. 'Lexi, it's kind of you to think of me, it really is, but addiction and me . . . we go way back. It's personal.'

I don't push him. 'Don't beat yourself up.'

'I wonder, Lexi, whether this is *your* addiction talking. If Saif doesn't deserve my sympathy because he was an addict, that means *you* don't deserve my sympathy either. What do you think?'

I actually laugh. A genuine laugh, from a place of fun. 'Oh, you wily old bastard, you get me every time.'

And now he laughs. 'That's what they pay me for.'

I see that it's coming to the end of the session and I haven't said anything about Sasha and Marcus. I have to decide. Oh, sod it, I'm going to wash my hands of the issue.

'Dr Goldstein?'

'Yes.'

'Can I talk to you about Sasha?'

'Yes. She'll be coming out of Isolation later today . . .'

'It's not that.' I sit forward. 'The night she cut her hair off, she told me something. She's probably making it up, or testing me, or I don't know what, but she told me Marcus had . . . molested her when she was sedated. I didn't know if I should say something or not.'

Goldstein doesn't blow up as I'm expecting, but his eyes darken. He processes for a second or two. 'Lexi, you did the right thing. It's not your responsibility to carry that information; it's ours.'

'What happens next?'

He exhales through his nostrils. 'It's a very serious allegation. And one that you can let me handle.' He gestures me towards the door.

'But wait,' I say. 'What if she's making it all up?'

He nods slowly. 'But what if she isn't?'

Ahmed takes us for Group. Since the morning of the sunrise, I've steered clear of Brady. My hands are like little magnets, I just want to touch him, and that's not good for either of us. Kurt feels a million miles away. Brady feels like a holiday romance, but a holiday in a fictional world where nothing I do counts. This *isn't* the real world – it's an ornamental snow globe. I'm somewhere between missing London and never wanting to return.

I feel safe here.

With Brady.

Sasha joins us for Group. She skulks in, looking thinner than ever. Her head has been properly cropped. Her skin is waxy, her cheekbones gaunt. She looks like she hasn't slept in about a decade. She slumps into the armchair. 'How's *Gossip Girl, Interrupted* going?' she asks.

I snigger. That about sums us up. Man, I miss *Gossip Girl*.

'Welcome back, Sasha,' Dr Ahmed says. 'Today we're talking about maintaining healthy behavioural habits, especially around food, exercise and sex.'

'I fuck and eat like a normal person, so can I go?'

'Sasha . . .'

'Sorry,' she mimes locking her mouth and tossing the key over her shoulder.

'Food and sex are difficult,' Dr Ahmed explains. 'They are just as addictive as drugs, but we need them to live. Yes . . . even sex. Some people abstain from sex for all sorts of reasons, but adult relationships, to thrive, need mutual intimacy and affection, if not intercourse.'

Now I suddenly find my fingernails *fascinating* as I do anything I can to not look at Brady. I can't stop thinking about what happened in the weird bunker in the forest . . . how hot we were together. When I touch myself in the shower, although I try to think about Kurt, my imagination idly drifts back to Brady.

'We have said time and time again in Group that it's not the trigger that's faulty, it's our individual relationship with it . . .'

It's Kendall's turn: 'For me, right now, I've just about accepted that I have to eat to keep my body alive. I one hundred per cent see food as fuel. I don't know if I'll ever be able to *enjoy* food. I think it's disgusting we rely on shovelling lard into our faces like hogs . . .'

After she finishes, Ruby speaks: 'I feel like here I don't have any control, so everything's real easy. I'm losing weight, I feel better, I like the food . . .' I examine Ruby, and she's definitely looking healthier. I guess the diet regime is working. 'But, Doc, you ain't gonna be sat in my refrigerator in Manhattan at two a.m. the next time I go on a binge. Who's gonna pull that goddamn chicken wing outta my hand?'

Then Guy: 'Maybe I have to simply accept that I can't get to grips with the most basic thought processes that everyone else takes for granted. I know terrible things won't happen if I don't perform my rituals, but thinking they *might* doesn't go away. The sooner I accept it, the sooner I can cobble together some semblance of a life. I used to think the goal was to get off medication, but now I think the goal is to live with it . . .'

And, finally, Brady: 'I hope I know the difference,' he says. 'I hope that when I finally fall in love for real, I don't mistake it for compulsion and let it go. But I don't know if I can do it. I was so far gone. Girls . . . guys . . . groups, it didn't matter. If I

260

was high, I'd go there. It was dark. I put myself – and other people – at risk. For me, sex isn't about "intimacy and affection" any more. It was just another razor blade.'

Jesus, I've never wanted him more. What is *wrong* with me?

'It's the same as anything else, Brady,' Ahmed says. 'It's about establishing parameters in which you can function safely. Maybe that means sober sex, maybe it means sex only in a relationship, maybe it means no sex. There *are* other things to a relationship. I've been married for six years, I can't remember the last time I had sex and it has nothing to do with abstinence!'

Dr Ahmed! Who knew? My mouth flops open.

Brady cracks a smile first and soon we're all giggling. Even Sasha.

I spend the afternoon taking Storm for a run on the beach. He needs it. I need it. The wind in my face blows all the fog off my brain. My hair feels salty and wild and mermaidy, and I like it.

Elaine – am I meant to call her Lady Denhulme now? – is amazed at the progress I'm making with Storm, but I'm saddle sore to say the least. With sweat gleaming on his flanks, I walk him back towards the stables.

Coming up the bridleway, I see the little red door to the stable cottage open, and instead of Elaine, the broad bulk of Goldstein pops out. I tug on Storm's reins and he reluctantly stops. 'Shhh,' I tell him.

Lady Denhulme emerges right behind him and my mind, never far out of the gutter, wonders what they've been up to.

Maybe it's nothing. Is Goldstein telling her what I told him about Sasha? Would she need to know? Only then he checks the coast is clear before kissing her lightly on the lips. She has to reach up on tiptoes to meet his mouth.

'Oh wow,' I mutter to Storm.

Well, this explains why both of them choose to spend so much time on this godforsaken – and there's a word I don't use often enough – island. And where's Lord Denhulme in all this, eh?

Mum and Dad; Goldstein and Lady Denhulme. I have to chuckle. 'Grown-ups are just as fucked as we are,' I tell Storm. 'And they're meant to know better.'

Back at the centre, I run a hot bath. After galloping around on Storm all afternoon, I needed a soak before I could function.

When I'm a wrinkly prune, I reluctantly climb out of the bath, dry off and change into a grey shift dress from All Saints and some stompy boots, and head down the corridor for dinner.

As I pass through reception I see Marcus, the boynurse, stride out of the front door, carrying a holdall. The door slams behind him. I hear his angry footsteps crunch over the gravel.

Uh-oh.

My stomach churns and suddenly my appetite for filet mignon is all gone. I find the others in the dining room watching through the window.

'Where's Marcus going?' Kendall asks.

'How should I know?' It comes out more defensive than I intend.

'Dude looks pissed,' Ruby comments before returning to her place. 'Did you tell Goldstein about . . .?'

I say nothing, confirming it. Sasha isn't here. I feel dizzy. This is because of what I did. I just hope I made the right call.

After dinner, we sit around the table talking about what we wanna do with the evening. I would gladly sell my soul for a cocktail at this stage. Brady suggests a swim. 'Come on,' he says. 'It'll be fun, like a pool party.'

'Oh yeah,' Kendall says. 'Trans people just *love* swimwear.'

'Aw, that stuff doesn't matter; it's just us.'

'It matters to me,' she adds quietly.

'I'll join in if you do,' I say. 'And I'll even wear gym shorts.'

Kendall seems to consider this. 'I'm not exactly in love with swimsuits either,' Ruby points out. 'But I'll sit my ass in that jacuzzi.'

'Awesome!' Brady grins. 'I've missed my pool back home.'

We agree to get ready and meet at the pool in twenty. It's never good to swim right after a meal anyway.

I step out of the dining room.

I don't see the shadow until it's too late.

It all happens so fast. I feel her on my back and my legs crumple. My knees and hands smash onto the cold, hard tiles and I cry out in pain. She grasps my ponytail and rams my face into the floor. I manage to twist to avoid smashing my nose, but my cheekbone makes painful contact. 'You fucking canary!' Sasha spits. 'You couldn't keep your mouth shut, could you?'

I hear someone scream and suddenly, from my weird position, I see feet come running down the hallway towards us. As I feel her weight being pulled off me, I see it's Kendall who's dragged her off and then Brady who holds her back. 'Get the fuck off me!' she screams through gritted teeth. Her eyes are wild, wide and white. She kicks her legs like she's treading water.

I pick myself up, but I'm dizzy, I cup my cheek with my hand. I've bitten my lip and can taste blood. 'Jesus. I was trying to help.'

'I don't need your help! I don't need anyone's help! Put me down!'

'You need to chill out, Sasha.' That's Brady.

She sinks her teeth into his arm. He swears and drops her. I brace myself, sure she'll launch herself at me again.

She looks like a cornered animal. 'You know what? I'm done. I'm so fucking done. I . . . can't . . . breathe! I'm suffocating. You are suffocating me! I have got to get off this bastard island.' She pushes past Guy and flees towards the back doors.

A little shell-shocked, we look at each other. 'What the hell was that about?' Ruby asks.

'You OK?' Brady says.

'That,' I say, 'is gonna leave a mark.' He hands me a tissue and I press it to my lip.

'I'll get you some ice.' Ruby heads towards the kitchen.

'Where are the nurses when you actually need one?' Kendall says, fuming.

'I imagine they were looking for her,' offers Guy.

'Wait,' I say. 'What do you think she meant? That she's done. You don't think she'll do something stupid, do you?'

We process. I see it in their faces. She *can* and *will* do something stupid.

'Fuck,' Brady says, summing it up.

'We have to go after her,' I say. I don't want to bring Saif into it, but I don't want to lose someone else. None of us do.

'Seriously!' Kendall now screams at the top of her lungs. 'Where are the nurses?' It echoes down the corridors.

'I'll go and see where they are.' Guy hurries upstairs.

'We can't wait,' I say. 'We better find her, come on.'

Kendall, Brady and I leave through the back doors. The lights only illuminate the lawn and she's nowhere to be seen. 'She must have gone into the woods,' Brady says.

'Which way do you think she went?' Kendall asks.

'Not a clue. We better split up. You go that way, I'll head down the drive.'

Kendall sets off down the path and I follow her, wrapping my arms around my body. It's bitter, but I don't want to waste time looking for a jacket. 'This is such bullshit,' Kendall says as we push through the gate on to the woodland path.

'Sasha!' I call. 'Come back! She'll get put in Isolation again. I'm not surprised she made a run for it. She must be going mad in there.'

'Going? It's a bit late for that, babe. Sasha! Where are you?'

'Like, where is she even gonna go?' I say as we trample down the path.

'Right? We're surrounded by sea.'

I stop and grab Kendall's arm. 'She said she wanted to get off the island.'

Kendall rolls her eyes. 'Oh, come on, she's not going to swim back to the mainland, is she?'

'This is *Sasha*. She might give it a go!'

And now Kendall's face falls. 'She might not have to swim . . .'

'What do you mean?'

'The docks.'

I remember taking that walk with Kendall and Ruby. There were boats. 'Oh shit . . . do you think . . .?'

Kendall shrugs. 'I think it's worth checking it out.'

Thankfully it's all downhill. We half run, half jog down the winding hillside towards the beach. 'Sasha has been on this island on and off for years,' Kendall pants. 'If anyone can escape, it's her.'

The moon is full and white, rippling on the sea. Up ahead, it illuminates a figure pelting towards the jetties. 'There. Is that her?'

'It must be.'

'Shit. Quick.' We sprint the rest of the way, feet pounding the path. 'Sasha! Stop!' I call. She doesn't even break stride.

The ferry must be back on the mainland. The only boats are the dinky rowboats we saw before. Sasha is heading right for them. She won't get far in those.

'Sasha, are you nuts?' I yell.

'You tell me!' Sasha screams. She awkwardly lowers herself into one of the boats, supporting herself against the pier. 'You know everything, apparently! Are you my social worker or something?'

We hit the jetty, my legs wobbly. I'm so not used to running like this. I can really feel all the tar shifting in my lungs right now.

'Sasha, get out of the boat before you drown,' says Kendall.

'I'm getting out of here. I'll swim if I have to. You bitches can't stop me.'

Kendall throws her hands up in despair. 'Let her go. This so isn't our responsibility.'

Sasha wobbles and teeters in her boat, trying to untether it from its mooring. A thought pops into my head. Before I can change my mind, I sit on the edge of the jetty and clamber in.

'What the fuck do you think you're doing?'

I take a seat and fold my arms. 'If you go, I go.' The words sound stupid and rectangular in my mouth, like a line in some bullshit buddy movie. I realise suddenly I remind myself of someone and that someone is Antonella.

'What is your problem, Blondie? You got a Caucasian saviour complex or something? I don't need you to save me.'

It's funny because, looking at her, that's exactly what she needs. 'Sasha, I'm not going. You need help,' I add so only she can hear.

'Fine.' She finally untangles the guide rope and pushes us off.

I was *not* expecting her to call my bluff. For just a second I must have mistakenly thought I was dealing with a sane person. The boat bobs and tilts from side to side as we float away from the jetty. 'Oh shit,' I say and grip the sides.

'Oh my god!' Kendall squeals from the dock.

I turn to face her. 'Kendall! Get help! Now!' I look back to Sasha. 'Sasha, this is a really, really bad idea.'

She picks up the oars, one of which is pretty much half an oar, and starts, clumsily, to row. 'Is it?'

'Yes. You're going to get us in so much trouble. Or worse.' The boat rocks and I grip the edges. Freezing cold water sloshes up over the sides in drunken glugs. I remember I get super-gnarly seasickness.

Sasha grins. 'Who are you gonna be? When we get to the shore? You can be someone new, whoever you want. I'm gonna be you: a self-loathing nihilist with great clothes and pretty blonde hair.'

I am literally clinging on for dear life. 'Sasha, please! Just take us back!'

'How does it feel? Not being in control for once in your life?'

I look at her darkly. 'When was I *ever* in control?'

'She's a victim,' Sasha smiles. 'We're all victims on this ship.'

'Look. What Marcus did—'

'Marcus did nothing you stupid, interfering whore! I felt him up! I tried to suck his dick! *He* rejected me.'

Well, that shuts me up. I vaguely recall offering a similar deal to Marcus. I was so out of it then, I'd have probably offered sex to Joyce for a fix. 'Why?' I say when the gentle lapping of the waves against the boat gets a bit awkward. 'To get out of Isolation?'

'No,' she says. 'No. I just wanted someone to touch me. I wanted someone to hold me in their arms, like Brady holds you.' She starts to cry. 'Of course, he said no. I mean look at me – I'm carrion, I'm repulsive. Even the mirror don't want me. I just wanted to feel some skin on my skin. That's what we do it for: skin on skin.'

'Sasha, I'm sorr—'

'No. No no no. You do not get to pity me. Pity costs nothing and you're minted.'

The boat feels like it's being tossed over the waves and I get the same sensation in my tummy as when I'm cantering on a horse. 'You are not repulsive.'

'Would you fuck me?'

'No, but only because I don't like girls like that.'

'Convenient.'

'Truth. Take it from me, you don't have to have sex to feel close to someone.' I remember what Dr Ahmed said. I remember laying close to Brady, feeling his heartbeat against my back.

'I'm not a virgin, or a retard,' she says.

'I know. The problem is that you don't let anyone close, Sasha.'

'And you do?'

'This isn't about me.' Right now, it really isn't. 'I *see* you. How much of it's real and how much is an act? Honestly?'

She stops rowing. 'I don't know any more.'

We bob. I feel sick. The salt air thickly coats my skin and lips. I wait for her to go on.

'I remember it starting. It was like rising damp, dark patches spreading through my brain. Normal thoughts went sour. I thought about being in my coffin; I thought my mum was trying to poison me; I thought people were following me home; I thought there was a man in my air vent. I knew it wasn't right. At first. I knew it was an illness.' She closes her eyes. 'But it just keeps getting worse. The dark patches keep spreading, no matter how many times the doctors and pills try to paint over them. It was too much, too hard to keep fighting it. So I laid down and let the rot sink into my bones and teeth. I submit. And now I'm too far gone. No going back. There ain't any clean left no more. I'm just rot.'

I shake my head and take both her hands. She lets me. 'You're not. You're *not*.'

She shakes her head, eyes down. 'There's nothing left of her.'

'I don't believe that. *This* is you. And even when you get lost in yourself, you can always get back. It just takes longer.'

'What's the point? Do you really think I'm ever gonna have a normal life?'

I shrug. 'Will any of us? What's normal anyway? I think the thing we all have in common is we all thought we were the first people to feel the way we feel. But we're not. We all think we're so broken. We all think we're the *most* broken.'

'Like that's something to be proud of.'

'I dunno,' I say, thinking. 'There's a Japanese art . . . kintsugi, it's called. I think.' I once saw an exhibition of it at the V&A. 'Artists fuse broken pottery together with gold lacquer. It's gorgeous. Instead of trying to hide the damage, they celebrate it, glorify it. I'm not saying we should be all like "look at me, I'm so amazingly fucked up". I'm saying that I don't think there are many adults who aren't in some way damaged by the time they're our age. Look at my parents, look at Goldstein, look at Elaine. They survived the breakages. So will we. I think we should embrace our wonkiness.'

Sasha pouts. 'What's it called again?'

'Kintsugi. Or something.'

'Kintsugi. I like that.' She nods. 'What about you, Blondie? Ready to embrace your imperfections?'

'I am not perfect. I never was. I never will be. But I would like to be a little bit better.' We fall silent. The boat continues to roll over the waves. My feet are wet. The wind blusters, tugging at my hair.

And then I think – why are my feet wet? I look down and, even in the dark, I see water swilling about in the bottom of the boat.

'Hey. Is that normal?' I try to keep my voice light.

'I don't know.'

'Was the boat in the water when you got in it?'

'No, it was sitting on the beach. I dragged it into the water.'

In the moment, my brain conjures the image of sharks circling us. I've seen too many movies. 'You didn't think to check if it floated?'

'I was in meltdown. Nuclear.'

I look over my shoulder. Sasha must be stronger than she looks because she's rowed us some way offshore. My heart starts punching against my ribs. My brain swooshes around my skull. I'm gonna lose my shit in any second.

No.

No, I've gotta keep it together. 'Right. Well. Start rowing us back, I'll see if I can bail it out.' I cup my hands and start tossing water over the side of the boat. Sasha joins me, but it doesn't seem to be helping. In fact, as we move around, more water seems to bubble up through a long, fine split in the hull. 'Shit!'

'Lexi, I can't swim,' Sasha mutters.

'What?'

'I can't.'

'You have got to be fucking kidding me.' The fear in her eyes says she's not. 'You row. Get this thing turned around and back to shore.'

In this light it's hard to tell how much water the boat is taking on, but all of my boots are now submerged. 'Keep rowing!'

Black water swishes and swills inside the boat, and it does now seem to be leaning. Water creeps up my calves. It's so cold. I wonder if the shock of the cold alone will kill us. I remember getting my roots retouched at the salon and reading an article in the paper about strapping young men who drown in reservoirs. The water is so cold their muscles seize up and they can't swim.

What a horrible way to die.

I keep tossing water over the side.

'Which would you rather?' It's Kurt, stoned on the Kensington Roof Gardens rooftop. 'Be burned alive or drown?'

'Burned,' I told him. 'I think you'd pass out quicker – the pain would be so intense. With drowning, you'd really know about it.'

I go faster.

The rim of the boat is now only inches from the water. The more water we take on, the faster it sinks. Figures, I guess, in a physics-lesson way. Shit. We're going under.

Don't panic.

'Sasha, we're gonna have to swim for it.'

'I can't swim!' she shrieks – a real shriek, no more Mad Girl Theatre.

'I can. Keep your shit together, OK? If you freak out now, you will kill us both. You could have killed yourself hundreds of times, but you didn't, which suggests you actually want to be here.'

Me and Antonella in our pyjamas in the pool. To go on the Year 10 trip to Brittany, you had to learn some basic lifesaving because we'd be sailing and canoeing. We laughed and laughed, taking it in turns to haul each other to the side. 'Girls!' The instructor blew her whistle, a shrill warning toot. 'Could you please take this seriously? This might save someone's life one day!'

I splash water at Sasha. 'What are you doing?' she cries.

'We have to get used to the water temperature before we get in. Get wet.' I close my eyes and scoop water into my face. It's cold, bitterly cold, and salty. It stings my eyes and nostrils. Sasha does the same, rubbing her arms and legs with seawater.

I can now feel the boat sinking out from under us. I take a deep breath. I push myself into the water. The cold snatches the breath right back. It feels like a slap, a slap everywhere. 'Fuck!' I cry, mostly to keep myself alert. There. I'm in. God it's cold, but I'm in. I need to steady my breathing. It now comes in fast, shallow pants and I doubt that's good. 'Sasha! Get in!' She's clinging to the boat.

'I can't! I can't swim! I'll sink!'

'You won't! That's not how it works. You'll float and I'll swim us back.' I can see the jagged outline of the cliffs, the broccoli silhouette of the trees. I think I can even see lights on in the mansion. But it's quite the swim. I don't know if I can make it.

But it's like I said to Sasha, I know I don't want to die. The fight almost surprises me. 'Sasha, you have to trust me. Get in, so I can get hold of you.'

'You won't let go of me?'

Oh, it's too cold to be cheerleadery. 'I promise.'

The stern dips all the way under and Sasha screams, flopping into the water. Her head dips under the surface, but I grab hold of her sweater. She thrashes around like a fish. 'Stop kicking!' I command. 'You need to be still or I can't do this.'

'Have you got me?'

'Yes!' I recall Antonella pretending to be unconscious. I remember looping my arms around her and swimming

274

backwards, towing her as I went. 'Lean back against me. I'm going to pull you. If you thrash around, you pull us both under.'

It's cold, it's cold, it's cold. Oh Jesus, it's cold. It saws to the bone.

I start swimming on my back. Sasha lets herself float. I let the boots slip off my feet and that makes things easier. With one arm around Sasha's tits and the other one pushing against the water, we start to move. Small mercies – the waves aren't too bad. I do feel the pull of the tide, but I just hope it's pulling us towards the shore and not further out.

We swim. I don't think we're going very far, very fast, but we are moving. If this was a heated indoor pool, we'd be at the side by now. If this was Grand Cayman, it'd be quite relaxing.

But it's neither of those things.

I can't feel my hands. My teeth clatter together no matter how hard I lock my jaw. With every stroke Sasha seems to become heavier like she's getting waterlogged. Or maybe I am. It's like swimming in superglue. We're just not going anywhere. Getting to the beach will take hours at this rate.

'Can I help?' Sasha asks quietly.

'Kick your feet up and down . . . like pedalling.'

She does so. It helps. 'This is all my fault,' she says.

'Don't start,' I say. 'Just kick.'

It's too hard. I'm not strong enough to get us both to shore. I doubt I'm strong enough to get myself to shore. I let out a little cry.

'What's up?' Sasha is panicking too.

My legs stop. I try to kick but it's too hard.

Oh god. This is it. I'm going to drown. I suppose it's better than a heroin overdose, but it's still pretty stupid. I wonder how Mummy and Daddy will spin it. Accident on holiday?

'Keep going,' Sasha says.

'I don't think I can. I'm too weak.'

'You're not! Lexi, you're badass. You're Lexi motherfucking Volkov.'

Wait.

'Wait what, darlin'?'

'Here's what's going to happen, Steve. I'm going to give you ten thousand pounds and you'll never come near me or Kurt ever again.'

'Is that right? But I want a blow job.'

'I'd take the money, if I were you. The other choice is I speak to my daddy. You know my name, don't you, Steve? Lexi Volkov. THE Lexi Volkov. My father owns that lucrative, if ambiguous, space somewhere between the mafia and the oligarchs. And look at you . . . a small-time dealer in a council flat in Battersea. So, before you threaten me or Kurt again, I'll ask you this: do you really *want to fuck with the Russians?'*

I laugh.

The noise jolts me back into reality.

'What?'

'Nothing,' I say. I go for a few more strokes, digging into strength I didn't know I had. We go another couple of metres, but then I have to stop again. My whole body is numb. My brain is telling my limbs to move but it's total paralysis. 'I can't do it. I'm sorry.'

'OK. Don't let go of me.'

I clutch Sasha tight. We float, skimming over the waves. I want to close my eyes but I know that'll be the end of both of us. Instead I look up at the midnight-blue sky, wispy cotton wool clouds are torn up between the stars. It's pretty. Despite everything, I'm weirdly chill.

It's like falling asleep. I don't feel the cold any more. I don't think that's a good thing. This is it. This is it. This is how I die.

And if I'm going to die . . .

So, that night.

That night was a fail from square one.

London goes soft in the summer. It was *hot*, like the skyscrapers and buses and pavements and trains were soaking up the sun and pouring it back out again in meaty belches. All you can do is head to the nearest bit of green. For us, that day in July, the oasis was Battersea Park.

Battersea Park is all winding paths and weeping willows and honking geese on the ponds. You can tell a lot about an area of London by the dogs you see. That day brought a pedigree mixture of Pomeranians, chihuahuas, pugs and French bulldogs sniffing at our picnic blanket.

It was rare to see Kurt in daylight hours and, like a vampire, he didn't once take his shades off. He quietly came down from last night's binge, lay flat on his back, hands behind his head. Every once in a while, I reminded him to apply sun cream or he'd sizzle like bacon.

Even though he was essentially unconscious, I claimed a minor victory that I'd managed to get him to come meet me and my friends. On our overlapping blankets were me, Kurt, Antonella and Nevada, and some St Barney's guys: Jack, Gay Jack and Troy.

God, it was so humid the air stuck to my tacky Hawaiian Tropic skin, my hair pure frizz. The butt-sweat situation was real. I wore a miniscule Dolce bikini top with some H&M denim cut-offs.

'Guys,' Troy said, shielding his phone screen from the sun with a hand, 'just got confirmation from DJ Apollo . . . there's a rave tonight.'

'Oooh, where?' said Nevada, nibbling a strawberry.

'Abandoned mosque in Catford.'

We all voiced the appropriate level of offence at that statement. '*Catford?* As if,' I said. 'Is that even London?'

Troy rolled his eyes. 'It's like twenty minutes from London Bridge, Lex.'

'Lexi doesn't do South East,' Nevada correctly added.

I smirked. 'Why don't we really go for it and just hit Aleppo for the weekend?'

'Well, I'm going,' Troy said sulkily. 'Apollo has basically said there's a surprise MC set from Lazarus.'

That got Antonella's attention. 'Oh my god, for real? He's gorgeous.'

Troy handed her his phone as evidence. 'No way! OK, I'm in.'

I gave her a look. 'I'm not going to Catford. End of.'

'Oh, come on, Lex! It'll be fun! When was the last time we went dancing?'

'Last Saturday!' I laughed. 'We went to *Sink the Pink*.'

'Oh yeah. But this'll be good too!'

'A rave in a disused mosque? God, how *Vice Magazine*. It'll be full of hipsters.'

'Hipsters and *Lazarus*! Please! I wanna make a baby with him! Think how cute it'd be.'

I nudged Kurt. 'Are you alive?'

'Yup.'

'What do you think? Apollo and Lazarus in Catford? You fancy it?'

He pushed himself up on to an elbow. 'Sure. I think some of the guys are going.'

'You knew about it? Whatever.' It's too sweltering to be pissy.

'Kurt,' Troy asked, 'think you can get us some beans?'

He flashed his eyebrows. 'Leave it with me.'

It was every bit as awful as I'd feared. Worse. Cash bar. I ask you. The organisers hired circus performers (standard) and you couldn't move more than a metre without crashing into some cunt on stilts or an out-of-work actress dressed as a 'sexy clown' trying to sell jelly shots. I don't know who thought 'awful kid's party' was something to aspire to in adulthood.

The Mosque – or what was left of it – was divided into two rooms. I guess one was the women's room and one the men's, back when it was functional. Now there was scaffolding all around the exterior and the dome had been taken down and covered with tarpaulins. The biggest hall was the main dance area, while the antechamber had a chill out vibe.

'Come on, Lexi, get into it!' Antonella screamed, tossing her mane back. 'Just go with the beat!'

The sound system was good, I'll give her that. I'd lost Kurt about half an hour ago. The queues for the (woeful) toilets were round the block, so he'd probably gone to find a bush.

Antonella was deep into her vibe, arms aloft, glo-sticks in hand. 'Just sink into it, darling.'

She gave me a lingering kiss on the lips. Jesus. Ecstasy. 'Are you high?'

'I dunno. Those pills Kurt brought are kinda bogus. I haven't come up.' She seemed pretty up from where I was dancing, but I said nothing. She sipped her mineral water. 'Did you take any?'

'Not yet. I can't find him.' I didn't want to come up without him around. 'Here, have mine.' I gave her the pill Kurt had given me before I lost him.

'You sure?' I nodded. 'Thanks! You can get some more off that girl over there, she's dealing.' She pointed across the mosque to a white girl with fire-engine red cultural-appropriation dreadlocks. I saw her place a pill on some girl's tongue.

We danced for a while. Even after night fell, it was still like twenty degrees, a sticky breathless night. I wore an oversize LA Lakers jersey as a dress with hi-tops and it was matted to my back. Antonella was blissed out. I figured her E had finally kicked in. She tipped her head back, hair damp with sweat. In the middle of the mosque, eyes closed, arms in the air, it was like she was lost in prayer.

I was about to leave. I always think that if you're not feeling the party, don't bring others down – just leave them to it. Nevada, Troy and a load of other people from St Agnes were there, so Antonella would be fine.

Except she wasn't.

I saw Kurt first, dancing through the crowd ironically. I could tell he thought it was shit and I loved him for it. 'Isn't this the worst?' I shouted over the bass.

'Have you ever seen so many twats in your life?'

I wrapped my arms around his neck and gave him a long deep kiss. 'Can we get out of here?'

'Abso-fucking-lutely.' He kissed me again.

I was so into the kiss, I wasn't aware – at first – of the commotion right over my shoulder. I just thought dancers were bumping into me. I didn't realise it was people pushing past to help Antonella.

I swear the music stopped. It didn't in real life, but all I could hear was my heartbeat pounding in my skull.

She was on the floor, flat on her back. She was shaking like there was electricity running through her body. Her eyes were open, but all white, like she was looking in on her brain.

People shouted, screamed, gathered around. Someone tried to make her drink water, like that was going to help.

Her face.

White shit bubbling out of her mouth.

Her face.

Every time I close my eyes I see

Her face.

'LEXI!' Sasha screams in my ear so loud it hurts. 'There's a boat!'

I don't remember passing out. I must have. I want to again. My eyelids are heavy, sleep pulling me back. Only it isn't sleep, is it?

'What?'

'Boat! There's a boat coming.'

I manage to push with my dead arms so I'm facing the other way. A light gallops over the waves towards us. It's coming quickly. 'We're here . . .' I manage barely a whisper.

Sasha is louder. 'Oi! Over here!' She waves her arms and I drop her for a second until she slips under the water and I grab her again. The light shines on our faces. 'It sees us! They can see us!'

Kendall. Kendall went for help. She knew.

I still might die. I think I'm broken. I might be too broken to survive. But I am glad we're not just going to be fish food.

It's all very trippy.

It's like when I first came to the island.

There is a boat. There are voices. I see a ladder. I'm too exhausted to use it. Someone has to get in to help us out. They save Sasha first. Strong hands hook under my armpits and drag me on deck. It's a lifeboat. The coastguard or whatever. They cover me in towels and blankets. Sasha is next to me.

They ask questions. I don't answer.

I'm cold.

There are stars.

Stay with us, Lexi.

I look at the stars.

'Lexi? Are you OK?' It's Goldstein.

'Yes,' I say. I'm too wiped to think of anything funny or clever. From the docks, a car brought us straight back to the house and I came round a bit. Now they're trying to establish if we need to go to hospital on the mainland. We're in the medical bay. It's the room next to Isolation. Both Sasha and I walk around in circles, swaddled in blankets – apparently it'll reduce the risk of hypothermia. In such a small space, I'm starting to get a little dizzy.

'How are you feeling? Take a seat.'

'Better.' It's true. My hands cradle a mug of hot chocolate and the sugar is bringing me back into this dimension.

'And you, Sasha?'

'Thanks to Lexi, I'm fine. Listen up, Doc, you gotta know it was all, one hundred per cent my fault. Lexi tried to stop me.'

'Sasha, Sasha,' he holds up a placating hand, 'we can deal with all of that later. All we need to do now is establish if you're physically all right.'

'Now I'm dry, I'm mint.'

I'm less sure. I'm not sure I'll ever be warm again. My bones feel blue and icy. 'I think I'll be OK,' I say. 'I'll take a bath.'

Goldstein pops a thermometer in my mouth. After thirty seconds or so he checks it. 'OK. More or less back to normal. I'll let the coastguard know they're OK to go in that case. But we'll be keeping a very close eye on both of you tonight. Understood?'

'I'll go in Isolation,' Sasha volunteers.

'There's no need.' Goldstein goes to speak to the coastguard, leaving us with Joyce and our drinks.

'Lexi. You came through for me. I owe you one. I owe you a lot more than one.'

I shake my head. I just really want to wash the sea off me. They gave us dry clothes but it's still all over my skin. I smell salty. 'You don't owe me anything.'

'Lexi,' Sasha says with a broad grin. 'We're *alive*.'

I spend a very long time in the bath. Despite having almost drowned, I submerge myself. I'm reminded of *The Bell Jar*, that quote about baths curing all of life's woes, but I can't quite remember it. The water is almost too hot, but I like it. My skin turns sausagey and pink, but I can feel my core defrosting. I take down the shower attachment and wash my hair twice, ridding it of stinky eau de seaweed.

A little worried I might still be dying, I don't dare close my eyes, at least until I'm out of the water.

There's a polite knock on the door. Gary said he'd give me some privacy. 'I'm conscious!' I call back. 'I'll be out in a sec.'

'It's Brady.' His voice is muffled by two doors.

'Oh,' I shout back. 'Give me a minute!'

I let the water out and grab a towel. I give my hair a quick rub and retrieve my dressing gown. My hair hangs in ratty tails and I haven't got a speck of make-up on, but I think I can face Brady. I look . . . well, clean.

I opened the door about an inch before he barges in and sweeps me into a bear hug. 'Oh Jesus, I thought you were dead.' He takes hold of my face and gives me a fierce kiss. I'm startled for about a second before I get my shit together and return the kiss.

'So did I,' I say between kisses.

'What the hell happened?'

'She got in a boat. I followed her.' I go and sit on the edge of the bed, my legs still like jelly. 'It was stupid.'

'Sasha is saying you saved her life.'

'I think we saved each other.'

'I was so worried,' he says, stroking my face. 'And I thought . . . I just thought how I was crazy to let you go. What if this . . . you and me . . . was meant to be, and there I am ignoring it?'

We kiss a little more. Gotta admit, I didn't see this coming, and I'm not complaining.

'Lex,' he says, 'when I thought about losing you, it felt like I was losing something *real*. I'm not high, I'm not drunk . . . and I think I love you. I think it's love. Real love.'

I roll on to my back and look up into his eyes.

What about Kurt?

What about love?

Instead, I ask, 'What about abstinence?'

'What if it's not addiction? What if it's just love?' He rolls on top of me and kisses me again. 'I think I . . . we . . . deserve that.'

He feels so warm. I want him to defrost me. I want him to make me feel again, feel like I haven't felt anything in a really long time.

Since that night . . .

'Brady, wait.' I push him off me.

His brow creases. 'What is it? Don't you want to?'

'No, I really, really do, it's not that.' I sit up and pull my gown together where it's come undone. 'It's just that you've been really honest with me and I haven't been honest with you.'

Now he really looks worried. 'What do you mean?'

I pad to the French windows and slide them open before I pull the armchair near the door so I can smoke. 'A couple of things. The first is that, back home, there was sort of a guy . . .'

'Can I have one too?' I hand him my cigarette and light another for myself. 'Sort of a guy?'

I take a deep drag, smoke the shit out of my lungs, and then exhale through my nose. 'The popular opinion is that this guy may not have had my best interests at heart. I may have also fooled myself into thinking I was in love with my drug dealer.'

'Oh wow,' Brady smiles. 'Sounds co-dependent.'

'Well, if you don't get the appeal, no one will.' It feels good to be honest. Again, cleaner.

'What was the other thing?'

'Brady, what you told me about the car crash must have been . . . Well, what I should have said . . . what I should have said a really long time ago is that I killed someone too.'

'Huh?'

I nod. 'I really did . . .'

I tell him about Antonella. Everything. The day she stepped on stage at St Agnes; the coffee at Bar Italia; and the night at the mosque in Catford. 'You ever taken PMA?' I ask.

Brady shakes his head. 'Don't think so.'

'It's similar to ecstasy, MDMA or whatever, but it's much stronger. Way stronger. The other thing with PMA is that it's slow-acting. Antonella thought she'd taken worming tablets or something, because she didn't come up right away like you would on E. So she took three. She took three super-strength ecstasy pills in an hour.'

'Shit.' Brady holds out his hand for another cigarette. 'And she died?'

'Not right away. She had hyperthermia and basically overheated. She had a heart attack and a brain haemorrhage. She was on life support for a couple of weeks . . . the bleeping thing and the oxygen thing, the works. We went to see her. She looked . . . she looked like a child. The bed, the machines . . . it all made her seem really little. This . . . little girl held together by tubes and tape. The doctors said she was unlikely to wake up, and if she did . . .'

'She wouldn't be Antonella.'

And that's the crux of it. A sob pops out of my mouth. It's such a strange noise it surprises me. 'And she was so good.' I cover my mouth with my hand. 'She was the best one and now she's gone. Her parents switched off the life support. You know, she would have gone on to do something fucking incredible. Not just impressive, but like Obama impressive. And we took her away from the world.'

'Hey.' Brady picks me up and sits, pulling me on to his lap. 'Lexi. You didn't kill her.'

I snort.

'You didn't. Did you make her take those pills? No – she made a choice, just like you did, just like I did.'

'Kurt gave her those pills, and I gave her Kurt. The pair of us are poison.'

'No! Did Kurt know they were PMA?'

I shake my head. He thought they were E. 'He said it's not his fault, but . . .'

'But what? He didn't know, you didn't know, Antonella didn't know. It was an accident.'

'I lied,' I say. 'I lied to cover for him.'

'Well, of course you did. Venus lied for me. Love makes us do shitty things sometimes.'

I try to speak, but if I do, I'll properly go. I just shake my head.

'How long have you been hanging on to that?'

'It was last July.'

'Ten months. That's a lot of guilt to hang on to.'

'I should have said. I should have said when you told me about the crash.'

Now he shakes his head. 'It's not the same, Lex.'

'It is, I think. Why is it that you don't blame me, I don't blame you, but we both blame ourselves?'

He looks me squarely in the eye. 'Because we hate ourselves.'

I smile a wry smile. 'Jackpot.'

'Maybe that's why we need other people in our lives – because we don't see ourselves too well.'

'Someone to love us when we can't love ourselves.' I say the words before I know what I'm saying, but now they're out. I kiss him before I can say anything else. The kiss is soft, nurturing somehow.

'That sounds very co-dependent, Miss Volkov.'

I shake my head. 'Nah. I think even Goldstein would agree that we all need someone from time to time. We won't get through this all alone.'

'Get through what?'

'Get through anything.'

'Such wisdom.'

'I read a John Green book once.'

He laughs and stands me up. He leads me back to the bed. He pulls my gown open a fraction and kisses the groove between my neck and shoulder. I tingle. More kisses up my neck towards my earlobe. Tinglier.

'Why don't you hate me?' I ask him, feeling utterly naked, even though I'm in the robe.

He looks at me for a long time. His hand holds the curve of my face. 'Because I can see you,' he says.

We kiss again.

I'm crying even though I'm happy.

A warm hand slides inside my dressing gown and cups my boob. His thumb traces my nipple and it instantly goes hard. His other hand slides down my tummy and doesn't stop. Maximum tingle. I catch his wrist before we pass the point of no return. 'Is this really what you want? I understand now; I understand if you can't.'

He kisses me on the lips. 'I love you for understanding, but I think this is OK. It's different.'

'OK,' I say, and he lays me back on to the bed. I can't believe I'm doing this: a couple of hours ago I almost *died*, I should be exhausted, but I'm fully awake. This moment is now. It's like an endangered butterfly or something and I don't want to scare it away. It might not flutter along again. Let's go, Brady Ardito Jr.

My gown falls open and he slides between my legs. Just the weight on top of me feels so good. As we kiss I realise this is the first time – maybe ever – I've had sex sober. I'm very . . . *aware*. Of everything: the scent of my shampoo; the taste of his kisses (spearmint); how much I want him inside me . . . it's almost an ache. 'Do you have a condom?' I ask. Turns out being sober also makes you sensibler.

'I do.' He fishes in his back pocket. Gotta love a Boy Scout – always prepared.

Health and safety done, we can focus on business.

You know what? I'm nervous. Like really, really nervous. Normally I'm too out of it to care, but this is different. I'm stone-cold sober, and also it's Brady . . . I want him to be impressed. I could care that I haven't shaved my legs – or anything else, for that matter – but I'm already too turned on.

This is happening. It hurts for a second, and then it's OK. Then it's good.

He's in me and it's right.

We carry on kissing.

We're so close, we're one thing.

I grab his bum – someone's been doing their squats – to pull him closer still.

'Fuck,' he moans.

He's almost hitting the spot. He's warming it up. 'Don't stop,' I whisper. 'Faster.' There you go.

'Lex, god, you're beautiful. Shit, I'm not gonna last long.' He grins. 'It's been a while.'

I laugh and roll him over. If we're taking the direct route, I need to be on top. I steer him back inside. He groans again. So do I. There, that's definitely the spot. I rock, finding a rhythm that suits us both. I arch my back and that's it. That is absolutely the one. I start . . .

'Brady . . . I love you . . .' Shit. I'll probably regret that.

. . . and we finish together.

I flop down on to his chest. He runs a hand into my hair and pulls me into a slow, soft kiss. 'Lexi, I love you too.'

Or maybe I won't regret anything. Not a single thing.

I wake the next morning, stretched diagonal across the bed. Creamy vanilla light seeps through the drapes and I feel the need to stretch like a satisfied cat. I remember falling asleep in Brady's arms, my head resting on his sticky chest. 'Brady?' I call, kicking my legs. I'm still naked, tangled up with bed linen.

I roll over and look towards the bathroom. The door is ajar and the light isn't on. The clock says it's 9:50. I've missed breakfast. I wonder if, after almost drowning, they're letting me rest.

Brady must have crept out to avoid one of the nurses catching us, I guess. Either that or he went to fetch breakfast, in which case he's both a hero and a saint.

I shower and dress: skinny jeans and a cream slouchy cashmere jumper I got at Bergdorf Goodman. I can't deny a certain spring in my step this morning, and not just because I got laid. I feel . . . *holy* somehow. Lighter, freer, absolved of sin.

I decide today is the day to tell Goldstein about Antonella. I think he has to promise confidentiality. Despite everything, I don't want Kurt to go to jail. I believe he didn't know he was giving her PMA. I don't even know if she bought more pills off the red-haired dealer.

I'm not an idiot. I know I held grief at arm's length. I fought it really hard. I haven't even started to understand how I feel about losing her. I love her, but I have lost her and it feels like nothing I've ever felt before. Maybe now is the time. It's going to hurt, but I think I'm ready.

I stick some ballet pumps on my feet and potter down the hallway. The kitchen staff are cleaning up breakfast, but I see Guy coming out of the gym. 'Morning!' he says. 'You look lovely.'

'Thank you! You know what? I feel lovely too. Have you seen Brady?'

'Nope. He wasn't at brekkie today. I wondered if he was . . . with you.' He whispers the last part.

'He was. Don't tell anyone. I'll go check his room.'

I trot upstairs and down the hallway to Brady's room. I knock on the door. 'Brady? It's me.'

There's no reply which is weird, because if he's not in the gym and he's not in therapy (Kendall and I have the 9–10 slot), then where the hell is he? Again, it's not like we live in a house with locked doors. I walk in.

I stop and try to take in what I'm seeing.

This can't be happening.

It just can't.

The bed is made. The wardrobes hang open, empty. Stray hangers litter the floor where clothes have been hastily pulled free and shoved in a case or bag.

I'm going to be sick.

I really am.

I push into his en-suite and drop to my knees in front of the toilet. I haven't eaten in hours so only produce hot yellow bile.

He's gone.

I crouch over the toilet for a minute, because my head is spinning and I might faint.

I swill my mouth out and return to the bedroom. I see a letter on the bed and I almost don't need to read it to know what it's going to say. However he words it, it's goodbye, right?

He has left me.

He fucked me and then left me.

I pick up the letter.

Dear Lexi

I am so sorry. Please don't hate me. I hope you, of all people, understand why I had to go.

I don't trust myself.

Last night, while you slept, I watched you. I couldn't take my eyes off you. I was imagining our long future together. I wanted to see the world with you . . . beaches and sunsets and Instagram moments. I wanted to wake up with you every day. I wanted to introduce you to my mom, my sister, my dad. I saw you in a wedding dress. I imagined our kids.

And that's how it starts. The obsession. I could feel it, like the bed was going to swallow us both whole. I can't do it, Lex. I can't do it to you – not when you're doing so well. The last thing I want is to rake you into my shit.

Clearly, I still have some recovering to do, and I don't think I can do that if my head and heart are full of you.

Keep on getting better. You are so strong – stronger than me, and stronger than you think you are. Thank you for sharing so much with me. Remember, it's not your fault and you deserve love and happiness, as do I. Who knows, maybe one day when we're different people . . . right?

Love B x

No way. There is no way he's done this. What time is it? How early did he leave? How many ferries leave in the morning? I guess there's one to bring staff over first thing. What time does it return?

I shove the letter in my back pocket and rocket downstairs towards the entrance hall. The receptionist blinks sluggishly like she's on about four Valium.

'Did you see Brady go?' I demand.

'Sorry?' she asks.

'Did you see Brady Ardito leave?'

'No, dear. I understand he has discharged himself though. I had a note on my . . .'

'What time does the ferry leave?'

'I don't—'

'Jesus! What time does the ferry go back to the mainland?'

'At about ten thirty, dear.'

I look up at the clock. It's 10:35. 'OK, thanks.'

I push through the main doors and slump down the grand stairs. In the distance, I see the ferry chugging across the sea, leaving white ripples in its wake. It's carrying Brady back to the real world and leaving me here.

'No . . .' My insides crush, fold inward like a tin can.

What's worse? Never having something, or having something and losing it?

I watch the ferry get smaller and smaller until it drops off the edge of the horizon.

I can't face therapy with Goldstein. I tell him I'm sick, although I do ask if I can check my phone.

There's a message from Kurt waiting for me.

Thinking of u a lot. Babe. Come home.

How? How is it boys magically know how to drive you maximum mental? Do they have a global whatsapp group?

The timing is perfect. It feels like a punch in the stomach. I relive folding onto Brady's sweaty chest, that bodily bliss.

I remember waking up one time to find Kurt watching me, his face pressed into the pillow. 'What?' I said croakily. Morning breath.

'You're pretty,' he said with a little grin. He was like a naughty school boy somehow.

I sit cross-legged on the floor in the middle of Goldstein's office. I make sure I'm facing away from owl-cam. Without making any noise at all, I cry.

STEP 8:
I ACCEPT I HAVE HURT
MYSELF AND OTHERS

I'm over it.

As my seventieth day creeps ever closer, I start to lose patience. Cabin fever sets in, the walls closing in like a funhouse.

I ride Storm most days, but I now know the forest hacks like the back of my hand. We're both going through the motions, he and I.

I've started many letters to Brady, and they're all crumpled in a wastepaper basket in my room. *I ~~love~~ miss you / This can work / Thinking about you / It'll be different for us / Let's give it a go . . .* I don't even know where he is; it'd be a message-in-a-bottle job.

I know it's stupid.

I knew him for less than two months. A lot of what we felt was probably brought on by this dollhouse we both found ourselves in. Holiday romances usually last as long as the flight home.

But I did feel *something* for him. And when I think about him now, I am sore. He's left me bruised.

I can't even think about Kurt. It's too confusing. I want him like I want heroin. It'd be good, but it's also bad. I'll deal with him later.

What's worse, the others are all leaving ahead of me. Guy went last week. On his last morning, he knocked on my door. I was on my terrace having a coffee.

'Come in,' I shouted.

'It's just me,' he said, shuffling into my room.

I rose from the sunlounger. 'Oh, is it time? Is your dad here?'

'No,' he said sheepishly, joining me on the terrace. 'There's something I have to give you.'

Sweet. 'A going-away gift?'

'Not quite.' He opened his hand and I see my McQueen skull ring is in his palm.

'Oh my god!' I grabbed it out of his fingers. 'Where did you find that? I've been looking everywhere . . .'

'I didn't find it.' He didn't look me in the eye. 'I took it. I . . . I'm sorry.'

'Oh. OK.'

'It's a thing I do.'

'I . . . sure.' Sometimes I wonder if Guy is a better-spoken, posh, white, male version of Sasha. So many knots, it's hard to know which to untangle first.

He shook his head in answer to my unspoken question. 'I don't really know why I do it. I suppose sometimes I like to imagine what it'd be like to be someone other than me. Anyone else, for a while, at least. So I take people's stuff. These little trinkets . . . I can't stop myself. I . . . well, I have to make amends before I leave. Step Nine and everything . . . so . . . I'm sorry.'

I tried to keep the shock off my face. Melissa's locket, Saif's watch, Brady's hat . . . I wondered if he took those too . . .

'Hey, it's OK. We've all done messed up things,' I said. He nodded, but looked so ashamed of himself. 'Guy, I mean it. I still think you're a good Guy. Get it?'

He gave me a smile. 'I don't wanna go,' he said in a very small voice. I suspect he'd retreat for eternity if he could; he's on the verge of becoming institutionalised. I gave him a tight hug and a kiss on the cheek.

I can't sleep – maybe because it's barely after eleven. With so few of us now, bedtime has been getting earlier and earlier. We're bored shitless. It also feels very female – almost like being back at St Agnes.

I head along the corridor towards the kitchen and see a shape sitting in the dark. Apparently I'm not the only one who can't sleep. 'Hello?' I say, wary of another kitchen altercation with Sasha.

'It's just me,' says Ruby. It's her final night at the clinic. I guess she can't sleep either.

In the dim fire-safety lighting, I see her sat in front of a Death-By-Chocolate chocolate cake.

'Relax,' she says. 'Before I go, I needed to prove I could do it.'

'Do what?'

She holds up a side plate with a couple of crumbs on it. 'Just have one motherfucking slice.'

I smile and see only one narrow wedge missing from the cake. 'Well, let me remove one more slice of temptation from your path.' I grab a plate from beside the sink and cut myself a piece. 'You ready for tomorrow?'

She sighs. 'I don't know. Maybe this time it'll stick. Imma level with you. This ain't my first ride at the rodeo. My first fat camp was when I was thirteen. I'm pretty over it; I can't keep doing this. I'm too goddamn old.'

I know what she means. I pick at the cake. It's a little dry.

'You know what the crazy part is?' Ruby goes on, sipping a glass of milk. 'She's mad as a shithouse rat, but Sasha's got a point. Don't you dare tell her I said so.'

'What do you mean?'

'Part of the problem is we're rich. And not just cash rich. *Time* rich. Time is a luxury item, don't you think? We have so much *time* and nothing to do with it. So I eat when I ain't hungry, you shoot up or whatever. If you ever read my daddy's autobiography – which he didn't write, by the way – he was working in his pop's grocery store at thirteen. He got early acceptance to medical school at seventeen. Always working, always had his eye on that prize. He didn't have no time to sit around thinking about his esteem and shit. Girl, I gotta get me something to do.'

'You've been busy looking after your mum . . .'

She shakes her head and her little diamond earrings twinkle in the dark. 'We got the best goddamn nurses in New York. I can't use that excuse no more. Like, what are you gonna do when you get outta here?'

I open my mouth but nothing comes out. 'I have no idea.'

'Well, girl, you better start thinking. Your time's running out too.'

She leaves the next morning. There's some slight excitement as a Mercedes with blacked-out windows crunches up the drive to collect her. We all gather around, wondering if we'll get a glimpse of the man a lot of people think will be the next president.

Alas, when the car door opens, a trim Kerry Washington type steps out and greets Ruby with a hug.

'Everyone,' Ruby says, 'this is my Aunt Rochelle.'

'Nice to meet you all.' She doesn't even take off her sunglasses. 'Where's Daddy?'

'Oh sweetheart, there was a funeral for the former senator of New Jersey. He had to go. You know how it is.'

'I do,' she says as the driver loads her luggage into the boot. Aunt Rochelle talks with Goldstein and Lady Denhulme. I overhear snippets; they're discussing a donation Dr Kidd wants to make to the foundation.

Ruby bids each of us farewell. Even Sasha.

'You OK?' I mutter as I give her a hug.

'I'm fine. It would have been weirder if he'd actually come,' she says. 'It means the world is just the way I left it. Maybe that's a good thing.'

As the ridiculous car heads towards the ferry, there are even fewer of us stood on the drive. I know my gift for making any given situation about me is especially gross, but I can't help but wonder if my world is the way I left it too.

And tomorrow is Kendall's turn. I'm gonna miss this bitch, and not just because she reminds me of Antonella.

For her last night, Kendall wanted a sleepover vibe, so we're in our pyjamas in the TV room, gathered around an extra-large pizza. Kendall helps herself to a second (small) slice with a sigh. 'Oh, my parents will be so thrilled,' she says ruefully. 'It's crazy. I can't believe I'm eating pizza. I . . . I didn't think I'd ever be able to.'

'And how is it?' I ask.

She swallows. 'I remember . . . I *used* to love pizza.'

'Pizza is one of your five a day,' Sasha says.

It's just the three of us. Some girl from off *The X Factor* checked in two days ago, but she's still in detox. Sleeping pills allegedly, but I think that's media spin for coke or smack to be honest.

'Are you nervous?' I ask.

'No, I'm excited. I think. I miss my friends. I can go back to college before summer term so Mum says I probably won't have to repeat the year. I wanna show everyone that I'm getting better too. Everyone thought I was crazy. "Tranorexia." LOL.' She continues to nibble on her slice of pizza. She is looking better than when I first met her. Skinny, yes, but no longer like a living corpse.

'It's gonna be weird when you're all gone,' Sasha says. I detect a hint of sadness.

'You'll be leaving soon too,' Kendall says, ever the pep-squad.

Sasha shakes her head. 'Sweet songbird, didn't you hear? I'm finally getting it.'

'Getting what?' I ask.

309

Sasha lays back on her duvet and convulses, shaking her arms and legs. 'Shock therapy!'

Kendall and I look to each other. 'Are you for real?' I say.

'Yep. The man with the electrodes has been after me for years. I finally gave formal consent. Not like anything else has worked, has it? Hours of therapy, basket weaving, a rainbow of pills. This is the last resort.'

'They zap your brain?' Kendall asks, agog.

'Like, I thought that went out with straitjackets,' I add.

Sasha smiles slyly. 'Nope. They strap you to the bed and make you bite down on a wooden spoon and then run a thousand volts through your head,' she laughs. 'Oh, look at your gormless faces. You pair of dicks! It's fine. They do it under general anaesthetic and it's only a low current. It changes the chemistry of your brain or something. But it might take time, so I'm not going anywhere soon.'

Not sure I'm buying what she's selling. It can't be that easy, or we'd all get it as a pick-me-up. They'd be doing it on Harley Street with Botox and collagen. I keep that thought to myself. 'And it's . . . safe?' I ask instead.

She shrugs. 'I dunno, Blondie. Goldstein said something about memory loss. And it doesn't always work.'

'What if it doesn't?'

She stares at the empty pizza box for a second. 'Well, then, that's it, isn't it? This is just how I am.'

'I'm sure it'll work,' Kendall says. 'It will.'

The following afternoon we're back on the driveway like the Railway Children. I give Kendall a long hug. 'Promise you'll email me,' she says. 'I'm only like half an hour outside London. We can meet up.'

'We will,' I say, and I mean it. I need to see someone from here in the outside world, I think, or this whole episode is going to feel like a fever dream. I'll need a reminder. 'I'll miss you.'

She smiles like that's all she really wanted to hear. 'I'll miss you too.'

Kendall gets into the back of her parents' car. They seem lovely – but both have the worn, embattled and sleep-deprived look of parents convinced it's all their fault. 'Don't be posting shit about me on socialite.com!' I say.

'I'm gonna sell your story to the *Daily Mail*,' she laughs through the open window. Her dad starts the car. 'Track him down,' she adds urgently. 'Just find him, Lex. He loves you. He does.'

Her words take my breath away. The car rolls down the drive and I can only wave her off.

Goldstein hovers at my side. 'Are you ready for your session?' he asks and I nod. 'Next week it's your turn.'

Going home. Home to maids and chefs and beauticians and other people who are paid to be nice. Mummy and Daddy don't even know where I've been. I don't know what I'm going home to. I don't even know if it's home.

It feels like I've been here forever, but it still feels too soon to leave.

'When was the last time you spoke to Kurt?' Goldstein asks.

It's my last week in the centre; my last week of therapy (at least with him). I don't know whether I'll miss it or not. I guess I've become . . . used to it.

I think about Kurt, out there living his nocturnal life, that urban fox of mine. For the last few weeks we've been messaging each other more than talking. He knows I'm coming home.

'We message every day.'

'Will you see him?'

'Of course.' But my tone is far from certain. I know I'll never see Brady again, but he has changed how I feel about Kurt. It feels more like seventy years than seventy days since we were last together. 'Things are different now.'

'You're different now.'

'Am I?'

Goldstein smiles. 'You've come a long way, Lexi. I'm not your warden, I can't tell you what to do. But we've talked at length about co-dependency and whether it was really in Kurt's interests for you to be clean.'

I flinch. It's hard to tell from texts, but with each day, Kurt seems to be – genuinely – getting more and more excited that I'm coming back. Once, I'd have taken this as some sort of victory over him, but now, I don't know. Does he really love me, or am I his personal cashpoint? 'I know.' I draw my feet under my legs. 'We have stuff to talk about.'

'Certainly. Have you thought more about what you'll do?'

I shrug. 'I can't exactly go back to St Agnes, can I?'

I was drunk on the day I wasn't expelled.

I'd downed half a bottle of vodka at lunchtime and staggered all the way to Religious Studies with Sister Bernadette. I sat by the window, falling asleep.

Antonella.

The last time I saw her in the hospital was tattooed onto my mind. Part girl, part machine, like something from one of Nik's horror comics. It was all I saw unless I got really, really blasted.

'Lexi Volkov!' Sister Bernie yelled. Imagine Mad-Eye Moody in a habit.

'What?'

'Ms Grafton's office. Now, please, hurry along.'

The whole classroom was gauzy. Swishy and blurry. 'Whatever.' I stood, only to topple on to Genie. I laughed. So did the other girls. I thought they were laughing *with* me. Now I'm less convinced.

I zigzagged down the long, lofty corridors of St Agnes, purposefully wasting time, keeping her waiting.

Somewhere in London, at that very moment, they were switching the life-support machine off.

Grafton was waiting, hands on hips, by her receptionist's desk. 'For crying out loud, Alexandria. In! Now!'

I waved at the mousy little receptionist as I sauntered past. 'Lookin' good, Bev,' I said with a wink.

'Sit down,' Grafton snapped. I did as I was told, slumping into an armchair. 'Just look at you! You're a disgrace!' My tie was skew-whiff, the waistline of my kilt rolled up. 'Have you been drinking?'

'No, that would be against school rules.'

Grafton pursed her lips, smoothed her skirt and seated herself.

'Is this the bit where you kick me out?'

'No, Miss Volkov. I'm assuming you haven't heard. This morning, the coroner ruled misadventure. No criminal charges will be brought against you or anyone else at this time.'

At once I felt absolved and guiltier than ever. Where was it? Where was my punishment? I . . . I had it coming. I earned it. I *deserved* it.

'Lexi?'

'What?'

'Are you all right?'

I shrugged. I couldn't even speak.

'Listen carefully. I've met with the governors to discuss your future and it's been decided that, whatever Results Day brings, you'll study for your A-Levels elsewhere.'

'So I'm expelled?'

'No, dear. Expelling you would only add to the deluge of negative publicity we've all endured already. We'll do absolutely everything we can to help you find an alternative school. I'll even write you a glowing letter of recommendation.'

Her room was spinning like a centrifuge. I felt nauseous. 'Why?'

'Because then you'll be someone else's problem. But more importantly, Lexi, hopefully you'll get the fresh start you so dearly need. After what happened to Antonella . . . well, perhaps you need somewhere where people know neither of you.'

It felt like a fist in the face.

She might as well have said it.

I needed to be somewhere where no one knew the story of how the Bad Twin killed the Good Twin.

I bowed out without a struggle. At the time, I was too messed up to fight it.

'Maybe you can return to St Agnes if that's what you want,' Goldstein says. 'Elaine Denhulme is a very powerful woman, as is her husband.'

I wonder what Lord Denhulme would do to Goldstein if he knew what he and his wife got up to in the stable mews. Who am I kidding – Lord Denhulme probably has a fleet of mistresses all around the world.

I'm filled with hope for a split second. Imagine . . . slotting back into that school, that kilt, those knee socks, that glorious routine. Nevada and Genie are still there. I sometimes forget I'm still only seventeen. Dog years. I guess I'd have to start a year behind them, but still.

The light fades as quickly as it came. No. Antonella haunts that school and I'd have to face her ghost every day. I'm not sure I can put myself through that. 'Yeah. Maybe,' I say.

'And your writing?'

'I've been working on some short stories,' I tell him. And it's true. They're not very good, mind. They're funereal and emo, however buoyant I try to make my prose. Bad, overwrought, teenage-angst writing. 'I want to get better.'

'Succinct.'

'I hope so,' I smile a little.

It's there though; the future. It was too dark before, but now I can see it. It's only visible through a pea-soup fog, so I can't see it clearly, but there's a *something* ahead in the tunnel and I'm chugging towards it.

I sit on the edge of my bed, surrounded by bulging, lumpy bags and an overstuffed case, straining at the zipper. The silver Miu Miu dress I arrived in, although laundered, sits at the bottom of the bin.

'Are you ready?' Nikolai asks.

I look up at my brother. It's so weird. He isn't thirteen and spotty any more. At some point in the last seven years, he's become a proper grown-up. When did that happen? And what does that make me, his little sister? 'Not really,' I say.

'Come on!' He offers me a hand and pulls me off the bed. 'It's going to be fine. Dad's in Moscow until Friday.' He scoops me into a hug. 'You look amazing, by the way.'

I laugh. 'Rehab is great. You should try it.'

Boynurse Marcus, back, and no longer under investigation, helps us with our bags. Nik's BMW waits on the drive. I faintly remember tumbling on to this driveway seventy days ago. God, I was a hot mess. I can't believe I've lasted this long.

The doctors – Ahmed and Goldstein – wait on the drive, with Sasha, like a weird family portrait. I don't want soppy goodbyes. I came, they fixed me, I left. If only it were that simple. I get through a hug with Ahmed with no problems, but when Goldstein hugs me, a little sob wracks my body. I don't know where it's coming from, but I press my face into his chest. 'Oh god, I'm sorry.'

He chuckles and pats my back. 'Don't be. Lexi, I'm very proud of the progress you've made.'

That makes me worse. 'Please don't say anything else nice. I can't take it.'

He holds me at arm's length and hands me a tissue. 'Now. Miss Volkov, you have my number?'

'I do.'

'You've got your follow-up appointment in London, but until then, you just call me if you need me. In fact, call me if you don't.'

I smile. 'I promise.'

I move on to Sasha. 'Ain't nobody here but us chickens,' she says.

'You won't be here forever,' I say.

'There are worse places to spend forever.'

I shake my head. 'You're gonna be fine.'

She smiles a psychotic smile. 'One day. Not today.'

'Be good,' I tell her, and then give all three of them a half-arsed wave before getting in the passenger seat.

'There's just one more goodbye I have to make,' I tell Nikolai.

I rest my head against Storm's head. I don't say any words. Partly because he's a horse, but also because I'll cry again.

I think he gets it.

'You'll be missed.' Elaine is standing behind me on the path, bucket of feed over her arm. 'I didn't think it was possible, Lexi, but you broke him in.'

I still don't say anything.

'Or maybe he broke you in.' Elaine smiles and ruffles his mane. 'Oh, it's all very poetic, isn't it? Unbreakable dark horse . . . and her friend, Storm.'

I laugh. 'Bit naff, don't you think?'

'I'm fond of naff.' She gives me a hug. 'People always pretend they've grown out of naff, but I don't think we ever do really. We all want the happy ending, if we're honest. If he gets out of hand, I'll be on the phone for tips. Don't be a stranger, Lexi.'

'Thank you,' I tell her. That does make leaving easier.

Nikolai drives us down the ramp and onto the ferry. There's only one other vehicle – a catering van bringing frozen stuff to the kitchens. 'This time you don't have to lie in the back,' Nik says.

'You know I don't enjoy a boat,' I tell him. Daddy has a yacht. I'm *really* not a fan. I'm *really* not a fan since what happened with Sasha.

'C'mon,' he says, unclipping his seatbelt. I reluctantly follow him out of the car and onto the observation deck at the front of the boat. There's a soft spring breeze, thick with salt. I tousle my hair.

Before long, the ferry chugs out of the docks. Behind me, the Clarity Centre gets smaller and smaller. In front of me there's a lot of empty sky and sea. I feel too small all of a sudden; vulnerable.

Nik takes my hand. 'It's gonna be fine, Lex. You're better now.'

I nod for his benefit, but I'm not so sure.

That's normal, right?

Through a lingering sea fret, the jagged silhouette of the mainland comes into view.

I'm going home.

It's boring country roads – fields, trees, roadkill – until we hit the M25 and then it's traffic jams all the way into Vauxhall.

London is still handsome in its rough-jawed way. I've kinda missed it. Nik follows the Thames and, as we cross Chelsea Bridge, I get a good view of Battersea Power Station, the Shard in the distance and Daddy's hotel. We're almost there. I take a deep breath.

We leave the car and luggage with the valets and head straight to our suite on the ninth floor, ignoring the England Rugby Team who are noisily checking out at the front desk.

It's exactly as I left it, only now a mountain of freebies brands have sent await me, piled on my bed. Goody bags from Clinique, MAC, Selfridges, Topshop, Apple, Moschino . . . and those are just the ones on top. The maids have tidied my room, but it's all pretty much untouched: dry-cleaning hanging on the closet handle; photobooth pictures of my friends blu-tacked to the mirror; old issues of *Vogue* and *Glamour* in a heap on the bedside table. They're covered in coke residue next to the old credit card I chopped lines with.

I shudder.

I wasn't expecting that. I've already – as part of my 'transition' – told Nik where he could find (and destroy) any drugs I might have dotted around the hotel. I remembered a baggy in an Alaïa clutch, a bottle of oxy in the bedside cabinet and some tabs of MDMA in a shoebox, but who knows what else I've forgotten.

'You OK?' Nikolai asks.

'Uh. Yeah.' I'll throw them away. It'll be OK.

'Sure?'

'What do I do now?' I say, genuinely unsure. Yeah, Goldstein and I talked about my writing, my *future*, but what about the *present*?

'Anything you want, Lex. You're free.'

The first thing I do with my freedom is make a cup of tea.

I call room service and ask for a salmon and cream cheese bagel.

Then I go to the living room – put the TV on because it's too quiet – and open my MacBook. I push a million throw cushions aside and sit on the giant suede flump of a sofa, legs crossed. Everything in our suite is tan, nude, sand or ecru – even the cascading vases of lilies. It's beige. Everything is fucking beige.

Last week, I was informed of major world events – spoiler alert, the world is still fucked – to prepare me for real life, so I'm not completely out of the loop, but I am completely out of *my* loop. First up, Facebook. I look up Kurt, but he's pretty off-grid. He's been checked into a couple of things by Troy, Adam Greenberg (Baggy), Flossy Blenheim and various other scene girls. I follow links to various pictures of parties and launches. He's been tagged in a couple, but always skulking in the background, not posing and gurning like the others are. Uh, he went to Mahiki. Really? God, he must have been desperate.

Nothing too dramatic seems to have happened. Nevada appears to now be in some sort of relationship with a shaven-headed musician girl called Fo – no surname – which is dimly interesting as I thought she was strictly into dick. Still, good for her. They certainly look achingly cool together.

God help me, but I load socialite.com. There's been very little movement during my exile. Xenia Blenheim currently reigns supreme along with the usual suspects: The Aziz twins, River Knox, Chastity Horowitz, Flossy, Sailor Birling. I, on a need-to-know basis, click on my own entry. There's nothing untoward. Someone has left a comment – 'Where has Lexi Volkov gone? She's super quiet rn.' There's no reply. Good.

Just in case, I google myself to see if any gossip columns have also noted my absence. In 'news' there's nothing. Well, there's a report from the Burdock & Rasputin party. I click the link. There I am, sandwiched between Gigi and Bella, looking like a washed-up corpse in a Miu Miu dress. 'God, I looked like total shit,' I mutter to myself.

There's a mirror over the fireplace. I look *better* than I did in February, but still a little creased. I sigh. I'm back now. Can't hide forever.

I pick up the phone. 'Hi. Is that Susannah? It's Lexi. Does Niall have any slots this afternoon? Cut and colour.'

The salon is in the basement, next door to the health centre. It's a windowless cell, tastelessly decorated in black and gold with sparkly tassel curtains draped everywhere, giving it the feel of Aladdin's brothel or something. But Niall is good – he's a session stylist who does three days a week at V Hotels. He comes out of his room to greet me. 'Oh, my god! Babes!' He plants a kiss on each cheek. 'Where the hell have you been?'

'Just with my mum,' I say.

'In Cayman?'

'Yeah.' My total lack of tan is a dead giveaway. 'The weather was shit.'

'Oh. OK. Right. Sure,' he says in his twinkly Dublin accent. I see some of the young beauticians eye me with suspicion. They're perma-tanned and over-contoured with draggy lash extensions. I scowl at them. I fucking pay their wages. 'Come on through, babes. What are we doing for you?'

I want a change. He fixes my roots and I ask him to tint it a shade lighter – a colder, icier blond. When the colour's been rinsed over the sink, he hacks a good six inches off the bottom, taking it to my collar bone. It looks sharp, new, fresh.

I look clean.

'Like it?' Niall asks.

'Love it,' I reply. 'It was time for a change.' He unwraps me from the cape. 'Hey, can I use the sunbed?'

He knows better than to ask why. 'Sure, babes. I'll just check if it's free.'

I have a healthy, golden tan when Daddy returns on Friday. You can tell when he enters a hotel because a nervous shockwave ripples through the building. The staff straighten their ties and adopt rod-in-ass posture. Daddy is pleasingly scary.

I hear him before I see him. Staff scurry down the corridor alongside him like pilot fish, no doubt trying to match his colossal stride. He's six-five and almost as wide. 'Later,' he snaps. 'It can wait. Tell them if they want to do business, they can wait one hour.' He enters the suite and throws his overcoat over a chair. 'There's my *myshka*! Come here and give your father a hug!'

I spring off the sofa and throw myself into his arms. He wraps them around me like tree trunks and I am four years old again. I feel tears sting my eyes, but I can't seem too emotional.

'Aw, what is wrong, *myshka*?'

'Nothing!' I say, wiping my eyes. 'I just missed you is all. It's been ages.'

'How is your mother? She still with that *durak*?'

I almost forget that that's my cover. 'Oh? What? Yeah, she's cool. And Jorge is good too.'

Daddy humphs. 'Jorge is a sissy man. When she wake up and realise?'

I roll my eyes. 'I dunno. How's Anja?'

He messes up my new hair by way of a warning. 'Anja is still in Dubai with her mother.'

'Best place for her,' I say with a sly smile.

Daddy can't get mad at me, I'm his *myshka*, his little mouse. Instead he gives me another big hug. 'Aw, I missed you much, *myshka*. I do not work for rest of day and we go to Sky Garden, yes?'

As basic as the Sky Garden is, there's literally nothing else I'd rather do, nowhere else I'd rather be. But this is fairly standard. Daddy is great at grand gestures: a pony! A Maserati on my seventeenth birthday! Drop everything for fancy dinner! Only then it's back to business as usual and I won't see him for days on end. All or nothing. Shit, I'm crying again.

'Alexandria? Are you OK?'

'I promise I am, Daddy. I'm just really pleased you're back.' He hugs me again and I realise how much, weirdly, I miss Dr Goldstein.

And Brady.

I miss Brady most of all.

The Sky Garden, a greenhouse at the top of a skyscraper overlooking The City, is a bit of a tourist trap, but the food is gorgeous. I have sea trout and – after a moment of hesitation – a bellini. I feel a little guilty for drinking and it goes right to my head. But drinking was never really the issue. At least, I don't think it was. Was it? I vow to just have one with lunch.

Daddy sees some people he knows – that happens everywhere we go – and I sip my drink and look out over London. It's so huge, people crawling through the street like ants. From so high up, I can see to the edges of the city, but however much I try to focus, I just think about him.

I wonder where he is right now.

I wonder what he's doing.

I wonder if he's thinking about me too.

St Agnes is smaller than I remember. It's the first time I've been back since *that* appointment. The smell, polish and school dinners, is exactly the same. I remember the final walk out of Grafton's office on the last day. I remember the girls looking on, their conversations abruptly tailing off as I strode past, trying to keep my head high.

She's the one who . . .

Totally her fault . . .

No, but she gave her the . . .

Today I've come alone. I thought it was important that I did. I'm wearing black cigarette trousers with Gucci loafers and a crisp white Chloé blouse. I couldn't look more penitent if I was wearing a fucking habit.

I wait outside Grafton's office in a stiff leather armchair, watching girls mill around the corridors, an uptight army of claret and gold blazers and kilts, knee socks and neckties. I feel so, so far removed from them, but what other choice do I have?

Some of them have spotted me, even though I kept my shades on. 'Is that Lexi?' 'Is she coming back?' 'I thought they expelled her ass?' I try to ignore them.

'Miss Volkov?' says Grafton's personal secretary. 'Ms Grafton will see you now.'

I enter the office. It smells of her *Eternity* perfume and strong black coffee. Oil portraits of past Heads judge me from all four walls.

'Good morning, Alexandria. Please take a seat.'

She's hard to read. 'Thanks for agreeing to see me,' I say.

'Of course, dear. Now, what can we do for you?'

My palms are clammy. I wipe them on my trousers. 'I was wondering if it would be possible for me to resume my studies in September.' She says nothing, but purses her peach-colour lips. 'We . . . we could say it was a year out. I feel ready to return. I . . . I want to get my A-Levels and think about university . . .'

Grafton holds up a hand. 'I'll stop you there, Alexandria. I received a phone call from Lady Denhulme last week.'

'Oh. So you know.'

'I assure you she was most discreet and so shall I be. I was pleased to hear you sought treatment.' She looks genuinely concerned; that's probably a good thing. 'That said, I'm afraid I won't be readmitting you to St Agnes.'

My heart plummets. I feel sick. 'You won't?' I just want to check I've heard right.

'I'm afraid not.'

'But . . . but why? I'm clean now.'

Grafton reclines in her chair. 'And I commend that, I really do. I don't for one second think that what you've been through is easy. But that's why I'm blocking your application. I once asked you, in this very office, when you were going to accept that your behaviour has consequences. Do you remember? If I welcome you back to the same school, with the same friends, it's like nothing ever happened. Once again, the last year of your life is conveniently erased without consequence.'

I want to fight, to argue, but I'm stunned. I wonder, honestly, if this is the first time I've ever been told 'no'.

'Alexandria, I have no doubt that, with your father's influence, you'll be accepted into any top-flight school in the world. But not this one, I'm afraid. I think it's important for you that last year happened, and this will serve to remind you.'

I will *not* cry in front of this woman. I push back my chair and grab my handbag. 'Fine,' I say.

329

'Alexandria, I'm sure you'll come to understand why . . .'

'I said it's fine,' I snarl. Like, what's the point? What's the point in everything I've done if no one else will forget what I did? I hold the pain in my gut and turn it into flames. 'By the way, my name is *Lexi* Volkov and maybe I'll *buy* this school just to watch you get fired. *There's* a consequence.' I stare her down as I walk out. She flinches first, because she knows I could.

I blast down the corridor towards the front doors like a hurricane. Two doe-eyed Second Form girls stare at me in awe as I put my sunglasses back on. 'What the fuck are you looking at?' I barge between them and back out into my London.

I'm going to burn this city down.

Because there's nothing else for me to do.

Red lips, red nails, red soles on my Louboutins.

I can't hide any longer. The hotel gets smaller by the day. Soon I'll be like Alice, my arms and legs sticking out the windows. I need to go out.

Yesterday I tackled Bond Street and bought a Vivienne Westwood LBD and Burberry biker jacket. Tonight, *Cramp Magazine* is hosting its Spring/Summer edition party at the hotel in Shoreditch. It feels like a safe bet. If it all gets too much, I can get a room or just come back to Vauxhall. Nothing bad can happen at the hotel.

I had my Bellini with Daddy at the Sky Gardens and I hardly noticed I was drinking; it just felt like the natural thing to do. I didn't suddenly want a whole ton of meth or anything. I think I'm safe around alcohol.

I take a hotel car from Vauxhall to Shoreditch. There are paps outside – of course there are – and it's like I've never been away. 'Lexi! Over here, Lexi! Lexi! Give us a smile!' Camera's flash like a strobe. I pose, hand on hip. Don't smile too much, it wrinkles your face. I wonder what magnificent journalism will appear in the Sidebar of Shame tomorrow. Will it be *Sexy Lexi reveals new do*? I'm not *showing off my assets* upstairs so it could well be *Lexi puts on a leggy display*. Their mothers must be so proud.

I do my twenty seconds before turning and heading into the hotel. The paps complain, but some other thirst queen will drag her boob job down the carpet in a minute or two.

The party is already throbbing. Canapé minions weave through the crowd, trays aloft. It seems during three months in rehab London hasn't moved on from serving miniature versions of infant party foods: I spy mini-burgers, mini-hotdogs, mini-ice-cream-cones. The DJ, some model who knows how to plug in an iPhone, pretends to cue tracks with big headphones.

Nothing ever changes. I lift a flute of champagne off a tray as one glides by.

I take a deep breath.

I can do this.

'Lexi!' I turn and see Genie pushing through the crowd, closely followed by Nevada who's hand-in-hand with Fo. Fo is wearing her sunglasses inside.

'Oh my god!' I gasp, already feeling like I'm playing the role of Lexi in some weird experimental theatre piece. 'Genie! How are you?'

Genie gives me lavish air kisses. Her red hair, padded out with extensions, falls in voluminous curls. She smells gorgeous. 'I'm super, darling! How are you? How was *Cayman*?' She doesn't really need to add a wink or a nudge.

'Great, thanks.'

'Well, darling, I must say, you look phenomenal.'

I'll take that. 'Thank you.' God, it's so noisy, I have to shriek over the music. 'Hi, Nev, how are you?'

She seems more guarded. She gives me just one kiss on my cheek. She looks as chic as ever. 'I'm everything. Lexi, this is Fo, Fo, this is Lexi.'

'Hi,' I offer her a hand. 'Nice to meet you.'

Fo, clearly on edge, shakes my hand and leans in for a kiss. 'You too, hon. Say,' she comes closer, 'you know where a girl can score some blow?'

332

I recoil slightly. Wow, that was quick even by London fashion party standards. 'No,' I say too sharply. 'I mean, just throw a canapé into the crowd, see who it hits and get some off them.'

'You not packing?'

'No. Sorry.'

'Cool. No worries.' Fo whispers something in Nevada's ear and vanishes into the crowd, presumably to score.

'She seems nice,' I say. 'So, you're a lesbian now?' I ask with a grin.

Nevada laughs. 'God, get into it. I'm sexually fluid, Lex.'

'Gosh, how radical.' I lick my teeth. 'She seems cool.'

'She's an asshole when she's on coke.'

'Who isn't?' It's nice to be back with old friends. 'Come on, let's get a booth.'

It's nice. Away from the speakers, I can hear them. They fill me in on school gossip, and – while I admit nothing – I tell them it was nice to spend some time away from London. A bottle of champagne doesn't last long between four and soon we've finished our second. I already feel quite merry.

The crowd is a mix of hipster writers and their club-kid friends (penniless art students ferreting finger food in their handbags for later), New Faces from Prestige and IMG, grime rappers who aren't very grimy, and us: the It Kids and minor royals. Eventually the club-kids, having had their fill of free food and drink, start to drift further east for their DJ slots or door-whore gigs.

'Where are we going now?' Genie says.

'I think I'm heading back to Vauxhall if you want to come? We can chill in the suite.'

Fo, who mostly communicates via Nevada, mutters something in her ear. 'There's a party in Chelsea,' Nev relays. 'The Aziz twins.'

I shake my head. 'They're brats. Aren't they, like, ten?'

'Duh, they're in Fifth Form.' The year below us. 'I admit I'm curious to see their house. Apparently their super-basement goes down five floors and they have a casino.'

'Gross.'

'Lexi! Come on!' Genie says. 'It'll be fun!' What she really means is, *don't leave me alone with Nevada and her mute, coked-up girlfriend.*

Oh, fuck it. 'Sure, OK.' To be fair, Chelsea is just the other side of the river from the hotel, so we have to head in that direction anyway.

Feet starting to hurt in heels, we totter out of the hotel and bundle into the back of a limo. I fight the urge to pull the Louboutins off. Once they're off, there's a risk they won't go back on.

As we pull away, Fo takes out a wrap of coke. 'You mind?'

Nevada and Genie look to me.

'Go nuts,' I say. I mean, it had to happen sometime, didn't it? Unless I want to become a recluse.

She chops out four lines on the silver tray reserved for champagne (and, let's be honest, coke). She snorts one with a rolled twenty and passes the tray to Genie who does a line too. 'Oh my god! That's good stuff!' She hands me the tray. 'You want some, Lex?'

I can't be the only person *not* on coke. That'd be unbearable. I'm so woozy from the champagne that a line of coke might get me through an hour of the party, and then I'll come down and go home to sleep. Yes, this feels like the sensible thing to do.

I'm proud of myself. I always knew, sooner or later, I'd have to manage myself around drugs.

I hold my left nostril shut and snort the line off the tray.

Coming up makes the journey from Shoreditch to Belgravia lightning fast. I'd forgotten how good the rush to your head feels.

'I heard,' Nevada says, 'that Waleed Aziz bought this place two years ago for a hundred and thirty million. And that was before they put the super-basement in.'

I'm unimpressed. Only poor people talk about money like that. Like, if you have to *count* your money, you don't have enough. I can picture the house before I've even seen it.

The limo pulls up outside a handsome townhouse. I step on to the kerb, unsteady in my heels. I already hear the gentle thud of bass from within, although the house is suitably soundproofed. This *is* Chelsea after all. Arm linked with Genie, we head inside.

It's an expensive house that desperately wants you to know it's expensive. The entrance hall is ceiling-to-floor marble, the sweeping staircase flanked by gleaming onyx Egyptian statues – the dog one and the cat one. Chandeliers drip gold from above. Tacky, tacky, tacky. You can't buy class.

All of the oil heirs are here. I think about Saif. These would have almost certainly been his friends. None of them seem to be in mourning, put it that way.

It's already heaving. I'm greeted mostly by people I recognise from school. I air kiss Reena Aziz, one of the twins, and thank her for having us. She's all hair and switchblade eyebrows. Truth be told, I'm a little terrified of her. She's one of very few people at St Agnes I wouldn't want to cross. She's in a good mood though. 'Wander! Get lost! Enjoy yourselves! Cinema and pool in the basement. Moschino swimsuits and towels for everyone!' She dismisses us with her gold nails. 'Go! Have fun!'

Cocktail waiters circulate with drinks. The martini glasses are filled with murky amber fluid. 'What is it?' I ask.

'Rattlesnake,' replies the pretty waitress. 'Whiskey, absinthe, lemon juice and egg white.'

Why the hell not? I take a glass and have a sip. Man, it's strong. Delicious though. 'Come on,' Genie says. 'Let's explore.'

The gaucheness continues as we descend into the basement. The kitchen and dining room backs onto an opulent garden party – decorated like some sort of souk with lanterns and hookah pipes. Belly dancers weave, shake and shimmy through the crowds. Guests are seated on low bean bags.

And that's when I see him.

Always the way, isn't it? Just when your guard goes down.

Kurt sucks on a hookah pipe, reclining in one of the Bedouin tents. The sight of him winds me. Shit. I don't know if I'm ready. Everything is slow motion. I wonder if I can retreat.

Too late. His shark-like eyes scan the garden and he clocks me. He too looks shocked for a second. I haven't *strictly* told him I'm back yet. I was building up to it. I swear.

He looks even better than I remember. The icy blue of those eyes, in stark contrast to the black lashes. He exhales a mouthful of swirling smoke and the corners of his lips curl. His left hand extends out, fingers like the barrel of a revolver and he shoots me. And I feel it. He got me.

'You want another line?' Fo says to Nevada.

I'm going to need one. 'Yes.'

After doing another line in a gold-plated bathroom, I figure I can't avoid him any longer. I return to the garden, but don't see him. I take another Rattlesnake from a waiter and wander through the crowd. Maybe it's psychological, but it smells of Marrakesh – of orange trees, honey tea and myrrh.

And then I feel his breath on my neck. Goosebumps. I somehow sense him. 'Nice hair,' he says.

I turn to face him. He kisses me on the cheek.

'Were you planning on telling me you were back?'

'Eventually.'

'Eventually?'

'Kurt. Guess what? I'm back.'

He reaches up and ruffles his quiff. 'I missed you, kid.'

It is and isn't what I need to hear.

'Aren't you going to say anything?'

I sigh. 'Let's get a drink, yeah?'

He waggles a half-finished bottle of Jim Beam. 'I'm all good.'

We find an abandoned love seat under a fairy-light infused pear tree. He takes a swig of bourbon and I sip my cocktail. 'Are you real?' I finally say.

He grabs my head and kisses me hard on the lips. 'I'm that real.'

'Kurt, don't.'

'Don't kiss you?'

'I don't think it's a good idea.' I down my cocktail and wince. 'Look, I met someone in recovery.'

He laughs cruelly. 'You hooked up in rehab? Classy, Lex, real classy.'

'Oh, fuck off, Kurt. Like you haven't fucked half of London while I was away.'

He actually looks hurt. 'Lexi, I love you. I missed you and I love you.'

I'm speechless again. Everything I wanted to hear at the exact wrong moment. Timing is such a bitch. Now, then, and Brady. We shouldn't have ever met. But we did. 'Things are different now.'

'Maybe I can be different. You don't know.'

'Kurt . . .'

'Do you love me?'

I push my hair off my face. 'I'm not sure what we have is love. It's too chaotic.'

Those eyes. God, I'd forgotten how handsome he is; how powerless he makes me feel and how much I enjoy the weakness.

'Love is chaotic,' he says. 'You can choose who you like, but you don't get a choice with love. That's why it's so cool. It's out of control.'

This isn't fair. 'Kurt, you never change!' I'm getting mad now. 'You let me drift away downstream, you get bored of me, and just when I'm almost free you reel me back in like a fish on a hook! It's not fair!'

'Hey . . .' He pulls me into a hug. 'I'm not gonna pretend I don't have shit going on, but it was never about you, OK? *You* I'm sure of.'

I wish I was. He gives me another kiss. This one is softer, more thoughtful.

'If you want me to give up junk, I will. I promise,' he whispers in my ear. 'I can't lose you.'

I pinch my nose, worried I might cry. 'Kurt, I need some time. It's been intense.'

'Sure. Sure, whatever you need.' We sit in silence, his arm around me, my head on his shoulder. I wonder if Kurt would ever leave me the way Brady did. I suppose, in his own fucked-up way, Kurt *needs* me more than Brady. 'Come on,' he says. 'Let's get drunk on the Aziz kids, yeah?' He stands and offers a hand.

'Sounds like a plan.' I take his hand and follow him down the rabbit hole.

We find the others gathered around a table in a yurt. They're sat in a circle, on velvet cushions, around a low bronze coffee table. 'What's all this then?' Kurt asks as we enter.

Nevada, Genie and Fo are there along with Baggy, Troy, Khalid Aziz – the other twin – and that model guy in the year below, Erik Something-Scandinavian. 'Blakeney,' Khalid leers, eyes glassy. 'Sit your ass down. You need to try this truly epic shit. It'll change how you see the world . . .'

We join them at the table. I see Nev give Kurt a death stare. She never did like him. Well, I think Fo is an utter cock so we're even. 'What is it?' Kurt asks.

'Just a cup of tea, my friend.'

Khalid hands him a little glass tea cup and Kurt takes a sip. His eyes widen and he smiles. 'That's my kind of tea.'

'Mushroom tea!' Genie giggles.

I panic a little. What the hell is this? A cornucopia of temptation? Give me a break, universe.

'Finest Amanita,' Khalid says. 'Speciality of the house.'

'Guaranteed good trip, man,' says Troy, smiling drowsily.

'Nice to see you looking so rested after your *vacation*, Lexi.' Khalid pours me a tea from an Ottoman teapot. 'To your health . . .?' His smile is spiteful, knowing. He's testing me. If I refuse, I might as well admit I've been through rehab.

'Thank you!' I say brightly, taking the cup. 'Bottoms up.' I figure it's hardly a cup of molten smack; it's just magic mushrooms. The tea trickles warmly down my throat and tastes like sunflower seeds. 'Delish.'

Kurt leans in to whisper something. His warm breath tickles my ear. 'There's my girl,' he says.

The trips starts after about thirty minutes. The others come up first. At first I observe them, bored and wondering if I wasn't going to come up at all. But then the room starts to turn like a fairground carousel – either I'm spinning or the walls are. It goes slowly at first but then gains speed. It's dizzying.

Up and down.

Round and around.

Genie is dancing with Baggy. She flops like a rag doll in his arms. Her boobs fall out of her dress.

She's like a painting.

She's Botticelli's Venus.

She's in a seashell. A great big seashell. Her red hair flows like water on fire.

Kurt is kissing me.

His tongue feels huge. My tongue is huge too. They're like two fat anacondas wrestling. It feels like my jaw is unhinging to swallow him whole.

Khalid is laughing. He's that clown puppet rocking inside a glass cabinet, laughing and laughing. I laugh with him. He's a clown! With red nose and white face. He's too close though. I push him back.

'Let's get some air,' Kurt says. I take his hand.

The garden is too much. Everyone has great big heads on skinny little bodies. Their shiny, marble eyes blink and roll in their skulls. They speak in strange cooing voices like Furbies. 'I wanna go inside,' I say. 'Take me inside.'

I see halls, endless marble halls. They stretch out in front of me like elastic toffee bubblegum being pulled out. Staircases and corridors. They all look the same. All around and upside-down. We're walking on the ceiling, surely? Like an Escher print. 'Where are we?' The marble swirls like whipped cream. I suddenly worry I'm sinking into vanilla ice-cream floors, but Kurt catches me.

'This way.'

The bedroom is cornflower blue.

How did we get here?

We were in a corridor.

Now I'm on a bed.

Everything is blue.

Blue walls, blue drapes. Mirrors. I see my reflection in the mirror to my left. Tilting my head takes great effort. It feels like a water balloon, glugging. I'm a little thing on a vast, king-sized bed. Kurt is on top of me, shirtless.

'I love you,' he says.

I feel kisses on my collarbone; my thigh; my hand. He sucks my fingers.

Each hand has ten fingers. I hold them up in front of my face. Red fingernails like talons.

My body has electricity on it. Lightning flickers and crackles over my skin. Kurt's body rubs against me. He's electric too. He pins my hands over my head and licks my armpit.

I look again in the mirror. Troy is here too? Huh? Why? He's on the bed too. He's shirtless too. His hands are on my body. He reaches into the Westwood and pulls my breast out. 'God, Lexi, you're hot,' he says.

I look up and Troy and Kurt blend into one. It swirls like oil on water. I can't work out if there's one or two of them.

Steve? Is that Steve? The dealer? No. No I don't want to . . .

343

Hands, fingers, all over my body. Fingernails run up my legs, over my face, my breasts. Ten fingers, twenty – I can't tell. 'Stop,' I say.

'I love you,' says Kurt.

Or maybe Troy.

'Troy . . .?'

Or is it Steve? Is Steve here?

Someone holds my face, squeezes it tight and kisses me. I'm melting into the bed. My face is pushed out of shape. My chin is on wrong. They moved my jaw. I can't speak.

'Stop.' The words sound slow. My tongue is so swollen and bruised. It's like he's rubbing engine grease all over me, leaving black smears.

'I love you.'

I open my eyes and try to push him – them – off. Is Baggy here too? I hear his voice. 'Fucking gorgeous,' he says, watching from the corner. 'Fucking . . . gorgeous . . . fuck her . . .'

'No . . .' I try to push him off again.

Brady is standing at the end of the bed. He looks so sad. *Look at her. What an epic disaster she is. I had a narrow escape. Near miss.*

Kendall is there too, sitting on a chaise longue. 'Gross,' she says. And Ruby, and Sasha, and Guy, and Saif – who is a dead body at the foot of the bed. A needle hangs out of his thigh. His dead eyes gape at me.

And Goldstein. 'Well, I must admit,' Goldstein says, consulting his clipboard, 'I can't say I'm massively surprised.'

'KURT, FOR FUCK'S SAKE GET OFF ME. GET OFF ME.'

I push myself off the bed and land in a heap on a sheepskin rug. I try to get to my feet and pull a huge lamp off the bedside table. I smash to the floor.

'OK, Lex. Just . . . chill . . . out.' Kurt's ginormous face looms down at me like something out of Studio Ghibli. 'You're tripping.'

'Don't touch me,' I say, standing up and leaning against the mirror.

'Lex, it's a bad trip,' his massive mouth says. 'You need to ride it out. It's gonna be fine.'

'You're disgusting,' I tell him. 'I'm dirty. You covered me in . . . Look at me!'

'Lex, you're not . . .'

'I'm dirty.' I have to get out of here. I have to get out of here right now. I see my shoes discarded by the bedroom door. I don't know where my jacket or my clutch bag is, but if I flag a cab it'll take me to the hotel. To Daddy. To Nikolai. They'll know what to do.

I put one shoe on and then the other. I push my way out of the bedroom. 'Lexi, come back!' Kurt calls after me. He's pulling his pants back on. I leave him and slam the door behind me.

I'm back in the corridor labyrinth. Did we come upstairs? Using the walls to support myself, I follow the sound of music. The corridors are long, swaying like we're on a cruise ship. I try to run but I feel like I'm running through wallpaper paste.

'Lexi! Wait for me!'

I have to get away from him. He wants to kill me.

My fingers touch railings. I see the chandelier. I'm on the balcony overlooking the entrance hall. I can see the front door. I just want to get out.

345

'Lexi! Stop!'

The staircase curves ahead of me. It seems to swing across the floor like a scarf in the wind. White marble rears up at my face. Rattlesnake.

No.

It's me.

I'm falling.

Oh god.

I hit the stairs.

So hard.

Hurts.

Ankles, elbows.

I roll.

My head.

I fall.

STEP 9:
I WILL MAKE AMENDS

'Are you an angel?'

'No. I was *never* an angel.'

'Am I dead?'

'You're on a lot of morphine.'

'Isn't that heroin?'

'Pretty much.'

'So you're like . . . a hallucination?'

'Sure. Why not.'

'OK. You good?'

'Lexi, I'm dead. You're just imagining all this.'

'Well you look *great*.'

'Thanks, babe. You've looked better tbh.'

'Bitch.'

'You really need to get over this, you know.'

'Fuck off.'

'Stop making *my* death about *you*. God, Lex, self-involved much?'

'But what I did . . .'

'You didn't do anything. I made my choices, I knew what I was doing. Well, I thought I did. I was stupid. You're stupid too.'

'Hello! I'm dying here!'

'No, you're not. Fucking drama queen. Nothing ever changes.'

'I really, really, really miss you.'

'I'm just a dream, but if I were real I'd miss you too. A lot.'

'Hems, what am I going to do?'

'Again, if I weren't a figment of your imagination, I'd say that you need to get your shit together. I didn't want to die. And neither do you. So you need to figure out how you're going to live.'

'But I don't know if I can . . .'

'Bitch, you can. Now wake up. You've got visitors.'

Turns out, all I had to do to get back on opiates is launch myself down the stairs at the Aziz mansion.

I don't really remember the next few days because I was doped off my tits. I had *the* most fucked-up dreams.

I'm in a private clinic in Marylebone. Everything is pastel peach, the colour of sugared almonds – including the nurses. They're very Stepford. They glide around like they're on rollers and speak in a soothing monotone, like they've been partially lobotomised.

I'm numb and I can't move much. I broke my collarbone, a wrist and my foot. I am, so they say, lucky to be alive.

When I first came to, I thought I was still tripping. Daddy, Mummy and Nikolai circled my bed like the trinity. 'There's my baby!' Mummy wasn't wearing any make-up. I hardly recognised her.

'*Myshka*? Can you hear us?'

Nikolai said nothing.

'Mummy?'

'I'm here, my sweetie. I'm here. We're all here.' That bit was lovely. My family, reunited.

A couple of days later, when I was stronger, things were less nice. The doctor, Dr Chandler, gathered them all in my room. 'Lexi, we need to have a serious talk,' she said. 'Your brother tells me you were recently treated for opiate addiction at a private clinic. Is that correct?'

I saw from their faces that this was no longer news to Mum and Dad. Nikolai had ratted me out. 'Yes,' I say. I sound like a guilty little schoolgirl, cookie crumbs all over her chubby cheeks.

'This has repercussions for your treatment here. We're going to have to be very sensible with what we prescribe you, OK?'

I nodded. Dr Chandler left us alone.

'Is this true, *myshka*?' Daddy asked. 'What your brother tells us?'

Daddy is on one side of the bed, Mummy the other. Nikolai paces at the foot. None of them look cross. They looked tired, *so* tired. And it's on me. 'I didn't want you to know,' I said.

'Drugs, *malysh*?' Mummy says. 'How could you hide that from us? We always teach you and Nikolai to come to us. We always understand.'

'We help you, *myshka*. If you need help, we will help.' Daddy's face is white with exhaustion. 'We thought you knew that.'

I have to believe I'm more than a cry for help, but here they are: Mum and Dad together at last. Thanks to me. It doesn't feel like a *Parent Trap* triumph though. I feel like they're finally seeing me for what I really am. Something putrid. I'm embarrassed.

I cry. Tears drip on to the bedsheets. 'I do.' Everything oozes out for them all to see. 'I need help. And I'm sorry.'

Later, I'm all alone. I'm feeling pain now. They won't give me the really good painkillers for obvious reasons. I ache all over. My teeth hurt, my cheeks, everywhere. That staircase kicked my ass.

There's a knock at my door. 'Come in.'

Nikolai enters carrying a goodie bag. 'Hey. I brought you some chocolate and a few books and stuff.'

'Thanks.'

He plonks them down. He seems pissed off.

'Are we OK?' I ask sheepishly. I wonder how many passes I'll get before he washes his hands of me for good.

'Lexi, you lasted a week and a half. What is wrong with you? I thought you said Clarity was good . . .?'

I stare out of the window at the handsome red-brick building opposite. 'Nik, please don't. You don't have to lecture me because *I know*.' I shake my head as much as my neck brace will allow. 'And it's not Clarity's fault. In fact, I should thank you.'

'For what?'

'For kidnapping me. For taking me to the island. You probably saved my life.' He blushes and looks at the carpet. 'You did,' I say again.

'It's what big brothers are for.'

'I was such a gigantic cunt,' I say. We both smile.

'Not gonna argue with that.'

'I'm so sorry, Nik. For everything.'

'None of it matters if you change, Lex. None of it. Clean slate.'

I nod. It hurts. 'I know.'

'And that asshole Kurt . . .'

'I'm not going to see him again.' I say without hesitation, and I know it's true. 'Clearly I can't. It's gonna kill one of us.' I take a breath because once I say it, I can't back out. 'I left the island too soon. I want to go back.'

This time I make the journey in the back seat again, but only because Mummy and Daddy want to come and meet this miraculous doctor I've been telling them about. We take about five wrong turns on the way to the ferry and they bicker. Of course they do. I don't know why I wanted them to be together. It's a nightmare.

Nik and I stand on the deck again as we approach the island. Mummy and Daddy are at the kiosk getting coffees for us all. The sky is turquoise but it's not quite summer yet. I don't have to wear the neck brace any more, but I'm still on a crutch for my foot, which is in one of those crazy plastic robot boots.

'I mean this in the nicest possible way,' Nik says, 'but this time don't come back until it sticks, yeah?'

'I promise.'

We drive up to the house. The nurses and Goldstein are waiting for me. I wonder if it's a novelty that they won't have to drag me inside, kicking and screaming. While Goldstein shakes hands with Daddy, Nik helps me out of the back seat with my crutch. When he sees me, Goldstein smiles the warmest smile and holds his arms open. If I weren't on one leg, I'd have run into them. 'I like your hair,' he tells me and folds me into a warm embrace.

I look up into his amber eyes. 'Can we start again?' I say.

STEP 1:
I ADMIT I HAVE A PROBLEM

'Where's Sasha?' I ask.

First full day back and I'm in therapy with Dr Goldstein. It feels good to be back on his sofa. Familiar like old slippers.

It's strange being here without the others. This time I'm staying in Kendall's old suite. Last night, at dinner, I didn't recognise any of my fellow patients – well, except her off *X Factor*. The others are a nineteen-year-old guy who's just been kicked out of Cambridge for getting blackout drunk daily (he's in a bad way right now) and a girl who's been sent by her modelling agency for a winning combo of anorexia and coke addiction.

Goldstein pauses for a moment at his filing cabinet, retrieving my old notes. Clearly this is confidential information, but he also probably knows we're not going to get much done unless he tells me. 'Sasha discharged herself.'

'When? Did she have the ECT?'

'Lexi, you know I can't discuss that.'

'So she did?'

'The week after you left. We took her to the mainland for the ECT and afterwards she decided not to return.'

'What? It went well? Or it didn't go well?'

'Lexi. I've already said too much.'

'Is she OK?'

'I hope so. I really hope so. Wherever she is.' He joins me and takes an armchair. 'So, Lexi. You said you wanted a fresh start. Why is that?'

My sweater flops off my shoulder when I shrug. 'I'll be honest, I'm not sure I *really* believed I had a problem last time. I mean, I *understood* I had a problem, but I'm not sure I believed it deep down. On some level, I thought rehab was just hoops to jump through; nothing about changing, y'know?'

He nods. 'So how are we going to make this time different?'

I bite my lip. 'I'm going to tell the truth.'

Goldstein smiles warmly and tips his head. 'Let's start at the beginning then . . .'

'OK.' I cross my legs up on the settee. I imagine I'm hooked up to a lie detector and an alarm will sound if I don't tell the truth. 'My name is Lexi Volkov. I'm seventeen. My family have a lot of money. My mum and dad always tried to teach me to be grateful, but I think it's really hard to be grateful for what you have when you've never gone without. Does that make sense?'

Goldstein nods.

I think I know me now.

I go on. It's time. I've thought it through and this is what I want to say. No. What I have to say. Deep breath, and I fall off the edge:

'It's really clear now that nothing ever really mattered. There was no risk to anything I did; there was always a safety net. I don't think I was ever even aware of it, but it was there. Maybe I did all that crazy crap because I was testing it, testing it to see if it would always catch me. I became a brat. At first, I guess, it

360

was just to see how much I could get away with. I don't really know when it stopped being an act and I stopped liking myself very much, but I just became this massive twat. Like, what's the point of anything I do? I just go to parties and shop and even charity stuff is mostly bollocks. I'm *embarrassed* to be me, and knowing that real people actually have real problems just makes me feel like an even bigger twat, you know?'

'You don't think you're a real person?'

'No. I'm acting. Acting the way I think people want "Lexi" to be. The one my Daddy wants, the one my friends want, the one Kurt wants. So I kept doing more and more stupid stuff. Like, what's the worst I can do before I hurt myself? I think I did hurt myself actually, in lots of different ways.'

He nods, ever so slightly. I pause and sip some water. This is good. I'm embarrassed. But this is it, this is the truth.

'Nothing mattered until something I did mattered. Grafton was right: one day something I did would have consequences. I just thought they'd affect me. And they did – I mean, look where I ended up – but karma came for Antonella first. I know, I know, it's not all my fault, but I think we were the same. She wasn't . . . none of us were saints or devils. I think we were both starting fires to see if any of them burned.'

I shake my head.

'After she died, I was like, *what's the point*? I didn't wanna know me, any version of me. So I pretty much hit the big red button. I just wanted to be out of it. And you tell yourself it feels nice, but actually how it feels is *numb*. It was anaesthetic.'

Dr Goldstein looks faintly proud. I feel like I've just performed for him. The version of Lexi *he* wants. I feel a bit grubby, but lighter somehow. A python passing a huge bolus down her body. 'And now you want to feel again?'

'Yes.' *Be honest.* 'Well, I think I should. But I might never. And that's weird.'

'Both the good and the bad?'

'People tried to shield me from the bad my whole life. It didn't work. So yeah, it's time to feel it all. All the pain . . . all the hate . . .'

Goldstein smiles, but his eyes are sad. 'Lexi. If you don't mind me saying, you seem quite adept at pain and hate. We have to teach you how to *love*. And you need to start with learning to love yourself.'

I want to make fun of him. I want to mime blowing chunks in his face.

But, of course, he is right.

I resign myself to the Ten Steps. Yes, it's a bit cult-like; yes, it's dogmatic; but it gives me something to focus on.

It's odd. I like Normandy, Dashiell and Celine – my fellow inmates – but this time I've learned not to get attached. I listen in Group. Normandy cries a lot and talks about 'being blessed'. Dashiell has the shakes most mornings, but is mostly guilty about what he's putting his loved ones through. Celine *really* doesn't want to be here. She's monosyllabic, French and smokes even more than I do. That's saying something.

I *contribute meaningfully* at Group. I'm slicing my guts open and everyone's having a good rummage in my entrails like they're browsing a flea market. But as the weeks crawl by, and as I offload more junk, I feel less ashamed and more unapologetic.

It's like I'm getting rid of unwanted, cumbersome baggage. I'm giving it away, for free.

I set my alarm for dawn each morning.

I know.

I guess I want to recapture that day we all watched the sunrise.

I've been learning yoga from Padma, the instructor. I'm getting pretty good at it. As the sun rises, I take my rolled-up yoga mat on to the terrace and run through a pretty hardcore sun salutation. Downward Dog, Cobra, Warrior Pose, *Tadasana*. I can do a shoulder stand and a headstand. Getting into my body takes me out of my head. I like it. I know it's a bit Notting Hill Yummy Mummy, but I can see my body changing. Instead of looking scrawny, I look lean and strong and healthy.

I ride Storm every day. He even lets Elaine ride him too now. He doesn't seem to like it always, and he's still an asshole to the other horses, but you know I'm a sucker for a bad boy. I'm totally in love with him; I wish I could take him with me.

In the afternoons, I work remotely with a tutor. We're working on English Literature and Creative Writing. I'm allowed to email him at Roehampton University and he gives me feedback on my work. I'm so, so rusty. The first essay – about representations of children as 'monstrous' in literature – was the hardest thing I've ever written. It's like learning to speak all over again. The last few years at St Agnes were too easy; I was phoning it in. This is like advanced Ashtanga yoga for my *brain*.

Sometimes I go down to the kitchens and hang out with Denise and Matteusz, the main cooks. Denise is an old battle-axe who worked under Gordon Ramsay back in the day, while Matteusz is talented but lazy. All he wants to do is take cigarette breaks and try insane new recipes. Between them, I'm learning a lot. I make a soufflé and perfect poached eggs. Matteusz shows me how to make a detox smoothie with spinach, ginger and cinnamon, and Denise teaches me pastry from scratch, which is more satisfying than it sounds.

It sounds *crazy*, and I guess I am an official crazy-person now, but it's pretty clear that I can't go back to London with nothing to do. I'll just get high again as soon as I'm bored. As corny as it sounds, I'm going to need a new *hobby*. The devil makes work for idle hands.

Dear Nevada

I hope you're well. I wanted to write to you to explain what's going on. I don't know what you've heard, what bullshit rumours are going around, and I wanted to set things straight.

Yes, I'm in rehab.

Yes, it's because I'm an addict.

I'm trusting you alone with this information because I hope I can rely on your discretion. See, if anyone else knows how I feel about Antonella, it's you. I never said this because I'm emotionally stunted (obviously) but I totally loved her and I didn't deal with her dying. Like, at all.

Anyway, I'm working things through and I'll be back in London at the end of summer. Probably.

I miss the old days, when we were young and everything was listening to music and kissing posters in your bedroom. Do you?

Love Lexi

PS – I'm not sure about Fo. Let's talk when I get back.

Dear Kurt

I'm going to keep this super chill, OK?

We are so bad for each other it's not even funny.

If you can't see that, I can't help you.

I'm feeling better and I want to – need to – stay that way.

We had fun in the beginning, but it stopped being fun a long time ago.

There's a horse here. He's called Storm. I had this strange need to break him in. I greatly romanticised it, but it wasn't love. What I really wanted was to control him, bend him to my will. That's a game we played too, and a game we're both losing.

I'm really glad I got help, Kurt. I can't tell you what to do, but I hope you get help too. The way we were living . . . we convinced ourselves it was OK, that it was normal, but it wasn't. You can only live that way for so long before the damage is permanent.

You're not going to see me for a while. It's not you I don't trust, it's myself. You know what'd be cool? In like ten years, it'd be awesome to see you on Primrose Hill with your gorgeous wife and adorable, floppy-haired kids. We'd be different then, and maybe we'll laugh about all this.

Love Lexi x

Hey there!

Lexi, girl, it's awesome to hear from you – and I'm so freaking proud of you! You take all the time you need. I kinda miss that place too. I'm doing pretty good. Diandra hooked me up with this new lifestyle coach, Guru Rachel. She's the best – she's worked with Ariana, Gwyneth Paltrow and Oprah. I know it sounds pretty phony, but I think she's helping me with empowerment and assertiveness. I'm hoping to convince Daddy that I should get my own apartment. I think being more independent and making choices for myself will help. I gotta stop feeling guilty about Mom too. That being said, I'm thinking about doing an internship on Daddy's campaign. I think it's time I stop denying who I am and where I come from. Sure, I'm kinda mad at my Daddy about some stuff from the past, but, to a lot of people, he's a hero. He's making a difference, changing the world. If he won't come to me, maybe I need to go to him. I keep thinking about our talk in the kitchen. Excuse the obvious fat joke, but maybe it's time to do something bigger than me, go fight the good fight. What do you think? Would that be cool?

When you get out, get on a flight to JFK! Come and stay any time! Say hey to Goldstein and Ahmed. Is Sasha's crazy ass still there?

Love you, girl

Ruby xoxo

Dear Lexi,

It's so lovely to hear from you! I'm glad you're getting the help you feel you need. It's nothing to be ashamed of.

I'm not doing too badly. My uncle is taking me on as an intern at his production company from September. Privilege, etcetera. I've always loved films so I'm quite excited. Anxious, but excited. I'm terrified I'll make a mess of it. I'm sticking to my OCD medication and I've decided to go tee-total for the time being. I thought it for the best. Father is disappointed I'm not going back to Cambridge, but I think he'll get over it.

I saw Kendall a couple of weeks ago, and she's excited to see you when you get back to London.

I'm afraid I don't have any contact details for Brady. I did get an email from him assuring me he was well (and sober), but there was no forwarding address which was quite frustrating. I think we need to respect his recovery, however hard that may be.

Please send my love to everyone at the centre and I'll see you soon. Give me a call if you need to talk, day or night.

All my best,
Guy Samson-Reed

'It's about time,' says Goldstein in our session, 'to start thinking about reintegrating you with your family.'

'So soon?' It feels like I only just got back, but it's been another eight weeks.

He nods. 'I think this time it'll be better, Lexi. You have the full support of your whole family and they can help in your ongoing recovery.'

'I know.' I now understand why Guy and Sasha so feared leaving the island – I can cope here. Few choices, no temptation. It'd be so much easier if I could just live out here with the horses.

'You can't stay here forever,' he says, apparently reading my mind.

'I know that too. I'm scared I'll relapse again.'

'You may do. And you know that a relapse is only a setback, not a reason to give up on recovery.'

We've spoken many times about this. 'I wrote to everyone,' I tell him. 'They all say hi.'

He smiles. 'I've been in touch with them all too.'

'Even Brady?'

He pauses. 'Yes.'

It's so stupid, but I want to cry. Just knowing he's out there fills me with . . . something warm and nice in my chest. 'Is he OK?'

'Lexi . . . you know I can't talk about other patients.'

'Please.' I wipe a tear away before it can roll. 'I think about him all the time.'

'Brady's fine.' Goldstein reaches over the coffee table and takes both my hands in his. 'He's working on his recovery, just as you are.'

I know he won't tell me anything more. I nod.

That night, I have a cigarette before bed on the lounger by the pool. It's warm enough to swim outdoors now. There are lights under the water and the turquoise pool glows and shimmers. It's a balmy evening. I wear only a baggy T-shirt and my pants. I'll go to bed soon, I have some reading – *Paradise Lost* – to do, but I can't stop thinking about Brady.

I need to stop.

Or rather, I need to start – start getting over him.

I'm going to drive myself crazy, just when I'm getting sane. I'm starting to see what he meant about love being an addiction – it takes over. Now I'm clean of Kurt, feelings for Brady have come rushing in to fill the void.

I fall asleep thinking about our big reunion (in my head, he's waiting for me in the rain as the ferry pulls back onto the mainland). I dream we're together in my bed only to wake up with a pillow in my arms. It feels a little like mourning, which is crazy because he was never mine to mourn. I guess we'll always have those few moments – the Witch House, the night the boat sank – and I should be grateful for them. This way, it never has to go stale. We'll never fight; he'll never stray; I'll never become his nagging shrew girlfriend.

I look up at the moon. I wonder what time it is where Brady is, and if he's looking up at the same moon.

STEP 10:
I UNDERSTAND RECOVERY
IS AN ONGOING, LIFE-
LONG COMMITMENT

Tomorrow I go back to London. Again. I'm shitting bricks. This time, I'm going back knowing full well I fucked it up the last time. I also know my old friends don't 'get it'. I'm not sure I can be around them ever again. I know that life *can't* be the same as it was. I know I have to avoid Kurt at all costs. Even so, I'm nervous. I can't go through all this again. I can't keep ricocheting back and forth to Clarity every other month.

I look around my suite. Clothes are strewn everywhere, half in and half out of my case.

I wonder what desperate, deluded, broken little creature will take up residence in here after tomorrow. I smile to myself.

In the desk drawer there's a pad of Clarity Centre paper and pen. I sit down and have a think.

TEN (MORE) STEPS

Welcome to Clarity! This is what I've learned during my considerable stay . . .

1. Make a friend
2. Make two friends for when the first is being a dick
3. Say YES to things. Except drugs: Just say NO to those
4. Watch the sunrise. Trust me
5. Accept help when it is offered. You do need help. Who doesn't?
6. Every day, brush your teeth, shower and get dressed. It means you haven't given up
7. Talk about yourself. Your story is as important as anyone else's. But also listen because your story isn't _more_ important
8. Go outside, at least once a day
9. Sleep enough, but not too much. Eat good food
10. Know there's nothing so broken you can't fix it

You're welcome. x

I take the letter and slide it behind the mirror. It doesn't fall out of the back. I don't know if anyone will find it, ever, but knowing it's there will amuse me greatly. And who knows, maybe it'll help someone, somewhere down the line.

Nikolai flops onto my bed like a beached whale. 'Lex,' he says, 'you have to leave the hotel. Your room smells like mouth.'

'Fuck off, no it doesn't.'

'It really does. You haven't been outside since Mum went home.'

Mummy wanted to check that the rehab had 'stuck' this time so had hung around for a few days, but she and her toy-boy are in the process of opening a chain of gyms on Grand Cayman so she had to get back. I'm not sure how my future relationship with Mummy and Daddy is going to look just yet, but we're trying. We're all trying. It feels like my parents used to manage me. Now I'm vaguely grown up, I see I'm going to have to manage them.

'So? I'm catching up on Netflix. I have like four boxsets to get through.'

He gives me a pointed look.

'Five days back and I'm still sober.'

'If you're just going to stay here and order room service, you might as well have stayed on the island.'

I shrug. Maybe I should have.

'Right. Get in the shower. We're going out.'

'Nik, no . . .'

'Do you want me to kidnap you again? You know I will.'

'Uh! I hate you and you smell of wee!' Under duress, I shower and get ready, not even bothering to wash my hair. I shove it in a messy ponytail and dress in some torn skinny jeans and my House of Holland T-shirt: *GET YOUR ROCKS OFF LEXI VOLKOV*. Henry Holland is a friend of mine.

Nik is waiting in the car and we drive towards Soho. It's one of those humid London evenings where hyena packs of braying

City boys spill onto the streets outside pubs, ties loosened. The pavements bake and giggly girls compare Tinder notes over Aperol Spritzes.

'Where are we going?' I ask. 'Ivy?'

'God, no.' He taps on the window to the driver. 'I think this is it. Thanks.'

We get out of the car and Nikolai leans over the banister to a basement underneath a theatre. 'What is it? A new cocktail place?' I thought London had seen sense over the whole 'hidden speakeasy' fad. If one more steampunk 'mixologist' tries to serve me gin in a teacup, I'll scream. 'Nik, it's exactly this sort of thing I'd like to avoid.'

He grins up at me, already halfway down the stone steps. 'It's not a bar. Come on.'

I follow him into the murk. We step into a little studio space. For a second I think he's brought me to amateur theatre and try to flee, but then I see everyone is milling around with cups of coffee in Styrofoam cups and there's a queue for a tea urn. 'Nik . . .?'

'It's an NA meeting,' he says. 'I downloaded an app that tells you where the nearest meetings are. There were loads, I just picked this one because it started at seven.'

I start to panic. 'Nik!'

'It's fine! You don't even have to say anything, and I'm allowed to stay. I figured it'll help me help you. Please? Stay?'

I roll my eyes. To be fair, Goldstein had suggested NA meetings before I left the centre. 'OK. Whatever.'

Chairs are set out in a circle. I get a cup of coffee and wait for the meeting to start. No one asks for my name and no one takes

377

a register, thank god. One can only hope they don't think anyone would be vain enough to wear a designer T-shirt with their own name emblazoned on it.

There doesn't seem to be a leader as such, but one woman – with a frizzy perm and deep tan – kicks things off by asking if anyone would like to speak. There's an awful silence before a handsome guy offers a hand.

'I'll go, thanks, Debs.' He doesn't stand up. 'My name's Ian and I'm an addict. I'm gay . . . I'm a primary school teacher, but I've always been up for a night out on a Saturday – XXL or Brut or whatever. I honestly can't remember when I first tried crystal meth – it just sort of felt like something everyone was doing . . .'

He finishes his story and then a younger black guy speaks. '. . . It got to the stage where I just wasn't going to lectures, you know? I was just staying in halls getting mashed on skunk . . .'

Then a woman in her early twenties with lots of hair extensions and collagen lips. '. . . I just didn't know what else to do. I could either sell sex to pay him or I thought he would kill me . . . I really thought he would kill me . . .'

And another young woman. She looks outwardly, well, respectable, except a notable chunk is missing from her nostril. 'I would honestly get into the office and do a line of coke in the toilet before I could even start the day. And I wasn't the only one, it was just the culture of the place . . .'

It goes on and on. Drugs, addiction, *illness* just ruining, decimating, lives. Some people have lost everything, some people got out just in time. I hope I'm in the latter camp. I get now why Goldstein wanted me to come to a meeting. I'm the youngest person here and I'm looking at a gallery of possible futures.

One woman's face is ravaged by meth, her face hollow, teeth crumbling, scabby sores. I cry, because I don't see any way back for her.

That's not going to be me.

I've been back about a month when Kendall has an appointment at the Tavistock Clinic so we arrange to have lunch at the Garrison on Bermondsey Street. I count down the days until I can see her. I'm starving for company. Since I got back, I've only seen Nevada and that was for dinner at the hotel. Safer that way. Fo, thank god, has gone on a US tour and they've decided to call it quits for now.

I'm early for lunch so I nurse a Perrier and read *The Bloody Chamber*. Kendall breezes in, wearing a nautical summer dress and red-rimmed Lolita shades. She too has had a few inches lopped off her hair and some caramel highlights. She looks *amazing* and I tell her so as I greet her with air kisses.

'Thank you!' she says. 'I *love* your hair!'

'Thanks! How are you? How was the appointment?'

'Good! Really good in fact.'

'Yeah?' I sit down and fan myself with the menu. It's almost thirty degrees out.

Kendall leans in. 'They said that if I can maintain a healthy weight over the next six months, they'll refer me for my surgery.'

'You mean . . .?'

'Yep! Finally getting my very own vag!' The diners at the next table look over in horror, but I couldn't give two shits. 'About time too!'

We both order squid and chorizo salads – perfect for this weather. 'How are you getting on?' I ask, nodding at the salad.

She shrugs. 'It's funny. I realised it's not about food.'

'What do you mean?'

'It's about me and my body. Hormones and stuff . . . everything was out of my control. Couldn't control two lots of puberty, but I could control calories. I think I was just supremely anxious about *everything*, but it was easier to pretend it was about food. I have to keep reminding myself that food isn't the enemy – I am. But this is more important, you know? I've worked so hard to be a woman, I don't want to be a dead one.'

I nod. 'You've changed.'

'Not really. You take your baggage with you, right? I have all the same issues that Liam did.' She's never told me her pre-trans name before. 'You know how a stick of rock has writing through the middle? At my core, I've always been exactly the same person. The transition isn't *me*, and neither is anorexia.'

I say no more, picking a bit of chorizo out of some rocket.

'Like you. Sure, you've gone through some stuff, but you'll always be Lexi Volkov.'

'Maybe that's the problem.'

'Shut up. Look at you. I remember them dragging you out of the car and into the house.'

'Don't! Not my finest moment.'

She sips her Diet Coke through a paper straw. I know they're environmentally friendly, but the feel of soggy paper on my lips turns my stomach. 'What are you going to do about Brady?'

I frown. 'Huh?'

'How are you gonna find him?'

'I'm not,' I say, giving up on my lunch. I'm suddenly not hungry. 'He doesn't want to be found.'

'OK.' She finishes her Coke with a slurp.

'Kendall . . .?'

'I'm just saying. I wouldn't give up on that one without a fight.'

'It's not that easy. You know it isn't.'

Kendall reapplies a cherry-red lipstick looking into a compact. 'Lexi, when I was super ill, I used to tip salt all over my food. Sometimes I'd put a dead fly – seriously, I used to collect fly corpses – or some hair or piece of glass in my soup so I wouldn't have to eat it.'

'And?'

'I'm not saying Brady isn't riddled with problems, but what if his *real* issue is that he sabotages his happiness because he doesn't think he deserves it? Him leaving Clarity – leaving *you* – was like me ruining my food.'

I hadn't thought of it like that. 'You think?'

'Isn't that what we were all doing? With the exception of Sasha – because who the hell knows what was going on with her – you, me, Ruby, Brady . . . Saif. None of us thought we deserved good things, so we created bad things.'

I smile. 'When the fuck did you become The Oracle?'

'I've been to therapy once or twice, bitch.'

We fall silent as a very cute waiter clears our plates. 'So, what would you do?'

'It doesn't matter what I'd do. The important thing here is WWLVD?'

'Huh?'

'What Would Lexi Volkov Do?'

After lunch, we walk towards Waterloo along the Southbank, following the Thames. It's almost aggressively sunny. I wear Dolce sunglasses and smoke. We get iced caramel lattes from a van. My feet sweat in ballet pumps.

We see tourists on the clipper boats, seeing London through selfie sticks. We pass a Latin American couple having a screaming argument outside the Tate Modern. In the end, she throws a strawberry ice cream at his head.

A businessman calls his assistant a cunt about fifty times while pelting past the HMS *Belfast*. He says if he gets fired, they're getting fired too.

A bundle of muscles in a tight yellow vest outside the National Theatre is freaking out on the phone to his friend because he had bareback and left it too late to get PEP.

A mum loses her shit at a kid because she wandered off to watch the boats. Through the anger I hear the shrill fear in her voice.

An Italian couple are basically having sex on a bench outside the Royal Festival Hall. A group of French students are non-too-subtly taking pictures of them.

On the lawns by the London Eye, a girl comforts her friend. Her boyfriend has got another girl pregnant and he's leaving her. Over and over, her friend tells her she's better off without him, but she says she loved him. She holds an engagement ring in her palm.

We don't really see much of London; we're too busy watching Londoners.

And that's when I get it.

All these people.

We aren't broken.

We're just alive.

Back at the hotel, I go to the roof gardens. An absolutely stunning gay couple lie side by side on sunloungers, hands held in the middle. They say nothing, soaking up the sun on the poolside. They're so silently in love it's noisy.

I want that.

I *deserve* that.

Not because I'm special, not because of my name or my money or because I'm an addict, just because I'm *here*.

If we're not here for love, what are we here for?

I go to the edge of the terrace and look out over London. The sun is starting to set and the sky is tangerine. North: Regent's Park and Camden Town. The cocktail bar with Kurt and Baggy. East: Shoreditch, Dalston, house parties, heroin. South: that Mexican. The bathroom with Kurt. West: Chelsea, the Aziz mansion. Everywhere I look memories are projected up against the monuments and skyscrapers. I once thought the island was the luxury cage, but I wonder if I was in one long before Nik took me to rehab.

I used to think London was all there was. I thought about living in Manhattan for a while, but always came back to London.

I'm *so* London.

Goldfish grow to fit the size of their tanks.

But Kendall was once Liam, and look at her now.

You know how a stick of rock has writing through the middle?

You take your baggage with you.

What Would Lexi Volkov Do?

The next morning, I make some calls.

I call Genie and ask for her brother's number.

I call him and he gives me another number.

That person, Tamara, gives me another number.

Jack tells me I need to speak to Rafe.

'Hello, is that Rafe? Jack O'Donnell gave me your number. This is Lexi Volkov from the V Hotels group. I hope you can help me. I need to speak with Venus Ardito.'

'Honey,' Rafe purrs, 'no one speaks to Venus.'

'Oh, I'm sorry, *honey*, you must have misheard me. I'll say it again. I'm Lexi Volkov.'

I've nodded off in the back of the cab. 'Miss?' the driver says, and I wake with a start. 'I think this is the place.'

I peer out the window. Forgetting my mascara, I rub my eyes. 'Roan Ranch?'

'Yes, ma'am.'

Since we left Eagle County Airport, twilight has fallen. Crickets and cicadas chirrup away like a little mariachi band. It's a sultry night. My bare thighs stick to the leatherette seat. Fireflies swarm around the lanterns that light the long, white-fence-lined driveway leading up to the ranch.

I wind down the window to get a better look. It's ... unexpected. It's *so* Americana. The middle of nowhere in Middle America. There's a front porch with crisp columns. A dainty table, with lace tablecloth, awaits afternoon iced tea. To my right is a vast training paddock, stables and, beyond the farmhouse, is a bright red barn from which stars and stripes billow. It all sits in the shadow of a snow-capped mountain. Even looking up at it gives me wobbles.

Remote doesn't begin to cover it; it takes about five minutes from entering the gates to arriving at the farmhouse. The driver gives a toot on his horn as we pull up. So much for the element of surprise.

Ten hours from Heathrow to Denver, another hour to Eagle County, an hour in the cab. I bet I look fucking amazing. Jesus. Here goes.

I step out of the cab. 'Don't go anywhere,' I tell the driver and hand him a hundred bucks.

I'm halfway to the front door, my Converse kicking up the dust, when it opens and Brady, wearing cut-off sweatpants and nothing else, steps on to the porch. His lips part but no noise comes out.

'Hey,' I say.

He shakes his head, ever so slightly.

'Aren't you going to say anything?'

'Am I tripping?' he says finally.

'No,' I say. 'I'm real.' I wait where I am between the cab and porch. I don't want to smother him, scare him away.

'I like your hair.'

I laugh. 'It's gone down a treat.'

Another pause. He pushes his hair off his face. 'Lex . . . what are you doing here? How did you even . . .?'

'I spoke to your sister. She's unexpectedly lovely. She's super worried about you. She told me you were here.'

'God, Lex. I'm almost impressed. You couldn't have called first?'

'You'd have run.'

He looks at his feet, the very same ones which would have fled given half a warning.

I take a deep breath. 'Brady, I know coming all this way makes me look batshit crazy, but I had to know. If I'm ever going to sleep sound ever again, I had to know.'

He says nothing. I carry on.

'You know what? I have lied and lied and lied. I've lied to myself and I've lied to everyone else. White lies, lies by omission, and outright, brazen, barefaced lies. I lie all the fucking time. But this – you and me – I think it might be real. And if it's real, we have a shot.'

'Lexi . . .'

'A shot in hell is still a shot! Let me finish, please. I'm almost done, I swear. I think. I'm scared. You and me . . . the way I feel scares the shit out of me *because* it's real. I get it that you're scared too, who wouldn't be? And maybe it'll go wrong. Maybe it'll be awful. But what if it's not? Maybe love is just scary! Brady, what if this is *love*? What if it's *good*?'

A tear runs down his cheek.

'If you tell me to, I'll get back in a cab, and catch a ten-hour flight all the way back to London, but at least I tried. I was honest and I will know.'

The crickets play on.

'OK, Brady, you're gonna need to say something now, you're killing me.'

'I bought a ticket, you know.'

'What?'

'It's in the kitchen. I bought a flight to Heathrow. I was gonna fly to you. I missed you so goddamn much, Lexi. I thought flying to London was a pretty crazy gesture . . .'

I have to smile. 'In that case, I guess I'm a little crazier than you.'

'No shit.'

A broad, brilliant smile conquers his face and he steps off the porch. I take that as my cue and tumble towards him. I fall into his arms and he holds me close. I'm gross and I smell, but he's sweaty too and I don't care. My face resting against his chest is the actual very best. 'I love you,' I whisper.

'I love you too.' He kisses me. 'But Lexi . . . I'm still working on stuff, and . . .'

'I know. Me too. We always will be, together or apart. But I'd rather do it together, wouldn't you?' I pull back and watch his face. 'Can we start again? Can we leave everything in the past and call this Step One? Let's strip everything else away and just be who we are in the middle.'

He nods. 'Yeah. Yeah I think we can do that.' He kisses my hand. 'Nice to meet you. I'm Brady.'

I smile. 'I'm Lexi.'

We kiss.

'Hey,' he says, 'does that dude have his meter running? You might wanna let him go . . .'

'He can wait a second.'

We kiss again under the moon and the mountain.

While that kiss would be the last scene in the film adaptation of my life, the credits didn't miraculously roll over the night sky. Is Jennifer Lawrence too old to play me now?

Anyway, life doesn't stop when you get a boyfriend. I got my ass to America, Brady didn't send me packing, and all of a sudden I was like, OK WHAT NOW? My plan only stretched that far.

Luckily, I settle quickly into ranch life. The barn at Roan Ranch was where Brady Ardito Senior played his first ever gig. Although it belongs to Brady's great aunt, she lives in Denver so is letting Brady stay as long as he likes. Alma, a housekeeper, comes up every day but she lives in New Castle town, a few miles away.

For now, I'm staying in a guest bedroom – big four poster bed and chunky rustic beams – but it doesn't mean we're not together.

There's so much to learn. After a few days, it really hits home that I don't really *know* Brady all that well and coming here was definitely . . . erm . . . impulsive. I dread to think what Goldstein would say. I feel like I *know* him on a witchy, deep, spiritual level, but like, what music is Brady into? How does he take his coffee? Moreover, why doesn't he own a fucking TV? Seriously.

Getting to know these little things has been fun though. We spend the days taking the ponies on hacks into the forests at the base of the mountain. It's breath-taking. I mean that quite literally: the further you get up the slope, the harder it is to breathe the thin air. Brady has three chestnut mares and one stallion, all absolutely exquisite, none as ill-tempered as Storm.

Brady teaches me how to fish in the river. I do *not* enjoy it, or appreciate the meditative effects, so like some fifties housewife, he catches the fish and I cook them – just as Denise and Matteusz taught me. Brady is hugely impressed.

Some evenings we drive into New Castle – they have a diner, a steak house, even a drive-through cinema. It's so retro, I love it. I have now been to an all-American mall. Less Vivienne Westwood and more K-Mart. Hilariously, even though I just turned eighteen, I'm not legally allowed to drink out here so I'm more sober than I've ever been.

I think I *could* have a wine or a beer though. Out here, there's nothing to escape from, I'm not trying to block anyone, or anything, out. I don't need to hit the big red button any more.

It stops feeling like a holiday after a few weeks. Nikolai and Tabby fly out to make sure I'm OK. They spend a week with us on the ranch before flying down to the West Coast for a road trip. Nik brought me the best housewarming gift: a television. Thank god. The cable is being installed next week.

One night Nik and I had a fag on the porch, listening to coyotes howl. 'Lexi, this is like being in a cowboy movie. How are *you* here?'

'I know, right?'

'You gonna stay?'

'Dunno.'

'What about Mum and Dad?'

I thought about it for a second. 'I'm not sure we owe them anything.'

He was about to say something, but then he just nodded. 'You've changed.'

'I needed to.'

'Don't change *too* much. I'd miss my sister if she went completely.'

I grinned at my brother. 'No danger of that, cunt.'

At the bottom of her heart, however, she was waiting for something to happen. Like shipwrecked sailors, she turned despairing eyes upon the solitude of her life, seeking afar off some white sail in the mists of the horizon. She did not know what this chance would be, what wind would bring it her, towards what shore it would drive her, if it would be a shallop or a three-decker, laden with anguish or full of bliss to the portholes. But each morning, as she awoke, she hoped it would come that day; she listened to every sound, sprang up with a start, wondered that it did not come; then at sunset, always more saddened, she longed for the morrow.

I'm reading *Madame Bovary* in the coffee shop in New Castle. I'm curled up on a battered leather armchair, looking out over the main street. While the coffee is passable, the pecan pie is extraordinary.

I stop reading, put an old Oyster card – a little memento of London – in the book to mark my place and rest it on my lap, suddenly convinced I've forgotten something. Did I leave something on back at the ranch? No, I don't think so. Have I missed a deadline or forgotten someone's birthday? No.

I wonder if the weird sensation is that, for the first time, I have nothing to worry about. I'm *happy*. A beautiful novel, good coffee, great pie.

'Can I get a refill please?' I ask the waitress as her ponytail swishes past my table. They don't know who I am here. I'm just 'Brady's English Girlfriend' and that's fine by me.

While I was finishing at the clinic, Brady threw himself into a project. Out here, developers are trying to bulldoze through land belonging to a Native American tribe. Gas pipes or something. After moving back, he lent his family name to drum up publicity, but felt it wasn't enough. He now spends some of his time either protesting on the reservation, or ferrying supplies to those who are peacefully occupying the land. I think it's been good for him. I know it has.

While I was in therapy, I thought that I was doing all that shit because I wanted to damage myself, but now I think it was chasing *bliss*. All those mock-highs I chased. It turns out the bliss I was looking for existed in books, coffee shops and pecan pie. And Brady, I expect.

Who knew?

I rest my head back into the armchair and, through the window, feel the kind sun on my face.

Time passes and it's Autumn. It can get brutally cold up here in the mountains, so most nights Brady and I build a big fire in the lounge. I enjoy nothing more than perving over Brady as he chops logs with an axe in the yard, chest and arms glistening with sweat. There's a great big sofa, but we rarely sit on it, preferring instead to lie on the shaggy rug, watch a movie, or Netflix, or sometimes just watch the fire burn out, as weird as that sounds. We talk and talk.

'I'm freaking out,' he said a couple of weeks ago.

'About us?'

'Yeah.' A slight frown. 'A little.'

I was nestled between his legs on the rug. 'How bad?'

'I think I can handle it, I just wanted you to know.'

'Do you want me to go away for a while?' I don't want to, but I've learned not to corner him.

'No. No, I don't think so. Just telling you feels better.'

And I knew that. I *know* he doesn't want me to go away, but I don't want him – or me – to feel trapped. We're together, but free. 'Cool. If you need me to, I can.'

'That means a lot, Lex. Love you.'

'I know.'

As fun as playing house with Brady is, I need to use my brain again. It turns out with a recommendation letter from Roehampton, I can apply to American colleges. I shop around and decide to enrol at Colorado State University.

'They have a pretty good Liberal Arts programme and I can study English Literature and Creative Writing,' I tell Brady over dinner, tonight – good old-fashioned steak and French fries. There's a great big dining room, but we tend to eat in the kitchen or on the porch where it's cosier.

'Cool,' he says. 'It's about a four-hour drive down the freeway if you miss traffic.'

I quite fancy the college-dorm experience, as absurd as that sounds. I'm hardly sorority material (they're definitely on Kendall's Periodic Table of Basic), but I'll stay on campus during the weeks and come back to the ranch on weekends. 'I'll need to learn to drive first. I tell you what, I never thought the thing I'd miss most about London is Uber.'

'I can teach you. It'll be fun.'

'Oh yeah, it'll be hilarious when I drive us off a cliff.'

'Can you apply for next fall?'

'Yeah. I have to write a short story for them.'

'What on?'

I grimace. 'It's called *What Made Me*. Pretty hideous, right?'

'You'll figure it out.'

The next day, while Brady runs errand in New Castle, I sit down with a pad of paper and a pen. The ranch has a gorgeous study that smells of decades-old cigars and whiskey, like they're engrained in the wood. I swivel around in the big leather desk chair. How did I go from hotel heiress to where I am now? I chew my pen.

What made me me?

~~My name is Lexi Volkov, heiress to the V Hotel Group fortune.~~

No.

~~My grandfather, Vladimir Volkov, was just a young man when Stalin seized power in Russia.~~

No.

That is not What Made Me.

God, this is impossible. I run my hands through my hair. They want a story. A beginning, middle and an end. But I don't know the end. I don't *want* to know it.

I think.

I remember.

Mummy and Daddy. Nik. Antonella. Kurt and my friends – old and new. Dr Isaac Goldstein. Lady Denhulme. Brady Ardito Jr. And heroin, and me.

We're a collage.

I once thought I was the star around which these satellites revolved, but no more. We were all stars, colliding.

I tear the top sheet of paper off the pad and start again.

CLEAN
By Alexandria Volkova

Face-down on leather. New car smell. Pine Fresh.
  I can't move.
  I'm being kidnapped . . .

Support

Clean is a work of fiction. Lexi is fictional, but many young people struggle with addiction – their own and that of their parents, siblings, friends or carers. Help is out there.

For more information on where to find support, you could consider the following sources:

Childline: Freephone 0800 1111
Frank: talktofrank.com
NHS: nhs.uk/livewell/drugs
Narcotics Anonymous: ukna.org

Acknowledgments

Thank you to the people who anonymously spoke to me about their experiences of addiction, recovery and sobriety. Your selfless candour is so important in removing the shame and stigma from mental illness and addiction.

Thank you to my wonderful agent Sallyanne Sweeney and all at MMB Creative for guiding me through a new phase in my career. Similarly, it's lovely to have found a new home at Quercus, a home that wasn't afraid to take on a novel as challenging as *Clean*. Thank you to Sarah Lambert, Kate Agar and the whole big Hachette Children's team!

Huge thanks to Samar Hammam for working tirelessly to take *Clean* global. It blows my mind that Lexi's story is being told so widely. Thanks also to Dominic Treadwell-Collins and Delyth Scudmore at Blueprint for seeing the potential for her story on television, and Anya Reiss for taking on the adaptation.

Lastly, as ever, thanks for my friends and family for putting up with me when I'm as obnoxious as Lexi.